living

at 40

L.B. DUNBAR

www.lbdunbar.com

L.B. DUNBAR

Cover Design: Shannon Passmore/Shanoff Designs
Cover Photo Credit: Regina Wamba
Editor: Melissa Shank
Editor: Jenny Sims/Editing4Indies
Proofread: Karen Fischer

Other Books by L.B. Dunbar

Scrooge-ish

Road Trips & Romance
Hauling Ashe
Merging Wright
Rhode Trip

Lakeside Cottage
Living at 40
Loving at 40
Learning at 40
Letting Go at 40

The Silver Foxes of Blue Ridge
Silver Brewer
Silver Player
Silver Mayor
Silver Biker

Silver Fox Former Rock Stars
After Care
Midlife Crisis
Restored Dreams
Second Chance
Wine&Dine

Collision novellas
Collide
Caught

Rom-com for the over 40
The Sex Education of M.E.

The Heart Collection
Speak from the Heart
Read with your Heart
Look with your Heart
Fight from the Heart

L.B. DUNBAR

View with your Heart

A Heart Collection Spin-off
The Heart Remembers

BOOKS IN OTHER AUTHOR WORLDS
Smartypants Romance (an imprint of Penny Reid)
Love in Due Time
Love in Deed
Love in a Pickle

The World of True North (an imprint of Sarina Bowen)
Cowboy
Studfinder

THE EARLY YEARS
The Legendary Rock Star Series
The Legend of Arturo King
The Story of Lansing Lotte
The Quest of Perkins Vale
The Truth of Tristan Lyons
The Trials of Guinevere DeGrance

Paradise Stories
Abel
Cain

The Island Duet
Redemption Island
Return to the Island

Modern Descendants – writing as elda lore
Hades
Solis
Heph

Dedication

For Adeline,
And summertime, strawberry picking, sunsets and strangers.

This book contains reference to a few medical conditions, of which I researched and discussed with others. While there are broadsweeping specifics about diabetes, my understanding is everyone's experience is individualized. Despite two family members with diabetes, I, myself, do not have personal experience with the condition, and therefore take responsibility for inaccuracies.

L.B. DUNBAR

1

[Autumn]

"I'd just like to have a baby."

Thud. The statement falls heavy after my sister-in-law brings up a previous conversation moments before the arrival of guests.

I want to have a baby. It is that simple and that complicated, and I'd been discussing such a thing with Anna since summer began.

My sister-in-law is the sister I never had. As the middle McCaryn child, she defies the stereotypes of siblings and birth order. She's the one with it most put together out of her clan. The handsome, devoted husband. The stable, loving marriage. The three beautiful, growing children.

On the other hand, I recently had a breakup with my longtime boyfriend, thus leaving me shy of forty years old without what I want most—a baby.

"Doesn't that typically involve having a husband?" my brother, Ben, asks as the three of us gather around the kitchen island inside his in-laws' home—the house his wife and her siblings inherited upon their parents' death. "Or at least a boyfriend?"

"Yes, well, there is all that." I glare at Anna for bringing up this topic now of all times and wave dismissively from where I stand opposite my brother sitting on a stool. Of course, there are the mechanics of producing a child, and as I've been on a dry spell since my breakup with Rick, actually making a baby might be a teeny, tiny issue for me at the moment.

"Is this because of Rick?" Ben asks, concerned for me. Ben Kulis is a great brother, like the best brother ever, and Anna totally lucked out with him. Me? I've had a string of losers. It seems to be my forte. *Don't have a job?* I'll pay for everything. *Don't have ambition?* No worries, I've been told I have enough for two people. *Need a place to stay?* Come live with me, eat my food, mess up my apartment, and then run off with someone else. All this passivity is left from my teen years, which happened twenty years ago, but whatever. Textbooks have been written about women like me and my issues in triplicate.

Fat girl. Lonely heart. Starved for attention. Ate cookies.

"I would prefer not to give Rick credit for this decision," I state, glancing at Ben before fiddling with an apple in the large bowl of fruit on the island counter. My brother worries about me. He wants me settled down. He wants someone to love me and take care of me in an emotionally supportive kind of way, and I want those things as well. I just haven't found anyone who gets me.

"That might be the first sound thing you've said," Anna states with a smile. My sister-in-law is also the best. She's the best of the best, like Ben, and she'll be the first to tell you how perfect she is in a teasing sort of way. She's not a snob. For a woman who was once incredibly shy and lacked confidence, she's grown bolder as we age, with a self-assurance I wish I had half of.

"Maybe we should discuss this another time," I suggest as my brother's three best friends are due to arrive for a two-week stay at the house at any minute. It's actually a cottage—Lakeside Cottage—but by most people's standards, the six-bedroom home on a cliff overlooking Lake Michigan isn't quite the quaint image that comes to mind when the word cottage is mentioned. On top of the sprawling home and glorious view, a coach house doubles as a three-car garage with a two-bedroom apartment above it. Anna's father was extremely successful in the sausage industry. This was her mother's dream home, a second home away from their modest family house just outside Chicago. Eventually, her parents sold the house where she grew up and moved here for their retirement. Unfortunately, they have both passed away.

"So, who all will be here again?" I ask Ben, hoping to redirect the focus from me to him. He's the one who wanted to gather his friends and for good reason, although that's another topic we aren't allowed to discuss.

"Logan, Mason, and Zack, plus kids."

"Minus wives," Anna says, wiggling her brows at me. It isn't that they don't have them, but Logan is a divorcee. Mason is the perpetual bachelor, and Zack has a wife equivalent to the Grinch. I swear her heart is three sizes too small.

"Jeanine won't be with Zack?" I ask, looking over at Anna as she hangs a dishtowel on the towel rod.

"She gave some lame excuse about travel overseas and sent Zack with Oliver and Trevor." Zack's twin sons are a handful.

As if summoning one of Ben's friends, the doorbell rings, and Ben claps his hands once. "Here we go." He sounds like a kid on Christmas morning. His body swings around on the stool, and he pops off it to stalk toward the hall leading to the front door like Santa himself will be standing on the other side.

"He's so excited." Sadness fills Anna's voice, and we both know why.

"It's going to be great," I assure her. Wanting to reach out for her arm with comfort, I stop myself, afraid I might cry if I touch her. Instead, I blink rapidly, willing away tears I'm not allowed to shed.

"So, we could always talk to one of the guys," Anna says, straightening the already artfully arranged fruit in the giant bowl. "Maybe Mason could sleep with you."

My head shoots up, and Anna's ulterior motive for bringing up this conversation today becomes more clear. "Gee, thanks. Let's beg the eternal manwhore to impregnate me." Mason Becker already had an oops a few years ago. I'd like to say he's a good dad, but I doubt it. I'd also like to hope I'm not that desperate. While nothing is physically wrong with Mason—he's cover model-worthy to look at—I just don't trust him. I've never been able to put my finger on it, but there's just something. Maybe it's the fact he tried to make me kiss a manhole cover when we were kids after he cheated at ghosts in the graveyard. As Ben and his friends are four years older than me, I was the tagalong little sister, annoying all of them, and Mason picked on me the most.

"I'm not saying you have to marry him. I'm just saying you could pull a *Big Chill*. Pick three guys, sleep with each, and then *voila*, baby."

9

The Big Chill was a popular movie in the early eighties, released a few years *after* my sister-in-law was born, but she's obsessed with all things from that decade even though she was an infant back then.

"I am not picking three random men to sleep with in hopes they give me a baby," I mutter. However, it wasn't an entirely awful idea. My baby plans hadn't been well-thought-out yet. It was just a thought.

I'd like to have a baby.

When Mason walks into the kitchen with his hair artfully styled in an I-just-ran-my-fingers-through-these-acorn-colored-locks way, the *Big Chill* idea has some merit. Mason also has bright blue eyes, which stand out against his tanned skin. If my child inherited his genes, that would be one beautiful baby, but Mason isn't the friend of Ben's who had my interest in the past.

"Speck," Mason calls out, reminding me of my childhood nickname from him. *A speck of dust.* Ben would argue it was short for spectacles because I wore thick glasses, but my brother was only being nice. It could have been worse, I suppose. Mason could have called me testicles.

Mason walks to me first, hugging me with a firm back slap like I'm one of the guys. Next, he gives a wrist-flip wave at Anna before slipping his hands into the pockets of his shorts. He never touches her, and I've always thought it strange. Anna jokes he only touches women he can grope, and as he considers Anna a sister with his best friend mister, he doesn't reach for her.

That sensation of something off about Mason ripples over me and reminds me why he should not be a candidate for baby-making. Not that I'm considering baby-making with any of the clowns joining us, but I am growing older, as my mother likes to point out, and the selection of available men in my life is slim.

Mason swipes his fingers through that luscious hair, disturbing the curls along his neck and over his ears. The motion strikes me as anxious, but I can't imagine what Mason and his playboy good looks would ever be nervous about.

A holler of greeting notifies us another friend has entered the house, and Anna and I look at one another.

"Zack," we call out together. Zack Weller is not eligible for the three men list Anna suggested as he's currently married, even though we all hope he divorces. It's not a nice thought, but his wife really is a bitch. As Zack is an intelligent man, there would be merit to him as a potential sperm donor. He'd offer brains over brawn though he's equally as attractive as Mason in a more business-suit porn, preppy weekender kind of way.

As I glance up from my spot near the island, I watch as Zack enters the kitchen area with another man to his right.

"I didn't know Zack was bringing a friend." As I speak to Anna, my eyes narrow.

"A friend?" Anna chuckles. "That's Logan."

Logan Anders?

"What?" I choke. Logan does not look like the man standing beside Zack. For one, this man's dark hair is professionally cut and almost styled. The Logan I remember, who had a babyish face as a young man, now sports facial hair which is more than scruff but less than a beard shaved to perfection. He smiles over at Ben, and two damn dimples the size of lighthouse beams blind me, and he's not even looking at me. His body is not what I remember either. He's filled out differently from the college boy who used to be overweight. He's solid in places I can see, like his biceps bulging under a tee and thighs in tight jeans, which leads me to imagine he's thick in other places I cannot see.

Do not consider the potential.

When the boys were in college, Logan was another friend of Ben's who tortured me for reasons completely opposite Mason. His teasing nature wasn't from dislike as much as it was a part of his personality, and I had the biggest crush on Logan. *The biggest.* I wasn't slim myself as a child, and I considered our similar physiques a good reason for Logan and me to be considered a good match. However, he only saw me as Ben's little sister and proved it one time to my complete mortification. He wanted beautiful, skinny women and typically got them because of his winning personality. He was funny. He knew how to flirt. He was also incredibly sweet.

When did he get so hot?

"That's Logan?" My voice rings a little too loud and with too much startled exaggeration.

"Yes," Anna hisses, turning to me with warning eyes to lower my voice. "He's worked really hard to lose weight, and I think he looks great."

Great is an understatement. He's smokin'. He's hotter than hot. He's the sun only rises for me hot. Unfortunately, Logan Anders will never look at me that way. I'll never be the sun at the center of his universe. I'll always be Ben's little sister. *Speck.*

2

[Logan]

"Who's the hottie with the body?" I mutter to Zack Weller as we enter the kitchen of Ben's lakeside cottage and stand side by side. It's been years since I've been in this home, and I already see the improvements Anna and Ben have made to the place. Clean lines in the kitchen. Practical beach house furnishings. Removal of the old drapes to allow in loads of sunshine through the plantation blinds.

Speaking out the side of his mouth, Zack mutters, "That's Autumn."

Autumn? *Autumn Kulis?* As in Ben's little sister?

"Speck," I choke out as I catch her looking at me. My hands slip into the front pockets of my jeans as I try to disguise the instant boner I seem to be sporting from just looking at her.

When the hell did she get so drop-dead gorgeous?

"Logan." Her clipped voice along with a weak wave isn't exactly the reception I'd expect to receive from my best friend's youngest sibling, but then again, it's been a while since I've seen her. In fact, I can't remember the last time I saw Autumn. It was sometime after all our weddings. Perhaps during someone's parent's funeral. When Ben told me his sister would be joining us for these two weeks, I'd pictured Autumn as she was at sixteen—a little fuller, a lot geekier, and a pain in the ass. She was always following us around, and Ben allowed it. He was just too damn nice to say no.

Thankfully, he's that kind of friend, too.

"Come to the cottage," he'd said when I took his call a month ago. It wasn't a strange request but out of the ordinary. We hadn't vacationed together in years, but this year, we had all turned forty. *"It's been too long."*

When Ben told me he was getting the four of us together, plus kids and wives, I hesitated. I'm a single dad and didn't know how I'd fit in with the old tribe. Then I remembered Mason is forever single, and Ben wouldn't take no for an answer.

"What's up, Mace?" I say, reaching for my former roommate. We hug as men do, clapping one another on the back before pulling apart. Ben comes to me next. He feels thinner than I remember, but it could just be that I'm not as bulky as I once was. It's been a rough eighteen months, but I'm proud of where my body is at. I'm healthier for it, too.

As Zack and I pulled up to the house at the same time, we've already said our hellos in the driveway, but the room is an additional eruption of greetings, hugs, and questions.

"Where are the kids?" Anna asks.

"Boys are scootering on the driveway. They have energy to burn." Zack has six-year-old twin boys, and they can be total terrors. We all blame it on Jeanine, his wife, but Zack could step it up a bit as a parent, too. He works too much, keeping him separate from his family. Jeanine didn't make the trip, and he didn't bring the nanny either, so it should be interesting how Zack handles his kids by himself. Ben's older boys were playing basketball in the yard when we arrived and agreed to watch the younger set before we entered the house.

"Lorna found Mila outside." My daughter, Lorna, and Ben's Mila are close in age and the only little girls in this crew. The girls haven't seen each other in a year, but Mila invited Lorna to follow her upstairs as soon as they saw one another, and I encouraged her to go. We have a lot of meaningful father-daughter time, but I want some adult space over these next two weeks, and Lorna could use girlfriend time as well.

When greetings settle, Anna barks out information in her teacherly voice, telling us who is sleeping where.

"Okay, Zack and boys in the coach house. Mason, Logan, and Lorna upstairs. Lorna can sleep in Mila's room. Mason, your room is at the top of the stairs. Logan next to the girls." Her own boys have a room up there as well. Ben and Anna have the master suite on the first floor, which leaves Speck.

"Where's your sister sleeping?" It shouldn't be a question. It shouldn't even be a thought, but it just pops out.

"Oh, I'm not staying here," Autumn admits.

"Of course, you are," Anna replies. "This is family time."

14

"I have a place in town, remember?" Autumn's sarcastic tone does not deter her sister-in-law. Union Pier is a quaint touristy town only a few miles away. If I remember correctly, Autumn owns a café between here and there, which makes sense that she lives nearby.

"You're staying," Anna hisses, giving Autumn a look of warning.

"I can't be left to fend for myself amongst all this testosterone." Her eyes widen more, if that's even possible, and it appears they're having some unspoken girl-talk I'll never interpret.

"Are Amelia and Archer here?" Zack asks. The McCaryn siblings—Archer, Anna, and Amelia—own this cottage; if one can call this cliffside haven such a simple word. It's a beautiful home with massive windows and a gorgeous view of Lake Michigan. It belongs in an architectural magazine, one of which I've been featured in. Their mother was best friends with Zack's mom, and his family used to own the vacation house next door. It's a complicated story.

"God knows where Archer is," Anna says of her brother, who leads a mysterious life. "Amelia had to work, but she said she'll try to make it next weekend. I'm not counting on it, though. But this is really Ben's holiday," Anna adds, which sounds like a strange statement. She looks over at her husband and offers him a slow, soft smile, and damn if my heart doesn't weep. I'm not an overly romantic guy, but Anna and Ben are just one of those couples where love emits around them like a fog of sugary steam. When they look at one another, you just know no one else exists to them. It's the kind of look I'd hoped to inspire and receive with Chloe, only I didn't.

"So, what's first?" Anna asks, looking at Ben as if he's the captain of this trip. In many ways, Ben was our leader by default. He's the one who brought us all together. Mason and Ben already knew one another when they met Zack and Anna. I'm the add-on as I was Mason's roommate in college. Zack and Ben lived next door to us in the dorms until the four of us rented a place during our junior and senior years of college. To say we were close doesn't describe how much these guys have meant to me over the years.

We've experienced marriages and births, divorces and breakups. It's been twenty-two years of incredible friendship with brothers from another. These men are family to me. We've been through thick and thin, and not just in our waistband. Out of all of us, Ben is the best kind of human.

Clueless Kulis, we lovingly called him when we were younger, but he might be the smartest of the bunch. He has the beautiful wife, a strong marriage, a thriving business, and a lovely second home on Lake Michigan.

When Ben called to invite me to the lake, he said we were the four points of a compass, and he wanted Lakeside to center us. He was calling us home to impart life lessons on us.

Live. Love. Loss. Learn.

It was a cycle, Ben suggested, and he was big on cycles as a landscape designer in the Midwest. He lived for the four seasons and believed we were on the cusp of autumn for ourselves. But, he warned, we had so much life still left to live, and that was his plan for these two weeks. It was a compelling argument.

"Beers by the beach," Ben announces, and Anna nods before turning to the fridge, snapping orders at Autumn.

"Oh, I see how it is. You want me here for free labor," Autumn says, chuckling, and that sound goes right to my dick. My hands return to my jean pockets and curl into fists. *What is this reaction?* I'm not hard up on the woman front, but it's been a while since I've found someone who interests me for more than a date or two. In fact, the dating scene is getting old. I work long hours, and as I share custody of Lorna, life is one big balancing act without a lot of wiggle room. When I pulled into the drive and turned off my phone, it hit me how much I needed this vacation.

Something is telling me I also need to learn a little more about Autumn Kulis.

"Speedos optional," Mason announces, and Zack groans.

"You put on a banana hammock, and we will disown you," I say.

"No one can ever own me anyway," Mason sing-songs, and Ben chuckles.

"True that," Ben says.

"True that?" I snark. "Are we speaking as we did in college?"

"Please don't speak as you did back then. We have young ears around here," Anna says while working to pull beers from the fridge and filling plastic bags with ice. A cooler appeared from somewhere, and the two women are working in sync as though they organize for a day at the beach on a daily basis.

"No swearing, no sex talk. That's pretty much my entire vocabulary," Mason teases, and Autumn laughs. While that sound is still doing strange things to me, I don't want Mason to affect her. I love Mason, but he's a dick to women.

"Will Autumn's boyfriend be joining us?" Not the smoothest of transitions to find out whether she has one or not. Last I heard, she was living with someone but never married.

"I'm single as a Pringle," she announces, and Mason smiles. His eyes focus on her. Oh no. *Fuck that.*

"Mason, how's Samantha?" I ask.

"Who?" he answers, still watching Autumn work alongside Anna. His eyes scan her ass as she bends forward to put something in the cooler.

"Your girlfriend."

Mason gasps and brings his attention to me. "Girlfriend? Dude, I do not do those."

"But you did," I mutter, recalling Mason got a woman pregnant. They tried to do the co-parenting thing, but it didn't work out, and he rarely sees his kid.

"Up top," Autumn says, standing upright again and holds her hand up palm outward for a high-five from Mason. Images of her as a geeky teen rush back to me. I don't recall her being so curvy and lush.

Mason doesn't respond at first, torturing her with his negligence by holding off just long enough for it to be awkward that her hand hangs in the air. Then he reaches over to smack her palm, only he doesn't smack it. He clasps his fingers around hers and gives her hand an awkward shake before lifting it to kiss her palm.

What the fuck?

The six shades of pink Autumn turn are a beautiful color with her oak-brown hair and coffee-colored eyes. Her choppy-looking cut accentuates the loose curls flowing around that blush-filled face. She's thinner than I remember and minus some seriously chunky glasses. Somehow, she got the nickname Speck from Mason. I had trouble remembering her name when we first met, but I was also twentysomething and mostly drunk. Her name should have been easy enough to recall. *Autumn.* A season of change. A new beginning. It's unusual and pretty and appropriate, considering Ben's dad was a landscaping man like Ben. She's no speck now other than a spectacle of beauty.

Fuck. Get your head together, man, and your dick. She's Ben's sister.

Mason releases Autumn's hand, and Anna gives Autumn a not-so-inconspicuous look, side-eying Mason, like they're once again having some secret conversation. Only Autumn shakes her head and chuckles.

"*No,*" she mouths, and I very much want to know what that rejecting word means and how I can turn it into a yes toward me. A *yes*, and a *please, more*, and those lips sucking . . .

"Logan?"

"Huh?" I shake my head to clear my thoughts.

"Are you going to change? It's suits and flip-flops attire here," Anna says as my eyes drift back to Autumn. *Is she putting on a swimsuit?* Further inspection of her shows the ties of a bathing suit around her neck and thin straps peeking out of her deep V-cut shirt. If she's wearing a bikini, *thank you, Jesus.* Then I notice Mason still watching Autumn, and I wonder if Ben's baby sister owns a muumuu as my mother used to call her cover-ups. No skin for Mason.

"You boys change. I'll get Calvin and Bryce and have them bring stuff down to the beach for you." As Anna speaks, Ben steps over to her.

"You don't have to do it all," he says, cupping her elbow and pulling her upright from her position bent over a second cooler.

"I want to do this," she says, her eyes avoiding his until his fingers tip up her chin, and she looks him directly in the face.

"Thank you." His words are quiet and tender, and I'm suddenly uncomfortable, feeling like I'm witnessing something I shouldn't see between a couple. I'm not the only one uneasy as I turn my head and notice Zack spellbound by our friends before glancing down at his feet.

"I'm going to get my bags," he mumbles, hitching a thumb over his shoulder before turning on his heels without a second glance back.

"I'm with you," I mutter but take another look at Mason standing close to Autumn. He's watching Ben and Anna while Autumn's watching him, and the salad I ate an hour ago isn't settling well in my belly. Once upon a time, I would have shared everything with my former roommate, and there was that one night with a redhead, but that would never happen again and certainly not with Autumn Kulis.

She's a woman you don't share. You keep her away from men like Mason and make her yours.

And where the hell did that come from?

3

[Autumn]

"I love you," Ben whispers to his wife, and my heart falls to my feet. Tears I'm not allowed to shed fill my eyes, and I quickly blink in hopes they don't escape with Mason so close. He's watching them as well, and when Anna responds with her own, "I love you," Mason glances away.

"I need a beer," he mutters.

"Not until the beach, pretty boy," I tease. "Grab a cooler."

"I need my suit."

"I thought you said Speedos were optional."

Mason chuckles, breaking free of his stupor over Anna and Ben's tender moment. He has no idea how important or valuable such words are to a person. Mason's never been in love. He's been too busy avoiding it his entire life.

"Give me five minutes." Spinning around, he quickly exits the kitchen for the front hall, and we hear his feet thunder up the stairs like he's one of Ben's boys. Awkwardly, I stand by the island, contemplating whether to give Anna and Ben space or stay in place. I'm afraid to walk away. Since our father's death years ago from a heart attack, Ben has been the father figure I should have had as I aged. He's my brother, parent, and friend, which is a lot on the shoulders of a sibling. Under the surface, I fear for the day I'll lose him, too.

"Coolers," I say, interrupting their intimate moment. With Ben's hand still cupping Anna's cheek, she snaps to attention first.

"Coolers," she says. "Okay. Beer. Snacks. What else?"

"Towels."

A small shed down by the water holds chairs and umbrellas plus water toys and other beach necessities. Still, it's a production to hike down the one hundred and fifty steps to the beach below.

"I just need a minute," Ben says, swiping his hand down Anna's back before kissing her cheek.

"How's he doing?" I ask as soon as my brother disappears.

"I promised him I wouldn't talk about it." The harshness in her voice startles me, and I blink once at the strong tone.

"Not even to me?" I question.

"No one. No talk of anything for the next two weeks."

I nod to agree. His reasons are understandable, even if I don't like them. These weeks are for him to hang with his friends and pretend he's twenty-one again, even if he turned forty this year.

"What's the story with Mason?" His palm kiss surprised me. If I didn't know better, I'd consider it intimate. However, this was Mason Becker I was questioning, and I half expected him to lick my palm just to be disgusting. He's also forty, and I'd like to hope that gives him a bit of maturity. *Nah*, I decide.

"He had that girlfriend a few years ago, and we all thought he'd finally found the one. When he got her pregnant, they moved in together, but we just knew it wasn't going to work out. Lynlee is four, and she's adorable, but it's a sad situation. Her mother tries to keep her from Mason, pulling punches at him by withholding his own daughter."

"Oh. I'm sorry to hear that." I hadn't known he'd had such an issue with his former girlfriend. I'd met her at my dad's funeral, but I wasn't in a frame of mind to evaluate her then.

"Some men just seem destined to be alone," she mutters, and I wonder if she thinks the same thing of me. *Will I always be alone?*

+ + +

My nephews, Calvin and Bryce, are miniatures of their parents. Calvin has dark hair like Anna and eyes just as deep, while Bryce is a mini-Ben with blue eyes and blond hair. At sixteen and fourteen, they're both on the cusp of manhood. They'll break hearts and have their hearts broken as they are both lovers in their own right. Mila, my niece, is the wild one, and she's my spirit child from another. If I were to have a girl, I'd want her to be just like the dark-haired beauty with eyes that match her father. She's a combination of Anna and Ben, and has heartbreaker written all over her, even at ten.

"Aunt Autumn," she calls out once I hit the beach with a giant bag of beach towels. "Come swimming." She's waving at me to follow her before I even set down my things.

"Give Aunt Autumn a minute." Anna chuckles as Mila turns and runs to the water. "Are you sure you want one of those things?"

"One of what things?" I question.

"A child." She laughs again.

"You're having a baby?" The masculine voice behind me chokes. I turn to find Logan dropping the cooler in his hands as if it slipped from his fingers. The heavy object narrowly misses his feet, but he doesn't move. He just stares at me.

"No. Yes. *No.*" My brows pinch as I glare at Anna.

"I thought you weren't dating anyone," he adds. His expression shows he's slowly recovering from the shock of what he overheard although I don't see why it would matter to him. *Baby. Boyfriend.* It's none of his business.

"I'm not. It's just . . . nothing." I wave a hand and bend for the bag of towels, hastily pulling one out to spread over a beach chair. I could throat punch Anna.

"My sister is *considering* having a child," Ben states, clapping Logan on the shoulder as he passes him.

"Way to blurt out something private," I snap at my brother, who only smiles at me.

"Just helping you along," Ben teases. I don't even know what that means.

"It's not like he announced you were on your period." Logan gulps after speaking and visibly shudders as if the thought repulses him.

"You always were so funny," I mock, giving him a death-beam glare like we're still children. Here's the thing about Logan—he was the funny guy in the room once upon a time, but I saw it for what it really was. He protected himself with humor because there's a fine line between being the sweet guy and the sexy one. The sexy one typically won, and Logan wasn't him among his friends. His sass sobered a bit as he grew older.

"Life of the party. That's me," he retorts, slapping his chest.

"I can loan you mine," Zack suggests, coming forward with the second cooler and placing it in the sand beside a beach chair. "They'll change your mind." On that note, Zack's two boys let out a whoop and a scream, chasing Lorna and Mila in the shallow waves. The wind whips around us, forcing white caps to form on the rolling water. It's a child's delight to have such crests to jump or dodge. Squeals of excitement come from all four of them, and it sounds amazing.

"It's just something I've been thinking about," I mutter, weakly defending myself.

"What have you been thinking about?" Mason questions, pulling up the rear with a bag of snacks.

"Autumn wants a baby," Logan announces, bringing us full circle.

"Really?" Mason's perfect man brows hitch. "I volunteer as tribute."

"What?" I say, my mouth falling open.

"What the fuck?" Logan hisses beside him, turning to glare at his old roommate.

"Not what I had in mind," my brother mumbles, taking a seat.

I turn to Anna, looking for backup in this train wreck she started. Her silence worries me, and she gives me one of her famous glares, hinting I should accept Mason's offer.

"*No*," I mouth to her again.

"No to what?" Logan demands, and I turn on him next, wondering how he saw me move my lips in the direction of my sister-in-law.

"I didn't say anything." With false innocence, Anna holds up her hands as she responds to Logan.

"It's nothing," I remark, but not even a heartbeat passes before Anna does speak.

"I think Autumn should make a list of three men, sleep with each of them, and let nature do its thing."

"Didn't that happen in *The Big Chill*?" Zack asks, and I groan.

"This is not the eighties, and why are we even discussing my sex life?" I sigh, my shoulders tensing.

"I'm good with talking about your sex life," Mason teases, taking a seat next to Zack, who tips a beer bottle toward the resident player, and they tap the glass necks.

"I don't think we should be discussing her sex life," Logan defends, lowering for the cooler at his feet, lifting the lid, and hastily pulling out a beer. He isn't even standing upright before the top cracks open, and the bottle is at his lips. He's swallowing with quick chugs, and his Adam's apple bobs. Watching that slight knob roll along his throat, I want to lick over that part of him and then rub my cheek against that scruff on his jaw. *I wonder what it would feel like between my thighs, up against my . . .* but there will be none of that. While I crushed hard on Logan Anders as a teenager, that infatuation ended with a crash and heartbreak long ago. However, I don't miss that he's defending me.

"Finally," I say, waving out a hand at him. "Someone's on my side."

"Oh, he'd be on your side alright," Zack mutters before tipping up his beer for another sip. Logan glares at Zack. I don't understand what they aren't saying, but I don't want to know. These guys are still buffoons, and I'm the little sister they love to tease.

"We're not discussing this," I huff, throwing myself onto a chair and staring out at my niece playing with the other children in the water.

"I'm sorry," Anna says, lowering to a seat beside mine. With my arms crossed, my body language reads like a petulant child.

"It's fine," I lie, but it isn't. Anna has it all, as does my brother, and it isn't fair. And I don't mean that negatively against them as I love them both, but I just want my own little share of life—a baby.

My hands roughly grasp the beach chair arms, and I quickly stand.

"I'm going for a walk," I mutter.

"I'll go with you," Anna says, shuffling to rise from her seat.

"No, you stay." These are her friends and a part of her perfect life. I just want to be alone for a minute like I always am.

4

[Logan]

"What the fuck was that all about?" I ask, watching Autumn's hips sway and her backside clench as she walks away. Her toned legs flex as she stalks over the sand, and my mouth waters. I want to lick up those hamstrings and nibble at the crease where her ass meets her legs. Then I want to press my face between those thighs and feast.

I'd like to say I don't normally think like this about women, and in many ways, I don't. But from the second I've laid eyes on Autumn, I cannot get my thoughts under control. Then I hear this about a baby.

"She's just struggling. I'd say it's a midlife crisis, but she's too young. Women don't have those until after forty," Anna states, glancing out at the kids jumping in the waves.

"And when do men have them?" Zack asks.

"Thirty-five," Anna clarifies like she's a psychologist instead of a middle school teacher.

"I think I missed mine," Mason states, and Ben laughs.

"That's because you'd have to grow up a little first before questioning what you've done with your life so far."

We all laugh, but Mason's eyes pinch. Ben's words have hit a mark. Mason is a cad with women, but he's also a good guy at heart, and I have my suspicions he's been in love with a woman who broke his heart. Assuming she was someone unobtainable or resistant to the Mason Becker charm, it's wearing on our friend that he can't seem to replace whoever it was in his life. In some ways, I know the feeling. I thought Chloe was my everything. I thought we'd be together forever. After Lorna was born, something changed. I worked hard to provide for my family, but it wasn't good enough, or maybe it was too much. Chloe grew distant and then indifferent. She didn't seem to care about me anymore, and one day, she said exactly that. Surprisingly, we divorced relatively amicably, deciding it was better to suck up our hurts for the sake of our daughter. Separate but together was how Chloe worded it. I never liked the phrase.

Gazing down the beach, I watch Autumn grow smaller and smaller on the edge of the shore.

"So what's with the list?" I ask.

"What list?" Ben asks.

"The one with three men."

Anna dismissively waves me off. "Oh, I just made that up. She doesn't have an official list. Not yet. I'm just suggesting she do it that way. Then she can keep things attachment-free like she always does."

"I don't want her unattached, though," Ben admits, and Anna catches his eye.

"I know, but you can't make her fall in love. Like you couldn't make any of those losers she's dated fall in love with her. You want her to be happy, but too often, she settles."

Ben nods, and a more serious discussion falls into the cracks of what isn't being said.

"Sounds like the very definition of a loser if they didn't love her," Mason states, surprising all of us.

"What happened to the guy she was living with?" I ask.

"Rick," Ben clarifies.

"What happened is, he put his dick into another woman," Anna bluntly speaks.

"I love when you talk dirty," Mason growls with a smirky grin before he takes a pull from his beer.

"Ouch." Zack winces at the suggestion of cheating before lifting his beer for a sip.

"Men suck," Mason adds, and we all chuckle. He hasn't been the most faithful of men. Then again, he hasn't been disloyal to women either. He's clear about being attachment-resistant. No commitments from him.

"Well, the right man is still out there for her. I believe that. I have to believe that," Anna says, gazing over at Ben. We've formed a circle of sorts with Ben and Anna across from one another and the rest of us falling in line minus the empty seat next to me. *A circle of friends* as Lorna would sing from some Girl Scout song. It's still amazing to me that our friendship has lasted this long.

"What's the plan for the next two weeks?" asks Zack, the most uptight and schedule-driven of us.

"Eat. Drink. Be merry," Ben states.

"Or do a Mary if we find one," Mason states.

"Dude," Zack hisses before laughing, and Ben smiles.

"No extracurriculars at the house," Ben warns. "I want everyone to relax and hang out. Feel like this is your home away from home. Come and go but don't disappear." It's all said in a fatherly tone. Ben's taking our time together seriously.

"To together," Zack says, tipping his beer to Ben, who hasn't been drinking one although it's open and poised on the armrest of his chair. Ben tips his beer to Zack's.

"To living, loving, losing, and learning," Ben adds.

"That sounds dull. To the four points of a compass." Mason lifts his beer.

"Welcome home," Anna adds, lifting hers in salute. They wait on me, but I don't know what to add.

"To forever friends," I say. Ben's eyes meet mine across our circle, and he slowly smiles.

"I like that," he says.

"You two sound like thirteen-year-old chicks," Mason teases.

"What's wrong with thirteen-year-old girls?" Anna defends.

"Nothing. If you're like an eleven-year-old boy," Mason counters.

"Why eleven?" Zack asks.

"Always trade up," Mason jokes, and we all groan. "What? I matured early."

"You never matured," I tease, but this time, Mason doesn't look hurt because he knows I'm right. He'll be a kid until he dies, and that's not a bad way to be. I just don't want him to decide he'll trade down and go after a certain someone's younger sister.

+ + +

"What do you think of Speck and all this baby business?" Mason asks as we enter the upstairs hallway after an afternoon of sunshine and too much beer. My head is fuzzy, and I need a nap before dinner, but that's not happening. I'll have to settle for a wake-me-up shower and a cold one at that. After a day of watching Autumn on the beach, lounging in the sun, and playing with the kids, especially Lorna and Mila, I've had a raging hard-on that needs a good beating. *Or three.* I cannot get Autumn out of my thoughts. Her laughter. Her smile. Her incredible body.

Fuck. It's crazy how consumed I've been by her all day.

"For one, I think you should stop calling her Speck." Said harsher than necessary, I realize I'm just worked up.

"I'd baby-make with her without the baby part," Mason states, wiggling his brows.

I'm not a violent person, but I drop the shirt I've been holding and pin Mason against the wall. Typically, I'd be a fumbling mess, but my strength has improved with my diet and workout regime. Mason gasps for air as he tries to speak with my forearm at his throat.

"Dude," he groans.

"Don't talk about her like that."

Mason tries to shove me off him, and I let him. Smoothing down his T-shirt, he glares at me. "I'd never do anything to Baby Kulis. I'm just stating a fact. She's changed. A lot."

I've noticed, but so has Mason, and it isn't settling well with me. He's been known to steal a girl or two from me once they get a look at him.

"Don't be a dick," I mumble, bending at the waist for my shirt on the floor.

"Want to tap that yourself?" he teases.

"Shut up," I hiss, turning my head to make certain no one else hears him. "I'm not going to talk disrespectfully about her."

"Disrespectfully? That's a big word." Mason holds up spread fingers waving them in a manner Lorna would call jazz hands. "I'm not being disrespectful. I'm just stating the four-one-one."

"Well, keep your four-one-one to yourself as well as your dick." Turning away from him, I don't want a response from him. Giving him my back, I reach for the knob of my bedroom door and slam it after I enter the room. Dropping my shirt again, I lay back against the wood and scrub both hands over my hair. I shouldn't be this worked up. *Baby Kulis*, as Mason called her, wouldn't be interested in me anyway. She'll always think of me as the funny one. The sweet guy in the crowd. A guy who might win a girl for his personality, but nothing else, like having a heart.

Like her, I've changed a lot, but one thing is still the same. She's Ben's little sister, which means off-limits.

5

[Autumn]

While I didn't appreciate my sister-in-law spilling the beans about my business to these guys, I couldn't stay mad at her. As always, Ben tried to smooth my ruffled feathers, and after an afternoon at the beach with everyone else's children, I was even more determined to come up with a plan. Life was short, and mine was not getting shorter. I wanted a baby, and despite not having a husband or even a boyfriend, I needed to make baby magic happen.

Then my mother showed up.

"I'm just here to say hello," she announces, appearing conveniently after dinner with desserts in hand.

Mrs. Kulis and *Mama K* ring out around the table to honor my mother. As the co-owner of Kulis Landscaping with my father, my mother knows these boys well. Mason began working for Dad before his junior year of high school, while Zack had been a family friend from the moment he was born. When Logan joined the group, he spent an entire summer with us when he had nowhere else to go after his freshman year of college.

"Hope you boys are all behaving," Mom adds as if they are still twenty instead of forty. My mother is a good woman even though she can be meddlesome, especially in my life. She and my father had a perfect marriage, according to her, while Ben and I know they had their difficult moments. *Being married is hard work*, my mother would say. *You seed. You plant. You grow. You harvest.* Sometimes, I felt her words of wisdom were directed at me as if I wasn't willing to work hard at anything. Then again, I'd been the office manager of the landscaping business for years before dedicating myself to my own business affairs.

"Mama K, heard you might be a grandmother again soon," Mason blurts, and I want to kick him under the dinner table.

"Really?" She turns to Ben and Anna as the obvious answer, but she also knows that isn't a possibility. Then she turns to me. Her brow tweaks, and I shake my head, wordlessly glaring at Mason.

Oh boy. Way to get me in trouble with my own mother.

"I can't stay. I just wanted to drop these off." She waves at the plates of cookies she brought. I'd already brought a fresh tray of sweets from my café, but one can never have too many desserts even though I try to be better about consuming sugary treats now that I'm older.

A round of begging her to stay follows, encouraging her to hang out a bit.

"I can't."

"Hot date?" Mason teases, and Ben glares at him next. Since our father's death, our mother has not been on a date that we are aware of. She'd be the first to say she's still young at sixty-three, but I'm not certain dating is on her radar.

"Knitting club," she replies to Mason.

"Gotta be careful around those sticks," he warns, wiggling his brows.

"Dude, you're so rude," Logan says while Zack just shakes his head at Mason's antics.

"Mama K is used to it from me." He winks at our mother, who pinkens just the slightest. She is used to Mason's crassness, but it doesn't mean his language doesn't affect her.

"Okay. Be good," she says to the table, but her eyes meet mine. "Autumn, walk me out."

"Dun-dun-dun," Ben mutters under his breath as I stand from my seat, and I smack him on the back of the head as I pass him. I should really reach over and tap Anna since she started this. The list has been another source of conversation during dinner, including Anna's recommendation I consider Bert, a local veterinarian. She gives me a sympathetic look, but it's too late as I follow my mother to the front of the house. The *seed* has been planted in Mama K's ear.

We haven't even cleared the front door when my mother turns on me. "Why is this the first I'm hearing of you having a baby?"

"I'm not having a baby." *At least, not yet.* She doesn't need to know the particulars, and I don't even have an official plan.

"Well, you aren't getting any younger," she reminds me.

"Thank you. I wasn't aware."

"No need to take that tone with me, missy." Spoken without ire, her position as my mother seeps into her words. She's open-minded about most things, especially when I moved in with man number three, minus an engagement ring. Still, she's meddlesome.

"What did Mason mean, then?" she questions. Standing on the driveway, she waits out an answer despite the oh-so-pressing knitting club.

"He's just being Mason."

My mother's eyes narrow, disbelieving my rebuttal.

"Well, as long as Mason isn't the father . . ." While my mother might adore my brother's friends, she didn't want me to end up with one of them except maybe Zack, which was never a possibility. His mother is her best friend, and like the sister she never had, they both would have enjoyed our families joining in matrimony.

"Mason will not be the father," I state, trying to assure her. I also want to move her along. "You should get to knitting. You don't want to be late."

"Yes, yes," she says, giving me a wave as she turns for her car. "My date with dueling sticks."

I softly chuckle, grateful Mason hadn't heard that statement.

+ + +

The next morning, I'm working at my current baby—Crossroads Café. The old pit stop was once a diner of sorts, run-down and in need of some serious tender loving care. The interior is white on white with white subway tiles on the walls and black and white square floor tiles decorating the place. Black racks hold the minimal dry goods, which complement our array of breakfast items, homemade deluxe sandwiches, and healthy snacks, along with some not-so-healthy but heavenly desserts. A short standing counter near a long window allows for indoor eating and beverage enjoyment.

I don't bake or make our products as much as I initially did, allowing my capable staff to work their magic. Still, I'm here every day working alongside them in whatever capacity I'm needed.

Morning times, the coffee rush has me behind the counter tackling the register.

"Welcome to Crossroads, may I take—" I stop short as Logan stands on the other side of the counter.

"Is this your café?" His eyes widen in surprise.

"I don't just pour the coffee." My sarcastic tone is unwarranted, but I'm still raw—and embarrassed—after yesterday's information dump on the beach plus the continued conversation at dinner. I don't need his judgment of my decision. I also don't need his approval. I'm a grown woman and can do as I please.

"This is incredible," he says, turning to look around him at the chalkboard menus, the coffee-complement station, and the standing-only counter. With his hands on his hips, sweat soaks a dark gray T-shirt covering his chest. His shorts suggest he's been out for a morning run.

"What can I get you?" I nod toward the long line behind him as I don't have time for his compliments, although I appreciate them. He eyes the desserts and the breakfast treats, which include scones, muffins, and croissants.

"Just a coffee, dark roast is great." His eyes wander back to the sugary goodies.

"Are you sure you don't want a raspberry breakfast bar? Maybe the chocolate croissant?" I tease. He certainly doesn't have his currently buff body from eating such delicacies daily, but he's on vacation.

"I can't. I have diabetes."

Standing straighter, I blink in surprise. "I'm so sorry. I didn't know." And now I feel like an asshole for pushing things that could be detrimental to his health.

He waves me off and pats his belly. "I'm better for it." Still, he can't be better if he has diabetes. Rocco heard Logan's order for dark roast and slides the to-go cup next to the tablet we use as a register. As Logan reaches into his pocket, I wave him off.

"Your money isn't good here," I say with a weak smile, feeling guilty for pressuring him.

"This is a legit business, so you need to take my green."

I shake my head, pushing the coffee toward him.

"I'll take his free coffee," the customer behind him jokes, and Logan glances over his shoulder.

"You're busy. I'll see you at the house." He lifts his cup in salute and steps aside, only I can't shake what he's said. *He has diabetes.* While I take the next customer's order, I ask one of my workers to take over at the register for a second. After slipping into the backroom, I step out the back door in hopes of finding Logan on the road. Crossroads Café is literally on the corner of Red Arrow Highway and Beech Street. Assuming Logan isn't taking the highway, I turn down the side street leading to the inner drive along the lake.

"Logan," I call out, catching him halfway down the road. As he stops and turns, I jog to him.

"Hey," he says as I approach him.

"I wanted to apologize. That was a dick move of me to push the treats. I didn't know . . ." My voice trails.

"No worries. I'm fine. Well, fine as long as I stick to a diet and exercise regimen. It's how I've lost weight, and I feel so much better."

"And you're okay?" I reach out for his forearm but quickly pull my hand back. Logan follows the motion with his eyes, and his brows pinch in question. I can't explain the real reason I'm concerned for Logan, but I am grateful he's physically taking care of himself.

"Yeah, I'm okay. Nothing brings me down, remember?"

Oh, I remember all right. I remember a college boy having a jolly good time at a fraternity party one night while I was visiting my brother. Left in Logan's care so Ben could sneak off with Anna for a while, I thought I'd fallen into a dream. Me, a high school kid, hanging out with Logan Anders at a college party. Only it all turned into a nightmare, and while I'd like to hope Logan forgot it all, I'm certain the basics are still somewhere in his memory.

"I remember," I whisper, meeting his eyes, but the spark in them doesn't hint at the past. Thinking anything that happened with me would be a blip on Logan's radar makes me just as foolish as I was as a teen. "I should probably get back. I just wanted to apologize."

When Logan doesn't say more, I turn on my heels, but he catches me at the elbow.

"Hey, I should probably apologize for yesterday." His hand still holds my elbow, his palm warm on my skin. His thumb strokes the inside crease of my arm, and I'm so focused on his touch I almost miss his words. "The baby-making business isn't our business, and I want to say I'm sorry on behalf of everyone. We shouldn't have been so cavalier in discussing it."

Surprised by the sincerity in his voice, I nod to accept his apology. "Thank you."

Logan stares at me another second, but when neither of us speaks, I step back as I really need to return to the café. His grip on my arm tightens.

"However, I am curious. Are you really making a list of men to sleep with?"

"Oh my God, are you serious?" I tug my arm free from his soothing grasp, suddenly feeling the sting of his touch instead of the heat. I take another step away from him, but Logan follows me, stepping closer to me. He's in my space, and the scent of sunshine and man fills my nostrils. It shouldn't be such an intoxicating smell, but it is. *Is it wrong to want to lick him?*

"I just want to know. Are you putting Mason on the list?"

"What?" I snap, staring at him like he's lost his mind. In fact, I say that. "Have you lost your mind?"

"I'm . . . I'm looking out for you," he states, and I laugh, a sharp, barking, unattractive yip.

"You're kidding me, right? Is this a Logan Anders joke?"

His brows pinch. "What do you mean?"

35

"As if you don't remember?" I have no idea why it's all coming over me now. After all these years, it shouldn't matter. *It doesn't matter*, I've told myself over and over again. It didn't matter that the boy I had a crush on rejected me. It didn't matter that when I threw myself at him, he not only retreated but turned my misery into a joke among his college friends.

Logan and I somehow found ourselves in a bedroom at that frat party. I had leaned in, and Logan pushed me away, the force enough to knock me onto the bed. I thought he was going to follow me down and kiss me like I'd seen in television shows where the couple falls to the mattress and passionately make out, only Logan didn't jump on top of me. He laughed. He laughed so hard tears came to his eyes, and I fled the room. He didn't follow me. He didn't chase after me and profusely apologize like some romantic movie. He turned my flirtatious pass into a hard pass for him and made a mockery of me to his buddies.

Fat chick upstairs hungry to be in my pants. Told her my sausage was more than she could handle.

"I have no idea what you're talking about." He shakes his head, his entire face pinched in question.

"Just . . . forget it. And it's none of your damn business who's on my baby daddy list." With those parting words, I spin away from him, and once again, Logan Anders doesn't chase.

+ + +

I'm off for the rest of the day, and the first break I get, I call Anna to beg her to let me skip dinner that night.

"I'm sorry again about yesterday. Please forgive me. We need you here. Ben wants you here." I'd like to say Anna was laying on the guilt, but she was only telling the truth. When my brother mentioned having his friends for two weeks, he also told me how much he wanted me present.

"But you'll be with the guys all the time," I whined to Ben a month ago.

"Anna will want your company." He shrugged. *"And I just want you around."*

I couldn't deny his request, but I needed one night away from the Autumn-wants-a-baby talk and who's-on-the-list discussion. There wasn't a list, and as I told Logan, it wasn't anyone's business, even if there was.

As Ben and Anna's home was along the inner drive lining the lake and less than a mile from the café, I'd ridden a bike to the café in the early morning hours. As late afternoon approaches and my day is done, I exit the building to find Logan standing near my bike chained to the fence in the back. He holds the handlebars of another bike.

"Hey."

"Hey," I grumble, not up for another confrontation with him. "What are you doing here?"

"I wanted to walk you home. Well, ride bikes home with you."

Uncertain why, I don't ask. Instead, I set about unlocking my bike and placing my workbag in the basket on the front. As I swing a leg over the bike, Logan stops me from moving forward.

"I've felt bad the entire day for this morning. I don't know what happened, so could you explain it to me."

Sighing, I stare off at the highway that intersects with the side street.

"I don't know where all that came from. I mean, I'm thirty-six. Something that happened when I was sixteen should not matter now." Logan continues to watch me, so I turn back to him and shrug. "Water under the bridge and all that."

Logan shakes his head. "Not good enough. Explain what I'm missing."

"Logan," I groan.

"Come on, Autumn." The strength in my name startles me as he's always called me Speck. A small shiver ripples over my skin at the determination in his tone.

"It's nothing," I say, suddenly embarrassed that I'm overreacting again toward this man.

"It's not nothing. You were really worked up this morning, and it's something I obviously did but don't recall. Saying it's nothing is a Chloe move, and I told myself I wouldn't ever let it happen again. I need to know what I've missed."

The mention of his ex-wife reminds me that Logan eventually went on to fall in love with a woman, even if they eventually fell out of love. I'm well-versed in falling into and out of love. I fall hard and fast—or at least that's what I think of myself—and have staying power for all the wrong reasons. It happened with Rick, and Kenneth before him, and Kevin before him.

I could point out Logan's comparing me to his ex-wife, which is unsettling, but the earnestness in his expression tells me he really wants the specifics.

"Remember when I came to visit Ben when you guys were juniors?" I take a deep breath, holding it for Logan's reply.

"Hardly." He laughs, and I'm familiar with that off-the-cuff sound he makes.

"Never mind. I can't tell you this. It's better that you don't remember." My foot hits a pedal, and I press forward, but Logan catches the handlebar, and I almost topple over.

"Autumn, dammit, tell me what I did." The serious snap of his voice stills me, but it's the concern in his eyes that softens me.

"I made a pass at you, and you turned it into a joke."

Logan releases the handlebar and almost trips over his own bike as he scrubs a hand over his short hair. "You what? And I what?"

"I tried to kiss you, and you pushed me away."

"I had to have been drunk." His gaze roams my body, and the perusal is a desperate caress, one frantic to remember me. His eyes outline my form as if given a second chance to touch me, only he never touched me in the first place.

"I didn't look like this then. I was just some fat girl who wanted your sausage."

His head snaps upward, eyes meeting mine. "I did not say that."

"Yes, you did," I bark, and then I take a deep breath. "Look, like I said, it was a long time ago, and it doesn't matter. I don't know why it's even coming up now but—"

"Whoa, whoa, whoa. First, I would never call you fat." His gaze skims up and down my body once more, and as much as I want to feel his appraising hunger against my skin, my teenage heart still aches from his harmful words.

"You did—"

"Uh." He raises a hand to stop me. "And if you ever kissed me, I'd certainly remember."

"Well, I remember, and you don't, and it was just stupid."

"Kissing me was stupid?" His eyes widen. His face horrified.

"We didn't kiss. It was stupid that I tried, and I don't even know why we are discussing this now."

"Because you're mad at me for something that happened twenty years ago, that I don't remember because I was probably drunk and acting like a twenty-year-old asshole."

His emphatic explanation does make sense. It's the rationale I'd given myself for years, so I don't know why I'm letting it get to me now. I've been with plenty of men since Logan's rejection—men who wanted me—at least for a little while.

"It doesn't matter," I state again, but Logan reaches out for my arm while still holding his bike in his other hand.

"It matters to you, so it matters to me." I almost cry at the tenderness in his words, but he can't mean them. He is just like every other man in my life—say one thing but mean another.

"Well, it's over now. I'm thoroughly embarrassed"—*and hurt*—"by the entire situation, and I'd like to go back to you not remembering it."

"Autumn, honey—"

"Oh no," I snap. "Do not give me some patronizing crap. I accept your apology, if there was one in there somewhere, and I'm sorry, too. I should have never assumed you'd want me to kiss you." Despite his arm loosely around my neck and his playful teasing of me throughout that night, I should have remembered it was who Logan was. He was flirty. He was funny. He was sweet. It didn't mean he wanted to be with me, and the memory always haunts me whenever I am around him.

Pulling my arm from his grasp for the second time today, I press at the bike pedal, propelling myself forward to give me some distance from him and set me on the road to Ben and Anna's place.

Logan quickly pulls up next to me but thankfully doesn't speak. Once we return to the house, one of the three-car garage doors is open, and I ride inside. Slipping off the bike, I hastily kick the stand to hold it upright. Logan pulls in after me, and right as I turn for the house, he catches me again by the arms, pulling me up to his chest.

"I want your kisses." The statement snags my breath. His dark eyes flame, but I'm still wound up.

"Because you don't want Mason to have them?" I have no idea where the sass comes from, but a competitive spirit has always run through the former roommates.

"Fuck Mason." Logan tugs me tighter to him. His nostrils flare and his breath assaults my lips, but he stills an inch from contact with my mouth.

Kiss me, I want to scream, but then again, I don't want it like this. I don't want it because he feels threatened when there isn't a threat. I'd never sleep with Mason Becker, not even for a baby.

Our chests heave against one another. My breasts swell and ache inside my Crossroads Café tee, and my nipples peak. His firm pecs tease those nipples, eager for attention. His fingers tighten on my upper arms, but still, his mouth keeps its distance.

A door slams outside the garage, and we both flinch, jumping apart as if we've been caught kissing. Logan releases my arms, and I step away, missing his nearness as if we were on the cusp of doing more than melding our mouths together. Shaky fingers come to unkissed lips that still sting with the potential. We stare at each other for another second before I duck my head, slip around him, and exit the garage, left with thoughts of what a kiss from Logan Anders might feel like and if it would ever mean anything to him.

6

[Logan]

"Hey, man, what's wrong with Speck?" Mason asks, finding me standing inside the garage trying to process everything. I have no recollection of what Autumn told me. Not her trying to kiss me. Not me insulting her. Jesus, I don't think I could have said such a thing about her, but that doesn't mean I didn't. A part of being the heavy guy meant feeling the freedom to pick on other large people. That's not to say it's politically correct or even personally acceptable, but it happened a lot in my college years while I was young, ignorant, and drunk.

A sense of humor and a hell of a lot of booze kept up a façade— that I was okay with my size—and I was, but I wasn't impervious. When other kids picked on me for it, I had to protect myself. Jokes made me acceptable to other guys. Humor was a form of flirting, awarding me the beds of several girls. It was a means to an end. It was also a forcefield around being sensitive to my size.

Then I met Chloe. I thought she accepted me. I thought we were equals in our attitude and habits, but after having Lorna, Chloe changed. She never wanted to go through *that*—meaning a pregnancy—again. She didn't want to be bigger. She worked hard at losing weight, turning her against me. Eventually, I repulsed my own wife. After we separated, she started dating. They weren't small, sleek and skinny but they were healthier than me. She swore she hadn't been unfaithful during our marriage. I suppose, I'm grateful.

The diabetes diagnosis changed my perspective on healthy habits. That and Lorna's fear I'd leave her. While Chloe and I did everything to assure our daughter we loved her and planned to parent her equally, Lorna worried I'd die when I learned about my health condition. A mind-reset and a new life course had to happen, and I'm happier and healthier for it..

"I . . . she's mad at me," I admit, scrubbing two hands down my face.

"Because you keep bringing up the baby thing?" Mason asks.

"I do not," I snap. Even though it's been on my mind, only second to how hot Autumn is now.

"You couldn't let it go at dinner last night."

I hadn't said a thing about it. Zack's the one who brought it up again, informing Autumn that a father would have rights to his child, and Autumn needed to take legal action if she formulated a list of men. In our litigious generation, Zack wanted her to protect herself and her baby.

"I can let it go," I growl.

"Keep lying to yourself. Tell me how that works out for you." Mason pats my shoulder and opens his car door, which happens to be parked inside the garage.

"Where are you going?" We aren't being held hostage, but Ben has made it very clear he wants us around for dinner every night.

"Anna's sending me on an errand. She said I should pick up condoms for when I sleep with Speck." Suddenly, I'm slamming Mason against the side of his car and he's chuckling while I pin him in place. "So much aggression." His brows wiggle as he shoves me off him. "And so fucking gullible. She can't get pregnant if I use a condom, dumbass."

However, even with a condom, Mason got Lynlee's mother pregnant. He's the one who brought up his super sperm last night, making jokes that his swimmers surpassed latex and the pill. I'm not impressed and I'm not reassured that Mason doesn't want to sleep with Autumn.

"Mason," I hiss, my insides unraveling as my fists clench. I've never been a fighter, but I'm turning into one where Autumn is concerned.

"Relax, man. I'm only looking for my sunglasses. Ben wants to hang at the beach before dinner."

I've never understood the friendship between Mason and Ben. Ben is just a great guy, kind and thoughtful, while Mason is thoughtless and selfish to the core. However, their history involves Ben's father also being kind and Mason's dad being a dick.

Without another word, I turn away from Mason and head for the house.

+ + +

After taking some time to cool off, I head to the kitchen to find Anna and Autumn with helpers in Mila and Lorna. My earlier bike ride started out as a ruse. I offered to take Mila and Lorna down the inner drive. On our return trip toward the cottage, I asked the girls if they wanted to stop at the café and wait for Autumn, secretly hoping they wouldn't. Lorna convinced me to let them ride the remainder of the way home without me, and I agreed, giving them space while I needed my own to pursue Autumn.

"Look at all the lovely ladies in this kitchen," I tease, kissing the top of Lorna's head before peering up at Autumn. She doesn't look at me. "What are we making?"

"Tonight is spaghetti," Mila proudly announces.

"I have whole wheat pasta I can make for you," Anna states, giving me an understanding smile. That's when Autumn glances up. She'd been dicing a cucumber.

"Can you eat the rest of this?" Her show of concern is heartwarming and a little reassuring that she doesn't completely hate me.

"It's all about portion control, counting carbs, and a hundred other things, but I'm good. If I don't want to eat it, I'll just double up on salad."

The kitchen is large, and the women surround the island with the girls kneeling on stools to rip up lettuce and drop in it an oversized bowl. I circle the island to be closer to Autumn. After running a hand up her back, I massage her neck. "Can I help?"

She stills under my touch, but I continue squeezing the back of her neck until she relaxes a bit.

"We have it all under control. The guys took the boys down to the beach for football," Anna says.

"I can take a hint," I state, tipping up my chin at Anna. My hand doesn't want to leave Autumn's tender skin, blanketed by her hair which is soft and tickles my arm, but I need to move away from her before I do something inappropriate against this counter despite the audience. I can't seem to stop myself from pressing a kiss to her temple before stepping away.

"I'm sorry," I mutter to her hair, inhaling her slight scent of pastries and coffee. When I step away, her head turns in my direction, but I don't glance back at her as I exit the house for the long walk down to the sand.

The strip of beachfront along the lake is serene, and the cliffs protect it from the noise of homes. On occasion, Anna's parents allowed her to bring the gang on a weekend visit, and we had some good times here. Watching the guys toss a football with the sons of our friends reminds me of those moments and makes me feel a little old. I always wanted more children while Chloe didn't. I love Lorna, but a son would have been fun, too. While I've never been upset about pink tutus and Girl Scouts, I'd love to toss a football like the boys are doing.

As I reach the sand, I wedge my way into the game, jumping to intercept the ball from Zack.

"Interception," I call out before running. I dodge around Mason, who does nothing to stop me, and pivot around Calvin, raising a fist in the air like I'm the king of sand football. Trevor, one of Zack's little hellions, tries to tackle me, but I leave him in the dust, slamming down the football to give my victory dance. My knees wobble together. My fists roll over each other. I shake my ass.

"You're never going to win a woman with those dance moves," Zack teases somewhere behind me, and I turn to face my friends.

"Don't need to win what comes easily," I mock, still doing my dance.

"You wish." Mason snorts.

"Trouble with the ladies," Ben jokes, wiggling his brows. "Calvin can give you tips."

"Dad," Ben's sixteen-year-old son groans.

"Got a girlfriend?" I tease, sounding like I'm sixteen as well.

"He has many," Ben states, and Mason offers Calvin a high five.

44

"Who cares about girls?" Trevor asks, digging in the sand with his little hands. He's covered in the stuff, and it can't be just from chasing after the guys with the football.

"He's only six. He'll get there someday," Zack says as I walk closer to them.

"Dad, hike it again," calls out Bryce, Ben's younger son.

"Let Logan do it. I need to catch my breath." Ben isn't out of shape, but he is breathing heavier. He looks great, but he also looks tired. He's holding his side like he ran a mile instead of tossing a ball, and he falls into a beach chair on the sand.

"You okay, man?" I ask, still holding the ball in my hands.

"Of course. Go play." He flicks his wrist like he's dismissing one of his kids, and I look up to meet Mason's eyes. He's been watching our friend as well, but in true guy form, we don't push it. I set up to hike the ball to Bryce, who sends it sailing through the air to his brother yards away.

"Holy shit. He has an arm," I say to no one and everyone. Turning back to Ben, I see him watching his son, pride in his face, but something's off in his eyes. "He going to play for the green and white one day?"

As alumni of Michigan State University, we've often joked about our kids attending college there and following in our footsteps. Anna's family is from Chicago, and although Ben moved to Illinois to be with her, his heart bleeds green and white.

"Hopefully," Ben whispers, his fingers coming to his lips and curling into a fist. He taps the side of his fist against his mouth a few times before he quickly stands. "I think I'll check on the girls."

We all seem to pause in our place as Ben gives us his back and walks the sand until he reaches the decking that leads to the one-hundred and fifty stair climb up the cliff.

"Is he alright?" I ask Zack, who is nearest me.

"He's been acting strange, but I figure it's just stress. This house is a lot to maintain from a distance. Although Autumn is nearby, she has her own business now and lives in town. Plus, it really should be Archer and Amelia picking up the slack. They're Anna's siblings." Archer McCaryn is kind of a vagabond, and Amelia is younger than Autumn with a high-pressure job in marketing in Chicago.

"Ben still doing okay with his business?" Ben is a landscape designer, and he could have taken over his father's business when he graduated college. Instead, he followed Anna to Chicago, where she got a teaching job, and he set up shop there, like an extension of his father's company. When his father died, Ben tried to remotely run both companies. His sister had been the office manager at the time and quit to start her business. It was a shit show for a while, but Ben found a new manager with his mom as point person to check on things.

"I think business is good." Zack pats my shoulder and calls out for his boys. "Trevor, Oliver, time to clean up before dinner." *Yeah, good luck with those monsters.*

Mason and I remain on the sand, tossing the ball with Calvin and Bryce a while longer, and all concerns for Ben dissipate as us older guys pretend we're teenagers again.

7

[Autumn]

After Logan's temple kiss, I sense Anna's eyes boring into the side of my head.

"What was that all about?" she asks when we both have our backs to little ears who could be listening. Mila and Lorna are miniatures of Anna and me, and it's been fun to have little girls around wanting to help. Still, I don't want to discuss Lorna's father and his strange behavior—and even stranger words—before her.

I want all your kisses.

"We had a little disagreement earlier. It's nothing." I shrug, stirring the pasta in the oversized pot while Anna sets wheat pasta in a smaller pot to boil.

"So." The word hangs between us, and I brace myself for whatever trouble Anna has brewing in her head. "What are your thoughts about Mason?"

"What about him?"

Anna glances over her shoulder to check on the girls. "He'd be perfect for baby-making."

Following her lead, I glance over my shoulder as well before answering her. "I am not making a baby with Mason."

"Why not? He's single with no commitments and no attachments. He'd be in, out, and out of the way."

I laugh. God love my sister-in-law, but that's not exactly how I want to think of this process. One and done is all I need, but truthfully, I wanted to share this experience with someone else. I'm more than capable of raising a child on my own, but I'd always hoped I'd find someone to be the other half of me, and as a couple, we'd raise a child together.

"Mason is hot, I'll give you that." He certainly is and always has been, but Mason also knows this about himself, and if personality is genetic, I don't want a child of mine being so self-centered. "But I just don't see myself with Mason."

I pause a second, adding sarcasm to my next comment. "And thanks again for yesterday. I blame you that Mason blurted out this baby-making business to Mom."

"What's there to see with Mason?" Anna ignores my sarcastic gratitude and checks over her shoulder once more. "It's only sex. I'd definitely put Bert the vet on your list. What about the hot guy who owns LickIt, the ice cream parlor?"

Ah, no.

Chuckling again, I respond. "I've never known you to be so cavalier like this." It's a fact that Anna and Ben were each other's first and only, and I admire that in a hundred ways, but I've always wondered if they were curious about others—how it might have been if they had at least one other experience to compare to. I'm the wild child between Ben and myself, and I've had enough sex to make up for the both of us, I guess. I'm no longer a one-night stand kind of person. There have been opportunities, but I'm more dedicated than overnight. However, I can count the number of committed relationships I've had on one hand.

"I'm not being cavalier. It's just . . . Ben and I want you to be happy."

"Who says I'm not happy?" I have a great life. I live in a condo overlooking the water. I own my own business. Life is good. It's just missing a few elements.

"I understand you're a perfectly capable, independent woman, but we only want what's going to make life better for you. Better than happy." Anna and I had a long discussion a year ago about my singlehood status. While I was living with Rick, there was no ring in the foreseeable future. I hadn't pushed for more from him because he wasn't capable of giving me more. It was my place he lived in. It was my business he worked at when he decided to show up. It was my livelihood he lived off, and I'd enabled all of it. I made excuses and believed him when *he* told *me* I needed him.

Anna also doesn't understand that not everyone can have what she and Ben have. No marriage is perfect, she'd tell me, but I doubt my sister-in-law has a sense of difficulty. She and Ben are a true partnership of responsibility and devotion on top of loving one another.

"You know it's important to Ben now more than ever." Anna's words hang between us, and I understand what she's not saying, but it's my life and my decision. Mason Becker is not the answer. Nor is Bert the vet or what's-his-name who owns LickIt.

"I appreciate your concern for my well-being, but let's leave me out of this for two weeks." I lower my voice hoping she doesn't hear the edginess inside. Since telling my brother and sister-in-law about my desires, the constant chatter around my plans drives my determination to accomplish it but on my own terms. "I'll figure my own life out, please."

Anna sighs, and we stand in silence for another second before she bumps my shoulder.

"I love you," she whispers. The words have become more important than ever to be said, and I blink away the sudden prickle to my eyes.

"I love you, too, you pain in the ass," I mumble under my breath, but it's loud enough she hears me and chuckles.

"What are all my beautiful girls making in here?" Ben says, startling us and pulling us from our conversation.

"Spaghetti!" Mila calls out as if shouting surprise at a party.

"Pasta. My favorite," Ben teases. It's not really one of his favorite meals, especially lately. The tomato sauce does a number on his stomach, but it's an easy meal for a large gathering, satisfies the kids in the mix, and Anna just modifies Ben's portion. Plus, there's always salad, as Logan pointed out.

This reminds me I want to ask Anna more about Logan's diabetes. My understanding of the disease is limited, but I know enough that people can live with diabetes. It just involves discipline and education to understand how to manage the disease.

"Alright, ladies. Go ring the bell for me," Anna says, and the girls scramble off their stools for a dinner bell in the yard near the cliff. It signals for the boys to come up for dinner. I step back to the island while

Ben walks to Anna and wraps his arms around her from behind. Her head tips to his shoulder, and I allow them this moment of privacy, keeping my back to them.

"You okay?" Anna says behind me.

"Yeah." Ben's muffled voice says he's either got his nose buried in his wife's neck or his lips pressed to her hair. Either way, the love surrounding my brother and his wife is sickening and lovely at the same time, and I'd love just a drop of whatever they have.

Within minutes, doors are opening, and loud voices fill the large family room-kitchen combination. Anna calls out for people to wash up for dinner, and chaos follows with serving bowls filled and dishes set in the dining room. At one point, Logan hands me a glass of wine before I've even asked for one. His hand finds its way up my back again as it did earlier, and he squeezes the nape of my neck as if this is normal for him, as if this is what we do. A shiver ripples over my skin, but I hold still, melting under his touch.

"Sit by me at dinner," he suggests as though we're teenagers needing seats saved at a cafeteria table. My face heats at the request, and I bite my lip.

"Sure," I whisper because my voice cannot be found.

Dinner is a cacophony of tales from the guys. Some stories are appropriate, and some are not so appropriate about their days together in college. Slowly, we lose the kids, and Anna and I pick up the dinner dishes.

"Girls cook. Men clean," Ben announces.

"You don't have to do that," Anna states while I'd like to interject that they most certainly do need to do something.

Ben intervenes. "I told you, you don't need to take care of us."

"If I don't, who will?" she teases, leaning down to presumably give him a kiss on the temple. However, my brother cups the back of her head, and the kiss lasts longer than proper for a dinner party.

"On that note," I mutter, continuing into the kitchen to relieve my hands of plates and return for more, only I find Mason directly behind me.

"We got this," he says, keeping his voice low, and I nod to accept his help. Starting the faucet, I rinse dishes for the dishwasher as the piles build. Mason steps up beside me, and we work as a team to load the dishwasher. With a hip check, he nudges me out of the way to wash pots and pans, and Logan takes over to dry.

"This really is such a great house," Logan says. The kitchen is now full of adults. As an architect, Logan appreciates the layout of this sprawling home with a large easy sitting room and kitchen combination but a formal living room and dining room for entertainment. An expansive stone patio runs the length of the open concept rooms, and Anna wanted to move the party outside later for the sunset. As it's late summer, the sun still hangs in the sky until almost nine. Today's been a clear day, so it's going to be a spectacular view from the patio.

"I'm so glad you think so," Ben states. "Because I have something to tell you."

I've been returning cookware to their proper place but drop the pot in my hand, and it clatters to the floor.

"Easy there," Mason teases, glancing at me over his shoulder while he is elbow-deep in the sudsy sink. With shaky fingers, I bend and retrieve the pot, handing it back to him to wash a second time.

"You're making more work for me, Speck."

Ignoring him, I hold my breath. This wasn't the plan. Ben didn't want to say anything to his friends until the end of the two weeks.

"Anna and I have decided to move here," Ben announces. Air whooshes out of me as I stare at my brother, whose hands rub up and down Anna's arms. He's perched on an island stool, and Anna stands between his spread thighs.

"What about your business?" Zack asks as a strange tension builds around the kitchen.

"I'm selling it."

"Why?" he questions.

"It was just time," Ben admits, pressing a kiss to Anna's shoulders. "I'm going to take back my dad's company here. Try to restore it."

Zack's brows pinch while Mason keeps his eyes aimed at the pots in the sink. Logan glances over at me and then at my brother.

"Were you in financial trouble?' Logan asks.

"Nothing like that. We're just looking for a change. Anna's been working hard to upkeep this house from a distance, and it just got to be too much. It was either our place outside Chicago or here, and we're happier here." Anna tips her head to kiss Ben once more.

Ben and I are from this area, growing up a half hour from Lakeside. We could never afford to live in this lakefront community, made up of homes owned by generations of families or the newly rich from the Chicago area, who make Lakeside a vacation home destination. Our father took pride in his independently owned business, but he was the hired help to these houses. He landscaped and maintained most of the properties, including this one, which is how Ben met Anna.

"What about Anna's teaching career?" Mason asks, keeping his back to the happy couple.

"I'm ready for something new. I'm actually going to look for a position here. I can't sit around all day and do nothing." Her eyes catch Ben's, and they share a weak smile. The decisions have already been made. Ben will consult on our father's landscaping business while Anna finds a new job teaching in the immediate area.

"That's kind of a big change with your boys in high school." Zack's comment is a reminder of one of the difficulties in my brother's decision to move. Ben and Anna didn't want to uproot the boys from their routine, but the move was presented as an opportunity and adventure. I doubt Calvin fell for it at sixteen, but he's been quietly supportive of the big change his parents are asking of him. He's smart enough to know there's something more to this decision.

"What do Archer and Amelia think of you moving here permanently?" Logan asks next.

"Archer doesn't have a say as he's hardly around and didn't lift a finger when our parents passed. Amelia is too settled in her job near the city and doesn't take time off to visit. I don't want the house to go to waste, and summer weekends aren't always enough time here," Anna admits. "Plus, summer is Ben's busiest season but my time off, and we want to be together *here*."

At one point, Anna's mother made the same decision, wanting this house to become their permanent family home instead of their house in Chicago. That decision came after the McCaryn children were all grown, though. Surprisingly, Ben seems perfectly happy to return to this area despite the big city contracts and extensive outlying suburbs his landscaping company services. He's looking forward to scaling down in business while moving here is scaling up in house size.

"Done," Mason announces of his dish duty, drawing our attention away from Ben and Anna's big announcement. Personally, I'm thrilled they'll both be closer to me, and I can spend more time with my nephews and Mila, but I still wish it wasn't for the reason they aren't sharing yet. "Time for a drink."

After drying his hands, Mason steps toward an alcove off the kitchen which houses a built-in bar area. The distinct pop of a bottle topper released from a bottle is heard, and the *glug-glug-glug* of alcohol being poured in a glass follows.

"Who else wants a scotch?" he calls out, and several of the guys groan.

Anna hops off Ben and heads to the counter for another glass of red wine, and Logan hands me another glass. With a glass of water in his hand, he taps my glass. "To adventure," he states half-heartedly and looks over at Ben again.

"Come sit on the patio," Ben tells his friends, and everyone falls in line to follow him. Only once outside, I notice Mason isn't present. His head bobs up and down as he descends the stairs to a landing halfway down the one-hundred and fifty steps to the beach.

"Go after him," Anna whispers, sneaking up behind me.

"Me? Why me?" Whatever Mason is sulking about isn't up to me to decipher.

"He's lonely. It's perfect. Just be with him. You never know where it could lead."

"Are you crazy?" I mumble, lifting my wine glass, and the words echo within it.

"You want a baby. He's your man. I'm telling you, ask him," Anna encourages.

"This is ridiculous," I say, stomping off the patio like a petulant child. I do not want to sleep with Mason Becker, but I also don't want to hear any more meddling from Anna.

8

[Logan]

I still couldn't wrap my head around the fact one of my best friends was giving up his hard-earned business to move to this area. Lakeside is a beautiful location, but his father's business does a fourth of what Ben's does in a larger city.

Even more pressing on me, though, is the fact Autumn followed pouty Mason down the steps, and they hadn't returned.

"I'm going to check on those guys," I state, offering no other explanation for following Autumn after ten minutes that felt like a lifetime. Mason had been flirting with her all through dinner despite her sitting next to me, and he continued the blatant perusal of her body while he washed dishes. *Kiss-up.* He's never washed a dish in his life. If anyone warranted maid service, it was Mason.

I only travel halfway down the wood steps leading to the beach before I see Mason and Autumn standing on a landing built as both a spot to rest from the climb and a private deck on the edge of the cliff for sunset viewing. Tonight's sunset will be spectacular as the golden orb sinks toward the water-filled horizon. Nothing impairs the sun from kissing the waterline, and kissing was strongly on my mind.

And the last thing I wanted was Mason kissing Autumn. However, his body's position—leaning his hip casually against the railing of the landing—said he was ready to make his move any second. Autumn faced him, holding her wineglass to her chest, and when Mason reached out to tuck her hair behind her ears, I almost tripped descending the short treads.

"Let's talk about this baby-making business." Mason's voice drifts up to me where only a few steps remain between them and me.

Let's not.

"Hey, guys. What are we talking about?" I fumble down the next couple of stairs and watch Autumn take a large step back from Mason.

Mason shifts his body to press his ass against the railing. Once I hit the landing, I step up to Autumn's side and look up at my longtime friend.

"Cock blocker," Mason coughs into his glass while I smile broadly at him before turning to Autumn.

"Am I interrupting?" I hope to hell I am because it sounds like Mason was on the verge of propositioning Autumn, and I'm not liking it one bit.

"Mason and I were discussing Ben's announcement." She smiles over at him and then back at me.

"It's a big change," I admit, still uncertain why my friend is making this move. He's only forty. Not old enough to retire, too young to sit idle, although he'll be anything but still if he works his dad's business.

Autumn only nods, gazing down at her wineglass held to her chest like a shield. When I don't move or add to the conversation, Mason takes the hint.

"I'm heading up to the house. Want another glass?" he offers to Autumn, who holds her wine up to show she still has a full goblet.

As Mason heads up the steps, taking them two at a time, I turn back to Autumn.

"Did I interrupt something?" I ask again, wondering if she wants him as her baby-maker. It would make sense. Women always wanted Mason, but for just once, I'd love a woman to pick me over him.

"No." She softly chuckles, twisting to face the lowering sun.

"Is Mason making the list?" The question tumbles out before I can stop myself, and Autumn sighs.

"I should kill Anna for opening her mouth."

Reaching out for her, I can't help but stroke up her back and under her hair as I did earlier, wrapping my fingers around the back of her neck.

"She always means well," I say, defending Ben's wife. Anna doesn't mean to meddle but just wants to help. She was the same way in college, always nudging people together, wanting them to find what she and Ben have.

Autumn chuckles softly and takes a sip of her wine. "I suppose everyone was pretty shocked by their announcement to move."

"I know I am, and I feel like I'm missing something." Autumn lowers her head as she sets the glass of wine on the railing. The unsaid weighs between us. However, I don't expect her to betray her brother's reasons if they run deeper than wanting a change of scenery. "But let's talk about us."

Her head swings upward, and she glances at me over her shoulder.

"I want you to know I would never call you fat. Not now, not then, so I'm sorry if that's what you heard—"

"Because that's what you said." Placing two fingers over her lips, I stop her from interrupting me further. Only, touching her lips scatters my thoughts, and I can only concentrate on the tender swell of her bottom lip and the curvy bow of the top one. Taking a moment to stroke over those lips, I stare at them, swallowing hard as I want a taste.

"Anyway." I finally recover, tracing over her mouth one final time before dropping my hand to hers. "I didn't think you were fat."

"I was solid, my mother would say," she mocks.

"I wouldn't have said that either. You were just younger than us. You were Ben's little sister."

"Yes, but I'm not little anymore."

"No." I pause, staring at those lush lips again. "You're definitely not." My fingers toy with hers while my other hand still cups the back of her neck.

"But I'm still Ben's sister." Said with hesitant sarcasm, a question lingers.

"Should that matter?"

"Does it?" she asks, and I bite my lower lip.

"I don't want it to," I admit, and we stare at one another. Those rich coffee eyes swirl with specks of cream, and I drink her in. When she doesn't respond, I confess even more. "I'd like to make that moment up to you."

"The moment when you called me fat or the moment you pushed me away?" she asks, her voice still tight.

"You're fucking beautiful," I say, and her eyes widen. "It doesn't matter what you looked like as a teen. We aren't teenagers anymore." I allow that to sink in because if we were still young, she'd never be attracted to me.

Then my head tilts, and I squeeze the back of her neck. "Why did you try to kiss me?"

She tries to look away from me, but my hold on her neck tightens, and I release her hand to cup her chin forcing her attention back to me. Her eyes close, and she licks her lips.

"I had a crush on you."

My own eyes widen in surprise, and I stare at her mouth, her pert nose, her closed lids. "What?" The word is a struggle.

Her eyes pop open, spearing me with their hesitancy. "I had this crazy notion that you and I were meant for each other."

Everything in me says to pull back, walk in a circle, take a moment to collect my thoughts, and return to her, but instead, the hold I have on her neck stays firm, and my thumb strokes her cheek. *This couldn't have been true.*

"What made you act that night?"

"This is so embarrassing. It doesn't matter anymore, like you said. We aren't teenagers anymore."

"Just tell me." I'm wound tight, and I need to know why this beautiful woman who was once an awkward teen thought I was her forever person.

"Ben asked you to hang with me, and you didn't complain. You just kept your arm around my neck and kept me close most of the night. You were funny. Sweet even. We went upstairs so I could use the bathroom, and you waited in an open bedroom. I thought that meant you wanted me to meet you in the room, and when I entered, I tried to kiss you. You pushed me away, and I fell on the bed."

Slowly, I release my hold on her, pulling away and missing her skin while hating myself.

"Did I hurt you?" *Jesus, I'm a fucking dick.* My hands clench into fists, one tapping on the railing.

Shaking her head, she drops her eyes to my chest. "Just my feelings by what you said."

LIVING at 40

I still can't believe I said such a thing, especially about her. "What happened next?" I ask, still forcing my hands to keep from reaching for her neck and face while my palms itch to touch her once more. Tell her how sorry I am for being juvenile and crass when I was young.

"I ran from the room because you were laughing."

"I laughed?" I choke. What could possibly be funny about a chick tossing herself at me? Those things never happened when I was in college. My humor lured a woman in, but I worked hard to get her to the next level—agreeing to sleep with me. Like in movies where the couple is funny in bed, girls would say I'm sweet, and I'd instantly be friend-zoned. They didn't take me seriously.

"Bent at the waist, cackling."

"Jesus." I hiss, turning my head away from her. I can't look at her. I don't deserve her looking at me, and I'm the one embarrassed. I'm mortified. Quickly recovering myself, I turn back to her. "I'm so sorry, Autumn."

Her breath hitches before she chews at her lower lip.

"I was a dick back then. An immature, overweight, obnoxious, probably drunk asshole, and I'm so sorry I hurt you." With her head tipping forward as I apologize, I bend my knees, tucking my body a bit so I can look up at her. "Forgive me?"

God, please forgive me.

She nods, craning away from me once more. "I do." My hands return to their previous position, cupping her jaw and wrapping around the back of her neck.

"Look at me and tell me you forgive me."

The setting sun reflects in her deep eyes, turning them a lighter brown speckled with gold. "I forgive you."

Slowly, I smile and bite my lower lip. We hold each other's gaze a moment before I speak.

"I'd like to make it up to you," I say, still unsettled by my younger behavior.

"You don't need to—" My thumb stops her, and we stand in this position another second.

"Kiss me," I whisper, gazing at my thumb stroking her lips. "I promise not to push you away."

Her eyes widen again, and the descending sun reflects in them.

"Let me rephrase," I say, leaning forward. "Let me kiss you. Don't push me away." My thumb lowers to her chin, pressing her face upward as I lower for her lips. She hasn't answered, but I don't wait for permission.

My mouth seeks hers, connecting with the softest lips I've ever touched. I intend to steal only one kiss, keeping it tender as I would have done when she was still young. Only, my brain kicks in, and my heart hammers, and the next thing I know, I've pulled her closer to me, opened my mouth, sought her tongue, and swallowed her gasp as we deepen our connection. Her lips mold to mine, following my eagerness. Her tongue swirls against mine as if savoring every stroke. Widening our mouths, we're hungry for more, and our heads tilt. The hand at her neck holds her in place while my fingers delve into her hair. Her breasts rub against my chest, her body melting into mine as her palms flatten on my shoulders but quickly curl around the back of my head.

"Fucking hell," I mutter to her mouth, quickly recapturing them and drawing them back to me once more before asking. "Did you kiss like this as a kid?"

She giggles against our joined lips. "I doubt it." Wanting to swallow that laugh, I press our mouths together again. I adjust her body, lining her backside up with the railing and devouring her more. If I don't slow us down, I'm going to hike her up on the ledge and strip her of her clothing, but I can't seem to stop. I promise myself I'll only take one more minute to kiss her, but her hands slip to my chest to tell me time's up.

Slowly, I pull back, and our eyes meet.

"I hope that makes up for things, just a little bit." Lifting her hand, she holds her forefinger and thumb close to one another, leaving only an inch between them.

"Maybe a little bit," she teases, and my eyes narrow. More than a little bit is happening in my shorts, and I have no doubt she can feel it through her summer skirt.

Softly chuckling, I lean forward for another kiss, quickly stealing it from her before she objects.

"The sun's almost set," she says, glancing over her shoulder, and I'm worried the kiss didn't have the same effect on her as it did me. That kiss was more than I deserve for treating her as I did, and something I'll long for the rest of my life if I don't earn another one from her.

Spinning to give me her back, she stares out at the lake, which looks as if it's swallowing the sun like I tried to swallow Autumn's tongue. She remains before me, so I risk running my hand up her back again, slipping it under her hair and cupping her nape. When she tips her head back, I slide my arm around her waist and hold her against my chest as we watch the sun disappear. Both quiet with our own thoughts, I'll spend the rest of my life making things up to her if she kisses me like that again.

9

[Autumn]

As we stand in silence, watching the glorious sunset, I smile to myself.

Wow. Logan Anders knows how to kiss a woman, and I accept that women were attracted to him for more than his humor. He had jokes to bolster his confidence, but once a girl got past the enticingly nice guy, a man who could seriously kiss existed.

"Please don't put Mason on your list," he mutters just below my ear as the sun disappears, but the afterglow still paints the sky in bright orange and vibrant pink. His words erase any aftereffects lingering from our kiss.

"Why?" I say, twisting my body so I can face him. "Why does this matter?"

Logan steps back and scratches at the scruff under his jaw. "I just don't think you should fuck him."

"Are you saying I should fuck you?" Logan flinches as I wave a hand up and down his body. The question is harshly stated because I'm instantly annoyed. "What is with this competition between Mason and you?"

"What competition?" he asks, his eyes narrowing at me.

"Mason's putting on the full-court press as well."

"What? Is he pressuring you?" Concern drips from Logan's voice as he steps back into my space, cupping my shoulders and stroking down to my upper arms. "Don't give in to him."

"Because I should give in to you?" My voice rises. I'm so confused. What in the— "Do you two have a bet or something placed on me? Is this some game to see who can get in my pants first?"

"What? No. Of course not."

"Because I'm not sleeping with either of you."

"Why not?" Logan asks, and I should be aghast, but there's something underlying his tone.

"Because this is important to me." This baby-making business isn't a joke to me.

It's when his body stills, and his hands release my arms that I linger on his question. *Why not?*

Why won't I have sex with either of them, or why won't I have sex with *him*?

"And I'm not important to you." The strength of his voice drops to that of a wounded kid, and his head lowers, eyes aimed toward my toes.

"Logan, why would you even want to sleep with me?" As his head lifts and his mouth falls open, I hold up a hand to stop his answer. "I want a baby. I want someone to get me pregnant. You already have a child. And I don't need a husband."

He takes a long second to stare at me before he answers. "You want no strings attached? You can use all this sexiness for baby-making." He draws a hand down his own body, emphasizing his value. I don't miss the part I need most straining behind his zipper. I'd felt him against my lower belly as we kissed. Logan definitely has the package I need, but can he deliver? And why would he want to? His teasing tone reminds me he can't take anything seriously.

"This isn't a joke to me." My voice lowers. I don't want no strings attached to be the theme behind having a baby, but as I have no dedicated significant other, I'm settling for the next best thing. Settling reminds me of what Anna's often said. I settle on being content when I should strive for more. Pushing away the thought, I glance back at the lingering line of rays just above the darkening water.

Logan's warm hands return to my upper arms, squeezing lightly. "Hey. It's not a joke to me either." Our eyes meet, but I can't read his thoughts.

"Logan, you love Lorna, right?"

"Of course." Surprised by the question, he blinks.

"And you'd do anything for her, right?"

"Definitely."

"She gives you purpose."

He slowly smiles. "Well, most days, yes."

"That's what I want. I want to love someone unconditionally. Someone I'd do anything for." My hands clasp together, coming to my chest as if I'm praying. I don't believe a child will replace that inner need to love someone as my equal, but a baby would still fill a hole. I don't want to miss my chance to have a little person because I don't have a bigger someone permanently in my life.

"I get that," Logan says, still rubbing my arms while looking over my shoulder at the darkening sky.

"Then let me do what I want and quit making a mockery of it."

His eyes draw back to me. "I'm not making a mockery of it."

"This thing between you and Mason is ridiculous. You guys are Ben's best friends. You're too close to him, to me. I'm not sleeping with either of you. I'll just find someone else."

Slipping around him, I attempt to cross the landing, but his hand catches the crook of my elbow and spins me to face him.

"Whoa, whoa, whoa. Let's not just find a random dude to hook up with. You want someone who has good genes. A brain not just super sperm and brawn, *and* you should have someone who can step in if you eventually need support."

I shake my head. "I have Ben and Anna's support. That's all I need." I don't need anyone's permission to do what I want to do, but I do want Ben and Anna to be behind my decision. Anna has questioned the timing, but I've assured her it's something I've been thinking about for a while. I'm not getting any younger like my mother reminds me, and this is something I want. I'm financially secure. I run a successful business. I own my own place. Ben and Anna have their own issues with the move but just knowing they'll be closer to me makes a world of difference. And of course, my mother might eventually come around to the idea.

Logan's gaze roams my face as if he's trying to read me, but I don't have answers to give him. Mason is a player with a solid reputation for sleeping around, not to mention his accidentally impregnating Lynlee's mother. *But Logan?* I just don't understand his motive. He already has a child, and he doesn't seem like the kind of guy to walk away easily from a responsibility. What I'd really like is someone to love me, so I don't want someone feeling beholden or obligated to me. I only want a baby.

"Good night, Logan," I say as we seem to be out of words, but I've only taken another step before he catches me again, tugs me forward, and crashes his mouth to mine once more.

His kiss is like a hit of something sweet and forbidden. It's raspberry jam smothering granola and drizzled with chocolate for an extra touch of decadence and naughty under oatmeal crumbles. Instantly, I'm intoxicated by his mouth on mine like I was when he first kissed me. *I want all your kisses.*

Heavy words mixed with heady kisses could make a weaker woman swoon, but I've been given pretty promises that fell flat before. I don't want to give in to a lingering crush and a lusty apology years later for a hurt caused when I was young. We're both adults. Baby-making is serious business.

Still, the warmth of his lips and the weight of his tongue stirs my insides up good. It's high-speed on a Kitchenaid mixer, and my hips thrust forward once as if my inner channel wants what's hidden behind his shorts buried deep within me. The idea of slipping over Logan, who is probably just as hot and firm down there as the rest of his body, has my hips rocking against him again. His hand slips under my hair, cupping the back of my neck as he's been doing all evening while his arm wraps around my back, placing a hand where my backside begins to curve. He presses me tighter to him, deepening the kiss, like he's afraid to let me go. I give in for another second, sucking at his tongue, drawing courage from his lips, and then I gently push back from him.

"Don't push me away," he mutters, but Logan once pushed me, and maybe it was a warning to my adolescent brain that Logan Anders could be very dangerous for me. He'd mess with my head and make my heart want more than he could give.

His mouth fights for mine, but I press once more, tugging my body free from the temptation of his lips and the thick length in his shorts. We both breathe a little heavier than normal. Lifting shaky fingers for my lips, I mumble against them.

"I can't do this with you."

+ + +

After running off from Logan and disappearing into my room, a soft knock comes on my bedroom door. It's late, and I've been trying to do everything to distract my thoughts from Logan's kiss.

"Come in," I softly call out.

"Hey." Anna steps through the door, leaning her back against the wood once she closes it. "You disappeared."

An unspoken question hangs between us. She wants to know details, but I'm not ready to share that Logan kissed me.

"Mason wondered what happened to you." *And* there's the reason. While Anna means well, she has her eyes on the wrong guy. Despite the hurt Logan inflicted when I was young, he always lingered in my heart, and I still found myself attracted to him. He dated countless girls who didn't seem right for him, and when he married Chloe, I got drunk at the wedding because I felt he'd missed an opportunity with me. They were the forever match when I wanted to be his. When they divorced, I was already wrapped up in Kevin or maybe it was Kenneth by then. I hadn't given much thought to Logan once I crossed thirty. We saw each other in passing at weddings and a few funerals. I'd accepted he wasn't for me.

"Anna, Mason is not interested in me."

Stepping toward the bed, I pull up my feet so Anna can sit at the end of it.

"You don't need someone interested, though, right? You just want his . . ." Anna waves at her lower region.

"His dick. You can say it. *His dick.*"

Her face heats, and she giggles like we're teens. "I know. I was just trying not to be so crass."

We're silent for a second, fighting smiles. "I bet he has a nice dick, though."

Her pinkened face turns a brighter shade. "I don't think about those things."

Chuckling, I say, "Come on. Not once have you wondered about someone else besides Ben?"

Straightening her shoulders and sitting a little taller, she's adamant as she says, "Only Ryan Reynolds." Then she falls over on the bed like she's revealed her darkest secret, and I'm laughing even harder as she covers her face in shame.

"You wild thing," I tease. Anna was quiet when Ben met her, shy even. While my brother wasn't necessarily a deviant, he wasn't innocent. He was outgoing, and he pulled Anna into him. They were opposites in some ways but mirror images in so many others. If she ever had considered Mason, she'd never admit such a thing, especially to me. I was still Ben's sister.

Sobering up a bit, she sits back up, leaning on one arm. "I just want someone decent for you." We stare at one another a second before we both break into laughter once more.

Another knock occurs on my door, but this person doesn't wait for an invitation. Popping his head inside, Mason appears with his model-worthy smile. "Sounds like I'm missing a slumber party."

Anna chokes, struggling to contain her laughter, as Mason helps himself to enter my room. He leaves the door partially open and steps up to the bed, waiting for only a heartbeat before tossing himself down next to me. With his back pressed against the pillows at the headboard, he crosses his legs, dangling his feet over the edge of the bed.

"What are we discussing? Our periods? Boys? Sex?" He drops his voice to sound like a young girl while each word rises an octave in excitement.

"Yes, our periods, so get out," I say, shoving at his shoulder, but he stretches his arm around me and tucks me into his side.

"Tell me all about it. Actually, tell me if you're ovulating. Is this a good time for you?"

"Oh my God," I blurt, pressing at his chest to release me, but Mason tightens his hold, and Anna chuckles. I'm not answering his question, but actually, now is a prime time if I were to calculate. I'm roughly two weeks out from having my period, and the signs will soon begin—

bloating, swelling breasts, daylong headache. Chocolate will jump to the top of the food chain along with salty products.

"You know, these are things to consider. The timing will have to be just right with whomever you select," Mason states, almost sounding like a doctor.

And we're back to discussing all things pertinent and personal for Autumn-makes-a-baby.

"Guys, I think I can figure this out."

"I can figure it out for you. I'm good at examining the female body," Mason decrees, and I groan. Anna squeals his name, and my door opens wider to reveal Logan. The smile on his face instantly slips away as he takes in my position with Mason. I'm on my bed, tucked under his arm with my hand on his chest.

"What am I missing?" Logan asks, but the suggestive playful tone he could have is devoid of any teasing, unlike Mason's when he entered my room. With Logan's eyes focused on me, the question admits he wants a different answer than girl talk.

10

[Logan]

To say my heart stopped when I see Autumn leaning into Mason is an understatement. My blood runs cold. Oxygen ceases to exist. I don't want her with him. I want her with me. It's primal in thought, but my Neanderthal roots beg me to stalk across the room and drag her from the bed.

She's mine. She had a crush on me when we were kids. She kissed me on the landing. She belongs with me, and everything in me is screaming of possession.

However, Mason curls his fingers against her arm, holding her to his chest even when she's pressing her hand to the tight tee he wears to show off that he's fit and has man nips. No one wants to see that business. My eyes narrow, and Mason tweaks one brow at me. He knows he's pissing me off.

Mason and I have competitive spirits, but deep down, I could never compete with him. He's got that cool hair and seductive swagger about him that draws chicks like magnets. He's a dick, but women love that shit, and nice guys finish last. Fat guys don't even cross the finish line. My solid stature and winning personality didn't beat savvy flirting and a slim stature. Although flirty humor could catch a girl's attention, I worked extra hard to prove I was worthy of keeping. Most times, it didn't work in my favor. The game has changed a little with my weight loss and a healthier lifestyle, but I'm still me, and it upsets me that with my outer shell improved, my gooey insides aren't seen as good enough.

Why would she sleep with me? It's a question I can't answer for myself. While I want to give her all the reasons—I'm loyal, dedicated, and I'd be good to her—that's not what she's looking for. She wants a means to an end, and maybe I'm not that guy. Maybe Mason is better. He can love 'em and leave 'em like no one else. He's been single his entire life. Still, I don't like the idea of Mason fathering another child and not being devoted to said kid in some manner.

As I stare at Autumn, asking my question—"What am I missing here?"—my meaning is twofold. What the fuck am I witnessing, and what's wrong with me?

Shaking my head to snap out of my thoughts, I change tactics like I always do. "Just came to say good night to all the pretty girls." I cross the room to kiss Anna on the top of her head. Stepping to the side of the bed, I lean over Mason and cup Autumn's face. With two hands on her cheeks, I lower and kiss her like I did earlier, claiming her with lips and tongue and the determination that Mason will not have her. She almost chokes at the eagerness I put into the kiss, swiping over her lips, stroking her tongue, and then quickly releasing her. With her eyes closed and her lips swollen, I'm satisfied I've made my statement.

Then I turn to Mason, who watches me. "Six point three-four for effort," Mason mocks. "If that wasn't so sloppy, it might have given me a semi."

Cupping his cheeks, I lean in as if I intend to kiss him the same way, but he's quick to remove his arm from Autumn and push me back from him.

"What the fuck, man?" he says, scrambling from the bed to get me away from him.

"Just wanted you to dream of me tonight," I tease, lifting my hand just under my chin and wiggling my fingers.

"If you kissed him, I'd never unsee that," Anna admits.

"If you kissed him, I'd dream of you both," Autumn states, and I turn to her, uncertain if she's serious or joking. Her wide eyes and lips still-moist from my kiss tell me she's teasing. Nipples peak through her thin sleep shirt, hinting at how turned on she is, and I want to tackle her to the bed, tug up that tee and suck at those breasts like a starved child.

"Jesus," Mason huffs while swiping a hand through his hair several times, mussing it up.

Take that, pretty boy. I turn my attention back to him until the corner of his mouth curls. He knows he's getting to me. He also knows I'm not giving up. I am more than just that funny fat guy. I'm more than a sweet personality. I can be everything to her, and with that thought, Autumn Kulis becomes a quest.

+ + +

The next morning, after a long run, I finally settle down a bit from the night before. After a quick jerk in the shower and a second time in bed, I fall asleep restless and unsatisfied. It isn't that I want to claim Autumn, but that I want the chance to get to know her better. As my best friend's younger sister, it's as if she's been in my life but not really a part of it. I know things about her, but I don't know her outside of the café owner and the desire to be a mother. I'm pulled to her in a way I can't understand but want to explore.

Still, there are so many questions. Why does she want to go it alone? Why *is* she alone? From the things I know of Autumn, she's loyal as hell to her family and a natural nurturer to her niece and nephews. My own Lorna couldn't stop talking about her when I went to say good night. Autumn apparently promised the two girls she'd take them on a special girls-only day trip this week. She's also capable of running her own business, making her self-sufficient and independent.

This quandary about her finds me in line at the Crossroads Café again, impatiently waiting my turn to approach the counter and greet her good morning. To my surprise, Mason's voice wafts over the subtle chatter in the crowded space, and I glance around to find Autumn standing beside him near the cream and sugar bar. Stepping out of line, I cut through the waiting people to edge closer to them.

"Hey," I greet, looking from Autumn to Mason. He lowers his head, shaking it side to side, while Autumn returns my greeting.

"Good morning." I watch her chew her lower lip, and my mouth waters for another taste of her. She's the cream and sugar supplement I'm no longer allowed in my coffee goodness. "Out for another run?"

My sweat-soaked tee gives away the obvious, and compared to Mason's untucked polo and khaki shorts, I'm a hot mess. Swiping a hand over my hair does nothing to improve my appearance.

71

"Mace, you're up early," I comment. Slowly glancing at me, he nods.

"Early to bed and early to rise makes a man healthy, wealthy, and *satisfied.*" I don't bother to correct him that the last word should be wise. He tips up a brow, insinuating his morning wood, and I'm grateful I'm not drinking coffee yet as I might puke.

"I think it's—"

"Don't bother correcting him," I interject over Autumn and direct another glare at Mason. "What are you doing here?"

Lifting his cup, he answers the obvious.

"Logan, let me get you a coffee, too." Autumn reaches out to touch my bicep and then slides her hand down to my forearm before releasing me. With a satisfied grin, I thank her and turn back to Mason.

"Dude, do you need to be so obvious? If you get any closer, you'll piss on her, and that will probably just piss her off," Mason snaps as soon as Autumn steps away.

"What the hell are you doing here?" I ask, knowing it's more than just the coffee in his hand.

"Look, not everything is about you or her, okay?" The sharpness to his tone surprises me, and I lean back a bit, staring at one of my best friends in a battle of strong wills. Autumn interrupts our linked glare when she hands me a coffee.

"I remembered you ordered the dark roast yesterday." She smiles up at me, and I swear my heart flips over like a happy pup wanting his belly rubbed.

"Thank you." Stepping forward, I lean my cheek next to hers, brushing my scruff along her soft skin before pressing a kiss to her jaw. She blushes as I stand straighter, and Mason shakes his head again.

"I've got to get back to work," she says, hitching a thumb over her shoulder, and Mason and I lift our to-go cups in tandem, saluting her.

"We'll talk later," Mason states, and I wonder what he means, but Autumn's eyes flick from him to me, and she fights the curve of her lips. Yeah, I definitely want to kiss her again, and something tells me she might want me to kiss her, too.

Following Mason's lead, we exit the café.

"What was all that about?" I snap as we turn to the side street, and Mason stops beside his sporty car.

"As I said, not everything is about you." He opens the driver's door but sets the to-go cup on the roof and rests his elbow on the doorframe.

"Okay, then talk to me. What's going on?" The shift in my voice has him leaning over the door, open as a barrier between us.

"I just have this weird feeling about Ben."

The mention of the man who brought us together has goose bumps rising on my sweat-coated skin. "What about him?"

"Something's off."

Now that he mentions it, I feel the same way, and it's not just the announcement to move back here.

"What are you thinking?"

"He's not drinking. Did you notice that? He opens a beer, but it just sits next to him."

"Are you thinking he has an issue?" Mason shakes his head in response. Out of all of us, Zack would be the more likely candidate for a drinking problem. Not that I think he has one, but he has a tendency to overindulge.

"Do you think something's going on with Anna?"

Mason shakes his head again. "I'm pretty certain the happy couple is still the happiest couple."

"But do you think she's pressuring him to stop drinking, or to move, or something else?" Anna McCaryn is the money in the relationship. The wealth of her family meant she'd never have to work if she didn't want to, but her generous heart made her want to be a teacher and deal with other people's children every day. Where she taught wasn't in the safest of neighborhoods in the Chicago area, but she loved her job, or so I thought, before this announcement to relocate.

"I don't know what it is. It's just a hunch." Mason casually leans over the car door, lowering his chin for his crossed arms.

"Hunch? Since when do you have a hunch?" I tease.

"Since I see the way you're nearly salivating over Autumn. Man, I get that you're single again, but you can't be desperate."

"Being with her isn't desperate," I defend.

"I'm not saying it's a desperate move. I'm saying you can't be that hungry." He eyes my body. "You still got it, right?"

"Are we talking about my dick?" I snap.

"Well. You certainly had me working a semi last night with that near kiss." He's teasing me. While there's no doubt Mason would share a woman with another man, he would not be interested in the other man.

"Fuck off." I laugh, and he chuckles, swiping at his hair.

"Seriously, what is it with her?"

"It's nothing," I lie, downplaying my rising emotions and my heightening libido at the mere idea of being with her.

"That's right. It's nothing. This is Ben's sister. Plus, she wants a kid. Are you really thinking you'd be a dad again?"

"Are you?" I bark. In my opinion, Mason's a shitty father, but I'm not about to call him out on his responsibilities. He's a grown man, and it's not my place to tell him how to act. I want to hope there's more to his story, but sometimes, I just don't know that there is.

"Autumn isn't looking for a daddy for her kid. She just wants sex to make a baby."

Instantly, my teeth grind at Mason so casually discussing Autumn's intentions and the fear that she and Mason have had a real discussion about the possibility of him fathering her future child.

"Is that what you meant when you said you two would talk later? You'd be talking about sex to give her a baby?" The question comes with all the passive-aggressive feelings I have on the subject of Mason hooking up with Autumn.

He tilts his head, taking a second to ponder me. "Don't you think we should leave it up to the lady to decide?"

"Fuck," I mutter again, turning my head from him. He knows she'd pick him over me any day, and I don't want to have an age-old argument about him leaving some women for us lesser men. Autumn isn't some woman. She should be someone's person.

"You really want her, don't you?" I don't see why he's surprised. Autumn is a catch, but I'm not looking to release her. I want her in a way I can't explain. Mason continues to eye me for a long time before he mockingly adds, "I'll be the first to congratulate you when you get engaged."

"Who's talking about marriage?" I scoff. "I'm not getting married again." *Pfft.* Is he kidding me? Only, I see in his eyes, he's not joking, and the retort tasted bitter on my tongue. Could I really have a baby with Autumn and walk away? Could I *not* marry her if I got her pregnant? Quickly, I remind myself I'd be doing what Autumn wants. She wants a baby, not a husband, and that's my out.

Mason tips his head in disbelief. "That's why I'd be a better choice. We both know I can walk away from shit. I've been doing it since we were kids."

"What the hell does that mean?" My eyebrows rise, and Mason lowers his eyes. His head shakes slowly again, dismissing his admission. "Forget it, man. It's never mattered."

"Mace, what are you talking about?" As I step toward the car door, he turns to retrieve the to-go cup from his roof and slips inside his fancy vehicle. I grip the door to stop him from closing it. "Tell me what you mean."

"I said it doesn't matter. As for Autumn, ladies' choice I say."

"Dammit," I mutter as he tugs the driver's door free from my grasp. Mason laughs, shutting me out with the click of the closed door. Staring after him as he reverses out of the lot, I fight old insecurities and talk myself into what I need to do.

I need to prove to Autumn I'm the *only* choice for her.

11

[Autumn]

The tension between Mason and Logan is titillating while frustrating, and I don't have time to think about either of them touching my tits. Between the two, Logan is the one I'm attracted to most although Mason isn't unattractive. He's just more the annoying brother you hate but love at the same time. It's all confusing, so at the end of the day, I gather around the two people who don't stir me up.

"Girls' night out!" I cry out as Mila and Lorna exit my sensible Hyundai crossover parked before the nail salon. We'll be getting manis and pedis in bright summer colors. It's fun to listen to the girls giggle and chatter although sometimes a conversation with me can be stilted. Instead, they whisper to each other about girly things, and it makes me smile. I don't recall being like this with girlfriends when I was a kid, but I must have been. Eventually, I was more the girl who had boyfriends. The one who dated for longevity but never ended up with the engagement ring. I was loyal to a fault which might strangely explain my still lingering crush on Logan despite what happened back when he was in college.

Dinner with the girls is ice cream although I'm certain it's not enough of a real meal, and they'll be looking for snacks later in the evening. This night is about breaking all the rules, though, with blueberry-flavored ice cream and a stroll down to the public beach in town. Deciding we don't want to ruin our freshly painted toes, we stick to the boardwalk before deciding to head back to the house. I promise the girls cartwheels on the beach before sunset after our toenails have dried.

As we return to the cottage, I glance at Mila in my rearview mirror. "Should we drive by the house?"

My niece smiles back at me. She knows which one I'm talking about. There's a little cottage home, not a sprawling one like the McCaryn family, that has my name on it someday. It's been on the market a while, but I can't afford it yet. It needs some TLC, but it's perfectly situated. You can see over the house across the street and out to the lake from the second-story window. It's not exactly lakefront, so the cost is much less than the neighbors across the street, but it's still the perfect house for me and a baby one day.

"There she is," I tease as I drive by the place, pausing to point out a swing dangling from a tree in the front yard.

"There's my swing," Mila says, as both girls glance out the window.

"Are you moving here?" Lorna asks.

"One day," I whisper, just like I've done about all my other dreams. One day . . . I will fall in love. One day . . . I will marry. One day . . . I will have a baby. I smile with hope in my heart that at least some of these *one days* will be sooner rather than later. After a final look, I return my foot to the accelerator and drive on.

As we enter Anna and Ben's, the guys are getting ready to head out. To give Anna a break, they're going into town for burgers and beer. Logan sits alone at the kitchen island, staring at his phone, but he shifts at our approach.

"Dad, look at my nails." Lorna holds up the back of her hands for her father to see the bright blue coloring with a daisy painted on each ring finger. The nail tech really is an artist.

"Blue? My favorite color." He leans forward to tug her to him, but she flips her hands to stop him.

"Dad, my nails."

Shaking his head, he dismisses her rejection. "Did you ladies eat?"

"We had ice cream for dinner but don't tell Mom," Lorna says, dropping her voice. My brows pinch as I meet Logan's eyes.

"Does she have a food allergy?" I didn't think to ask if she was allergic to dairy or any food for that matter, nor did I consider she might have a health restriction that doesn't allow a cheat with ice cream.

"No," Lorna answers for herself. "I just promised Mom I'd eat a salad a day and not skip the vegetables at meals."

A deeper crease forms between my brows as I glance down at the beautiful eleven-year-old girl before me. Everything about her matches her father, which means she has broader shoulders and solid legs. It's an athletic build, and she doesn't need salads.

Mila says something to Lorna, and they excuse themselves from the kitchen as Lorna calls over her shoulder, "See you, Dad."

"Bye, honey." He waves although she isn't looking back at him, and he watches her disappear in the front entryway. "I don't know how I'm going to handle it when she turns into a teenager."

"I'm sorry about the ice cream. I just thought it would be fun to say we had it for dinner, but I'll see that they eat something healthier later."

Logan waves a hand at me, and I take a moment to note his appearance. He's wearing a dark tee and khaki shorts that droop on his hips. He looks sexy for the single dad at forty, and suddenly, I'm nervous that young things will hit on him when the guys go to the bar.

"Don't worry about the ice cream. I hate when Chloe *enforces* Lorna's eating habits." He air quotes the word enforces, further mocking the term as he speaks.

"Right? Who wants salad at eleven?"

Logan swipes a hand through his hair. "Chloe just worries Lorna will grow . . . large like I was and develop diabetes."

"She's not fat," I blurt.

"It's a sensitive issue. Even Lorna gets upset that she's bigger than some of the other girls in her grade, but she's also a year older than them with a late birthday, and she just has solid genes." While Lorna might still have baby fat, puffing her knuckles and thickening her belly, she isn't large by any means. She's eleven. She's healthy and active from what I've seen, and any concerns aren't warranted. But I remember how I was when I was her age. I was fuller than others and self-conscious about it.

"Has she gotten her period?" I ask although that's a bit intrusive.

"Not yet." Logan looks at the ceiling. "God help me when that happens."

"You'll be fine," I tease, stepping toward him. With his foot planted on the footrest and his knee pointed to the side, I step into his space. "You're a great dad." My hand lands on his chest, smoothing down his tee. As if I can't control my own body parts, my palm lingers on the warmth seeping through the cotton and the firmness underneath that I witnessed on our first day at the beach. My fingers splay over his pec and stretch toward his nipple. *What am I doing?* However, I can't seem to pull my hand away until Logan catches my wrist. Slowly, he lifts my hand for his face and presses a kiss to my palm.

"My nipples are sensitive," he says in all seriousness while his eyebrows dance. Heat forms between my thighs. Logan lowers his fingers, reaching for the edge of my denim miniskirt, curling under the hem and playing with the frayed material at the edge. He's also brushing his knuckles on the skin of my upper thigh, sending small currents of need straight to my core. It's embarrassing to admit, but if his fingers drifted north under my skirt, he'd find me wet.

"Again, I'm sorry about the ice cream." Needing something to do with my own hands, so I don't grab his wrist and force his fingers higher up my thigh, I reach around him, leaning my breast against his chest as I stretch for an apple in the permanently stocked bowl of fruit on the counter. As I lean back, my eyes lower for his crotch, wondering if our nearness is having any effect on him like it's having on me. The knuckles just under my skirt intensify their stroking, and I take a bite of the crisp apple, eyes still focused on his zipper region. Here's the thing, Logan is tall—like six-four—and if he's proportional, he has to have a long *thing* behind those shorts. I've experienced where someone isn't proportional, and let's just say the relationship was short-lived, every pun intended.

We remain quiet, although the sound of the crunching apple seems to echo around the kitchen. Logan watches me chew while I'm nearly salivating around the fruit on my tongue. I'm not a big one for giving head, but I really want a taste of him. I want to know if he's salty-sweet and a little juicy as he hardens. My thighs clench, and Logan stills his fingers. We both breathe unevenly, staring at one another until he stands quickly. His hand rushes up my back and under my hair, curling around my neck, and my body is flattened against his. He leans forward, and I anticipate our mouths meeting.

"Logan, are you . . ." The sound of Ben's voice stills time, and then we break apart. Logan knocks the stool back, causing it to screech loudly against the wood floor before colliding with the one behind it. I step away from him and drop the apple I was holding, feeling as if all the blood has drained from my veins and the use of my muscles isn't something I can control. What was I thinking? I almost climbed on his lap right here in the kitchen and begged him to take me.

Briskly stroking his fingers through his hair, Logan's eyes shift from me to over my shoulder, where my brother stands somewhere behind me.

"Yeah, I'm ready." His hand drops, and he adjusts himself, which would normally be inappropriate, but it's an admission. He was getting as turned on as I was. Stepping up to me, he leans forward and offers a chaste kiss to my cheek.

"See you later, beautiful. Behave yourself," he murmurs before pulling away, and my eyes follow his retreat like a left-behind puppy.

"You too," I whisper, fear filling my belly that he'll meet someone younger, hotter, and easy to please for one night, and I'll be left with all these roiling hormones. Not to mention my desperate need to use said hormones and work on making a baby.

The thought snaps me out of my lusty haze, and I turn my back on the guys as Logan follows Ben to the front door. Logan is not the man to sleep with me. I need a man who can let me go after giving me what I want, and I'm afraid *I* wouldn't want Logan to leave if we'd done the deed.

+ + +

After another evening down on the beach, where I prove I can still do a cartwheel at almost forty—although I give myself a little vertigo from doing one—the girls need showers, and then we watch a movie. I've given Anna the night off, telling her to go do something for herself while I cater to two little beings full of giggles.

"I feel guilty not spending time with Mila," Anna admitted. Calvin and Bryce have graciously agreed to take on Zack's hellions and have them quarantined in the apartment above the garage for a night of video games.

"Let me do this for you. I love playing the greatest aunt in the world because I can always return her to you," I teased. The truth is I don't want to have to return children to their parents, as wrong as that sounds. I want a child of my own, to keep close to me.

As we watch some girly movie starring an actress I don't know, I reflect on Logan's interaction with Lorna. I realize one day a baby will grow into a teen and eventually leave me behind as my mother often complained Ben did to her. But I also accept that's the way of things. If I do my job as a parent, I should be able to set the human being I've groomed and loved free into the world as a responsible citizen and decent person.

Considering the ice cream dinner, I question my ability to parent for a full three seconds. I'd never want to put a child in harm's way. The fact I didn't ask about allergies concerns me. There are a million factors that could go wrong in parenting. Not to mention, I'm aging, although I'm not ancient. Still, over thirty-five and pregnant is considered a risk, and I don't like to think about how something might happen to my future child because I've waited so long to have him or her. The thought almost paralyzes me by the time the movie ends, and I'm saying good night to Mila and Lorna. I should seek out Anna, but she has enough on her plate, and this two-week holiday has already turned into a little bit of Autumn wants a baby more than Ben's big hurrah.

Slipping into my room, I change into the loose boxers I wear to bed and a thin cotton camisole. The breeze coming off the beach is pleasant, and I keep the windows open, listening to the rush of waves echoing up the cliff as I climb onto my bed. I try to read, but my thoughts keep wandering, so I skip back to a favorite in my ebook collection and find a section that's hot torture. My sex pulses. My thighs clench, and I slip my fingers down my belly and into my shorts. I'm almost to the promised land when my door flings open and then quietly closes with a click. My hand moves so quickly out of my shorts it knocks into the ereader in my other hand, forcing me to drop it and smack my chin with the device. Glancing down the length of my body, I can't move. My eyes find Logan standing with his back to my door. His head tips toward the ceiling. His chest rises and falls.

"Was I interrupting something?" His teasing tone tells me he caught me, but his refusal to look at me hints he'll let me deny it.

"What are you doing in here?" I whisper although we're the only two inside the room. Perching up on my elbows, I stare at him over my feet which seem to frame him in as he's plastered to my door.

"What the hell are you wearing?" He swallows hard, and I watch his Adam's apple roll as I did the first day on the beach when he guzzled a beer. I want to lick him there. I want to feel the edge of his scruff against my tongue and then rub my cheek along his, allowing the soft scratch to tickle my skin.

"Pajamas," I state of my attire.

"Whose boxers are those?" The old pair is something I've had for years. The traditional male boxers with small polka dots on the blue material are comfortable and all mine.

Tilting my head to the side, I ask, "Why?"

"I . . ." He licks his lips as he stares back at me. "I can't fuck you in another man's briefs."

Holy . . . *what?*

"Excuse me." Still perched on my elbows, I'm frozen once again but blink in his direction. Logan presses off the door and comes to the side of the bed. His fingers twitch as he reaches forward for my knee and then stops himself, curling his fingers into a fist and returning his hand to his side.

"Put me on the list."

"Logan," I groan, falling back on the bed and covering my face with both hands. He hisses as I do this, and I spread my fingers to allow me to see him through the slats. His eyes focus on my breasts, un-bra-ed and nipples pert through the thin material of my cotton shirt. Falling backward, the camisole shifted, and a strip of my belly is exposed.

"Please," he groans, closing his eyes.

"Logan, you do not want to be the one to get me pregnant." My arms fall to my sides, feeling self-conscious in this position of him staring down at me as I lay across my bed.

"Why not?"

"Because you have Lorna."

Pausing for a moment, he takes a deep breath before responding. "You don't need me to be the dad. You just want my sperm." He's trying to tease me, but his eyes scan my body. He chews at his lower lip. Instantly, I'm as heated as I was standing before him when he sat on the kitchen stool earlier this evening. My head says deny him while my body screams for release, wanting more than my own fingers to perform the finishing act.

"Fine," I mutter, sounding petulant even though I'm anything but. My hands curl to fists as I lie on my back.

"Why do you look like you're gritting your teeth? Would it really be that bad to sleep with me?" His softening tone puzzles me. He reaches forward, connecting with my skin this time by stroking one finger over my knee and circling the cap before dragging it down my shin. "I'd want you to enjoy it."

Yes, please, I think as his finger retraces its path and drags over my knee again, heading up the length of my thigh to the hem of my briefs, which is high on my leg. Reaching the edge, he slips his fingertip just beneath the material at the center of my thigh where my leg meets my hip.

"I don't want you to feel like I'm doing you a favor."

Please, do me a favor. *Do me.*

Logan pulls his finger away and stands taller. "I get it. I'm not Mason, but I still think we'd be good. I'd be good to you." His eyes avoid mine as he slips his hands into his short's pockets. He pauses a beat before turning on his feet and heading for my door.

My body vibrates but watching him walk away, everything in my body screeches to a halt. He can't leave me like this. I'm too wound up

L.B. DUNBAR

between his touch, and the book, and earlier. Plus, my hormones are raging, and my gut says this is the time. I'm between my cycle.

Scrambling to my knees on the bed, I follow his retreat, crawling on my knees as he stalks to the door.

"Wait." The word rushes out of me as I reach forward, nowhere near able to catch him with my touch. "Don't . . . leave."

A foot from the door, Logan turns back to me.

"I don't want Mason."

My chest heaves as we stare at one another. I can't read his expression. *Am I really doing this?* "But we need some ground rules."

Logan tilts his head as his hands come to his hips. "Okay."

"It's only sex. You get in and stay in until I say to move."

Logan chuckles, reaching up for his mouth and scrubbing his fingers around his lips. "Never heard that before, but okay."

"I'm clean. Rick left me over eight months ago, and I got tested right away when I found out he cheated on me."

"Fucking bastard," Logan says, and the harshness actually warms my insides. He's pissed on my behalf. "I haven't been with anyone in over a year."

I stare back at him, shocked. "But you're so . . ."

"What?" The sharpness in his tone the second time forces me to admit how I see him.

"Hot." Slowly the edge in his expression melts away and he grins a sheepish boy grin.

"You're fucking hot, too, sweetheart." *Oh God, call me endearments and I'm mush.*

"You don't need to feel responsible for medical expenses, holding my hand during delivery, or anything thereafter for the remainder of the child's life."

"Jesus," he mutters as I return us to the rules. Turning his head away from me, he stares out the windows where the sky is a deep bruising color of blues and approaching black. "Fine."

He looks back at me. "I have a rule as well."

"Okay," I hesitate.

"Nothing held back. You let me say what I want, do what I want to your body."

Holy shit, yes.

"Be up front now if there's a hard limit. I'm not doing safe word shit. You can stop me in the middle of anything, but I'd like to know now where I can't go."

Blinking at him, I swallow around the admission. "I've never had anyone in the back, and I don't know how I feel about that. I also don't think I'd be into sharing, even if it's been a fantasy."

"Sweet Christ," he hisses, stepping back to the side of the bed. I shift to follow him, facing him still on my knees on the mattress. "I'd never share you." The heat in his words scorches my skin, making me feel wanted more than I've ever felt.

"What about you?" I ask, my voice croaking as I speak. "Do you have any limits?"

"I want to be the only one who fucks you. If this doesn't work"—he points between our lower bellies—"you can move on . . . to the next guy. But for two weeks, give me a try and be only mine."

Wetness floods the plank of the briefs. My core pulses faster than my heart, and my thighs tremble.

"Logan." His whispered name is full of my agreement and my need for him. In an instant, his hand is behind my neck, and my mouth crashes to his. I'm up on my knees, flattening myself to him as his other hand smooths down my back, cupping my ass with a hard squeeze. I rock against him, feeling the hint of his length behind stiff material, but it isn't close enough. My fingers rush for the edge of his tee, pushing it up his chest, breaking the kiss only long enough for him to tug the material over his head. Our lips quickly return to each other's, tongues seeking connection. His skin is warm, seeping through the thin material of my cotton camisole as my hands skim his sides. Suddenly, I stop.

Disconnecting our kiss, I glance down at the device attached to him. "Do I need to be worried about anything? I won't hurt you, will I?" The last thing I want to do is compromise him.

"It's my insulin pump. It's durable and doable to go around it. If it freaks you out, I can remove it for a while." Cautious eyes meet mine.

"No," I blurt, cupping his scruff-covered jaw in hopes to reassure him. "I'll just be careful near it."

I lean forward for another kiss, and all thoughts of his pump are forgotten.

His fingers find my shoulders and loop under the thin straps of my cami. Logan tugs at the ribbon-thin material, lowering them down my arms, and leans away from me as the top catches on my breasts. He watches as he pulls the straps even lower, allowing my breasts to spring free. Hissing, Logan dips for one breast. Cupping it in his palm and hitching it upward to meet his mouth, he opens and sucks hard. His tongue swirls around the nipple before he draws his lips inward, pulling the hard nip to a peak. Quickly, he moves to the other one, repeating his movements as I comb my fingers through his hair. He stands taller and forces down the remainder of my shirt to my waist.

Still on my knees, his hands flatten on my thighs, his fingers curling into the short boxers.

"Thank God these aren't someone else's," he mutters, leaning in for a kiss.

"Why?" I mutter against his mouth, but he's already told me he can't fuck me in someone else's briefs. He doesn't answer me as he guides my lips into another mind-dazzling kiss. As his knuckles stroke at my skin like they did earlier in the day, he inches closer to my center. Suddenly, he pulls back.

"You aren't wearing anything underneath." It's not a question as much as confirmation when a finger swipes through the small patch of hair and tender folds aching for him. "You're also soaking wet."

"It's embarrassing," I admit as I'm nearly dripping with need.

"It's fucking hot," he says, slipping a finger into me and returning his lips to mine. His tongue invades my mouth as his finger delves deep. The kiss is steamy and quick. "Clothes. Off."

He reaches for the shirt bunched at my waist and tugs it plus the boxers to my knees.

"Stay like that," he demands of my kneeling position, and I work the clothing over my legs, quickly returning to my knees. "Now, where was I?"

He kisses me once more, deep and lush, before leaning back and watching his hand cup me between my legs. Two fingers enter me in a rush, and I grip his shoulders to steady myself.

"You're so wet," he marvels as though he's never felt anything like it. Looking up at me, he says, "Never be embarrassed with me."

As quickly as he speaks, he returns his gaze to his fingers, and we both watch as he enters me over and over with two thick digits. I'm full but need more of him.

"I want you to come inside me," I blurt. I've never been so bold. I'm not sheepish in the bedroom, but I'm not the demanding one either. I'm not the one who admits what I want, but I want him more than I care to admit.

"We'll get there, beautiful, but first you'll come. On my fingers. On my tongue, and then all over my dick buried deep inside you."

Sweet raspberry bars. My head tips back at his words, at his focused attention, at the feel of his fingers working their magic. I rock into his palm as the heel of his hand massages the sensitive nub that will trigger the first command on his list. "I've never had three before."

"Commence mission *not* impossible," he mutters to himself, his teasing tone mixing with his serious intention to perform a miracle with my body. Dancing against his hand, I release within seconds of his words and his mouth captures mine, absorbing my gasps of surprise. It's sensory overload to kiss his lips and fuck his fingers, and I can't concentrate on any one thing. My entire body hums. I don't know that I've ever released so fast.

As my hands skim down his chest to his waistband, he lifts his fingers coated from me and sucks them into his mouth. Watching me, he swirls his tongue around his own fingers as I unbutton his shorts and tug at the sides, forgoing the zipper. They easily slip from his hips. Boxer briefs in a deep green rest underneath, barely containing one of the biggest dicks I've ever seen. Logan is definitely proportionate.

My thumbs hook into his waistband, but he stops me with a hand on one wrist.

"Logan, I need you now," I warn him.

"We'll get there, sweetheart. When I'm ready. Now lie back on the bed."

12

[Logan]

A fantasy of mine has always been a gorgeous woman breathless and eager for me. While I found Chloe incredibly attractive when we married, that attractiveness wore off over time through her changes in physique and attitude. I like curvy women, and Autumn was curvy in all the right places. Her ass was rounded to perfection. Her hips swelled with enough for me to really handlebar her and her breasts—her breasts made her a goddess. Her body is something some ancient sculptor would cast in marble and jack off to all day. She was that flawless, and she was mine for the remainder of this vacation.

I refused to allow the question in my head of what the end of two weeks might mean. I didn't want to think about her walking away with my child inside her. I only wanted to revel at this moment where a gorgeous woman was panting for me.

She lies back, her hair billowing out on the bed, and a hand covers her belly. "None of that," I command, wiggling free of my khaki shorts. I entered her room barefoot, and I climb over her on the bed, tugging her hand free of her waist. Pinning her wrists by her head, I lean forward and kiss her again. I'm a kisser. I like kissing, and I like how Autumn kisses me back. I really like how she lingers once I pull away, like she's tethered to me and follows my retreat as if chasing my kiss.

"No hiding yourself from me," I warn her. "I think you're fucking stunning."

Her breath hitches as her eyes widen. "We can't let anyone know." Her comment surprises me.

"You want us to be a secret." I fight the sharpness piercing my tongue.

"I just don't need everyone knowing what we are doing because they know *why* I'm doing it. It's already too much that Anna shared my thoughts with everyone."

In hindsight, Anna was insensitive, although she did try to backtrack, warning all of us not to keep mentioning it, and telling us it was a private matter she should not have shared in the first place. Our teasing of Autumn that first night was only because she was Speck. She was Ben's little sister, but I wasn't thinking of her like that now. Underneath my straddled legs was a woman who knew what she wanted and was going to enjoy getting it.

That declaration is also a good reminder that this is nothing more than sex.

"Okay," I acquiesce although I'd love to shout from the rooftops that a gorgeous woman is eager for me to enter her and give her everything in me.

My hands skim down her arms near her head, coasting along her sides as I shift until my broad body is between her thighs. Angling my hands on her hips, I demand, "Open for me." Her knees bend outward as her legs spread wider, and I stare down at a beautiful sight of moist skin and curled folds. My mouth waters, and I lower to lick across her seam. She flinches, but I smile against her, slipping over her sensitive skin again and again. My fingers squeeze her hips, and my arms angle in a way her thighs are pinned down. She can't move, and it heightens the anticipation. My tongue thrusts forward, circling around her before delving inward, and my dick throbs. I'm so hard, and I'm ready to release, but I want this. I want her to explode on my lips, marking me in one more place with her essence. She's musky and sweet, and I lap it all up until her thighs quiver.

"Logan. Oh God, Logan. It's going to be—" Her warning cuts short as I suck at her clit and her back arches. The tension in her body tells me she's coming, and it isn't stopping. I shift my hands under her thighs, licking her everywhere, soaking up every drop of her until her hand comes to the top of my head. "Enough."

I'll never have enough of her, and I can't explain the sensation. I've known this woman more than two decades, and I want to kick myself for not seeing what's been within my reach. A brief flash of Lorna reminds me I wouldn't change one thing in the past eleven years, but now I need to seize what's in front of me. I scramble off the bed to remove my boxers and quickly return to my previous position. On my knees this time, I hitch her lower body up my thighs, watching as my bare dick stands at attention. I've never been so hard or so nervous. I want to give her what she needs from me.

With my hands curled under her knees, I lean forward, watching as I fall against her slick folds. The moisture coats my throbbing shaft, and I'm not certain I can wait another second to enter her.

"Logan," she pleads. "Please."

Begging me. She's begging me to be inside her, and I don't want to disappoint her. Stroking over myself once for good measure, I drift my gaze up her body to find her watching me. Her eyes are glazed over like she's had a sharp hit of something potent. Her hair tumbles over her shoulders. She's radiant, and I watch her face as I guide myself to her entrance.

"You're so huge." It's every man's dream to hear such things, but from her mouth to my ears, it's a live wire of electricity. Sparks fly as I slip into her wet heat, jolting alive as if I'd been dead inside. I slide to the hilt, sparing no time to surround myself with her.

"You okay?" I question, worried I'm too much for her. She's tight, and I'm snug inside her.

"This is amazing."

Jesus, she's a dream. I pull back, struggling with the sudden friction, eager to repeat the sensation. Surging forward, I'm engulfed in her heat once more, and I watch as I disappear inside her. It's titillating to watch, like live porn. Only this isn't obscene. This is otherworldly, and this beautiful woman is transcending me to a place I've never been. I'm almost embarrassed how quickly this might end.

"I . . . you . . ." I can't find the words as she embraces me in her body, and I slide through liquid heat. Dropping one hand forward to balance myself near her hip, I keep her lower body raised to my thighs and thrust. She yelps, and I glance up at her face. Her head has fallen back to the bed.

"Take what you need from me. Don't be gentle."

"Autumn," I groan as my hips flex and my pelvis moves. I rock into her on repeat, surging with sharp, short jabs as her channel rubs my shaft, and the friction heats everything. Too quickly, my lower back tightens. My balls seize, and I thrust forward, holding myself deep inside her. My dick jolts and jets a fountain of relief. Aftershocks follow, forcing every drop from me, but I don't move. I don't want to waste a single drip, and I remain over her with her hips tipped upward and my dick filling her.

I look up at her to find a tear slipping from the corner of one eye.

"Did I hurt you?" I push upward by the hand balancing me, but she's quick to slap her hands to my shoulder blades, holding me over her.

"I'm not hurt." Her voice croaks, and she swallows as another tear slips free. "I know it couldn't possibly work this quickly. Like the first time would be a miracle, right? But something inside me feels different already."

Chewing at my lip, I fight all the things that come to mind like maybe this means more than just a mission. Maybe this could be more than a means to an end. Maybe she could want more from me, but I keep all those extra thoughts to myself.

"Tell me when you want me to move," I remind her as another tear falls. This one is larger, and I can't help leaning forward to swipe at the drip rolling to her hairline.

"Autumn, look at me." She's been staring up at the ceiling, but her liquid-filled eyes latch onto mine. "We have eleven more days, and we'll do this again and again until we're certain it sticks, okay? We'll do it extra times just for good measure, and once more for good luck."

She slowly smiles before giggling a little. The jostling of her body jiggles me inside her, but I'm softening. I'm not as young as I used to be, and I'll need a little recovery time before we can go for round two. *Will she want round two?*

As her hands slip from my shoulder blades, I lean forward to kiss her, not wanting our connection to end but sensing the finish line. *Will she want me to leave?*

"Let me get you something to clean up." I slip free from her and instantly miss her body. As the house is older, she has a powder room, not a full bathroom in this bedroom, but I find a washcloth in a basket and soak it with warm water. Returning to her, I wipe her up and toss the cloth back to the sink like I'm shooting for a basket from half-court. The slap of wet cloth against the porcelain tells me I made the shot, and I feel like a king. I just had sex with a beautiful woman who begged me to come inside her, and all I have to do is hope my seed plants. Turning back to Autumn, she's pulled the sheet to her chest, holding it over her covered breasts and staring up at me.

"I'm not leaving." I'll fight her on this, but after the intense experience we just shared and the silent hope between us that it worked for her, I'm not walking out of this room. She nods, and I send up a quiet prayer of gratitude as I curl into bed beside her. We face one another, and I brush back her hair, staring into her deep, sated eyes. "Close your eyes, baby. Sleep."

She nods again without a word. After leaning forward for one more kiss, I watch her lips remaining puckered when I pull back and whisper to her, "Sweet dreams."

+ + +

"What's all this?" As I look up from my position by the kitchen counter, seeing Autumn takes my breath away. I wanted to stay in her bed a little longer, but as she mentioned last night, she doesn't want anyone to know about us and what we were doing because they'd already know the reason. So, I snuck out before dawn and crashed in my own bed for a few hours. However, I promised Lorna I'd make pancakes this morning. It's been great hanging with the guys and letting Lorna have her time with Mila, but we needed to check in about the ice cream meal and her comment on eating salads.

Talking weight with a pre-teen girl is a tricky subject. I don't want to belabor her size as I view her as healthy and wise to weight issues, and I don't have concerns. The doctor assures us she's in a normal range, just on the high end of it for her height and age. I'd be more concerned if she wasn't athletic and only sat around playing video games, but she doesn't.

She plays soccer and used to dance ballet. We live in a small community, and that means the competition is minimal for sports at her age.

Autumn steps closer to me, and I turn to give her a smile. Her eyes are bright this morning, and I peek over my shoulder to see who is close enough to hear me.

"Sleep okay last night?" Her eyes lower as she turns for the coffee maker and pours herself a cup.

"It was okay," she teases, chewing her lip as she looks up at me over the rim of her mug.

"Just okay?" I glance over my shoulder once more. "Need to work on that tonight then."

Her smile grows before she takes a sip of the morning goodness. As she lowers the mug, I take one more check over my shoulder before leaning forward for a quick kiss to her cheek. I want it to be more. I want her lips on mine and my arms around her, but we have little eyes nearby and ears that can miraculously hear well when they want to versus when asked to unload a dishwasher or do their homework.

"I need to get to work."

"You work too much," I state, instantly regretting how possessive it sounds. It's exciting that she runs her own business. I'd always dreamed of owning my own architectural firm, but the place I work pays well, with benefits, and allows me the flexibility I need to be with Lorna. Without being married and having Lorna only half the time in a week, work is all I have, so I know if I had my own business, I'd overwork and forget to take time for the fun stuff.

"I can't help it," she says. "It's the center of my life."

A baby is going to change all that for her. Her child will become the axis of her world, and every decision she makes will revolve around her kid. Parenting is a tough job to do alone, and I'm fortunate Chloe and I are amicable about Lorna, although some days it's rough being a one-parent show.

"Don't you have any days off?" I'm curious because I'd like to make plans with her, maybe steal her away for a day, and give us more alone time. For baby-making purposes, of course.

"I promised I'd take time off around the weekends. Saturdays and Sundays are our busiest days, so I can't skip them, but I have Thursday and Friday, and then Monday and Tuesday next week."

"Keep a day for me," I say, glancing over my shoulder once more.

She chews at her lower lip, and I immediately recall kissing her there, sucking at that tender curve and melting into her lips. "We don't need to date," she whispers, her eyes shifting to the island where the girls are chattering to one another while waiting on more pancakes.

"I still want to be alone with you, away from here." The griddle sizzles, and I turn my attention back to the pancakes in need of flipping. A tender hand comes to my arm and slides down it to my wrist.

"I'll see you later. Have a great day."

The second she walks away, her sweet words hit home. These are the things I've missed most about being a couple with someone. The little words of encouragement. The tender touches before parting. I miss random text messages and sporadic conversations throughout the day with that person you thought would always be there. I took those things for granted with Chloe, and they became rote instead of special moments.

I watch as Autumn disappears through the front entryway and then check out my girl sitting at the island with a smile on her face. She's looking back at me, and I wonder if she can read how I feel about the woman walking away.

"Who wants more pancakes?" I call out.

"Me," Mila blurts.

"Are there more?" I glance at the entryway to see Zack with his two boys in tow.

"Have a seat." I nod to the island. "Coffee's here." Zack steps over and scrubs at his hair, which stands up on end.

"Rough night?" I question.

"Rough morning." His voice is groggy as he pours himself a cup of coffee. "They wouldn't let me be."

"I didn't think you slept anyway." Zack is a workaholic. Everything is on the clock and by the book. That's how he runs his life. The lawyer in him wants all things legal, timely, and tidy.

"I don't actually. I've been awake since three. I should have brought the nanny." Zack sips at his mug while leaning his back against the counter near where I cook.

"Is she hot?" I tease.

"She's young." He huffs and scrubs at his sandy-blond hair again.

"Jeanine approves," I wonder.

"Jeanine hired her. She got her from some service. Half the time, I can't remember their names because they come and go so quickly." He sighs, knowing the reason his babysitters quit. His kids are out of control.

"That's mine," Mila cries out, and Zack steps forward, intervening as one of his boys has stolen a pancake off Mila's plate. I turn to restock the serving plate and set it before the boys who lunge for it like starving vultures. Returning to the grill, Zack follows me, walking backward. He puts himself back in his prior position against the counter, staring off at his boys.

"The boys are a mess. My marriage is a mess."

"What's wrong?"

"Jeanine's having an affair."

My head pops up, and I stare at the side of his face. "How do you know?"

Zack shrugs. "She said she had a business trip in Europe when she didn't have anything booked on her calendar. Her assistant confirmed it's an official vacation. I caught her packing lingerie. Do you know the last time I saw my wife in lingerie?" He turns his head to look at me, and I don't really want to answer him. I don't really want to know. We all agree his wife is a scary woman—intense, bitchy, and downright judgmental—and those words aren't a cover-up for her being ambitious. She's rude. Thankfully, Zack doesn't want a real answer from me and offers one himself.

"Never. She's never worn something seductive in her life." He scrubs at his hair again. "How did I end up with her?"

"You got her pregnant at a conference." It's the truth. Zack weakly smiles, but it's full of regret. Who would have thought a law conference would get him hot? Apparently, blowing off steam included a few too many shots and an extra key to her hotel room. Zack did what he thought was the right thing to do. He claims fatherhood isn't his forte, throwing himself into work, but his issues with fatherhood run deeper than his legal position.

"That's why this business with Autumn concerns me." Zack turns his back to his boys, placing his hands on the countertop. "She needs to be careful who she selects to father her child. I don't want some asshole screwing her over."

I swallow at the thought. As I promised her last night, if what we do doesn't take, I'll walk away, but the thought makes me feel like an asshole, and it's the last thing I want to happen. Already I'm in over my head, fighting to remember it's only sex and nothing more.

"I think Autumn's sensible enough to make her own decisions," I defend, protective of her decision to sleep with me last night.

"I'm just getting a strange vibe from Ben."

"Does he disapprove of her idea?" Ben's always been a protective older brother. He often allowed Autumn to tag along when they were kids, and she came to visit us while we were in college. That reminds me, I still can't find a memory of her making a pass at me and me rejecting her, and it's eating me up that I did such a thing.

"It's weird, but I think he greatly *approves* of it. He mentioned how he just wants her taken care of, which seems like a strange comment as she's taking care of herself, running her own business, living in her own place. He says she's a natural-born caregiver, and she needs Operation Autumn 2.0 in her life." Zack peeks over his shoulder. "Maybe she'll stop hooking up with losers."

Former jests and jokes poked at me for my heavier weight or my lack of ability make me bristle at the term loser. For a moment last night, I thought Autumn would reject me because I didn't meet her expectations. I would be a loser once more.

I fight the instant grin wanting to curve my lips as the night turned out to be anything but losing.

"Well, I think we should let Autumn live her life the way she sees fit. She obviously has reasons why she didn't get pregnant before and why she wants a baby now."

"It's called desperation. She's approaching forty."

"Don't be an ass. Maybe she has other reasons for wanting a baby." I flip the next batch of pancakes and step over to the island for the serving plate. Returning to the griddle, I waited a beat too long to turn them over, and the fluffy batter browns quickly. Scooping up the new set, I fill the plate and hand it to Zack.

As Zack's son Oliver knocks over a glass of orange juice and the liquid streams to the edge of the island, he mumbles under this breath. "I don't know why anyone would want one of these monsters."

He doesn't mean it, but I understand his frustration. He hasn't had to deal with his children alone enough. Maybe he's the one who needs to get rid of his *loser* wife.

13

[Autumn]

In the middle of the night, I wake to a sudden press of kisses on my shoulder. A warm hand palms my upper arm, and I smile despite the long day.

When I finally made it back to the cottage, Anna sat alone on the patio.

"Where is everyone?" The quiet made me suspicious.

"The guys thought they were twenty-one and decided to down a few gin and tonics after a long day of sunshine. Zack bribed Bryce to watch his boys again, and he took off with Mason about an hour ago."

Uh-oh. That sounded like trouble waiting to happen.

"When I went to check on Logan, he was facedown on his bed, passed out and snoring, and Ben was sick."

Shit. I lowered to the seat beside Anna. "Is he okay?" Ben should not be drinking.

"He's living his best YOLO, he tells me." The hardy sip she takes of her wine tells me she disapproves of his actions, and I have to agree with her.

"Will he be okay?"

"He'll have a wicked hangover as I imagine they all will. At least tomorrow they're going golfing for the day." Anna stared off at the descending sun.

"I'm sorry I was late."

Rolling her head on the back of the patio chair, she gives me a weak smile. "You have your own life to live, Autumn. You don't owe anyone an apology."

"But I promised I'd be here to help out."

"Oh, they did this to themselves." She snorted, lifting her glass and taking another drink. I helped myself to the bottle, and we sat in silence as the sun disappeared beneath the waterline.

Eventually, I made my way to bed, worrying that drinking might not be best for me if I'm working on getting pregnant. Then I was just agitated because I found myself upset that Logan wouldn't be joining me after all this evening, and I'd been looking forward to another round of sex with him. I shouldn't have been as eager as I was. It's only sex.

Yet here he is, waking me with kisses over my shoulder and up to my neck. At least, I hope it's him.

"Who is this?" I tease, and he freezes.

"Logan," he cautiously states. "Were you expecting someone else?"

"Ryan Reynolds but he's taken," I joke.

"Ah, are you a *Deadpool* girl?" he mumbles, returning his lips to my neck.

"More like his calendar girl girlfriend, which reminds me this day is lost." I hate the sour tone I take, reminding myself he is kissing me. "I was sleeping, by the way."

"No time to sleep. We have plans."

"Sounds like you already enjoyed the day," I mock.

"I'd enjoy it more if you gave me a blow job."

Instantly, I roll on the bed, falling to my back and peering up at him beside me. "You get drunk, pass out, wake me up, and now you want a blow job."

"Sure. It will restore me to rights, and we can get back to business."

"Are you serious?" It's one of those moments when he could be joking, but I can't see his face well enough in the dim light of the room. My blinds are open, and the moon is out in the sky somewhere, illuminating the bedroom in a dusky dark blue.

"Well, you are just using me for my sperm." His hand slides down my arm and curls around my wrist. Lifting my arm for his mouth, he sucks at the pulse point of my wrist before scraping his teeth over it.

"Is that what you feel like? I'm using you." I shift my head on the pillow, trying to get a better look at him.

"I feel like I need your mouth around my dick to get me pumped up, and then I need to bury myself inside you."

I gasp, but his lips cover mine, swallowing the air I expel. He steals my breath as he shifts his body over mine, straddling me before releasing my lips and shoving down a pair of athletic shorts. He's not wearing anything underneath the thin material, and despite the dark, a perfect outline of his dick forms. He squeezes himself, and I see he's already hard. He doesn't need me to pump him up, but perhaps his ego needs a stroke. I don't want him to think I'm just using him for what his body can give me. That is part of what we're doing, but I also haven't felt as alive as I felt with him last night. He's stroking my ego more than he knows.

Giving in to his request, I tip up my head as he walks on his knees over my body. Falling to one hand to balance himself over my head, he holds himself just above my lips.

"Suck me." I shouldn't be so turned on by his command. Deep down, I know if I told him no, he'd move off me, but somehow, I like how demanding he is, and last night I promised him anything he said, anything he wanted to do to me, I'd take it.

Opening my mouth, he traces over my lips with his tip, and my tongue comes forward, giving the slit a lick.

Logan hisses. "That mouth." He groans, and I lift again, encouraging him to enter my mouth. He holds himself at the base for a moment before I brush his hand away and take over, pulling him to the back of my throat before hollowing my cheeks and sucking him hard.

"Shit," he mutters, combing his fingers through my hair, petting me almost as I slide up and down his thick length, drawing him deep before slipping to the crown. My tongue swirls around the ridge before I swipe over the head once more. Opening wide, I take him deep again.

"Okay. Enough." He pulls out of my mouth and moves down my body, kissing my neck before lowering to my chest. He tugs the straps of my cami to the sides, locking my arms while exposing my breasts. Eagerly, he sucks at each one before leaving me in this position and moving to my briefs. Drawing them dramatically down my thighs, he pulls them from my ankles and tosses them over his shoulder. I don't have a second to comment before he flips me to my belly.

"Okay with this?" he asks, testing me. A warm hand rubs up my spine before he grips each of my hips and props me up on my knees. I'm a rag doll of submission and a raging bundle of hormones. He accused me of using him, but he's proving he's using me just as much, and as wrong as it sounds, I'm okay with this. On my knees, elbows pressed to the mattress, he swipes the thick head of his dick along the seam of my backside. His thumb follows, teasing me, and I clench.

"I'd never force you into anything you were uncertain of." The serious tenor of his voice gives me pause, and I try to glance over my shoulder.

"I know," I croak, not in a position for a chat.

His slick head moves lower, and he hisses again. "You're so wet. It's like you were waiting for me."

I was waiting for him, ready for him, hours ago, but it's even more than that, and I can't divulge the emotions I shouldn't have behind what we are doing. I don't want to begrudge him his time with his friends. He isn't here for me. He's here for Ben, but I selfishly want a slice of that time because I've never experienced what I'm experiencing with Logan.

Suddenly, he rams into me, jolting me forward, and I gulp, swallowing all thoughts of anything other than our position at this moment.

"Autumn." He exhales on my name. "Crisp air. Colorful leaves. Cooling temperatures." *He's a poet?* For a second, I'm wondering if he's still drunk, but his steady rhythm keeps pace with my heartbeat, and we fall into a dance of him sliding into me, drawing to my entrance and surging forward into my depths. It's not a position I've regularly been in, but I'm not complaining. It's different but fulfilling in another means.

"I'm so deep like this," he explains. "The angle. I feel like I touch every part of you. And fuck." He's all over the place with his thoughts. With his breathing ragged, the sound of us coming together fills the room.

"Do you have any idea how happy I am to finish inside you?" At first, I don't know what he means, but as his hand strokes over the lower portion of my back, I realize under different circumstances, he'd need to pull out. He'd cover my skin and leave his mark in another manner, but for what I want, he needs to remain inside me.

"Come on, sweetheart," he demands, but in our rush to please him, I'm faltering. I'm not as close as I need to be. Surprising me, he leans forward and slides his hand over my belly, pausing there a moment. "I'm going to give you everything you want."

Christ, his words. I rock back, forcing him deeper. His fingers stretch forward, plucking at my clit, eagerly strumming me in hopes I'll reach the end goal. With thighs shaking and hips moving, I suddenly feel as if I've lost control of myself. I'm working over him without thought, striving forward on pure pleasure.

"That's it, honey." The tone of his voice and the sound of friction between us, plus the wetness coating my thighs, sets me off in a way fireworks dance before me. I scream into the pillow, curling back like a stretching cat, and Logan follows by thrusting forward once more before stilling inside me. My channel clenches as he pulses, and I don't know that I've ever experienced a simultaneous orgasm before. If I have, it's never been like this. I'm floating and dripping and weightless and wet. I'm a mess, and it's more than my body as I fight tears once again. Last night, I was so emotional after three orgasms, and I promised I wouldn't be so reckless again. But something about the connection with Logan pushes me to the very edge of my being as if I haven't been living before him.

I collapse to the mattress, and Logan follows, smothering me for a moment before perching up on an elbow to take off some of his weight. He isn't heavy, but more like a comforting blanket, and I want him back over my body. Instead, he remains attached to me.

"We don't want to miss a drop." His voice dips into the teasing tone he has, and I almost let loose the welling tears. I don't want him to feel like there's only one mission, although that's what I told him I wanted. I don't want him to think I'm using him when, deep down, I know I am. And I definitely don't want him to know how much I'd like more from him than what we are doing.

He's giving me what I asked. I can't ask for anything else.

Eventually, he slips to my side, flipping to his back. An arm comes over his eyes for a second before he lets it fall to his chest and he turns his head to face me. I remain on my stomach, staring at him.

"Do you have any idea how incredible you are?"

His serious tone causes me to giggle. "No."

"I don't think I've ever been with a woman like you. No, I know I've never been with someone like you." He shifts to his side. "Women don't see me as a sex god."

"Who says I see you as a sex god?" I tease, smiling at him.

"You must because goddesses only give themselves to gods."

Goodness. "You're so sweet."

Without responding to me, he leans forward and proves his sweetness by tenderly kissing me. His fingers comb my hair around my ear as he did last night.

"Are you still drunk?" It should have been the first question I asked.

"Only on you, sweetheart. Only on you."

+ + +

I wake alone again, as I had the day before, and I send up a silent prayer that what we've done works. It would be ridiculously soon to take a pregnancy test, but I feel different with Logan. Reminding myself not to get caught up in sweet words and bodily sweat, I roll from the bed, feeling slightly sore from his eager actions last night.

I've had generous lovers in the past, but none quite so enthusiastic as Logan. It was refreshing although sad. Why had it taken so long to find someone like him, and why was it so wonderful? Perhaps it was that a plan was in place. We agreed it would go no further than what we were doing. That defense didn't settle well with me, but I had no other explanation for the thrill in my belly when I think of Logan or the ache between my thighs to be with him again so soon.

I'd missed him the day before, which felt like a schoolgirl sensation or a hopeless crush, and I'd already had one of those on Logan. I worried

I was in grave danger of falling into a decades-old habit of pining for someone unobtainable.

The summer Logan spent with us, he was always so funny, but he was also kind to me. He didn't see me as other boys had, or maybe he did see me, and we shared a kindred spirit because of our sizes. I didn't want to be sour that I wasn't good enough for him when I was sixteen because I was only sixteen to his twenty at the time. He was a silly college boy, and I was a curious teenage girl. We aren't those same people, and I shouldn't want to define what we are now almost twenty years later. Not defining us might be part of what's so exciting between us.

As I stand in the shower, I'm interrupted from my thoughts as the bathroom door opens. I swore I locked it, but the barrier moves, and a body slips inside the small space. Logan stands with his back against the door as he had when he snuck into my room the other night. Through the foggy glass panel, I stare at the outline of his form. He's so solid, and it's not just his size but his heart. I've watched him interact with Lorna over the years, and it's evident he's a good father. When he and Chloe divorced, he worked at continuing to participate in Lorna's life despite separate households, unlike Zack, who seems completely at a loss with his boys who live with him day in and day out. I can't even comment on Mason.

"What are you doing in here?" I whisper, leaning around the glass partition.

"I just had to see you before we head out for golf. I don't know why we have such an ungodly early tee time." Logan looks like he's still wrecked from last night, and thoughts of him being drunk concern me. Is it safe to drink so much as a diabetic? He presses off the door and moves closer to the foggy glass. "And I hate that today is your day off, and now I'll be gone half the day."

"You're here for Ben," I remind him. "You're here for all of you to be together again."

"But I want to spend time with you." He actually pouts, lips protruding like a petulant child.

"Come here," I whisper because he's just too cute. Leaning forward, I kiss him while my body hugs the glass separating us. I don't want to get him all wet. When I release his lips, pulling away from him, he catches me by the back of the neck and tugs me back to him. Our mouths fuse together, harder, firmer. Still pinning me to him by the hand at my nape, his knuckles trail down my body, over my sharp nipples, and along my belly.

"You aren't being fair," I mutter to his mouth against mine. He's turning me on before he walks away.

"I can be fair," he says, slipping his fingers lower.

"Logan," I warn, catching his wrist. I don't want to be a hot mess, longing for him all day. I'll take matters into my own hand if I need to and something in my glare must warn him of my thoughts.

"Don't you dare fucking touch yourself. Save it for me." He can't be serious, but as his eyes narrow, I see he means it. Pushing off the glass, I step back to the tile wall, keeping the steamy distance between us. The only way he can stop me is if he walks into the shower and he's already dressed for the day. Leaning my back against the cool but moist tile, I slide my hands over my breasts, squeezing them together, circling them before pinching the nipples already hard and pointed from his kiss.

"Autumn," he warns, but it's too late. I turn my head, giving him the side of my face. I can't watch him watch me, but I allow my fingers to coast down my belly and between my thighs. "Fucking hell."

Lightly tickling at my folds, I give in to the sudden need for release. Stroking harder, I rub two fingers at the pleasure point, my breath comes faster. My heart races. My other hand flattens against the tile. I've never been an exhibitionist, but the curses and gasps coming from Logan spur me on. My hips begin to rock into my palm, and I risk a glance at him.

He's holding the partition with one hand while his other lay on the edge of the tile. His focus is glued to my fingers, strumming at myself.

"You're wet, aren't you? Dripping with need for me. Only me." His gaze lifts, and fire dances in those eyes. There's nothing I want more than for him to strip and enter this shower, but it's also extremely empowering that he can't, or won't, and he can't stop me from taking what I need from myself. I buck against my fingers.

"Show me how hard you are for me," I demand, feeling bold. He scrubs a hand down his face and then unbuckles his belt, loosening his shorts and revealing his strong, thick length. As far as penises go, his is huge, solid and long, and my mouth waters as I recall his commands from last night. Licking my lips, I stare at him as he strokes himself.

"Logan," I warn, gasping on air. "Logan." My hips dance, and my fingers flicker. My belly flutters, and I still, slapping my other hand against the tile at my back. Spreading my legs, I let the orgasm take me, biting my lips to hold back the moan of relief. Logan continues to stare at me, rocking into his hand.

"Coming in my hand feels like a waste. I need to be inside you."

"But you're already cleaned up for the day."

"Fuck it," he mutters, pushing his shorts and underwear to his bare feet and tugging his shirt over his head. He steps into the cooling shower, rushing me with a hard kiss to my mouth as he cups my jaw. Bending at the knees, he positions himself between my thighs.

"I'm too heavy." He can't lift me, but he slaps a hand to the side of my thigh and hitches it high against his hip. Thrusting into me, he kisses me again, swallowing my gasp.

"Gonna be quick," he mumbles as his lips remain on mine, and he surges into me, sharp and fast. Within seconds, he stills, tugging at my thigh. He pulses into me, and the relief of him coming inside me almost brings tears to my eyes again. I'm turning into such a sap, and I don't understand all the emotion wrapped up in us having sex.

He pulls out of me almost as fast as he enters, and a gush of wetness follows. *Dammit.*

"Dammit," he says as if reading my sentiments. His fingers swipe at the mess as if he can place it inside me, but it's too late. "No more standing sex. It's a waste of good sperm." He's joking, of course, and his smile shows he's trying to make light of the situation. This was pure need, not intention, and I shouldn't have been so foolish. Still, a man has never pushed me to my limits as Logan has.

"I hate to fuck and flee, but I really have to go," he says, kissing me before I can respond to him. Once he releases me, I chase the kiss, and he softly chuckles. "I love how you linger as if you want more of me."

I do want more, so much more than I should, but I quickly wipe away the thought. This isn't about anything other than making a baby together. Although, the sex we just had won't lead to that end goal. The sex we just had only seems to prove my point. I want more from Logan Anders than just a baby, and that's a dangerous desire.

14

[Logan]

As I exit the bathroom, I'm greeted with, "Good morning." Turning with my hand on the doorknob, Mason stands in the hallway. He pauses before me as I still with my back to the bathroom door.

"Is that the shower?" Mason tips his head, listening as the sound of rushing water seems to echo into the hall. "Who's in there?"

I swallow, ready to deny the sound, but Mason levels me with a stare that pins my back to the door, still clutching at the handle behind me. His eyes narrow.

"Did you fuck her?" I don't care for his tone or the implication—although it's true—as he swipes a hand through his perfectly sculpted hair. His body tenses. "Dude, she's like our little sister."

"You made comments about her yourself, how you wanted in her pants," I remind him as those first days he made his own quips about being with Autumn and giving her what she wants.

"I wasn't serious. Sure, she's hot, but she's . . . Speck. I just don't see her that way."

"See who how?" We both turn at the sound of Ben's voice as he clears the staircase and walks down the upper hallway to where we stand before the bathroom.

"No one," I say.

At the same time, Mason states, "Autumn."

Ben looks from Mason to me and back at our friend.

"What's going on?" he questions, his brows furrowing.

"Tell him, man. You owe him the truth on this one." Mason can be a total prick, and this nudge is almost as bad as tattling on me. I tip my head back on the barrier between me and the bathroom, unable to look one of my best friends in the eye.

"With your blessing, I'd like to sleep with your sister. I promise it won't be more than giving her what she wants—a baby." This has to be one of the most awkward things I've ever promised.

"Fuck," Ben mutters like the slow drip from a faucet. The word softly echoes down the hallway as Ben's gaze roams my body. "Seems like even without my blessing, you've already slept with her." He pauses for effect. Without admitting anything, I've just admitted everything.

"And you think I don't want more for my sister?" The edge to Ben's voice lowers my head, and I meet his glare. "I want her to find true love, get married, and be happy. I want someone who cares about her, not just shacking up with her in my house to fulfill some harebrained idea of sleeping with a bunch of guys to get pregnant."

"I thought you were on board with this baby-making business," I state, not knowing he disapproved of it.

"Because I thought it was a phase, like all the guys she dates. She'll move on to something else soon enough."

Not a winning vote of confidence for his sister, and I defend her. "She's not a child. It's not like she'll grow out of wanting a baby. She's a woman and on the verge of being too old to have a kid."

The door at my back suddenly opens, and I almost fall into the bathroom. Moving aside, Autumn steps into the hallway wearing only a towel around her middle. She clutches her pajamas to her chest while water droplets still linger on her shoulder. I do not want to think about taking her in the shower only moments ago, but my damp hair hints at what we did.

"If you all are done talking about me, I'd like to leave the bathroom," she snaps, directing her glare at her brother. "As for you, thanks for your vote of confidence, Ben. Just because you have the perfect life doesn't mean it comes easily to others, and it also doesn't mean I don't want the same thing."

"My life isn't perfect," he states, matching his sister's glare. Something under the surface hints at a secret, and that hunch Mason had suddenly feels more like intuition.

"You're right. I'm sorry. But I'm also not blabbing it all over the place, nor am I losing faith in you," Autumn argues, her voice softening as hurt laces her words.

"What is she talking about?" Mason asks, his gaze moving from Autumn to Ben.

"Nothing," Ben mutters, keeping his eyes fixed on his sister.

"What are we missing here?" I ask next.

"What you're missing is I don't need you to defend me. Not my age. Not my intentions," she says to me before turning back to her brother. "If I want to have sex with him, I will." However, the way she says her piece does nothing to calm the roiling sensation in my stomach. I'm not fucking her just to fuck her, and I'm not having sex with her just to give her a baby. I don't know what I'm doing anymore other than feeling like I'm falling down a deep well without a way to climb out of it.

+ + +

Bloody Marys don't help relieve the hangover most of us carry nor dull the pain in my gut at the awkwardness of the morning. Between Ben's disappointment and Autumn's hurt expression, my golf game sucks as I can't concentrate. Mason is uncharacteristically quiet but screw him. Maybe he's upset Autumn chose me, but I don't care what his problem is. *Ladies' choice*, he said. She chose me for now.

"What will you do if she does get pregnant?" Ben eventually asks me as we stand out on the green while the other two are ahead of us. "Are you going to marry her?"

"Fuck no," I say a little too adamantly. "She doesn't want that, remember? The goal is only a baby."

"The goal is to have someone love my sister as she deserves. An adult-someone which is different than having a child love her."

I get what he's saying, and I agree, but that someone isn't me. That's not what she wants from me. I could joke about her need for a sperm donor, but I can't find the humor in the thought nor do I think Ben will appreciate such a thing said about his sister.

"Look, I'll be whatever she wants me to be. If she wants me hands off, I'll keep my hands off."

"Seems a little too late for that," Ben mocks, lining up for his swing.

"If she needs money or wants support, I'll give what I can." The statement does not make my rivaling emotions settle any better. Do I really want to just throw cash at her and walk away from a child, *my* child?

"Not really a glowing recommendation." Ben swings and watches as his golf ball takes off.

"What do you want me to do?"

Ben peers back at me, squinting his eyes in the bright sunlight. "I want you to stay away from my sister." There isn't much bark behind the biting words, though, and his shoulders fall. "But Anna's been pushing that it be one of you guys. She thought it should be Mason."

"Why?" I question. "Why Mason?"

"She's worried he's lonely. She probably thought he'd sleep with Autumn, and he'd fall in love with her, like my sister has something magical between her legs."

"Don't talk about your sister like that," I snap. Ben watches me, brows arching at the aggression in my tone.

"Well, I'm not certain how to explain it without being totally grossed out myself. Still, Anna thought any of you would be better than some random sperm donation because at least we'd know the history of the father."

Autumn hasn't mentioned artificial insemination in all the conversations where her baby-making decision has come up, so I assumed the list was her plan. I don't like the idea of her baby's father being someone random or coming from a frozen test tube. She's beautiful enough to get a man to sleep with her, and I'm a willing volunteer at the moment.

"What happens when this doesn't work? She isn't going to get pregnant after one time," Ben questions.

My head lowers as it's already been three. "It only takes once."

"Don't talk like you're the poster child for sex education." Ben's voice turns bitter as he leans on his golf club. "It could take months for this to happen. You're only here until the following weekend, and then what? Back to Indiana for you."

And she moves onto the next guy. The thought churns in the pit of my stomach.

"I don't know what's next," I admit, squinting off at the end of the fairway, avoiding his questioning gaze. I keep telling myself I don't need to think about what's next because Autumn only wants what's now. She only wants the effect, but not the cause itself. The truth is, I could easily fall for her, but she doesn't want that, and I'm not about to admit my conflicting feelings to Ben.

"I don't even know how she thinks she's going to be a single mother and run her business. She works all the time, hardly taking time for herself."

I might agree. I'd had the same thought, but Autumn seems capable, and as having a baby is a priority, I also think she'll work out what she needs to do in order to parent. While I didn't have to do such a thing when Lorna was a baby, I've certainly had to re-arrange my life now as I co-parent. It's manageable.

"She says she has you and Anna for support," I tell Ben, turning back to him. He shakes his head, lowering his face to glance at his feet.

"Yeah, well, that's not a solution." Suddenly, I feel like we're back to the second half of the conversation this morning in the hallway where there were hints of Ben having a less than perfect life. Admittedly, no one has it stellar. We've all had money concerns, or marital issues, but out of the four of us, Ben has it the most together.

"Is something going on with you and Anna? Paradise is still intact, right?" I question, wondering if this is one of those rare moments for him.

"Yeah. Anna and I are fine." He looks up and stares down the fairway as I had.

"Good, because I need to believe true love does exist, even if it isn't for me," I tease. Ben softly chuckles.

"Who says you can't have love?"

I stare back at him. "Dude, divorced guy. Already tried that, and it didn't work." I like to think I loved Chloe, and I'm certain I did. I always will in some ways, as she mothered my child. *But true love?* Yeah, I'm not so confident in that concept because if true love were the case, Chloe would have loved me in return no matter what.

"Doesn't mean it can't happen again." Ben pauses, peering back at me. "Or for the first time. Maybe for real this time."

If Ben's implying I'd love his sister, or she'd love me, he is living in a dreamland. This is just sex. We don't even live in the same state, plus I'm already a father, and Autumn doesn't want a dad for her kid. She wants a man to father one with her, and that's it.

"Ben, I don't need your permission. Or I should say, your sister doesn't. She's a grown woman. It's her body, and she can do what she wants with it."

"Please, spare me the details." He holds up a hand.

"But I'd still like your blessing to give this a try with her, for her."

"If it works," he mutters, pausing a second before speaking next. "I'm not saying I approve of this method, but if I had to choose between you and Mason, my bet would be on you. I love you both, but you're the better fit for her."

His words surprise me, and I recall what Autumn said about thinking I was made for her as a teenager. Does Ben know she had a crush on me? Am I the only idiot when it came to Autumn's feelings?

"Why?" I ask. *Why me?*

"Because deep down, I know you're the best of men. You'll do the right thing, if necessary, and you aren't really taking advantage of my sister. Plus, you're reliable, respectable, and reasonable."

Jeez. Why doesn't he just say I have a good personality?

"What I'm most worried about is the practice it takes to get pregnant. It's never just sex. Someone is going to get hurt." Ben subtly taps his chest, indicating his heart.

"No one's going to be hurt. We both know what we've gotten into." That's actually not one-hundred percent true, though. I hadn't planned on all the emotions I have rolling around inside me or the way she makes me feel when we're together. I'm alive in a way I've never been. She makes me feel . . . like a new kind of weight has been lifted. I'm free yet whole, which doesn't make any sense to me.

"We can never know anything for certain," he says, sounding cryptic once more. Zack calls out to us, waving a hand for us to hurry up, and Ben walks away, leaving me wondering what he meant.

15

[Autumn]

My body hums with nervous energy after this morning's altercation in the hallway. I don't know why Ben said what he said, other than he doesn't believe in me. I'm the flighty, little sister who can't find a man. While I'm smart enough to manage our father's business for years, and then open my own, I'm not sensible enough to make an intelligent decision for myself, my body, and my needs. Ben can really piss me off even though I love him.

The idea of a day in the sun does not sound like a good plan to me. I don't have the wherewithal to sit still and chat with Anna, but I can't leave Anna as she's suddenly responsible for all the children again. Mila and Lorna. Oliver and Trevor. Bryce and Calvin have been relieved of kid duty as Calvin has a job working for the local location of Kulis Landscaping. Bryce was allowed to hang with some kids he knew in the area. Both boys will be making new friends come fall. When the two weeks at Lakeside Cottage are complete, Anna and Ben plan to return to their home to pack up the house. It's already on the market with some eager interest.

To add to my dismay, my mother arrives once we settle on the beach. "I just want a little time with my grandchildren," she announces.

Anna and I lock eyes. My mother is here on a fishing expedition and not the kind that involves a hook and a pole.

"How are the boys?" she asks, helping herself to a chair.

"Calvin and Bryce, or do you mean Ben and friends?" Anna asks of her mother-in-law, knowing how to play the game with her.

"Let's start with the older set."

"They're all hungover and paying the price by golfing." Satisfied that walking a golf course in the day's heat is punishment for yesterday afternoon's behavior, Anna huffs.

"Is Ben okay?" Our mother has never hovered over Ben as she does over me, mainly because she trusts Anna to keep him in line. I'm the problem child. Still, I understand her current concern.

"He's fine," Anna lies, not wanting to worry my mother. "He's having the time of his life with these guys, and that's all that matters." Her firm tone brooks no argument from my mother, who actually thought getting the guys together would be good for the soul.

"And how are my girls?"

"Do you mean Lorna and Mila?" I ask, teasing my own mother. She's taken on Lorna as her pseudo-grandchild as Logan doesn't have living parents.

"Well, them too, but how are you two holding up?"

"Everything is under control, Ruthie," Anna addresses my mother. She never quite got the hang of calling my mother Mom as she had her own until a few years ago.

"That's my girl," Mom directs at Anna, having adopted her as a second daughter. Then Mom turns to me. "And how are you?"

"I'm good," I admit, finding it very true despite all the morning's hullabaloo in the hallway. I feel amazing.

"You have a certain glow about you today," she adds, eyeing me, and for half a second, I feel like a teen again, wondering if my mother knows I had sex last night. "Still thinking about having a baby?"

"Uh, Mom, I can't talk about this right now." I gaze over at the four kids digging in the sand. Using them as my excuse, I dismiss a conversation I don't want to have with my mother today, tomorrow, or months from now. It's not her business, although I'm certain she'll have plenty to say about it.

"You should sleep with Mason."

"Mom!" I shriek. "Weren't you the one saying *as long as Mason isn't the father*."

She waves a dismissive hand at me. "What? He's good looking, and we know he's virile." My mother wiggles her brows, and Anna snorts.

"Mother!"

"I'm just suggesting that if you're going to shack up with someone to make a baby, at least pick a beautiful looking man as well as one sexually appealing and strong."

"This is not happening." I glare at Anna because if she hadn't opened her mouth, Mason wouldn't have opened his.

"I'm sorry," my sister-in-law mouths to me, but at this point, she can beg forgiveness to the end of time.

"I'm going to help the kids build a sandcastle." Pushing off my chair, I walk over to Oliver and Trevor. They have the energy to burn as do I suddenly, and I follow their lead to dig in the sand. Eventually, we walk along the beach and play in the water, splashing around as though I'm a kid myself. Thankfully, my mother disappears while I'm walking the boys down the shore.

Trevor is the wilder one of the two boys, while Oliver is a bit tinier than his twin. Once we leave the refreshing lake, Oliver shivers, and I wrap him in a towel, tugging him to me to warm him up. Settling in a chair, I pull the boy onto my lap, and he tucks his head against my shoulder. With an arm stroking up his back, he snuggles into me.

"When did she leave?" I question of my mom's absence.

"A while ago. She said she had a lunch engagement." Anna's been reading a book but closes it with a snap. We're silent for a second, and I decide I might as well get this conversation over with.

"I suppose Ben told you," I mutter, not wishing to disturb the little one on my lap.

"Told me what?" she questions, glancing over at me. Usually, I'm good at reading Anna, so I can't tell if she's pretending—acting as if she doesn't know anything—or if she really doesn't know what happened this morning.

"I just assumed . . ." As Anna stares at me, she shifts in her seat.

"Well, now you really need to tell me." Her eyes drift to Oliver on my lap, and I realize we aren't in a position to discuss anything in detail. However, Anna has this way of having a cryptic conversation. She says you develop it as a mother, and I better learn the language if I plan to be one.

LIVING at 40

"Logan and I . . ." I wave a hand around my midsection. Anna's eyes widen.

"What about Mason?" she questions.

"It was never going to be Mason." I laugh, jostling Oliver, who is out like a light, and I shift him over my lap for more comfort.

"Why Logan?" Anna isn't asking to be facetious. She's truly curious why I chose him over Mason the manwhore. The virile, sexually appealing one, as my mother called him.

"I've always had a crush on Logan. We had this silly misunderstanding back when he was in college, but I've never really lost the infatuation with him."

"What happened in college?" Anna asks, concerned.

"I might have . . ."—I check that Oliver isn't listening—"tried to kiss Logan at a party and he rejected me."

Anna's brows lift. "I can't imagine Logan ever rejecting anyone. He isn't desperate but he also wasn't the one girls went for first. In fact, Logan really struggled because once a girl met Mason, nine times out of ten, she'd go for Mason instead."

Not liking the comparison, my lips purse. "Well, I never wanted Mason more than Logan." My thoughts drift back to the incident with Logan and his dismissal of that night. His negative comments about the fat girl wanting his sausage. His humor was his coping mechanism and I'm sad at the thought he needed to protect himself. He was a great man, and any girl would have been lucky to handle his sausage back in college.

"If you have feelings for Logan, are you sure this is a good idea?" Anna asks. I'm still waiting for her shock or disapproval of my intentions to have a baby.

I thought it was a phase, Ben's words rang through the closed bathroom door loud and clear this morning.

"It's what I want," I whisper, leaning forward and pressing a kiss to Oliver's little head. He's more than a baby, but these are the moments I want in life with my own child. The sense of security and comfort this wild child must feel with me as he's crashed out on my lap.

119

"And what does Logan want?" Anna glances off toward the lake water, and I turn my head enough to see Lorna dancing in the waves with Mila.

"He's been more than willing to participate," I joke, but a bitter lump forms in my throat. Logan already has a child who adores him, and he worships her. Will he really be okay with giving me a child and walking away? I could never ask him to stay with me. Suddenly, I'm wondering if we've made a mistake. If *I've* made a mistake, allowing Logan to have sex with me for a baby. Maybe I should have asked Bert the vet, propositioning someone I don't know half as well as I know Logan. Logan is someone too close to our group, and I've brought him even closer to me. "Do you think I'm doing the wrong thing?"

"I think you're an adult and can do what you want. Just make certain you're doing it for the right reasons."

And what are those reasons? I don't need to ask her. She can't answer because she was married when she had children. She was younger. She doesn't understand the burning desire I have now as I'm growing older. The fear I might have missed opportunities in my past, and the concern I might not have other chances in the future. I need to do things my way, which is this way.

"I'm keeping everything in perspective," I say as if that's an answer to her statement. Anna nods, opening her book once more, and I'm relieved our conversation is finished. I have much to think about, but for now, I close my eyes and let the sun heat my face.

I'm not certain how much time passes before I hear a male voice.

"How did you get him to do that?" The quiet question flips my lids open. Disoriented as I'd been dozing, I follow Zack's gaze to his son on my lap. He's still asleep against me.

"I don't know," I whisper, not wanting to wake him but finding my neck aches from the position I've been resting in.

"Let me take him," Zack says as the other guys circle our messy setup on the beach. Chairs, coolers, and towels cover feet of the sand. Mason has a spike ball game in his hand, and Logan carries a football with a case of beer. Ben brings up the rear, looking exhausted.

"I've got him." Leaning forward, I press a kiss to Oliver's head. The little boy snuggles deeper into me.

"Well, I'm jealous," Logan says, falling directly into the sand beside my seat. He stares off at the water as if he didn't speak to me.

"Of what?" I mutter.

"A six-year-old," he teases, glancing over his shoulder at the little boy resting against me. I'd ask about his day or their golf game, but a strange tension surrounds the guys, and I don't want to trigger any conversations revolving around this morning. I just want to sit still and hold this boy.

"Spike ball. Who's in?" Mason calls out, and Logan presses up off the sand at my silence. Anna glances over at me, noting Oliver still on my lap.

"It's a nice look for you," she says.

"What is?"

"A child on your lap and a man interested in you." Tears prickle my eyes. It isn't fair as neither the boy nor the man are mine.

+ + +

Coming out of my bedroom after dinner, I have a book in hand as a decoy. I'm hoping to head to the landing for some quiet after a busy afternoon and another chaotic meal. The guys seem restored to their old selves after a rousing game of spike ball on the beach and beers with burgers for dinner. Ben and Zack are taking all the younger kids into town for ice cream, giving Anna a break for a bit.

As I enter the hallway, Logan steps out of his room and crosses the hall to me.

"Hey," he whispers, reaching out for my hand.

"Hey."

"You okay today? You were pretty quiet during dinner."

Glancing away from him, I blurt my thoughts. "Am I making a mistake?" I turn back and continue with a fountain of questions. "Am I doing the wrong thing? Should I just accept that it's too late?"

"Whoa, whoa, whoa," Logan says, reaching up for a section of my hair and brushing it behind my ear before sweeping his hand under the weight of it and circling my nape with his warm palm. "Why would you say all this?"

"Is Ben right? Did I leap before looking? I have a habit of doing such a thing. It's how I ended up taking care of Kevin, then Kenneth, and most recently, Rick. I average five years each. Do I lack commitment?"

"Hey," he says again, squeezing my nape and ducking his head, forcing me to look at his eyes. "Let's get out of here."

"I was going to read," I tell him, weakly lifting the book.

"Run away with me instead. Lorna's with the kids in town. Let's take a walk on the beach."

I nod though I feel guilty he's taking me away from here. Or maybe it's that I'm taking him away from his daughter. What was I thinking falling into bed with a man who already has a child? I thought it would mean a lack of responsibility for him, but he's one of the most committed guys I know. He knows the difficulties of raising a child and the attachment one should feel toward their own kid.

Logan takes my hand, and I willingly follow him as he leads me down the staircase. Entering the kitchen, we find it empty, and Logan helps himself to beers in the mini fridge in the bar alcove. Clutching two bottles between his fingers, he takes my hand again and leads me down to the beach, where we walk a bit to remove ourselves from the immediate space below the house.

Eventually, Logan stops and folds down to the sand, tugging me down after him.

"Here." He pops the top of one bottle, handing it over to me, and then unscrews the second bottle for himself.

"To you," he says, tapping the neck of his beer to mine. He salutes the lowering sun with the cold brew and lifts it for his lips. Following his lead, I take a small pull from mine and then settle the bottle between my crisscrossed legs.

"What if I can't do it?" I whisper. "What if I'm not a good mother?"

"Autumn, you will be. I saw you today with Oliver and Trevor, and those kids are hellions."

"But I can return them to Zack."

"I've also seen you with Lorna and Mila. The nail painting. The cartwheels. You were braiding their hair earlier tonight."

"That's just girl stuff." I snort, dismissing my actions as I pick at the label on my beer.

"It's mom stuff," he offers. "And before you say that's the easy part, I know you'll be great at the hard stuff too." He pauses to take another drink of his beer. "Look, I don't really want to get into your past relationships, but obviously, you're loyal. Ben mentioned how you took care of those guys, doing everything for them, and it leads me to think you're nurturing."

"To a fault," I mutter.

"Why is that a fault? So you like to take care of people? That's admirable."

"But Ben would think it's irresponsible because I let them walk all over me." I'd heard the unspoken. Ben blames me for enabling the behavior of the men in my past, allowing them to live rent-free, job-free, commitment-free with me.

"It's different with a child. It's not enabling. It's teaching and learning. Lorna's taught me so many things about people and life. Her attitude and behavior are humbling sometimes. But parenting is a commitment where you expect to give not receive. You'll receive in so many other ways. In different ways."

I nod as I know what he means. I've seen it with my nephews and niece. It's all the little things they do with Anna and Ben—the hugs, the apologies, the helpfulness, and the small gifts of gratitude. It's a trade-off that's unbalanced but still rightfully weighted as a parent should give more than a child.

"Would you really be able to walk away?" I ask. "Am I asking too much of you? What if I do get pregnant by you?"

I glance over at him as I speak, taking in his casual posture. He sits with his knees raised, arms dangling loosely around them. In profile, he's magnificent with a strong jaw, firm nose, and high cheekbones. His dark eyes sparkle, reflecting the sunlight dropping in the distant sky.

"I'll do anything you ask of me," he says, turning to face me. "I'm not saying it won't be difficult to know you have my child and want to raise him or her on your own, but I don't think I've mentally gotten to that step in the process. I only want to give you what you ask of me now. Making it happen is the first step."

"You're a good man, Logan Anders." He snorts, and I tip my head to his shoulder. "I didn't really plan to do it all alone. I'd always hoped one day I'd find the right man who would love me and want to be with me, want to have a family with me. I'm sorry if I've asked too much of you." I hate the pity party I'm having for myself. He turns and presses his lips to my head.

"You haven't asked of me anything I didn't want to do for you."

Staring out at the sun, he finishes his beer and takes mine, finishing it as well.

"What are you thinking?" I eventually ask.

"How I want to lay you out on this sand and watch the sun reflect on your body while I eat you out and hear you scream into the breeze."

"Jesus." My core clenches at his directness. Lift my head from his shoulder, he glances over at me.

"See, I'm not thinking about nine months from now or even two weeks. I'm only here in the present, and that present includes you as a gift."

"You really are sweet," I admit.

"But I can also be dirty, and I want to be dirty with you."

"It's broad daylight." The sun is setting, but it's still bright, and the beach is populated enough that sex on the sand would be obscene. Still, the thought of it flutters my insides.

"Maybe we should head back before I do something I don't think you want to do tonight." Sorrow fills his voice, and I chew the corner of my lips. I'm not saying I don't want to continue having sex with him, but it does seem unfair to ask it of him.

He quickly presses upward, standing before me, and reaches down for my hand to tug me off the sand. As I stand, he catches me, wrapping his arms around my waist for a firm hug, and the embrace nearly breaks me. With his hand under my hair, against my neck, and his other hand lower on my back, it's so nice to just be held, and Logan isn't letting go. We stand like this for several minutes until a little voice interrupts us.

"Daddy?"

16

[Logan]

The troops have returned, and Lorna stands feet away from me with Mila next to her. In the distance, Ben and Zack are stacking wood in a fire ring. The night is breezy. The air temperature has dropped just enough to hint fall is right around the corner. The first week of August is almost over, and time seems to be speeding up.

"Hey, honey. How was town?" I ask, stepping away from Autumn and feeling the loss of her against me.

"We bought stuff for s'mores and some Moose Tracks ice cream." Her eyes shift to Autumn and back to me. Without looking, I sense Autumn putting more distance between us.

"I've never mastered Moose Tracks in a cookie bar. Maybe I need to try again? Think you can help me with that someday?" Autumn says to Lorna, distracting my daughter from the question written on her face. *Why are you hugging my dad?*

"Sure," my daughter answers, not sounding too enthusiastic about baking.

"I'm going to head down to the boys," Autumn whispers before walking forward. She hesitates near Lorna and Mila. "Hey Mila, come with me."

I tilt my head for Lorna to follow me. "Come take a walk with me."

Lorna steps toward me, and we turn for the shoreline where the water laps over the sand. Walking a few feet in silence, I start the conversation.

"Having fun this week?"

"Yeah."

"You like hanging out with Mila, right?"

"Yes, Dad." The hint of teenage sass grates on my nerves, but I continue.

"What's on your mind?" A look crossed Lorna's face when she saw Autumn and me hugging, and something is rolling around in that brain of hers.

"Nothing." Is there any worse word in the English language when it comes from children?

"You know that Ben is one of Dad's best friends." She doesn't respond. "And we've been friends for a long time, which makes his sister Autumn my friend, too. And friends hug sometimes."

"I'm friends with Mila. Bryce is her brother. We don't hug."

"Umm…" Her quick deduction surprises me. Glancing over at Lorna, I see her head down, feet kicking at the sand as we walk. "Do you want to hug Bryce?" *Lord save me.* There are only three years between them, but I'd like to think they are young enough the span makes a huge difference. When I was fourteen, I was not looking at eleven-year-old girls.

"No." Her face pinkens.

"Okay, well, Autumn is . . ."

"Dad, if you want to take Autumn on a date, it's okay." Her directness trips me up, and I scratch at the back of my neck, knowing there's no way I will explain to her what I'm actually doing with Autumn. I also don't date around Lorna, keeping those moments to the weekends when she isn't in my house.

"Yeah. I don't think dating will work as she lives here, and we live in Indiana. But I like spending time with Autumn. We're all spending time together," I say, hoping to suggest there's nothing unusual in the mix of gathered friends.

"I know, but Mom's dating Peter." She shrugs. I'm not a fan of my ex-wife's new boyfriend, Peter, pronounce *pe-tear*, like derriere. Chloe and Peter have been together for a while, and Lorna doesn't complain about him, but I still don't care for him. He spends lots of time having dinner with them or hanging around on the weekends Lorna is with her mom. He's in international sales, working in the United States for some overseas company. I'm certain one day he'll return to France where the company's headquarters are located, leaving Chloe behind.

"You'll always be my number one girl," I remind her, slipping my arm around her and tugging her to my side.

"I know."

I press a kiss to her head and stop walking. "Should we head back?"

"Sure." She shrugs again, and I keep my arm around her as we return in the direction of the fire Ben and Zack built. "Dad, did you know Mila's moving here?"

"I did know that. How does Mila feel about it?"

"She says she's scared to start a new school, but she's excited to live here. Her room is bigger in this house, plus it has a bathroom in it. She says Lakeside Cottage is her favorite place in the world."

"Wow. Lucky girl then."

"Do you think we could move here?" The question gives me pause.

"Why would we move, honey?"

She shrugs once more under my arm. "It's one of my favorite places, too."

"Yeah, but you'd miss your friends, right?"

Shrugging happens again, and I wonder what I'm missing. Is she not happy at school? Is something happening with her friends? Chloe has warned me that starting middle school this fall will come with all kinds of transitions and changes for Lorna. We need to be aware of Lorna's potential to struggle with a new building, new schedules, unfamiliar students, and the possibility of her friend group shifting.

"You know you can talk to me," I remind her. She shrugs once more but doesn't offer anything more. Glancing in the distance, we both see that our group has grown and gathered around a now crackling fire. Without a word, Lorna takes off, slipping out from under my arm, and jogging up the sand to meet Mila. The two eagerly step over to the ingredients for s'mores placed on a rock to begin the business of roasting marshmallows.

"Everything okay?" Autumn asks as soon as I rejoin the group.

"I will never understand teenage girls," I mutter, collapsing down to the sand while Autumn sits in one of the permanent chairs on the beach. "Even when I was a teenager, I could not understand them."

Autumn softly chuckles, and I want to tug her down to me. I want to wrap around her again as if we are teenagers. Glancing over at my daughter working a marshmallow on a stick, I watch as Bryce asks her if he can help her, and Lorna hands the stick to him. Her head lowers as she does, and her face turns pink once more. *Fuck.* Shifting on the sand, I sit upright, observing them.

"You okay?" Autumn asks, and I turn to her. Looking back at Lorna a second, and then at Autumn, my chest pinches.

I'd always hoped one day, I'd find the right man who would love me and want to be with me.

Fuck! Is this how Autumn felt as a kid when she was around me? She told me she always thought she and I were meant to be together. Did I disappoint her? Of course, I did. I pushed her away when we were young, and she tried to kiss me, and that hurt. I know it hurt, based on the number of rejections I've received from girls not wanting the fat guy in the group.

Oh my God, Lorna, don't look at Bryce. Don't desire your best friend's older brother. It's all going to lead to heartbreak. He's going to be a dick one day. He's never going to deserve you. A cold sweat breaks out on my forehead despite the heat of the fire.

"Logan, are you okay?" Autumn reaches out for my forearm, and I stare up at her. "Is it your diabetes?"

"I-I'm good." I lie because I'm not. I don't want my daughter falling in love because love can hurt. It can hurt so much. That's why I'm keeping things in perspective with Autumn. I don't need to love her. I've already hurt her, and I just want to make it up to her with a baby.

"Whatever happened with the house next door?" Mason asks, scattering my thoughts. Zack remains quiet, but Ben answers.

"Some old guy owned it a while back. He rarely came here. We heard he has a wife twenty years younger than him or something like that."

"Lucky bastard," Mason teases, lifting a beer for his lips.

"I do not want to hear this," Zack mutters.

"Anna heard the old man died. He had kids, probably around the same age as his young wife. We haven't seen anyone there this summer, though."

Zack shakes his head, and I remember that the house next door to Lakeside Cottage belonged to Zack's family when he was young.

"What a waste," Mason mutters.

"Don't be a dick," Zack says, turning on Mason.

"What? I just meant it's a shame a house with this view is sitting empty." Mason's words are insensitive, but I understand what he's saying. As a construction guy, he knows the property is worth millions, while the house isn't worth half as much after all these years.

"I have a dick," Zack's son Trevor blurts. Mason snorts and leans over to fist-bump the kid.

"Me too, kid," he says.

"Please don't encourage him," Zack mutters. "Trevor, remember what I said. We don't say such words around other people."

"What's wrong with dick?" his brother, Oliver, asks, and Zack tips his head back, thudding lightly on the chair back.

"On that note, I think it's time to get you monsters to bed." Zack stands, and I turn to Autumn.

Her face glows in the light of the fire. She's so beautiful. I could love her. I could be that man she's waited for, who wants her and wants a family with her. Then I glance across the fire and see Lorna and hope inside me shatters just a little bit.

+ + +

The rest of us remain around the fire until darkness coats the sky. Ben and Mason decide to hang out a little longer, but Anna eventually tells Mila it's time for bed, and I tell Lorna the same. Lorna and Mila head up the long staircase first with Anna and Autumn behind them, and I follow, deciding I'd like to tuck Lorna in tonight. As we reach the landing halfway up the difficult climb to the house, I catch Autumn's wrist, and she stops walking.

"Let me hold you tonight." In the darkness of the trees hovering over the landing, it's difficult to see her eyes. "We don't have to do anything more tonight if you need a break. I just want to hold you close." She nods, chewing the corner of her lips. I want to lean in and kiss her so badly it hurts, but Lorna is up ahead, and Anna paused on the staircase.

"You guys coming up?"

"We'll be right there," Autumn says, leaning in and stealing her own quick kiss from me before breaking free of my hold and taking the steps upward.

After a shower, teeth brushing, and a second drink of water, Lorna is finally settled into Mila's room, and I head to Autumn's bedroom, sneaking inside as I've done the other nights. Crawling up behind her on the bed, I find her hair wet.

"Did you shower?"

"I smelled like smoke. I don't like when it lingers in my hair."

"Should I shower?" I tease, slipping my arm over her waist.

"Nope. You can stay right here." My lips find her shoulder but long to move lower, into the dip of her neck. However, I promised nothing more tonight, so I just hold her, inhaling her scent and marveling at the fit of her body against mine. We lay on our sides, her back to my chest. Unfortunately, she squirms a little bit, and her firm ass brushes against my front where I'm rock hard.

"You are not making this easy," I tease, nuzzling my nose into her hair.

"I can't seem to help it. My body likes how you feel behind me and responds accordingly."

"Yeah. Like when I had you on your knees last night, pummeling into you?"

Her breath catches, and now I'm just torturing myself with the images of me behind her, sliding in and out of her.

"Yes," she whispers breathlessly, and I squeeze her tighter to me.

"And how is your body responding to mine right now?" I whisper just below her ear.

"I'm wet, and I want you. I ache for you, actually."

Jesus. "We cannot have that. My body is your plaything. Take what you want from me."

She shifts a little to glance at me over her shoulder. "I don't want to disappoint you, Logan."

"Nothing about you could ever disappoint me," I admit, laying her on her back and climbing over her. "We need to make up for this morning."

"What was wrong with this morning?" We both recall how I rushed her in the shower.

"Standing up sex is not an option if we want to get pregnant." *We?* "I mean, you. Everything dribbled out of you, and we need to keep the goods inside until the seed is planted."

"Are you likening me to a garden?"

"I want to see you bloom." I lower my hand for her belly, shifting to my side as we both gaze down at my palm covering the full, flat expanse of her stomach. For a moment, I imagine it. I see her swelling and us together sharing the experience, but that is not her plan. That's not the direction she wants things to go.

The path we need to take is sex—again. However, somehow things feel different as we slowly remove each other's clothing, taking our time to kiss and nip at one another until we're both naked and on fire with need. She's dripping, as she said, and I touch her until she gives me her first orgasm.

Pushing me to my back, she rolls over me and moves between my thighs, holding my shaft upward at the base and devouring me with torturous, teasing laps before sucking until I'm on the verge of erupting.

"You need to hop on pop before I burst," I tease, although my voice is soft, strained even, and she chuckles. Climbing back up my body, she straddles me, sliding over my length with the heat of her pussy. She takes her time to lower over me, drawing me into her depths, making me feel like I belong there. I was made for her.

"Jesus," I hiss, clutching at her hips. I'm going to blow, and we need to shift, but she doesn't let me move. She works up and down my dick, taking her time to fill herself before dragging to the tip once again. "Autumn," I warn her. It's too much. The slower tempo. Her teasing hum. Her hands coast over my chest while her hips rock, moving in small, sharp circles at first before slipping up my rock-hard dick and slamming back down again. She presses herself upright, completely swallowing me into her, and she scratches her short nails down my chest. Straddling me, she gazes down at me buried deep within her. With moonlight streaming over her lush body, she looks like a goddess again, and I want to know what deity I need to pray to to deserve her.

"You're so beautiful." I reach up for the tips of her hair, which fall over her shoulders as she undulates back and forth. Her clit rubs my pubic bone, and I know it feels good for her, but I can't hold off.

I jackknife upright and flip her to her back. She lets out a squeal, but I smother the sound with a hard kiss to her mouth. My hips begin to hammer at her while her legs wrap around my lower back.

"Can't. Go. Slow." I can't make love to her when this needs to be about sex. When this needs to be about her and what she wants as an end goal. I move faster, drive harder, delve deeper, until I can't take another second. I still, and a fountain of release explodes within her. I don't move other than the racing of my heart and the jolting of my dick, both pulsing in a rapid rhythm. One part of me wants to give her so much more. It's a part that can't be seen or even felt directly. It's wrapped in faith, trust, and a belief that love exists. That I can love her if she'd let me.

L.B. DUNBAR

17

[Autumn]

Logan and I fall into a crazy routine of sneaking into my room after each day's activities. Boating and jet ski rentals. Fishing and tubing. More golf for the guys. Lunches, dinners, and drinks. The days are packed to keep people busy but relaxed, and all the while, I check off the minutes until Logan and I can be alone having the best sex of my life.

Something shifted the other night. It was more than the depth of him inside me, but deep in my soul, I felt something different. Then he flipped me as if trying to get back to who we were instead of stepping forward into who we could be. Admittedly, I could love Logan Anders. I always have in some way. There was no going back to being just friends. He was no longer my brother's best friend, nor was I just Ben's younger sister. Every moment alone was a new adventure between us and burrowing the idea of us deeper and deeper into my heart, allowing him where I shouldn't want him.

He had Lorna. He lived in Indiana. He had a life outside of Lakeside. He was only doing what I asked, and I was certain I was pregnant, but it didn't stop me from enjoying him, taking from him, using him to satisfy some fantasy in my head that we could be a family. That we were moving *toward* something together.

As time sped up, we neared the end of our two-week holiday, which no one wanted to discuss.

"Let me take you out on a date at least once," Logan teases on Thursday morning. The guys are scheduled to leave on Sunday. Logan will head south to Indianapolis while Mason returns north to Traverse City. Zack will return east to the Detroit area, but Ben will stay here, and we will navigate being a brother-sister family living in the same city once again.

"How will we explain a date?" I chuckle in the early hours of the morning. Logan stays longer and longer through the nights, setting his alarm for dawn to sneak back to his room.

134

"As Mason and Ben know what we are doing, I don't think it will be much of a surprise. I feel like I owe dinner to the woman giving me a million star-seeing orgasms."

I laugh into the pillow. "Star-seeing, huh?"

"An entire galaxy," he says, shifting to face me as we've just completed another universe-rattling moment of morning sex. He's so hard when he wakes, and I don't want to waste the eagerness with which he wants to release. Sometimes I need to allow him to go first inside me before he gives me attention, but I'm okay with that arrangement. Everything Logan does, he's doing for me, and he never leaves me unsatisfied.

"Anna also knows," I say quietly.

"If I could let you scream, the entire town might know we're together." With Lorna only doors down the hall, screaming with the orgasms he gives me is not an option, but I'm stuck on the words he's spoken.

We're together. How I wish it were true. Only a few days remain, and that leaves us with three nights.

"Okay," I say, staring at him as he strokes back my hair. "Dinner tonight then."

+ + +

Driftwood is a popular restaurant and bar closest to the public beach. It's a beautiful August evening, and a rooftop setting allows patrons to see the lake in the distance. A slight breeze cools off the hot day, and Logan secured us a corner table for privacy.

"I don't remember the last time I was on an official date," I state, grateful for this evening. With Rick, we always ate meals I cooked at home after preparing food for others at the café all day. In addition, Rick hardly ever had money, so treated meals were a rarity. Surprisingly, he had plenty of money for drugs, alcohol, and another woman.

"I wish it could be fancier." Logan glances around the packed rooftop, full of patrons loudly laughing and imbibing. A bottle of wine has been placed on the table, and Logan pours us each a glass. "This area needs a good steakhouse."

One can order steak here, but Driftwood's fame is its burgers and sandwiches.

"I'm not worried about the menu. Just here for the company," I flirt, reaching for my glass of wine.

"I don't want the company to disappoint you either." He lifts his wineglass and tips it at me before adding, "I've been on too many dull dates, and not many led to seconds."

As Logan drinks, his comment reminds me of my conversation with Anna about Logan being a second choice to Mason. I've never felt that way myself, but I can understand how Mason might appear better than Logan, with an emphasis on appearance. As I've aged, though, I've learned repeatedly it's the inside of a man who counts, and a sense of humor is more stunning than a pretty face.

Wishful thinking brings hope Logan doesn't have second dates because he doesn't find the women he dates appealing and not the other way around. Unfortunately, Logan will leave here and go back to random dating, eventually meeting the right woman and settling into a routine with her. They'll date on the regular and have wild sex when they can. Maybe he'll fall in love again. Maybe he'll marry her.

I don't like the thought of any of it.

"Do you date often?" I hate that I'm asking. We promised only sex, but I'm still curious. Who will he see when he returns to his home?

He shrugs, reaching for his glass of wine. "Not like I used to." He avoids looking at me, but I wait out more explanation. "When I first divorced, a few guys at the office encouraged me to date right away. Get laid, they said. You'll feel better. Only I didn't." His finger circles the rim of his glass. "I didn't like feeling like I was stepping backward in time. Starting over to discover someone. Learn their likes and dislikes. I understand that's dating, but I just didn't want to do it. I guess I was too comfortable being married."

"There's some crazy statistic I once read that said men are something like eighty percent more likely to remarry than a woman. It's the comfort factor you just mentioned." I'm not judging him, but it makes sense to me. All the men I'd dated liked the fact I took care of them. It made them too comfortable in their situation but not comfortable enough to be with only me.

"Why aren't you married?" he asks, as long as heavy conversation seems to be on the table.

"I could say I never found the right guy. But I think it's more the right man never found me." I glance away from him as it's more than I wanted to share, but the truth pours out. I blame it on the wine and the company. "I'd find a man, fall hard fast, and think he must be the one. But I like to think the one would have found me just as well, and it hasn't happened." I shrug, lifting my glass for my lips. "Maybe it never will."

"You don't believe in destiny, fate, love?" he questions, arching a brow. "I thought that's what all women dream of."

"Logan, I'm going to let you in on a little secret." Both eyebrows hitch as I crook my finger, beckoning him to come closer to me. "I do believe in destiny, but I think mine missed me."

His mouth falls open, but I lift a hand to stop him.

"While all girls want Prince Charming, they don't want to feel like they have to do all the seeking. A woman wants to be sought. She wants to feel like she's more than a fleeting moment to a man but the woman he absolutely cannot live without for a lifetime. She's perfectly capable of taking care of herself, but she doesn't want to feel like she has to do it all alone. She wants to feel needed but not have him be needy. She wants to be taken care of but not be smothered. Hold her hand. Hold her up. It's a lot of pressure, but the right man . . . he knows how to do it."

"I'll never measure up. It's a constant line of contradictions." Crestfallen, his expression suggests he really believes this about himself, and I feel guilty I've imparted wisdom that comes across as an impossibility. Maybe my sights have been set too high, but that can't be the case, considering the lowlifes I've had in past relationships.

"We aren't called the contradictory sex for nothin'," I tease. He reaches for his glass and finishes the remainder of it.

"I thought you were supposed to be the gentler sex," he says, not fully teasing me.

"I am gentle, but that doesn't seem to get me anywhere. Honestly, I'm not married because no one ever asked me."

This lifts his dropped lids, and he stares at me. "Were they insane?" His sharp reproach of my exes makes me laugh.

"Actually, I think *I* was a little bit crazy. It's my nature to nurture, and men who need that kind of tuck-them-in-bed and spoon-feed-their-ego is who I seem to attract."

"Jesus, you must think we're all dicks," he mutters.

"Not at all. And I like a dick." I wink, hoping to draw us away from this depressing conversation. He chuckles softly, but his laughter isn't coming from his belly. "What about you? Why aren't you remarried?"

"I haven't found the right woman who can take on me *and Lorna.*"

I nod as if I fully understand, and in many ways, I do. It takes a special woman to accept a man who had children with another woman. "Did you love Chloe?"

As he pours himself more wine, he explains. "I thought I did. When I look back on our beginning, I really think it seemed like love. With hindsight, I'm not convinced it was the type of love I wanted it to be. I mean, we seemed to be the sort of people who understood one another. The weight. The eating. The humor. Chloe changed. Or maybe I did, and it just wasn't that long-lasting love I'd always hoped I'd find." He crooks his finger at me. "I have a secret to tell you."

I giggle as I lean closer to him. "Men believe in love, too. It's why when we think we've found it, we're so comfortable with it. We want to be taken care of but don't want to be mothered. We want to appear strong but realize we can be weakened by the right woman. There's a desire to be wanted as if a woman feels she can't live without us. We dream of being the center of her world, but deep down, we know it's the other way around. We can't live without her."

Slowly, I smile at his teasing voice. I've done my part to center someone else inside my world, but then again, I've been headstrong enough to know a man isn't ever going to take care of me like I need, so I do things for myself. Like the café. Like wanting a baby.

"Well," Logan states, double-tapping his fingers on the table. "Now that we've imparted all the wisdom we have as experts in relationships, it appears the magnitude of *impossible* between men and women leaves us with the only thing men and women find of value in one another, and that's sex."

I snort. "And even that can be questionable. Present company excluded, of course." I wink at him.

Logan laughs as well, and just like that, our serious conversation ends. We talk about safer topics instead. Logan tells me how he likes his job, but he's been longing for a change. I tell him about the café and how I'm living my dream. He tells me more about Lorna, and it's clear how much he loves his daughter. For a moment, I'm saddened that my child won't have the fatherly figure every kid needs. My father is deceased. Ben has his own children to parent, and whoever does get me pregnant won't be present to be a dad. I've told myself I'm strong enough to be both mother and father but listening to Logan discuss his child, it hits me that a valuable piece of my child's upbringing will be missing if I don't have a man in my life. It's the contradictory line between mother *and father*.

We finish our meal with a second bottle of wine, and to say we are tipsy might be an understatement. We sway as we walk, bumping into one another as we exit the restaurant. Logan loops his arm lazily over my shoulder, tugging me into his side, and instead of leading me to his car, he steers us toward the beach.

"I want to make out with you," he blurts, and I giggle like a teen. "No sex. Just kissing."

"You already made up for the lost kiss," I remind him, recalling his mouth on mine on the landing less than two weeks ago. How did we get to only a few days from the end so quickly?

"This is . . . different," he says without more explanation. We step off the boardwalk leading to the public beach and cross the cool sand. It's late and dark, and technically, the beach is closed. Before us, a lifeguard hut stands on pillars a few yards from the shoreline and faces the black lake.

"Let's go up," Logan whispers.

"I don't think that's legal," I warn him, noting the sign listing all the things not allowed at the beach, which probably includes climbing up the short ladder and standing on the landing around the square structure. I don't know for certain as the letters blur together a bit. Logan doesn't reply to my concern, but he places his hands on my hips, guiding me to the ladder and hoisting me upward. I squeal.

"Shh," he warns with a chuckle. "We don't want to get caught."

This makes me giggle more as though I'm a rule-breaking teenager once more. The thrill of getting caught ripples through me as I climb the short distance, and Logan follows. We aren't exactly hidden, but it isn't obvious we're up here when Logan sits with his back to the building and drags my legs over his lap so my shoulder rests near his. We only sit like this for a minute before he's scooting me over one leg, and my backside falls between his spread thighs, draping both my legs over his left thigh. His hand coasts up my spine, and I shiver in the cool evening breeze coming off the lake.

"Make out with me." It's such a strange request yet another shiver slips over my skin, making the fine hairs stand erect. Logan's palm cups the back of my neck as his mouth crushes mine. We both taste like wine and the sweetness of comfort and familiarity. He doesn't need to discover me because he's known me most of his life. He's circled around me enough to know the basics of who I am and what I do, and in some cases, why I do those things. On a deeper level now, he knows me intimately, also understanding how I like things, what my body can do to his, and why I want what I want.

Our kissing grows deeper, but his hand doesn't leave my neck. His other arm wraps around my waist, but he isn't turning me, isn't shifting us, isn't making me straddle him. I remain between his thighs while his mouth savors mine as if getting drunk on the wine flavor coating my tongue.

Eventually, the hand at my waist coasts slowly up my side, like a hesitant adolescent, eager to fondle me yet nervous at the same time. Slowly, slowly, slowly, his fingers seek until he cups the underside of my breast, gently nudging the swell upward.

"I thought you said only making out," I mutter to his mouth, teasing him.

"Wouldn't be the real thing if I didn't try to cop a feel," he teases back, returning his attention to both my lips and the weight of my breast in his hand. His palm presses upward, massaging before squeezing the globe tighter and pinching at my nipple.

"Let me touch you," he whispers, and I giggle again. I don't recall make-out sessions like this as a teen, but perhaps that's the point of our position. He's building a memory. The way he's kissing me tells me he's taking this moment very seriously. He's intent on absorbing every movement, every touch.

"Only third base," I mutter to his lips as if questioning him. His fingers release my breast and move to my kneecap. Slowly, he begins his descent. He bunches up the edge of my skirt, and shaky fingers coast up my inner thigh. His anxiety makes me giddy and a bit confused. We've been together for almost two weeks, having sex in numerous positions and speeds, but this has him uneasy and almost shy. I lift my hand for his cheek, and his fingers complete their cautious journey up my inner leg until his knuckles brush over the wet plait of my underwear. He hisses against my mouth, and I echo the sound. While I anticipated his touch, I'm startled by the tender brush and sudden rush of desire. Something is happening here, and I can't get a read on it because I'm drowning in his kiss and his slow-stroking knuckles. Moving back and forth over the damp cotton, he's teasing me in a way tears prickle my eyes. I need more from him.

"Logan," I whimper before his fingers curl around the barrier and gently stroke my sensitive folds.

"Want to be needed but not needy," he whispers. It takes me a moment to register what he's saying. "Too bad I'm a greedy fuck when it comes to you."

L.B. DUNBAR

With that, two fingers dive into me, and I respond with a quick gasp despite my desperation for his touch.

"Capable of taking care of herself," he mutters, once again quoting me as his fingers deliciously drag back and forth inside me. "But I want to be the one to take care of you. My fingers are the only ones that can touch you like this. Yours do not do it half as well as mine." He increases the pressure while remaining torturously slow in the drag and dash of entering me. He also isn't lying. While I can get myself off, his fingers do it so much better.

"And you are more than a fleeting moment because I do not know how I am supposed to live without you after all this ends." His words almost ache as they leave his lips and fall against mine, but his fingers have me dizzy, and his mouth has me spinning. I'm circling him in a sense. He's the center of everything right now, and I don't want to fall out of the orbit he's created of himself.

"Logan," I cry softly to his mouth, on the cusp of something bigger than me. He's brought me to orgasm so many times in the past few days, but whatever is happening right now is going to shatter me. As I crest, I balance on the edge, holding on to the thrill before the rush of release.

"I will never be a prince, but I'd treat you like a queen."

With another gasp, I break from his mouth and fall apart, but he chases me, seeking to keep the connection as best he can with his fingers buried inside me and his tongue in my mouth. I'm drowning under him as wave after wave of release coasts over me. My legs tremble. My heart races, and all the while, he's kissing me, thrilling me with his fingers and his tongue and his beautiful heart.

My God, I love him. Tears prickle my eyes once again, and I don't know how I can let this end. How can I walk away from him? How can I live without him?

18

[Logan]

For the first time since we started this crazy venture, I don't follow Autumn into her room but kiss her in the hallway outside her bedroom door before holding it open for only her. Her expression is puzzled. Her eyes seek mine with one question, but I simply shake my head, offering a weak smile. The beginning of the end is coming, and I need to pull myself away from her. Something happened while we were making out. Something inside me broke while my fingers stroked inside her.

I felt myself slipping, falling, drowning in love with her and the desire to keep her. But that wasn't what she wanted from me. I'd never measure up, and while I teased her with my ridiculous secrets about men, I wasn't kidding.

We were simple creatures, and all we really wanted was to be loved. We wanted to be the center of another person's world, but Autumn didn't want to orbit me. She wanted a baby. That little, beautiful human being we hopefully created would be her sun. A baby was what she wanted to feed her need to nurture without all the craziness of a man taking from her.

The others were all fools.

I was an idiot.

Closing the door to my own bedroom, I fall onto the bed, heart heavy and head muddled from the wine, the taste of her on my tongue, and the scent of her on my fingers. She surrounded me in all the places it would hurt most, and I would take the punishment as it was the first time in years my heart thumped this hard. Making out with her was almost worse than making love to her. The patience to go slow. The desire to speed up. The contradiction was the thrill, just as it was with any woman—the contradictory sex—frustrating and fascinating. Despite all the confusing thoughts circling my head, though, I only wanted to think of her because too soon, thoughts were all I'd have.

+ + +

Wine headaches are the worst, or so I thought until Friday night arrives. It'd been a day of rain and gloom, which adds to the lingering sense of ending. Autumn had to work, and I'd spent time playing board games with crabby kids and sore losers. Mason can be the worst when someone purchases Sears Tower in an older edition of the game *Chicagopoly*. After the kids have all gone their separate ways for bed or movies, depending on their ages, Ben asks us to meet him in the sitting area off the kitchen.

I'm tired and want to call it an early night, climbing into bed behind Autumn and falling into her as we soak up the last hours of this vacation. I have no way of knowing if she's pregnant or not. She explained to me how the timing was right, and we were playing a bit of Russian roulette in hopes something happens. Thinking of her with another man, working at becoming pregnant with someone else, makes me sick to my stomach. I don't want her to move on, which doesn't feel fair of me to ask. We made no promises to one another. I'm going back to Indiana on Sunday. She'll stay here. Life will go on.

"So, you're probably wondering why I've asked you to hang out again," Ben states, his voice uneasy as he rubs his hands over his upper thighs. He's sitting on an overstuffed chair that holds two people, and Anna sits beside him. One hand of hers is stroking up his back, and another wraps around his wrist.

While those words in that combination should mean nothing other than sounding too formal, there's a quiver to Ben's voice that has the hairs on the back of my neck standing on end. He swallows, and I can almost hear the roll of his throat across the room where I sit beside Autumn. We sit closer than necessary for such a large couch. Her thigh presses against mine, and I want to wrap my arm around her shoulder, tucking her into my side, like Anna is doing with Ben in a sense. I fixate on how the wife of one of my best friends strokes up his back and tightens her hand on his arm. She's staring at the side of his face, as if holding her breath, hanging on the precipice of what he might say next.

"There's no easy way to say this, so I'm going to blurt it out and then go backward." His voice cracks, and his lids blink a few times rapidly. He swallows once more before speaking. "I'm dying."

A deafening silence fills the room, and I'm not even certain I've heard him correctly. He must be joking, and I begin to smile, ready to say as such to him. *You fucker, that's hilarious.*

"Aren't we all," I snap, chuckling to myself, reining in my sharper retort. We're forty. We're entering a crossroads in our lives. *Over the hill* is what people used to call this time period.

Heaviness falls among us despite my joke. Anna closes her eyes, and Zack sits forward, resting his elbows on his thighs. He swipes both hands over his mouth. Noticeably, two people not reacting. One is Autumn who sits perfectly still beside me. With her thigh pressed against mine and her hands folded in her lap, white-knuckled and stiff, I know that she knows whatever the fuck Ben is talking about. She's his sister.

My head swivels from her tightly clasped hands to Mason, who also sits still with his head lowered and his fingers clutching the cushions on either side of his thighs. That fucker also knows what's going on.

"Am I the last to know?" I blurt, but Zack's quick neck crane in my direction informs me he had no idea either. My heart races while my hands turn cold. "What's happening?"

"I'd been experiencing some stomach trouble, and I attributed it to stress. The doctor told me I was suffering from acid reflux, but the pain was getting worse, and I just wasn't feeling right." Ben's expression pinches as he waves a hand over his midsection. "I kept ignoring it. Taking more antacids. I didn't have time to slow down, as the doctor suggested. I worked out and sometimes thought maybe the pain was from intense ab work. Maybe I was pushing myself too hard."

Ben takes a deep breath, glancing at Anna as if she can confirm all he says, or maybe he's looking at her as his strength, the center of his world, the woman who takes care of him.

"I was diagnosed with pancreatic cancer."

Zack presses just the tips of his fingers over his lips while his elbows still balance on his knees. I remain slouching into the couch cushions as if they support me, propping me upright. I don't know what to say. I don't know what to think. I don't know enough about this disease.

"The mortality rate is high. I've already had some rounds of chemotherapy, but it didn't work to reduce or destroy the cancer cells. Typically, once cancer latches onto the pancreas, it isn't letting go." Ben bitterly chuckles, and I wonder if he's quoting what he's been told.

"How long?" Zack asks, the question choked out of him.

"They're giving me less than a year."

"Fuck," I hiss and notice Mason closing his eyes. I can't look at Autumn. I can't process that she hadn't told me. My best friend is dying, and she didn't mention it.

"This is why you're moving," Zack states, calm, conscious, and controlled. He's listing things in his head, sorting the reasons outside of our best friend having a life sentence on him. "But why here? Wouldn't you get the best medical care in Chicago? This is a small town. This is a resort area." His voice is slowly rising, struggling with the tension.

"We discussed it." Ben looks at Anna, finally placing a hand on her knee and squeezing. "And I don't want the best medical care. I want the best life." He turns from his wife to us. "I want to spend my time in a place that makes me happy. I want to come home."

It's strange to think Ben considers Lakeside his home. He's been living in Chicago almost twenty years, giving up his father's business to start his own and be near the woman he loved.

"Do the kids know?" I ask, recalling that moving in and of itself seemed like a big change. They were giving up the familiarity of a house, schools, and friends, but now they'd live in a new place, starting over, and eventually losing their dad on top of it. Instantly, I think of Lorna and my own mortality. I wouldn't want to leave her behind, yet the natural course of life says I should go first. I *will* go first but hopefully not at forty. Hopefully not while she still has so much life to live. I want to be there for all of it. Dances and dates. Wins and losses. High school. College. Jobs. Love. Motherhood. I want to be a grandpa someday, and

I realize I'm so far ahead of myself, and my friend will miss out on all of it. He's going to lose everything, including his life.

"They know I'm sick. An internet search could give them answers, so we had to be honest, at least with the boys. They know I don't have much time. Mila only knows I have cancer, and it's not contagious. We haven't discussed death as much with her. We don't want her to worry before it's time."

Silence fills the room once more as Zack closes his eyes, fingertips still at his lips. Mason continues to stare down at his legs, and I'm scanning the room, still wondering what's happening to us, to him.

Is any of this real?

"What can we do?" I finally ask, no longer thinking of myself. I scoot forward on the couch, balancing myself on the edge of the cushion. "Tell us how to help. What do you want from us? Anything. Ask it." Two fingers double-tap at my wrist. Does he want my blood? Need a transplant? Want a . . . I don't know what, just what can I do to stop this from happening to him? Ben Kulis is one of the best people I've ever known, and this cannot be happening to him.

Only the good die young. It's been said, and it has never felt truer than at this moment.

"I just wanted you all to know, and it felt easiest to tell you all at once." Ben clutches at Anna's leg. "I want you to stick together as friends and help Anna if she needs it."

"Ben," Anna whispers, but it's Mason's reaction that turns my head. He's glaring at Ben while Anna lowers her eyes.

"Be here for Calvin and Bryce when they need a man and help Mila when she needs a father." He swallows hard once more, and I know what he's thinking. He won't attend another father-daughter dance or walk her down the aisle. He won't be able to yell at her for leaving her cleats in the hall or watch her play another softball game. Will he be gone by next spring? Will it happen in the summer?

"Is this why you asked us here?" I don't mean the sitting area. I mean Lakeside Cottage. Are we here because he wanted to tell us he was dying?

"Yes. I wanted to spend one last time being us and acting as if we'd never grow old . . . together. I just wanted to hang out and forget."

"Have you been feeling okay since we've been here?" Zack asks, and I recall each of our concerns about Ben looking tired and not drinking alcohol.

Ben only shrugs.

"Why didn't you mention this earlier?" Zack snaps. "We wouldn't have pushed so hard. We . . . we wouldn't have interrupted your vacation." Zack glares at Ben.

"But this isn't a vacation for us. This will be our home, and I wanted time with you guys before it might go . . . bad." Ben pleads with Zack to understand.

"What about your mom?" I ask. Ruthie is a hoot. She was devastated when Ben's dad had a sudden heart attack and died. She and Old man Kulis were so in love. It wasn't fair. In the natural progression of things, the parent goes first. I don't know how Ruthie will survive this. How will Autumn?

Spinning to face her, I snap, "You knew, didn't you?"

Her mouth falls open, but I turn away from her before she can answer. I can't tackle this fact. I already know the truth.

"My mom knows. It's another reason we're moving here. I want Anna and the kids closer to her, and I want to re-establish the business as best I can, so everyone is provided for."

"You sold your business. You're moving here. You've given up on medical treatment—"

"Not medical treatment," Ben interrupts Zack. "I'm just not going to be aggressive in finding a solution that will strip away the time I have left."

I know enough that chemotherapy isn't fun, but it could help even if Ben has already said the treatments haven't. I understand not wanting to be all drugged up or sick all the time, but there must be something. *God, let there be something.*

"So what? You just hang out here and . . ." I can't bring myself to speak the word. The anger in my voice feels unwarranted, but I'm not able to help myself. I'm angry. I don't understand. How did this happen to him?

"Logan," Autumn whispers next to me, but I turn on her.

"Don't," I snap. Turning back to my friends, I ignore Autumn hoisting herself off the couch and leaving the room. This is her brother, but this is my friend. The man who took me in like a brother from another. When I no longer had parents and humor was all I had left, he assured me I'd always have a friend in him. He'd be my family. His family would be mine. In the back of my head, it's an explanation for why I didn't respond to Autumn all those years ago. I can't remember that moment, but my reasoning had to be that Ben was family. I couldn't disrespect him by taking advantage of his sister. I hadn't been friends with him as long as Zack or Mason, but Ben made me believe it never mattered. He'd always bring us all back together, keeping us a family.

"What's next?" Zack asks as if reading my earlier thoughts.

"We just live." Ben entwines his fingers with Anna's, bringing their collective hands to his lips and kissing them.

"Pretend nothing's wrong?" Zack asks, flabbergasted. "How can you ignore this?"

"I'm not ignoring it. I'm just choosing to embrace what I have left before it literally eats me alive." Ben chuckles, but I don't find the humor in what he's said. With my own condition of diabetes, it's not a laughing matter. Mason must agree with me because he stands and heads to the bar area just off the kitchen. Ice clanks against a glass, and a bottle glugs as liquid pours.

"Bring me one of those," I holler over my shoulder, not even questioning what he'll bring me.

"Make it three," Zack adds.

Anna presses a kiss to Ben's temple, mutters something to him, and stands. Ben stands with her, cups her neck, and kisses her hard and passionate before us. Zack stares. I look away. A glass breaks near the bar.

Anna pulls back and pats Ben's chest before turning to leave the room, and Ben returns to his seat.

We wait for Mason to return. He brings four glasses of amber liquor with him, dispensing one crystal tumbler to each of us before lowering the bottle under his arm to the low table before us.

"I'll drink yours if you won't," Mason tells Ben.

"I'm counting on it," Ben mutters to the glass, and Mason downs his first round. There's always been a layer of animosity mixed with the love of friendship, but something is even more off than usual between the two of them.

We each remain quiet, taking turns to lift a glass and drink after mouths open and shut, words unable to find any of us.

"This is stupid," Mason finally speaks. He's downed a second lowball, filling it higher than his first. "You want a better quality of life at the end of your life, so be it."

Startled by Mason's interjection into the silence around us, Zack shifts on the couch, looking over his shoulder at our friend.

"Okay . . ." Zack turns back, facing the glass in his hand, and swishes the liquid inside. "Okay. You're right. This is Ben's life." He speaks as if Ben isn't present before addressing him. "We'll do things your way, but I want a promise."

"Jesus, Zacker," I hiss, shaking my head.

"If things get really bad, you promise me you'll get medical attention. You won't just let yourself suffer in pain but do something to aid yourself. Do something to lessen it."

"Maryjane for medicinal purposes. She's my kind of woman," Mason teases.

"Isn't it legal here in Michigan now anyway?" I question, no longer up on which states have legalized marijuana use.

Ben chuckles. "I promise I'll use something. I'm not that much of a martyr."

We're quiet for another second before Mason chimes in again. "Remember when we were young . . . er . . . younger, and we had a plan."

Zack glances over at me.

"We were going to be our own business. No dads. No bosses. We'd be in charge. Logan would design houses. I'd build them. Benny would make them pretty outside, and Zack would make sure we stayed out of trouble. At least, legally." Mason laughs. Vaguely, the details come back to me. It was probably a night just like this, somber and silent, when we were drinking too much, discussing fathers and futures. Ben already knew he didn't want to take over his dad's business because he wanted to follow Anna. He didn't want her to give up her dream for his. Mason never got along with his father, which is how he found himself working for Ben's in the summers during high school, and Zack had his own issues with his old man, a known criminal. My dad was dead and had been since I was five.

"What happened to that dream?" Mason asks.

Zack chuckles, bitter and ironic, while Ben admits, "I married Anna."

"Yes, women. How fickle they can be." Mason takes a hearty pull of his drink. Ben narrows his eyes at Mason but doesn't speak to contradict our friend. "We were the four seasons."

"The four points," Ben corrects. "We were going to name the business The Four Points for the direction each of us came from." Mason was north. I was south. Zack was east while Ben was west. We sounded like Power Rangers, and if anyone suggested we wear matching outfits in bright colors, it might have been me, making a joke about the glory of wearing a morph-suit. But as I recall that conversation and we sit here some twenty years later, I wonder . . .

"Why didn't we do it?" It was more than Ben marrying Anna. Why didn't we ever follow through on that dream to work together, to be a team?

Ben shrugs, but Mason stares down at his glass. Zack is just thinking. It's written in his expression. He might have even zoned out of this conversation, but he's still sitting here, listening. He's uncanny like that.

"To The Four Points," I say, lifting my glass like the Power Ranger-wannabes of the past. Mason slowly smiles.

"To The Four Points," he adds, raising his glass as well.

"To the future," Ben whispers.

"And the past," Zack adds as if shaken out of his revelry. "And friendship."

To that, we all drink, even Ben, who takes a small sip of the sharp alcohol, and then coughs, reminding us that dreams fade, life shifts, and it could all end sooner than we think.

19

[Autumn]

Accepting the early fate of my brother was difficult. Ben told me months ago when he'd learned the truth and began chemotherapy treatments. The prognosis was desperate. The outlook inevitable. I wanted to curse God, poor genetics, and the universe, but the diagnosis came down to cancer is not selective. It seeps into anyone, at any time, without explanation or reason. We were a healthy family. We were heart attack and stroke people, not cancer victims. Our father died of a heart attack. Our grandfather died of an allergic reaction to something. Even on my mother's side, her family simply died of advanced age. The men in our family had not been subject to cancer, yet here it was in Ben.

As I sit in a rocking chair inside my designated bedroom in Anna's family home, I peer out the window at the lake in the distance. The sun is going down earlier every day. The sky closes in on another day, and it's hard to imagine that one day, Ben will not exist. I swipe at an errant tear. I cried often when he first told me. I'll cry again when it actually happens. When I watch him suffer. When I watch Anna. When I see the lost look on their children's faces. I'll be here for them because life will never be the same without Ben.

He wanted these two weeks to hang with his friends. To remind himself that life is short, and we need to be thankful for what we have and who we have in our lives. He wanted one more time to tell them all he loved them, but not only with words. He wanted final memories for all of them. Without even suspecting it, he'd given me final memories as well. I'll be forever grateful that my brother called Logan Anders to join him for these weeks, and through some miracle and the meddling of Anna, Logan ended up in my bed, hopefully impregnating me. He'll give me a new life to focus on when my brother is no longer present.

I swipe again at another slow tear.

I'm not upset at Logan's harsh, "Don't." He'll come to understand it wasn't my place to tell him about my brother's condition. Ben wanted

L.B. DUNBAR

to do it himself, and he wanted to do it on his own time. He planned to tell them as he had, hoping to give them a night of thoughts and concerns, maybe ask questions tomorrow, but eventually remember two weeks of fun. He didn't tell them at the beginning because he didn't want anyone worrying about his condition, enforcing naps, or questioning every step they took. He wanted to keep living even while he was dying.

Knowing Ben, he'll push himself until the final hours. That's part of this decision to move to Lakeside, in a house he's always loved, in a town he's missed. He wants time with his young family. He wants to enjoy himself.

When I think of Calvin, Bryce, and Mila, I fear for all they'll give up by leaving the only home they've known. School. Friends. Activities. But they seem to be taking it all in stride. Calvin and Bryce understand. They're honoring their father's wishes even if they harbor some resentment for the decision. Mila isn't clueless, but she's welcoming the adventure and is thrilled to live here full time. Anna's more difficult to read, but she's accepting what Ben wants, saying they're only moving their future up by years. Years she'll live, and Ben won't.

My door eventually opens, and Logan walks in. His eyes are glassy, and I can't decide if it's sadness or alcohol. Either way, I'm here to offer him whatever he needs from me. I want to wrap him in my arms and assure him everything will be alright, but I can't.

He sits on the edge of the bed, facing me. His eyes lower for his lap, where he clasps his hands together between his strong legs.

"Do you want to talk?" I ask, equally content to sit in silence.

He shakes his head, rolling his lips. He appears angry, and I understand the emotion. I was angry myself when I first learned of everything. I'm still angry in many ways, but anger will not keep Ben alive.

"You understand it wasn't my place to tell you, right?" The last thing I want is Logan to be upset with me, and I need to know where he's at.

He nods, but adds, "A little forewarning would have been nice, though." Sarcasm drips from his lips, and it's not a good sound from him.

However, I understand the hurt, the surprise even. I'm still in shock, and it hit hard again when Ben explained it to his friends. Reaching out a hand, I wiggle my fingers at Logan. I want him to come to me, and thankfully, he does. He collapses to his knees before me and wraps his arms around my waist, tucking them between my back and the rocking chair. His head falls to my lap, and I spend minutes combing my fingers through his hair, trying to soothe the ache in his heart. I should say something, but words escape me, and I figure silence is better for the moment.

I'm not certain how long we sit in this position before Logan nudges his face lower, working his nose to the edge of my dress which hits mid-thigh. My legs were pressed together and off to the side to accommodate him, but he shifts, wedging his broad shoulders between my knees and forcing me to spread.

"Logan," I whisper, as his hands come to my lower back and his teeth clamp on my dress, moving it upward the final inches my spread legs do not offer. His face falls squarely between my thighs and his nose drags over the thin fabric of my underwear. His hands tighten on my back, squeezing once before lowering to my ass and tugging me forward enough that his face is firmly against my core. He slips a hand forward to push my underwear aside and then spears me with his tongue.

"Logan," I hiss. Now doesn't seem to be the time for this.

"Don't." He growls against sensitive folds before clamping his lips around them and sucking hard. His tongue splits me open again and dips among the juices he's creating. I accept the invasion, strangely understanding his need for connection. Despite the rocking chair, I'm held firmly in place as he laps and licks like a starving man, desperate for his last meal. I ignore the uncomfortable knowledge he's using me and quickly breach the edge of release but don't break over it. Abruptly, he stops as if he knows I'm right there. I whimper but don't complain.

Reaching for my hands, he tugs me forward, and I fold to the floor, uncertain what he wants from me or where he wants me. I'm like a rag doll at his disposal as he guides me to my back. He makes quick work of opening his shorts and shoving them down to his knees. Brushing aside my thong, he positions himself at my entrance and rams forward. I bite my lip as he moves in sharp, rushed thrusts, lifting my legs so my ankles are near his shoulders. I'm nearly bent in half as he surges inward, grunting with the effort to keep my legs upward and his knees pressed into the thin rug under them. He doesn't speak. There are no words of endearment. No tender caresses. He isn't even looking me in the eye. I take the rush of him filling me and allow him to lose himself inside me, disappearing for the minutes it's going to take before he implodes. He's going to come before I do, and I accept I might not get there.

Holding myself back, I clutch at the rug under my fingers with my knees near my shoulders. Logan strains forward, groaning once his release hits him. In this position, I'm the perfect angle for every drop of his seed to move forward, to fill me, and reach where it needs to go. As I'm hopeful I'm already with child, this night shouldn't matter, but every time we're together, I take it for what it's forth—an opportunity to be close to him. A chance to pretend that we are a couple, and we can be a family.

Logan holds his position once he finishes, but he doesn't touch me other than his hands on my shins. He lingers while he catches his breath, and then he pulls out. He doesn't bother to straighten the awkwardly pushed aside thong. Offering me a moment of reprieve, he tucks himself into his shorts before he holds out a hand to help me sit upright. He still doesn't look at me.

Swiping a hand over his face, he curls upward, standing to his full height. His eyes remain dazed, and I'd like to think he's upset over what just happened. The rush, the rapid release, the disconnect between us which we haven't felt since we started having sex. However, this wasn't sex. This was fucking, and Logan doesn't have a hint of regret on his cheeks. Without a word, he turns and exits the room.

And it hurts more than losing Kevin, Kenneth, and Rick combined.

20

[Logan]

I wake early, alone, and fighting off the disconnect with Autumn last night. While I went to her room, wanting comfort from her, I hadn't expected the anger I felt. I can't say she lied to me as she hadn't, but she withheld the truth, which bothered me almost as much. Chloe did those kinds of things. Not wanting to admit how she felt or how she was changing in both body and mind, she withheld information until nothing was left to salvage between us.

I don't like feeling as if Autumn had done the same thing and spent most of the night tossing and turning over it. As I reason with myself, I conclude there is no ulterior motive to Autumn's lack of information. This didn't pertain to her goal. This was about her brother, my best friend, who announced he is dying. And it wasn't some drunken, we're-all-going-to-die-one-day speech. This was immediate. We all knew the older we got, the faster time sped up, and a year wasn't a long time in the grand scheme of things, especially when considering someone's life ending. Twelve months was not enough time remaining.

Admittedly, I shouldn't have used Autumn as I did. I should apologize. I should beg forgiveness, but I don't know what to say. I don't understand my own actions. I went into her room seeking solace and left feeling like shit. I should have stayed to comfort her. She was losing her brother, but I hadn't found it inside myself to stick around. I was used up and wanted to escape her rather than hold her after I fucked her on the floor.

Jesus. I fucked her like I didn't care about her. Like I only thought of myself and my aching heart for my friend. That had been the crux. I had been thinking only of me and not her.

I swipe a hand down my face, and her scent still lingers although I hadn't touched her. Not really. My mouth reacted to the scent of her, eager and willing to taste her despite my mindset. My body took control, but only one part of me needed to connect with hers. I fucked her, and I hate myself.

Rolling from the bed, I slip into day-old shorts and find a semi-fresh tee draped over the chair in my room. Slipping it over my head, I comb my fingers through my hair and head to the bathroom in my room. A quick brush of my teeth, and I decide it's as good as I'll get to go grovel at Autumn's feet. We only have one night left, and I promise myself I'll make it up to her. I'll just hold her in my arms and give her the comfort she deserves with this devastating news about her brother.

Unfortunately, when I step into the hallway, my plans are shot to hell by Mason.

"Hey. I'm glad to see you're up. Want you guys to take a drive with me." Mason claps me on the shoulder, and I point over it in the direction of Autumn's room.

"I was just—"

"Listen, loverboy, you can give it a rest for a few hours. Just a drive. I have something I want to show you guys." Mason's voice rises softly, but it's full of excitement. A touch of anxiety also underlies his tone. He's nervous but eager to show me whatever is so damn important it can't wait.

"Zack's already up, and I told him he could bring the boys. Ben is meeting us downstairs."

It appears plans have been made without me. I'm not certain I'm intended to be included in Mason's little sightseeing venture, but I grumble my consent and follow him.

As we enter the kitchen, coffee is brewed, and pastries are set on a plate on the island. My diet has been dismantled on this trip with the additional sweets and too much alcohol. These are some of the reasons I need to wear an insulin pump. Then I consider the incredible sex I've had the past few days and assume I've burned some calories with the rigorous activity.

Fuck, I really need to apologize to Autumn.

Instead, I gladly take the coffee offered as I need to caffeinate and follow Mason outside with a to-go cup in hand.

"We aren't all going to fit in your tiny Barbie mobile," I mock, noting Mason's sporty little BMW in the driveway. For a tall man, he drives a squat car, and I sometimes wonder if it's a direct reflection of his anatomy. Then again, the man gets a lot of tail, which doesn't happen without a big dick.

"We can take Anna's SUV," Ben states, stepping onto the drive.

"I wanna ride with the top down," little Oliver admits, and Mason high-fives him.

"Well, there isn't room for six either way," I snap, feeling petulant and pissy this morning. I really should have stayed the night with Autumn. "Where are we going again?"

"It's a surprise," Mason states, wiggling his brows at a bouncing Oliver. "I'll put the top down. You grandpas follow in the SUV."

Ben and I look at one another. "Grandpas?" I snort.

"He's implying we're old." Ben laughs.

"Is that even funny?" I bark, worried about Ben's emotional state and the fact forty isn't old. In fact, Ben isn't going to reach old age. He isn't going to be a grandfather either. Mason is a fucking prick for being so insensitive.

"It's hilarious," Ben states, giving me a reassuring smile that says he isn't offended by Mason. "Don't be awkward." The warning is clear. He wants me to treat him as I usually would, but I can't. I don't know how to react to my friend dying. I should be used to death. I lost my father when I was too young to remember him. Then I lost my mother before I went off to college, leaving me an orphan throughout my university years. I couch hopped during holidays and summers until finally landing an internship with an Indianapolis architectural firm. I've worked for them ever since.

Ben and I climb into Anna's SUV, and we follow Mason.

"Do you know where we're going?" I ask, trying to calm myself.

"Not a clue, but Mason was rather adamant we all join him."

"I missed the memo," I mock, sipping my coffee while Ben drives.

"He brought it up after you left the room last night."

"Are you certain I'm included then?" My voice falters with the possibility, and disappointment strikes. Maybe I'm an afterthought in Mason's scheme.

"Absolutely." Ben shifts his head a second to look at me. "What's going on with you this morning? Don't be weird."

I snort. Don't be weird that my best friend is dying. Don't be weird that I fucked his sister. Don't be weird that I've been trying to get her pregnant for the past ten days.

"It's already weird."

"The fact you're sleeping with my sister?" Ben admits.

"Among many things," I mutter, taking another sip of my coffee.

"How's that going, by the way?"

I choke before peering over at him. "You want to know how sleeping with your sister is going?"

"Yeah. I mean, is she pregnant?"

I huff. "I have no idea."

"But you've been going at it like rabbits on crack."

"Ben," I mumble. Speaking of awkward, this is awkward.

"Well?"

"I cannot discuss this with you," I groan.

"Why not? Because she's my sister?"

"Yes." I bitterly chuckle.

"I'd like you to discuss it with me *because* she's my sister. Because I love her, and I want her taken care of. I might not agree with this practice . . . hook up with a few guys to get pregnant . . . but I want her to have what she wants. I want her to have a child if that's what she thinks will make her whole, fulfill her life, and bring her happiness. I'd prefer it wasn't from some random man but one of my best friends. At least, I'd know who the father is and know he was a good man."

Just layer that guilt like butter on toast.

"Won't I be shit if I leave her to do it alone?" I've been wrestling with this thought more and more lately.

Ben glances over at me again. "Would you really let her do it alone?"

160

LIVING at 40

My head thuds back on the seat. "I don't even know if this worked. And if it did, I guess I'd cross that hurdle when it happens. It's not like we live next door to one another, though."

"Life is full of sacrifice," Ben says, but his voice teases me.

"You want me to move here and take care of her? That's not what she wants. She wants a kid, not a husband. She doesn't want me."

"Are you sure about that?" Ben asks, and I'm curious if Ben knows something I don't. I try not to be bitter that the Kulis siblings are good at keeping things from me when it concerns the other.

"I . . . I'm following her wishes." I have my own wishful thinking, though. I want to be with her. I want to sleep with her, and I want to give her what she desires most—a child. She hasn't mentioned a husband, not once, and she hasn't asked me for more.

"What if my wish was for you to marry her if she's having your baby?"

"Ben." I groan again. "Man, that's a lot of pressure."

"I see something between you two." He sounds like a woman, and I worry Anna's rubbed off on him in the near twenty years of their marriage.

"Don't do this to me," I whine.

"What?" Ben innocently asks, tilting his head to glance at me once more.

"Don't make it a dying wish for me to marry your sister." The silence that falls between us is like the windshield suddenly shattering. We're surrounded in the awkward plea I made to him, and Ben's hand tightens on the steering wheel. He takes a moment to collect his thoughts, and I'm opening my mouth to apologize as my shit mood is not what he needs, but he speaks.

"My dying wish is that my sister finds love as I've had with Anna. I want her to have a family to mother and smother and take care of instead of all those losers she's dated. It doesn't have to be you, Logan. If you don't want those things for yourself, it doesn't have to be you. But I want you to be happy as well. And I'm willing to bet my sister could be it for you, too."

161

"I am happy," I quickly retort, ignoring the hope in my heart at what he's said about his sister. I am happy enough . . . until I consider the dead-end dates, the chaotic schedule of sharing Lorna, and the fact my ex-wife has a boyfriend.

"Are you?" Ben asks with sharpness in his tone.

"Fuck off," I whisper, with a weak smile. I hate how well Ben knows me.

"Just looking out for you, friend," he says. "I love you, man."

"Ben," I whisper-groan again as my nose prickles and my eyes sting.

"Gotta say these things while I can," he admits, forcing a smile on his straight face. The false bravado is like a stab to the heart.

"I promise I won't let anything happen to her." Caving just a little on his request, I find it not so difficult to admit. I'd never let anything happen to Autumn, and I'll keep in touch, wanting to know how things are proceeding. The idea makes me sick, though. Her with another man. Her eventually pregnant all alone. Her being a mother by herself.

"And I love you, too." The words are thick in my throat. I agree that the phrase should be said more often, and not just from the fear of never saying it again.

Tipping back my head, the weight of these two weeks crashes down on me, and I'm almost ready to go home. Almost.

+ + +

When we arrive at our destination, it's thirty minutes north of Lakeside. I don't recognize the area, although there's a lake before us.

"What's this?" I ask as I exit the SUV, and Mason stands next to his vehicle, waiting for Ben and me.

"It's Lake Liberty."

"Never heard of it," I admit, glancing over at Ben, who looks equally confused. Mason tips his head, and we follow him. It's a quick walk down a gravel drive to find a clearing with a shit home on the property.

"What do you think?" Mason asks.

"What do we think of what?" Zack questions and then yells at his boys. "Don't go in the water!" The two race to the edge with such speed there's little doubt they're about to project themselves into the clear liquid. Surprisingly, they stop short of the edge.

"I want to buy this property," Mason says.

"O-*kay*." Zack drags out the word.

Mason draws his focus from the lake to face us with a beaming smile. "May I present the first investment of The Four Points?"

"What?" I choke.

"This is it. It's time we join our collective knowledge and invest together."

I blink at Mason, uncertain I've heard him correctly. "We don't even live near here." None of us do, not even Ben when he moves to Lakeside in a few weeks.

"We don't need to be close. We can just take turns overseeing the portion of the process that belongs to us." Mason is not deterred as he turns back to the decrepit house.

"I can build it if you'll design it." Mason waves a hand at the currently collapsing structure. "Zack can handle the legal stuff, and Ben can make the outside beautiful."

"I can't work the land," Ben mutters sadly.

"I don't know the first thing about designing houses. I design buildings and high-rises," I retort but my heart races. What is this? What's happening here?

"You've mentioned in the past how you're overworked. Plus, how much commercial building is really happening where you live? Who needs another high-rise, stacking people on top of one another? This would be a home. A permanent residence or maybe a second house for someone. It can be affordable living with sustainable products. You could be creative."

"Mason, I can't design a home." However, the idea is tempting. It's not that I can't. It's that I'm out of practice. Structural engineering is different for a house, but renewable energy sources could be the same.

I'm creative with my current projects, but I understand what he means. There's a different level of artistic design here.

"What's the investment?" Zack asks, surprising me that he's even minutely interested in this suggestion.

"I was thinking a quarter apiece. All the properties I've looked at are in foreclosure. It's not the house, but the land we seek." He sounds like a pioneer, and I don't miss the pride in his voice.

"Properties? As in, more than one?" Zack doesn't miss the particulars.

"I have five locations scoped out at the moment."

"Five?" Ben chokes.

"I wanted a variety of choices. We can even dispense with one and make it so we each invest in only one at first but share the responsibility with each project. Design. Build. Beautify and business." Mason points at each of us and our perspective role in such a venture.

"Mason," I groan. "I don't have that kind of cash." I'm not a rich boy like the rest of these guys. I didn't grow up with daddy's money like Mason. The comparison isn't fair to Zack as his father eventually lost their wealth, but he's still spoiled in his own right. Ben has Anna's prestige backing his name, but I don't. "I can't. I'm out."

"We can't be The Four Points without all four of us. Come on, man. This was our dream," Mason pleads, swiping a hand through his artful curls. His freaking model looks make him appear too polished to actually do any demolition on a place or understand the meaning of hard work.

"We were drunk," Zack reminds us.

"We were young," I clarify.

"We did have a dream," Ben says, slowly smiling.

"We have all the parts. You have your dad's company which you want to restore," Mason says, directing his attention to Ben. "No heavy lifting for you, just consult. And I have the construction crew," Mason adds for himself.

"Logan, you can share designs via the internet, and Zack could do the same with contracts and such. It wouldn't be the same as working together, but we'd still be in it collectively."

"And what about when we disagree?" I ask, knowing that as much as I care for Mason, we can butt heads like the best of bulls.

"It's bound to happen, but we'll have everything legal and legit. That's Zack's side of things. We're a team, but it's business."

I shake my head. It's too much. I just can't envision it. And between Autumn and now Ben's announcement, I can't wrap my thoughts around another venture. "I'm still out. I can't swing the cash, let alone find the time." I work overtime only because I throw myself into it. It fills the void when I don't have Lorna.

Mason sighs. "Just think about it. We don't have to do anything immediately."

"What about these properties? How long will they sit on the market?" Zack asks.

"A few have been on the market a while, and they're eager to dump them, but we don't have to rush. Others will pop up."

"And if they don't?" I ask. The other side of this idea is what if we fail? What if we purchase but can't flip the house? What if we invest but don't find other prospects?

"This is waterfront property," Mason snorts. "There's miles of it in this state."

"Are you thinking we'd work all over Michigan?" Ben asks, obviously overwhelmed at the thought.

"I'm thinking we'd only work the properties along the immediate coast. We can turn these over. I know we can." Mason's faith in the process is a bit inspiring, and I've never seen him so excited by the prospect of doing something like this.

Ben rests his hands on his hips, glancing at the lopsided house. "I'd have to speak to Anna. We have a lot going on."

Mason's shoulders fall. "I understand. I thought maybe she'd like to be in on it, too. Give her something to look forward to. The boys as well. In a few years, who knows, Calvin might want to be a part of the company."

Ben slowly nods, and I want to punch Mason again. He's being considerate while inconsiderate at the same time.

"I could do it," Zack says. "I don't need Jeanine's permission," he teases of Ben.

"Logan?" Mason questions.

"I'd have to think about it." It's not a firm no, but I already know there's a strong possibility I won't say yes. Still, I glance over at the house and slowly envision something more modern with energy-efficient windows and solar panels to help aid electricity. This venture could be that something different I've been wanting for a while, but I can't leave Lorna behind. Autumn crosses my mind, but I'm not certain what to think regarding her.

"I guess that's all I can ask," Mason states, breaking into my thoughts and slipping his hands into his pockets. His shoulders hunch, and his eyes lower for the ground. "I just want you guys to consider it."

What am I missing? I don't know why Mason would want to take on such projects as he already runs a very successful construction company with his father. Located a few hours up the coast, they build multi-million-dollar homes and make bank in the process. However, I'm on overload and trying to figure out Mason's motive is beyond my scope of brainpower today.

"Who needs a drink?" Mason finally asks.

"I do," Oliver says, reminding us that two little boys have been running around someone else's property.

"Daddy, I'm thirsty," Trevor adds, and Zack reaches down for his son, hoisting him up to his hip.

"Okay, little man. Let's find us something to drink."

We step forward, returning up the gravel drive, but I take a final glance back at the house, finding Mason doing the same. His head slowly shakes side to side, disappointment on his face, and I realize there was a lot at stake showing us this property. A lot more than I understand. I wish I could give in. I wish I could make a gut decision, but I just can't.

21

[Autumn]

The final day was strange. There was no other way to describe it as I lay in bed trying, and failing, at reading a book. The men had disappeared in the morning, and all Anna knew was their destination was a mystery. I had to work, so I didn't have an afternoon in the sunshine like the rest of them. Dinner was somber. Ben didn't want it that way, but his friends tiptoed around the elephant in the room. I sensed a giraffe, a panda, and a purple spotted dragon might be in there as well, as each man seemed to have something weighing heavily on his mind. After helping Anna with the dishes, I excused myself, not in the mood to witness a final sunset with the rest of them. They are the friends—Ben, Zack, Mason, and Logan—and even Anna. I am the outsider. Just Ben's little sister.

As my bedroom door opens on a rush and then shuts on a soft click, I sit upright, startled by the sudden intrusion.

Across the room, Logan and I meet eyes as his back presses against the door, and my breath hitches. We haven't spoken directly since sometime yesterday. On my bedroom floor last night, he didn't speak as we did what we did. He didn't say anything to me at dinner other than "pass the potatoes, please." But, there's apology, panic, and something else written in his current expression, and as he crosses the room in three large steps, I climb up to my knees, meeting him at the end of my bed, and we embrace one another. My arms wrap around his neck, drawing his face into the crook of mine while he circles me with his arms like a vise grip, holding me plastered to him. Unable to release one another, we tumble back to the bed, ignoring jabs to the back and a soft choking sound. We continue to hold tight.

Logan's weight blankets me, and I refuse to let him move. With his nose at the side of my neck, he's breathing heavily, inhaling my summery scent. Without words, he moves down my body, nestling himself between my legs which spread to accommodate his broad shoulders. He stops short under my breasts, lowering his forehead for my stomach and

L.B. DUNBAR

pausing. Turning his cheek to my belly, he closes his eyes, and I reach for his dark hair, combing through the soft locks. His hand comes to my tummy, and he spreads his fingers as he flattens his palm. Shifting only enough to press his lips to my rumbling stomach, he kisses me once near my belly button and then returns his cheek to my abs. We stay like this for a long time. Long enough that Logan's weight grows heavier, and he dozes over me—his ear to my belly, his hand on my side.

At first, I can't sleep, so I just continue to stroke over his hair, wondering why this sweet man came into my life now and accepting the sad fact that he's leaving. I'm not opposed to long-distance relationships, nor is separation by miles an issue with cell phones, internet, and video chats, but it's not the life I want to lead, and it wasn't the deal between us. The goal was to get pregnant and nothing more. He already has a child. He has a home and a job hours away from here. This was about me and included me not involving him. My heart feels so differently.

I want him to stay with me. I want to be good to him. Last night was an anomaly. He was hurting, confused, frustrated even with the idea that Ben is dying. It's a lot to take in, especially when we've spent these two weeks trying to create a life—a baby—a little person for me to love.

Slowly, I drift off to sleep, but it's more a heavy doze, the kind that leaves you conscious of your surroundings but unable to move in reaction to anything you hear. However, when Logan shifts over me, pushing up my cotton cami and pressing kisses to my skin, I'm alert while drowsy. His mouth continues to move over my belly, sucking at the loose flesh before lowering and sliding my boxer shorts over my hips.

"What are you doing?" I softly question in a raspy voice.

"One more time for good luck," he mutters into my stomach as he shoves my shorts to my knees. *We'll do it extra times just for good measure and once more for good luck.* I swallow around a sudden lump in my throat. One more chance to root if the seed isn't already planted. My dad would love the gardening metaphor but maybe not the process of this plan. I'm sleeping with a man in hopes he'll get me pregnant, but he won't stick around to raise the baby. And I can't fault him. This is what I asked.

As I shake the bitter thoughts away, my fingers return to combing through his hair. He quickly removes my shorts and underwear before pressing his nose through the coarse hair at the apex of my legs. His tongue comes forward, cautious as he caresses me with tender strokes. He swirls around me, lapping everywhere but where I need as if memorizing me with the trace of his tongue. Finally, he narrows in on the bud, sucking hard before paying it homage. The torture is too much, and I shatter in a gentle release like waves slowly retreating to the lake. It's not a crash or a rush, but a stretch of sensation, crackling and bubbling like the water leaves the sand as it returns to the larger body of liquid. *I'm* liquid when he finishes, feeling weightless and undone. We've been together so often, in so many ways in the past two weeks, and each time I think it can't be different, it is.

We've had sex. We've made out. We've fucked.

But this night, we're making love as he enters me in a slow dive before dragging back to my entrance, teasing me, testing me. Repeating the motion over and over again, he takes his time to fill me. My back arches, and I lift my head to meet his mouth with mine. My hands scan the scope of his body, not wanting to miss an inch as I cover the plains of his back and the firm hills of his ass. My palms coast over his shoulders and biceps and down to his wrists. His hands rest beside my body, but he entwines our fingers, lifting them above my head. His body stretches over mine, and we move as one in the most sensual dance I've ever danced. With tender thrusts and swaying surges, I follow his lead.

"Autumn," he whispers. "The scent of leaves. The color of change." He strains a second. "An ending to something I don't want to end." His mouth crashes to mine before I can respond, and I swallow around the invasion of his tongue and the lump in my throat. Our bodies begin to stutter, colliding faster, breaking the slow beat to pick up the pace. His hands clutch at mine, and I respond as if holding on for dear life.

"Will you get there?" he asks, hinting that he needs to release my hands in order to touch me. He'll slip his fingers between us and rub where I need his touch, but I don't want him to let go. I don't want to release him.

I shake my head on the pillow. "Come for me," I whisper to his lips only an inch from mine, and he stills his body while he pulses inside me. Once. Twice. Three times he jolts, and I'm so full. It's more than the depth of him joined within me. It's more than the idea of what could be happening inside me. It's my heart that's near bursting, and I don't want to lose this moment. So, I squeeze his hands tighter, and we pause time as he remains over me until he's gone soft and slips outward.

And if ever I thought a conclusion has occurred, it's this moment. He climbs down the length of my body, pressing kisses to my breasts, my belly, and one last spot between my legs before scooting off the edge of the bed. Slowly, he tugs his shorts back on before picking up his T-shirt.

"Thank you," he whispers to me, holding my eyes for only a second before turning for my bedroom door and leaving me alone for the rest of the night.

+ + +

While my body should feel beautiful from the way Logan handled our final act, my heart is black. Breakfast is a chaos of rushed eggs and forced waffles, and I take orders for every request to keep my hands busy and my mind absent. As dishes are cleaned, commands are given to start packing cars and picking up loose items lying here and there. My mother arrives to say goodbye to the boys as she continues to call the forty-year-old men who are friends.

Before I know it, it's almost eleven, and we stand in the driveway among Zack's car and Logan's SUV. Mason stands nearby with his hands in his shorts.

"Why aren't you ready?" Logan asks of him, and Mason turns his head to glance at Ben before facing both Zack and Logan.

"I've decided I'm staying." His announcement is like a wrecking ball colliding with the house.

"What?" Logan snaps.

"What?" Anna adds, turning to face Ben from her position tucked under his arm.

"Why?" Zack asks.

"I'm the only one single. Ben's eventually going to need help. I can offer strength for things his boys shouldn't do, and Anna can't muster."

My thoughts race to things like bathing my brother and lifting his body.

"Are you calling me weak?" Anna barks, her tone expresses her shock mixed with a touch of irritation.

"You're the strongest woman we know," Ben says, pressing a kiss to her forehead, and I try not to let the comment sting. "But Mason has offered and . . . we'll talk."

The dismissal tells the rest of us it's not up for discussion, and Ben doesn't wish to explain further. Did he ask Mason to stay? If he did, I don't understand. I thought he wanted time for his family.

"I'll be staying over the garage," Mason announces as if to clarify how he'll be separate but ready when Ben needs him.

"What about work? What will your dad say?" Zack asks as Mason works with his father in their construction company.

"He'll just have to understand. This is family."

Tears well in my eyes. Mason can be an ass, but Ben sees something in Mason the rest of us don't. It's the only explanation for why he's remained friends with Mason all these years.

"All right then," Zack says, holding out his hand for Mason. "You call us if you need support." The handshake is met with a half hug like guys give, but when Zack moves on to Ben, he holds a little longer. Anna gets a full embrace, and I'm reminded that Zack's and Anna's families have been connected the longest. Hugs are passed around, even to his little monsters.

"You be good for your daddy," I warn Trevor and Oliver, pressing kisses to their heads before they start fighting over who gets to sit where in the back seat.

Logan steps up next, back-clapping Mason. The pounding from each of them sounds harder than necessary. When Logan steps over to Ben, he captures my brother's face in his large hands and holds it.

"You need anything. *Anything.* You call me." His eyes shift to Anna. "Anything."

Anna nods, and Logan pulls Ben against him, holding a little longer as Zack did. Next, Logan wraps around Anna, and finally, he lifts Mila.

"Thanks for letting Lorna crash in your room."

"She can come stay with me anytime." Mila's little voice sounds grown-up and polished like her mother. Logan presses a kiss to her forehead before lowering her to the ground.

"And stop growing up," he teasingly warns her.

Lorna wraps her arms around me, and I hold her head to my breasts. She's almost as tall as me, and when I press her back, I brush her hair behind her ears, looking her right in the eyes.

"Ice cream for dinner is our secret," I tell her. "And practice your cartwheels."

Lorna laughs.

"I'd also say stop getting so beautiful, but I know you can't help yourself."

Lorna beams at my compliment, displaying how beautiful she is. Someday, the boys will notice too, and Logan will have an issue on his hands. Lorna moves over to hug Ben, Anna, and Mila while Logan shifts to me. His arms wrap around my neck, and he holds me against his chest.

"If I said I had the time of my life, would you hold it against me?"

I chuckle into his neck as the tears I didn't want to shed begin to leak.

"I'm just thankful you held me against you," I whisper and choke a bit to fight the sob threatening to break next.

"Dammit, Autumn," he mutters, soft and broken. "This is not goodbye. We're still friends. I'll see you . . ."

When? And whenever it is, it won't be the same, and we both know it. I might be pregnant with his child, and I might not. The next time I see him could be the loss of someone we love or the beginning of a new life, but we will never be just friends. We'll always have this summer. Hopefully, we'll share something else, but it won't be something we share together if that makes any sense.

I nod to agree. "Thank you," I whisper to him as he did to me last night. Our gratitude for one another is certainly for different reasons. I'm grateful he gave me this chance. I have no idea why he would thank me. Pressing a kiss to my temple, he lingers a moment. I want him to kiss me, but I know it won't stop there. I'll want one more kiss, and then one more night, and then more time in general.

"Let me know when you know something," he mutters directly against my forehead, and I nod again, unable to find my voice. We could be pregnant. Correction, *I* could be pregnant, and the thought fills my eyes with blinding liquid.

"Okay, loverboy, time to break," Mason crassly interjects, and Logan pulls back. His hands cup my face similar to how he held Ben, and his eyes search mine, but mine are too clouded to read his. When he pulls away from me, I still feel the heat of his touch, even as he gives me his back. Even as he climbs into his SUV. Even as he backs out of the driveway.

Mason slips his arm around me, but I don't feel it across my shoulders. I can't find the strength to lift my hand and wave as the SUV pauses at the end of the driveway before turning onto the road, leading Logan home.

Goodbye, whispers through my head.

"Aunt Autumn, why are you sad?" Mila asks, and I tip my head to look down at my niece. She was leaning against Anna but stands upright to face me.

"I'm not sad *sad*," I tease, forcing a smile. "These are just happy tears because it was a great adventure but over too soon."

Mila stares at me as if she has no idea what I'm saying, and I admit I don't either. My thoughts are everywhere and nowhere.

"Okay, sad sad happy girl, let's go back inside." Mason presses a quick kiss to the top of my head and then releases me, stepping forward to Mila, who he picks up by her arms. She squeals in delight.

I don't know what Mason is doing by staying here. I don't know what Ben was thinking if he asked him to stay. I only wish I'd had the strength to tell Logan I didn't want him to go. After a final look at the empty driveway, I head back into the house to collect my things. It's time I return to my home as well.

22

[Logan]

The three-hour car ride home was difficult between my own distracted thoughts and Lorna's silence. Watching Mason wrap his arm around Autumn as I pulled out of the driveway was almost enough cause to force me back to the drive and kick his ass. He looked all too happy to be next in line if my sperm didn't take, and I can't explain how badly I want it to happen. I want her baby to be mine. I want her to be mine.

But that isn't what she wants.

Last night, I dozed on Autumn's belly, willing whatever miracle needed to happen to have happened. Willing my little swimmers to get where they needed to go, and at least one break through the necessary barrier to seal the deal. I'd thought of nothing past planting my seed in Autumn but driving away had me heartsick over leaving her behind.

What if she was pregnant? What next? It wasn't like I wouldn't see the kid. I'd be attending whatever function we planned next as friends. Thoughts turned morbid, and I prayed the next occasion we gathered was not a funeral.

My head is not in a good space as Lorna and I cross into Indianapolis, so to say Chloe dropped a bomb on me when I returned Lorna to her mother's house is an understatement.

"Hey, so I wanted to tell you I've decided to move to France with Peter."

I stare at her as if she's spoken French. "You're leaving Indiana?"

Chloe shrugs, and I wonder what I ever saw in my ex-wife. She was so beautiful when we met, but she changed so much in the course of our marriage and the years afterward that I don't recognize her anymore.

"What about Lorna?" How could she leave our daughter behind?

"What about her?"

The unspoken lingers between us before I connect the invisible dots. *She'll be going with Chloe.* "Over my dead body," I snap.

"I can't leave her with you."

175

I stare at my ex-wife, flabbergast at both her incredulous tone and her distrust in my ability to care for our daughter. Not to mention, she is not taking *our* daughter outside the country *to live.*

"Chloe, I don't think this is the time to discuss this." Standing on her front stoop, I have just kissed Lorna goodbye. She has soccer practice during the week, and I'll be the one taking her, so I'll see her in a few days.

"A decision has been made, Logan. I'm moving to France in two weeks, and Lorna is coming with me."

Two weeks?

"Does Lorna know you have plans to do such a thing?" I'd like to believe my child would tell me, even hint at the idea, that her mother was moving them out of the country. When Lorna suggested moving to Lakeside, it would have been the perfect time to mention how she might be moving away, and she hadn't. Ironically, we'd talked again on the car ride home about Lorna's desire to move to Lakeside, how lucky Mila was to live there all year, and I had to explain that even *if* we ever moved there, we wouldn't be living in Mila's house or even a house on the water. I can't afford a million-dollar home.

"It just sort of happened." Chloe sweetly smiles, excitement written on her face.

"What do you mean *it just sort of happened*? When?"

"While you were away. Peter learned he needs to return to France, and he doesn't want to go without me."

"And Lorna," I growl.

"Well, of course, Lorna." But that's not the answer I want to hear, nor will I let another man take my child to another country. I have accepted that I might have to share Lorna with a stepfather one day, but I've never been good at sharing.

"Did he propose to you?" The question comes out harsh and bitter.

"Well . . . not exactly." Chloe clutches at the door, her eyes rapidly blinking as she shifts her gaze away from me a second.

"What *exactly* did he do then?" I question, grinding my teeth with the discomfort that we actually are having this conversation on her front stoop.

"He asked me to move to France with him."

"With Lorna?" I hiss again.

"Yes, Lorna."

I don't believe it. Peter might want Chloe, but he doesn't want my daughter. He can't have her.

"I don't approve." My arms flap to the side and slap my thigh for emphasis.

"Do you need to approve?" Chloe stammers, staring at me.

"Yes. When it concerns Lorna, I do have a say. We agreed we would share in the parenting responsibility." I exhale. My heart is racing. I don't like to fight with Chloe, considering it bad form for Lorna to see us at odds, but this is beyond anything we've ever encountered in co-parenting. Taking a deep breath, I try to soften my tone. "I don't want to deny you anything, Chloe, but you cannot take my daughter from me."

"*Our* daughter," she reminds me, but it appears she's the one who forgot we *share* her.

"Maybe we should ask Lorna how she feels," I demand, no longer patient with this information. If Chloe wants to do this on the front stoop, then I want Lorna present.

"She won't really have a say, but I'll be talking to her tonight."

"Jesus, Chloe, we just got back from a vacation. An emotional vacation. You were the one who told me before we left that we needed to treat her like a budding teenager, on the cusp of womanhood." I shiver at the thought of Lorna growing older but accept that it's inevitable. "She should have a choice."

"What happened?" my ex-wife asks, ignoring my plea for Lorna's decision-making ability. Chloe releases the door and crosses her arms over her chest. Her voice rings with concern but not sympathy. It's more of a *what did you do* question.

"It's . . . nothing. We just had a lot of fun, and . . ." I take another deep breath. I don't want to tell Chloe about Ben yet. She liked my friends well enough, but she never felt she belonged when we shared vacations or attended weddings, funerals, or reunions. I never understood as everyone was nice to her, but she said she didn't fit. "We should talk to Lorna together."

"I think I can handle it."

Like she's handling this? "I'm not saying you can't." Although, my jaw clenches as I'm suddenly questioning her ability. On top of learning about Ben and leaving Autumn, this is the last thing I need. It's also my first priority. "But you cannot take Lorna to France."

I glare at Chloe, hoping she reads the warning in my eyes. I will not let my daughter go.

"Just let me talk to her," Chloe adds, lowering her head. "I'll have her call you after we talk."

I do not like this solution. I want to see Lorna's reaction. I want to be present when Chloe springs this bullshit on her, but most of all I need to know if Lorna might want to go. Would she really like to move to France? She hinted at her fears for the future in middle school. *Would crossing an ocean be a solution?*

After swiping a hand through my hair, I cup the back of my neck. "I want a call from Lorna as soon as you are done talking."

Chloe smirks at me. "Fine."

"Is Peter here?" I should have asked this first. I'd like to throat punch him. He doesn't want my daughter, and I'm certain of it.

"No, he's at his place. I wanted to talk to Lorna alone. Break the news between the two of us first."

The only breaking that's going to happen is skulls if this woman thinks she can take my child across the world, but I tamper down the fear, biting back the threat of lawyers. We've never had to go this route, and I don't want to start, but this is too much.

When I finally return home, the weight of everything hits me hard. The two-story walk-up is too quiet. After a rowdy vacation with a dozen people in a spacious home, I'm suffocating under the silence and the small size of my place. I miss Autumn immediately, and I can't settle my concerns for Ben. Now this fuckery with Chloe and the possibility of losing Lorna, and I'm coming out of my skin. I reach for my phone, hovering over Autumn's contact number.

Staring at my screen's background image, which consists of a sunset from Lakeside, I hesitate before tossing the phone on my kitchen island. I can't call Autumn because that's not what we had. That's not what we were about, but I need to talk to someone. I need to scream and shout and wipe away the ache in my chest at the potential of losing too many people I care about—Autumn, Ben, Lorna. Their names circle on repeat until I pick back up my phone and press a different contact.

"Zack, I need some advice."

+ + +

Three days later, I'm standing at my desk when my assistant knocks on my office door. "There's someone here to see you, boss."

"Okay . . . uh, give me a minute." With all the chaos of dealing with Chloe's bomb drop and asking Zack for legal advice, I'm struggling to keep my thoughts on work. My current project includes a multi-level apartment and shopping complex in a once run-down area of Indianapolis that's being rejuvenated. My architectural firm not only designs commercial properties for the immediate Indianapolis area but has also created libraries for universities and an entire hospital.

My wandering concentration is also a result of not sleeping well in my quiet house and empty bed, spending most nights thinking of Autumn until the thoughts turn to memories, and I'm whacking off like a teenager again.

In the three days since I left Michigan, I've wanted to call her a million times but haven't known what to say. Our last two nights together, we were out of sync, and I didn't know how to right the pieces or if there was even a chance of mending whatever it was that happened. Perhaps we just came to an end as was expected. Only, I didn't want it to end—not by a long shot—but what could I do about it? Now, I have this Lorna mess.

Tossing down my pencil, I stalk to my office door and freeze.

"Autumn?" I blink once and glance left, confirming I'm standing in my office and not dreaming of her presence. "Autumn, sweetheart, what are you doing here?"

I rush forward at the panic on her face. She's so fucking beautiful despite the fear in her eyes and the washed-out coloring of her cheeks. She's wearing a long overcoat which makes no sense on such a summery day. Then I notice she has on flip-flops and decide something is seriously wrong.

"Joseph, we'll just be . . ." I point at my office as I reach for Autumn's elbow and guide her into my space. Once inside, she takes a few steps away from me, staring out the window and wrapping her arms around her middle as I shut the door. Then she turns to face me.

"You have a nice view." It's an odd statement. Glancing over her shoulder, I look out at Indianapolis's cityscape, which isn't bad but isn't as great as seeing the lake.

"Autumn, honey, I'm assuming you aren't here for the view. And I won't believe you were just in the neighborhood."

She lowers her head. "I got my period."

Staring at her, my brows pinch. *Shit.* "Sweetheart." I step up to her, but she steps back, and I halt.

Okay, then.

"You drove three hours to tell me you got your period." I'm only trying to confirm that although she doesn't want me to touch her, she drove some two hundred plus miles instead of calling me to tell me our little experiment did not work.

"Yes." She looks up at me, dazed and confused as if even she can't explain why she drove here instead of calling.

"Why?" My voice cuts. I saw her standing with her arms around Mason as I hit the end of Ben's driveway. Or rather, Mason had his arm over her shoulder. It's all semantics. We didn't create what she wanted, and now it's up to the next guy. My heart races, and I clench my hands.

"I just thought you should know." She shrugs as she twists her lips, and her eyes avoid mine.

LIVING at 40

"So you can move on," I snap, hating how I sound. Of course, Mason will be the next guy. He was always the one to steal girls away from me, or they fell for him after me. Suddenly, I'm that fat college kid once again not feeling good enough. My swimmers weren't the sharks they needed to be and hadn't gotten the job done. Maybe Mason already knows Autumn isn't pregnant, which does not seem logical as I face the distraught woman before me, but suddenly, I can't think straight.

Her head pops up at my sharp reply.

"No," she states. "No, I just thought . . . I don't know what I thought . . . you said you wanted to know. And I guess this means you're free of any obligation." She waves a hand between us.

"I didn't realize I'd have an obligation." She didn't want me to be obligated. She just wanted me to make a baby with her. Swiping a hand through my hair, I'm frustrated and upset with myself for my unkind words.

"I-I shouldn't have come." She steps forward, but I block her path.

"Why did you then?" I question once more, holding up my hands to stop her retreat. She'll have to go through me to get to the door.

"I just thought you should know." Her voice shakes, and her lower lip quivers. Her arms tighten around her middle. "It didn't work. I knew it probably wouldn't on the first try, but we . . . and so many times . . ." A tear slips down her cheek. "Something happened between us, right?"

Guilt smacks me in the cheek. I reach for her, pulling her to me and wrapping my arms around her. Her hands cover her face as she buries it in my chest.

"Shh." Her body trembles against mine, and the ache inside me is an open geyser, overflowing with sorrow.

"I knew it wouldn't be so easy as to happen on the first attempt, but I also felt so certain that it had. It seemed like it just had to have happened. There was something. I felt it."

Her head pops up as she speaks, her voice confident in her conviction while her hesitant eyes search mine.

"There was something there," I whisper, confirming what she said. We had a connection, and it was more than just baby-making.

"Let's get out of here," I say, stroking my thumbs over her tear-stained cheeks.

"I don't want to get you in trouble or anything."

"You just drove three hours to tell me something huge, and I'm not letting you out of my sight. Where are you staying?"

She shakes her head. "I hadn't gotten that far. I just noticed . . ." She waves at her lower body. "And got in my car, heading here to tell you."

Leaning forward, I press a kiss to her forehead. "Okay, honey. We'll go to my place." Keeping my hands on her shoulders, I wait for her to acknowledge what I've said. I'm taking her home with me.

She nods to agree, and I pack up a few things. I can work from home later, but first, I need to take care of this woman.

23

[Autumn]

I don't know why I drove all the way to Indianapolis. I mean, I know *why* I drove here. I know what happened, but I don't know why I drove here. I could have just called Logan, but I needed to see his face. I needed to see his devastation if he was devastated. I was being ridiculous, and I knew that, but I couldn't seem to stop myself. I had to see him.

After following his SUV to his townhome, his place isn't what I'd expect him to live in. For a man who designs buildings, the skinny-looking rowhouse doesn't say home to me. It's quaint but obviously a modern rendition of something old and metropolis. I park on the street while he pulls into his singular driveway. I don't have a bag or even my purse, just a tote where I dropped an entire box of tampons, my cell phone, and my wallet. I'm dressed like a homeless person in an overcoat despite the heat of mid-August and flip-flops. I'm wearing a pair of shorts that have seen better days and a Crossroads Café T-shirt.

I'd called in sick, which I've never done in the five years I've owned the place.

Logan waits for me as I walk up his short drive, and then he wraps his arm over my shoulder, tucking me into his side as he leads me up the front steps and into his place. The inside is nice but stark, bright but dull at the same time. It doesn't look lived in, and I briefly wonder where are the signs he and Lorna spend time here.

After dropping his keys on the kitchen island, he leads me directly to his couch, and we sit facing one another. He takes both my hands with his.

"Okay, let's back up. What happened?"

"I got my period." It's that simple.

"Okay." He releases one of my hands and nervously scratches at the stubble under his chin. "How are you feeling? What are you thinking?"

"Honestly, I'm thinking Ben was right. What was I thinking? I can't sleep with random men and hope to get pregnant. I don't *want* to sleep with a list of men, and the more I think about getting pregnant, the more I realize I don't want to do it alone."

I want a child, but I want someone by my side as well. I'm thirty-six. I'm not too old. It could still happen. It's just taking me longer than most. A late bloomer, my mother would say, although I matured early, developed young, and feel like I've been having sex with the wrong men forever. Before me sits the right man or at least a man I'll measure every other man up against from this point forward.

"Thank fuck," Logan snaps, surprising me. "I don't want you sleeping with random men either." His expression sharpens. "If you still want to have a baby, though, you can do it. You can do anything you set your mind to. You can raise a child on your own, but you won't be alone. You'll have Ben and Anna." We meet eyes, knowing I'll only have Ben for so long. Plus, Ben is my brother. He isn't who I want by my side. "And I'll give you all the support you need."

The sentiment is sweet, but I don't know what he means. His thumb strokes my knuckles, distracting me, and I recall every touch, every caress, every kiss of the past weeks.

"What changed your mind?" he cautiously asks. "About the random men and your list."

"You," I whisper, swallowing around the concern he won't like my answer. "I know that's not what we promised. That wasn't the deal, but I can't be with anyone else right now. I don't know that I ever want to be with anyone else. There was never a list, Logan, but if there had been, there would only be one name on it."

Logan's eyes slowly widen, and I'm freaking out that I've gone too far. I've arrived at his work like a stalker, dressed like a deranged one at that. And now, I've admitted my feelings for him. Feelings we weren't allowed to factor into the equation. I've complicated matters that were never intended to be complicated, and Logan continues to stare at me.

Slowly, he lifts a hand and curls it behind my neck. His fingers squeeze, tightening even.

"I'm sorry if it's not what you want to hear. I understand it's—"

A fierce kiss cuts me short and nearly forces me backward on his couch. His fingers delve into my hair, gripping a chunk, loosening strands from the messy bun on my head. His tongue invades my mouth. He tastes like absence, and I've missed him so much. He also tastes like everything I'd ever want, and I don't know why I didn't tell him how I felt before he left.

"No random men," he mutters against my mouth, and our teeth bump. "No list. Only me."

Slowly, I smile against his mouth pressed over mine but not kissing me. The demand seeps into me, and I swallow the thought, drinking it in like a magic elixir.

"Only you," I repeat against his lips.

"We'll just try again, and again, and again." He kisses me once more, softening it only a little. "I'll give you all the babies you want."

We continue to make out on his couch, falling back against it. Logan has a hand up my shirt, holding his palm against my warm belly. One of his thick thighs is between my legs as his body partially covers mine, and we continue to kiss like love-starved teens until I remember my condition.

I have my period.

"We can't . . . do that," I mutter as his thigh nudges upward, adding tension to an area that both aches for him and doesn't want him anywhere near me. "But I want to be clear this isn't only about sex. This isn't about making babies. At least, not for me."

"Why not?" His pause should make me question everything, but I steamroll ahead.

"I can't ask you to make a baby with me."

"I think we might be a little late for that," he teases, returning his mouth to my jaw.

"Long-distance is difficult. I don't want to put pressure on you, on us."

"Ask me," he whispers as he nears my ear, nipping at the lobe.

"Ask you?" I question.

"Ask me to make a baby with you. Ask me to keep having sex with you. Ask me to fill you with babies, Autumn, and I will."

"Logan," I groan, uncertain if it's his commands or his nibbling down the side of my neck that make me shudder. Quickly, his mouth covers mine, kissing me like a man hungry and needy. No, not needy but wanting me.

"How will this work?" I finally ask, feeling like I'm dropping a sledgehammer on our reunion.

"We'll work it out. It's going to involve some creative scheduling, but I want this. I want us."

The words bring on the biggest smile. It's everything I want to hear, and the weight of concern along with the reality of not becoming pregnant lifts a little.

"I want us, too," I tell him. His mouth returns to mine, tender and sweet, slowing our pace. Then he pulls back. His hand continues to roam my stomach, slipping to my side.

"What the hell are you wearing?" He softly chuckles, shifting to eye my unseasonal coat. He grunts, and I giggle as he works it off me. My fingers find his tie and begin to unknot it, tugging it loose before simply pulling it over his head. Next, I unbutton a few buttons on his dress shirt, but while my fingers work, my thoughts race. His job. My café. His place. My place. His daughter.

"Where is Lorna?"

Logan bitterly chuckles, swiping a hand through his hair as I tug his shirt free of his pants. "Funny you should mention Lorna. The day I came home, Chloe hit me with a whammy. She wants to move to France and take Lorna with her."

"What?" I snap, lowering my hands to the warmth of his back. He works at kicking off his shoes while he balances over me.

"When I dropped Lorna off, Chloe laid it on me that her boyfriend asked her to move with him to France. Her boyfriend, not fiancé, not husband. This could be a dead-end relationship, and she wants to move to France with our child."

Dead-end relationship. I've hit plenty of dead ends in the relationship department, so I'm an expert in knowing sometimes things don't last forever. Look at Ben and Anna. They could have had forever, but their forever will be cut short, only proving my point. Even Logan and I aren't guaranteed, but I'd like to see where we go. As if reading my thoughts, he speaks.

"I don't know where we'll go, but I know I'll always kick myself if we don't continue. If we don't try."

Chewing at my lower lip, I slowly nod as my fingers trace over his spine.

"I'm so sorry this is happening with Lorna. What are you going to do?"

"I called Zack. I don't want to take legal action against Chloe. We've never been that cutthroat with one another, but she can't take Lorna from me. She's all I have." His hand coasts under my chin and along my throat, tenderly touching me while we discuss such an upsetting subject.

You have me, I want to say to him, but he needs to think about his daughter. She's a part of him, and I can't imagine him giving her up.

"I shouldn't be here," I whisper, torn between the thrill of his touch and the ache in my heart for his daughter. "You need to take care of Lorna."

"I will take care of her." His brows pinch. "But right now, I want to take care of you."

He's sweet, and guilt peppers my heart.

"We should reconsider unprotected sex. Now isn't the time to get pregnant."

"Why not?" His eyes leap to mine. His hand stills on my chest, smoothing over my T-shirt but not reaching a breast.

"Because you live here. Lorna's here. Your job is here. Your home is here."

"If Chloe gets away with taking Lorna, I'll have nothing tying me to this city." His voice is laced with acid, and I'm frustrated for him. I don't want him to lose his daughter. I don't want him to give up his job or his home. He's vested here.

"Chloe isn't going to take Lorna away from you," I state, hoping to reassure him and keep a good vibe out in the universe that this loving father will not lose his daughter.

"Damn right she's not."

"Is there something I can do to help with Lorna? What did Zack say?"

"He has a lawyer friend looking into the custody agreement, but he's pretty certain moving out of the country is out of the question. Chloe either needs to stay here without Peter or relinquish Lorna to me."

"Wow. You'd have her full time." Lorna is amazing, and I have no doubt Logan will be a wonderful single parent. He's already doing the single-dad thing, but he's still sharing time with Chloe. Having Lorna all the time will be a new challenge, especially as she enters middle school. A girl needs her mother, but I can't deny Lorna needs a father like Logan in her life as well.

"That's what I want." His firm tone tells me he'll do everything to battle Chloe if she tries to take Lorna away, and I love how protective he is of his child. I'd love a man to be just as protective of mine . . . and me. I'm at such a crossroads, and the name of my café sounds rather prophetic. I still want a baby, but I sense even more how now is not the time with Logan.

"I'm sorry I made you leave work," I admit as he remains propped on an elbow wedged between me and the back of his couch. His hand continues to skim down my body. He's gone through the valley between my breasts and landed on my belly, kneading the soft flesh.

"I'm not worried about work. How are you feeling?" His head lifts, and his eyes scan mine. "Cramps? Headache?" *Is he really concerned about my period?*

"It's just the usual. Cramps. Headache." I repeat for him, excluding that ugly, heavy flow in the first days. I feel sluggish, even sleepy, but I would not trade the position I'm in right now with him next to me on this couch.

Logan hums—an ominous sound.

"What?" I tease as his hand lowers, returning under my shirt to touch my skin. His fingers curl into the waistband of my ratty, old shorts.

"I'm on my period," I state, eyes widening at him.

"I'm not afraid of blood."

"Oh my God. You did not just say that to me." I scoff.

"I'm saying this. Shower. Now." Logan hops over me with the agility of a cat, landing on two feet beside the couch. He lowers both hands for mine and hoists me upward.

"Logan," I warn, but before I can add further reprimands, I'm up in his arms, and he's carrying me off for the bathroom.

24

[Logan]

We didn't have sex, but we did other things to get much-needed relief from the tension surrounding us when Autumn first arrived.

I ordered in from a favorite barbecue place downtown and selected a movie to watch, although I'm not really paying attention. Autumn is seated between my spread thighs on the extended settee portion of my couch. Her body leans against my chest, and I toy with her hair. Wearing one of my tees with a blanket over her legs because of the air conditioning in my place, I like seeing her in my clothing, and I love having her in my home.

My place isn't filled with art or trinkets like most houses. I have pictures Lorna made magnetized to the fridge and photographs of us here and there, but for the most part, my place looks like a bachelor pad with a large screen television on the wall and the oversized couch with an extended end. The rooms here could use some color, and Autumn could be it.

I'm comfortable in how we sit, and I wish we'd had more moments like this at Lakeside Cottage. We weren't necessarily fooling anyone about what we did at night, but we tried to keep a respectful distance during the day. Most likely, the shared looks and occasional sneaking off for a quick kiss in a hallway or behind trees on the walk up the cliff didn't miss anyone's attention. Still, we never cuddled on the couch like we are now. It feels like a normal date-night-in which reminds me we've only been on one date.

"Three hours isn't that far of a drive," I say as I try to reason with myself that we could work.

"It's not too bad. Pretty direct," she states as if confirming my words.

"So how soon can we do this again?" I question, tightening my arms around her, realizing I don't mean the sexy stuff, but hanging out with one another. I want to date her. I want to know her better. We've spent decades in the same circle but circling one another. It's time to make her the center of my attention.

The best solution is a rotating schedule of visits. The complication comes in having Lorna. I never miss her activities, and I don't want to start. However, I can't ask Autumn to come to me every other weekend.

"When do you have Lorna next?" Autumn thoughtfully asks.

"As I just had her for two weeks, it's Chloe's weekend in a few days. The following weekend is mine." I hated the idea of rotating weekends and limited visits during the week when Chloe and I first divorced. It didn't seem fair. I wanted Lorna in my home when I woke and when I went to bed. I wanted all the little moments and the big ones between, but eventually, I had to learn to share. Chloe and I kept up with monumental steps, and it's one reason Chloe's recent betrayal stings so much.

"So, the weekend after that?" Autumn asks. That's nearly two and half weeks away and sounds too long to go without her.

"How does that work with your cycle?" I tease, bringing us back to our original mission. After what she said to me earlier, though, I'm relieved to hear we're both on the same page. I don't want her with random men. I don't want a list for her. However, I still want to give her that baby she desires. I want to give her so much more, but I need to tackle this issue with Chloe first.

Autumn's head shifts off my shoulder before she sits upright and angles her body between my thighs to face me. Her eyes lower to my chest, and she flattens her palm to my racing heart.

"I'm not talking about sex," she whispers, tracing her finger over the cotton covering my left pec. "I want to date you or whatever you want to call it."

Can this be real? It's my same thought.

"I want to date you, too." I lean forward for a kiss, but she pulls back too quickly to make it anything more than a soft peck.

"I will not distract you from Lorna, though. We need to be cognizant of her. She has a lot going on."

I nod to agree, nearly loving this woman for her concern for my daughter. I hear what she's saying, but I'm also feeling strangely like Chloe—a little selfish. How is it fair that my ex gets to date? She wants to move to France, and I can't even figure out when to see Autumn again.

"We'll work it out," I state as I said earlier. Leaning forward, I capture her lips as I didn't like the too-quick kiss or the way she pulled away from me. Our mouths meet and slowly move together. Tongues twirl. Teeth nip. She grips my jaw, and my fingers wrap around the back of her neck. We're both hungry for more when we can't go much further than heavy petting tonight.

God, I want this woman. It's only been three days since I last saw her, and I'm desperate for more. This feeling of wanting her so much is near dizzying, and the fact she wants me in return is mind-blowing. I'll never have enough of her, and it's more than diving into her body. I want her smile. I want her heart. I want us.

We must make this work.

+ + +

In the middle of the night, I get a call from Lorna, sobbing into the phone.

"What's wrong, honey?" With Autumn tucked next to me, I'm groggy with sleep. I shift in order to concentrate on my daughter, and Autumn rolls toward me.

"Don't make me go, Dad. Please. I don't want to go to France. I know it will be awful in middle school, but I promise I won't complain. I won't be upset about anything, just don't make me move somewhere where I don't know the language and won't like the food."

"Calm down, baby," I say, trying to get a grip on my bearings. Scrubbing a hand down my face, I eventually roll from the bed and stand. "No one is going to make you go anywhere you don't want to go."

While my daughter might have been apprehensive about middle school, she'd rather face the torture of it than travel halfway around the world. And while France is as civilized as they come and full of food she'd grow to love, as well as a language I'm certain she'd master, I understand her apprehension.

"Dad, please let me live with you." Her plea breaks my heart.

"You know I want that, right?" My constant concern since Chloe told me her plan is that she hasn't been totally forthright with our daughter, and the hairs on the back of my neck bristle. "I told Mom you could live with me."

Another sob has my heart ripping in two.

"Lorna, did Mom say something differently?"

"She just keeps telling me I have to go with her. It will be an adventure, but I don't want an adventure. If I wanted to move somewhere, it would be Lakeside."

"Oh, baby," I whisper, knowing it can't be this difficult or this easy. If Lorna was on board to move, I just might be persuaded to race back to Lakeside. *Does Mason still want to open a business together?*

Spinning in a half-circle, I face my bed where a sleepy Autumn is watching me. I adore this woman, and I want everything with her. Would it be ridiculous to give up a good job with the firm? Could I uproot my entire life? My thoughts race to Ben and his situation. He just wants to be happy in his final days. He wants to live where he wants to live, love who he loves, and slow down a bit. Would any of that be wrong?

"Honey, nothing's going to happen tonight. Mom and I need to talk, and we will. Tonight, you need to calm down and go to bed." *What is she even doing up this late?*

"But Dad—"

"No, but Dad. You aren't going to France, and I'll be speaking with Mom tomorrow." My voice hardens. I don't understand how Chloe can do this to us. We might not be a couple, but we had an agreement. We'd parent together. We'd make choices for our daughter *together*. We'd been agreeable so far in our arrangement, but this is too much. I am not backing down.

"Fine," Lorna moans, and the hint of impending teenage years creeps closer.

"I love you, baby," I say to her, watching Autumn watch me.

"Love you, too, Dad." With that, my daughter hangs up, and I stare down at Autumn.

"Lorna, right?" She slowly smiles in the dim light of my room. Streetlamps cast a glow through the blinds.

Softly, I chuckle. "Yeah."

"You're so sweet when you tell her you love her." Her voice softens, and I collapse back to the bed, sitting on the edge.

"I don't toss those words out lightly," I tell her, brushing a hand down her arm. "My daughter is the love of my life."

Autumn sighs, rolling away from me to look up at the ceiling. "I can understand that." She blinks. *Does she understand?* Everything I do, I do because of my girl. I want what's best for Lorna despite wanting a little slice of happiness for myself.

Continuing to stare at Autumn, I consider something else. She deserves someone who can love her, someone who can commit everything to her. She deserves a man who can be by her side.

I hadn't thought about it before, but maybe this is where all the baby business comes from. She wants a certain someone to center her life. She wants to give all the love inside her to someone special. However, loving a child isn't the same as loving your soul mate. Lorna is my everything, but she isn't a replacement for the other half of me.

"Loving my child isn't the same as loving a partner." My voice remains low, as if I'm imparting great wisdom. I need Autumn to understand that having a baby isn't going to fill a hole in her.

"I know that," Autumn states, an edge to her tone as her head rolls on the pillow and her eyes focus on me.

I should stop talking, but I can't seem to stop myself. "A baby won't replace a man in your life."

"A man in my life?" Her eyes narrow; her voice turns edgier. "I thought that's who you would be."

Stroking up her arm with my knuckles, I hum in response, biting my own tongue. I want to be that for her, but suddenly, I'm not certain how that will work. We've discussed the calendar and haven't come to any conclusions. Autumn needs someone present, and I'm going to be a distance from her.

We've discussed how Autumn didn't really want to raise a baby on her own. She hasn't been alone by choice. She's been alone because she dated idiots. I don't want to be one of those men who let her slip out of my hands, but I'm also not certain how I can keep her. It doesn't feel fair to her.

Sadness weighs heavy on my shoulders, as I suddenly don't know how to make us work.

25

[Autumn]

"So, what's happening with Logan?" Anna asks as we sit in the nail salon getting late summer pedicures. In the interim of the two-week guys' visit, Anna and Ben returned to Chicago to tackle the laborious task of packing up their belongings and moving their personal affects to the Lakeside house. Dozens of boxes, including pictures, mementos, and valuable items of their previous life, litter their future home. Their furniture is scheduled to arrive Saturday. They are keeping only the most sentimental pieces and parting with the rest. Their house in Chicago is under contract.

"Nothing's happening with him."

A man in my life? That's who I thought you'd be.

I'd misunderstood everything. To my surprise, he hadn't called since I left his place, despite his professions to date me. Unable to help myself, I'd called him. *Three times.* Then I wanted to kick my own ass. I swore I'd never do it again. I wouldn't give in to the temptation to nurture. I only wanted to check on him and Lorna, but each time I called, it went to voicemail.

Hey, saw you called. Will call you later. Nothing followed his first and only text. No phone call occurred.

I hadn't tried to call again. It had been eleven days and roughly twelve hours since we last spoke, and a thousand times a day, I'd check my phone or hover over his number before tossing the device to the side. Just once, I wanted a man who chased me. Who wanted me. Who wanted an *us* with me.

I had my answer to Logan's commitment. Considering his situation with his daughter, my need to nurture was crawling under my skin. I fought the urge to contact him again because it's what I do. I hover, sympathize, tug a man into my arms, and soothe him in my bed. Then I cook, clean, offer money, and lose my heart. Not that I really thought Logan would need all that from me. I was getting ahead of myself, but I recognized the signs and didn't want to go down that path again.

Instead, I'd taken time to reflect on my rash decision to rush to his home and tell him my situation instead of just calling him.

I wasn't pregnant.

Perhaps it was the reality check I needed. What was I thinking? Sleeping with Logan Anders in hopes to get pregnant—*ha*. He's not the type of man I could ever walk away from without a deep scar. He's my brother's best friend whom I've always crushed on, and suddenly, he was in my bed—in my heart—even deeper than those younger years. I was an idiot.

Besides thinking we were made for each other as a teen, I couldn't ever really explain why I crushed on Logan as much as I did. He was one of those men who you can't put your finger on why exactly you like him so much. You just do. It was more than his sweet humor, his handsome looks, or his large heart, or perhaps, it was a combination of all three that made him feel like a gift in my life. His devotion to his daughter only added to his appeal. His determination to keep her. His sweet voice when he spoke to her.

I'd fallen even further down the rabbit hole of desire for him.

However, Logan and I are at different points in our lives, and I'd assumed too much. I fell for pretty words and bottomless promises. He said he didn't want me with other men, but he wasn't the man present with me. He said he wanted me, but he hadn't called. I'd heard it all before, and I'd slowly come to accept I'd misinterpreted everything. Everything he'd said was out of sympathy for my condition.

I wasn't pregnant.

He told me what I wanted to hear. *He wanted to make babies with me. He wanted to try again. He wanted to date me.* I was such a fool. He'd given me that elusive sausage from his college jest, and he'd been correct. I hadn't been able to handle it.

"Are you going to see each other again?" Anna hesitantly asks, rolling her head on the massage chair beside mine to gaze over at me.

"I wanted to." I blink up at the ceiling, willing away tears that had been falling for days as I admit the truth to my sister-in-law. "I really wanted to continue being with him somehow, but his silence speaks volumes. And I could never ask him to continue with the plan. I can't ask for more from him with these new concerns for Lorna."

Mason, Ben, and Anna kept me informed of Logan and Chloe's issues. I only wish Logan had been reaching out to me instead. As for the plan, Anna already knows I got my period, and baby-making step one did not work.

"And you told him what happened?"

"I told him," I remind her. She doesn't know I went all crazy-ass and drove to Indianapolis to tell him of my fate. She doesn't know I'd spent another night in his arms, giving in to his touch and taking his words for what I thought they were worth. I also didn't have the heart to mention I'd tried repeatedly to get in contact with him. His silence spoke volumes.

"It just doesn't seem like Logan. I saw how he looked at you. He couldn't keep his eyes off you." Her brows pinch as she questioned what I've already questioned. I didn't understand what had happened.

"I guess he changed his mind." To say I was disappointed would be an understatement.

"It has to be this thing with Chloe." Anna nods to emphasize her thoughts.

"Maybe."

I didn't care for Chloe. We'd met on several occasions when she was Logan's wife, and I never liked her. There wasn't anything wrong with her. When she married Logan, they seemed like a good fit. They were the couple I'd always envisioned Logan and I being. The couple destined for one another because of size, shape, and silliness. However, Chloe changed after having Lorna. She lost weight, and her personality shifted. Everyone was convinced she was having an affair with her personal trainer. I didn't wish for Logan to divorce her, but no one was surprised when they did separate. His devotion to his daughter kept him near his ex-wife, establishing a friendship with her that seems rare among divorced couples. Chloe's desire to move to France and take Lorna with her really rocked their relationship.

I didn't want to be selfish. His daughter was at stake. He had bigger issues than dating me, and I didn't want to bother him. Still, I wanted to call. I wanted to know if he was okay, how was he handling things, or if he just wanted to talk. Apparently, he didn't.

"You should call him," Anna states as if reading my thoughts. "He could use a friend."

Friends. I scoff. Logan and I could never be friends again. I was the tagalong sister coming and going here and there with *Ben's* tight-knit group. I was an outsider, and I was feeling my position. And I couldn't go backward. I couldn't pretend I hadn't felt more for him.

Our two-week commitment was finished. The bargain broken. I hadn't gotten pregnant. I'd made the misstep to rush to Logan with my news. *Was I pregnant or not?* He only wanted to know the facts. I wasn't. Despite pretty words to try again, we wouldn't. In time, we'd act like we never slept together.

As the only man on my so-called baby-making list, the list was now empty. I was as alone as I'd been before Logan. Maybe even more lonely as I'd had a taste of what I thought would be a good thing, only to have it be just sex.

Wasn't that what I'd asked of him? *Oh, the irony.*

"I don't know what I'd say." I really should call one more time and ask about Lorna. She must feel torn between parents, and that had to be difficult. The thought reminds me how fortunate I was that my parents loved one another and gave Ben and myself an example of a hardworking, devoted couple. It wasn't always easy for them, but their love always shone through. Ben had been lucky to replicate that kind of relationship. I wanted the same thing for myself.

"Logan really isn't like the rest of them." Anna gives me a knowing look as if she can read my thoughts. I consider the crazy physical connection between the two of us and this strange disconnect we have now that our vacation tryst is over. Perhaps chemistry was all we had, and we lack the deeper attraction needed to sustain a relationship. Or maybe I just don't warrant that type of commitment from a man.

"Do I really know that?" I question. "I went along with this crazy scheme and then built up a fantasy in my head." I believed what Logan said to me when he was only trying to be nice. I wasn't pregnant and I was sad. He comforted me. He wrapped me in his arms and said what I wanted to hear. I took it to heart. This was all on me.

"I'll just move down the list," I flippantly state, finding no conviction in my tone.

Anna's eyes widen. She doesn't believe me either. "You don't mean that. You didn't even have a list." Her sassy tone suggests she hopes I don't continue this phase, as Ben crudely called it.

"Who would even be next?" Her breath hitches as if she has an idea, and then her eyes narrow as if she doesn't like it.

"Not Mason," I scoff while Anna stares at me. "I was thinking Archer might be a candidate." I burst into laughter after suggesting her older brother, and Anna lifts the nail polish bottle from the tray, acting as if she'll pitch it at my head, which she'd never do.

"Very *not* funny." She snorts. "I'd have to know where my wayward brother even is to endorse him, which I don't. He'd make a terrible father."

"Ah, but that's the point. I don't need a father. I just need a stud." I wink at her, and she laughs again. The truth hurts. The plan started because I only wanted a baby, not a man. I didn't think I'd want a dad for my child, just a father to produce a baby. My heart aches at the conflict within me.

"You don't really feel that way, though, do you?" Anna softens her voice, knowing me well. Like I've often said, she's the sister I never had, which gives her the right to sometimes be a pain in the ass.

"No. I don't." My voice lowers. Despite the live-in boyfriends, I'm a traditionalist at heart, and I want to be married someday. I want a man by my side, and I want a baby in my arms. Neither is in the cards for me yet, and I'm tired of wallowing over it.

"Enough about me. How is Ben? How is the packing and unpacking and moving?"

Anna sighs at my dismissal of this conversation but spends the remainder of our pedicure time explaining the stages of their move and how she'd like everything settled by Labor Day, which is only a few days away. The kids will start school the following Tuesday, and life will forever be changed for all of them.

26

[Logan]

I was a fucking idiot.

Nerves were eating me up inside, and I was sweating more than usual. The guys had planned to surprise Ben by arriving in time to help move in the furniture and unpack boxes. We'd even coerced Anna into allowing us the chance to repaint rooms if need be, especially for her boys. They were giving up a lot as high schoolers, especially Calvin, to make this change for their parents.

Anna knew of the plan, but Ben didn't, and he looked exhausted when we invaded on Saturday morning. I was a hot mess of anxiety, working on little sleep and too much coffee. And at some point, Autumn would be here. I hadn't called. She'd reached out to me, but I hadn't returned her calls.

I was a fucking schmuck.

With Zack's help, I gently but firmly informed Chloe she could not take our daughter out of the country to live. This led to a huge argument, but I wasn't willing to give in. Lorna was just as much my child as hers, and I was beginning to question whether Chloe wanted her child for herself or because she was growing angry with me.

Finally, we came to an agreement. Last night had been painful on a multitude of levels. Lorna was strong until the final boarding call. The tears and sobs seemed inconsolable, and I finally had to tell Chloe to just leave.

At a small dining table in the sitting area off the kitchen, I nurse another coffee and a cinnamon swirl danish I have no business eating. Mason, Zack, and Ben also sit with me. The table is tucked into an oversized bay window with a great view of the lake in the distance, but my eyes keep wandering to the front hall. My hands anxiously rub down my shorts because sweat moistens my palms. I don't remember being this nervous before my own wedding or at my child's birth, but I'm melting under the anticipation of Autumn's appearance.

When she finally does arrive, it's in a rare second I'm not glancing over at the hallway, and all conversation slowly comes to a halt. Autumn stands completely still near the kitchen island, which is only feet from me but feels miles away. She is so fucking beautiful it takes my breath, and I decide at that moment to do whatever it takes to deserve another chance with her.

"Hey." Her voice cracks as she addresses all of us but stares at me. With another swipe of my hands down the thighs of my shorts, I choke around a weak response.

"Hey."

We stare at one another, and the heat crackling from over there to over here turns up my body temperature by one thousand degrees. Then she looks away from me.

"Don't just sit there, dumb ass. Go to her," Mason mumbles under his breath. Unfortunately for me, Mason's been chastising me about my poor communication with Autumn. He's been a good friend, checking in daily on the Lorna situation, as he called it, and then dropping hints about Autumn.

She looks sad.

She misses you.

You should call her.

Maybe I'll have better luck with her.

This final comment was meant to torture me into motivation, but Lorna took all my energy. I didn't know what to say to Autumn, and the more time that passed, the less I knew how to recover us.

Slowly, I stand, swiping at my shorts one more time. With our eyes locked once again on one another, I approach.

"Autumn." Her name is too stiff against my tongue. "It's great to see you again," I weakly state, feeling the daggers at my back. Ben wants to crack me over the head, and Zack exaggerates a cough. Mason is ready to laugh his ass off when I fail with this woman.

Leaning forward, I go in for a cheek kiss, but Autumn turns her head in my direction, and some force of nature has our mouths meeting. We still for a mere second before our lips slowly move, molding to one another's, working in sync. The kiss slowly builds, like a pot of water set to boil—little bubbles appear, jostling the liquid until atoms erupt and the water rises in a furious froth.

Autumn is in my arms before I know it. Our mouths suck and nip, and my arms wrap around her middle, securing her to me. When her legs hitch up over my hips, I hike her up against my body and walk us out of the kitchen area to give us some privacy.

"I'm so mad at you," she mumbles with her mouth still against mine. Her fingers tug at the back of my hair. The pinch is a live wire to another part of my body that's desperate to reconnect with her.

"I'm sorry," I mutter back, wanting to remain attached to her. We aren't close enough, but I don't deserve to be inside her yet.

With her arms around my neck and my hands at her ass, holding her against me, we move into the front hall. Our mouths connect once again in a scorching kiss. Anger. Frustration. Reunion. When her back hits a wall, she pulls her head back and her feet drop to the floor, but I pin her in place with my lower body.

"We should talk." My voice is hoarse with my need for her. I just want to bury myself inside her, forget the past two and a half weeks, and start fresh.

"I talked to Lorna outside." The mention of my daughter is both a reminder of the past miserable days and the ice water I need to calm down. Pressing my forehead to Autumn's, I sigh.

"About that . . ."

"Tell me everything," she quietly demands. Cupping the back of her neck, as I just want to touch her, I pull back from her forehead and begin.

"Zack helped me find the legal means to tell Chloe she could not take our daughter out of the country."

"Did you give her an ultimatum?" Autumn's voice rises with concern and surprise.

"No. I gave her a choice. Peter or Lorna." Chloe felt guilty deciding. She never wanted to be seen as a bad mother, and she hadn't been other than her nagging concerns for our daughter's weight. I tried to assure

Chloe I wouldn't judge her for choosing Peter. She deserved happiness for herself, but it had me thinking I deserved it as well. While Lorna was the center of our lives, she wasn't selfish. She wasn't demanding we put her in the middle. We each deserved more for ourselves. Still, I would never part from my child. "I told Chloe she should go. Rather than me be the one to live without Lorna, it should be Chloe, and maybe Chloe should use the time apart to determine what she really wants in life."

Autumn's breath hitches. "Does this mean you have Lorna full time?"

"I do." Slowly, I grin, proud of myself for not backing down to Chloe. I'm happy while equally scared to have my budding teenage daughter all to myself.

"What if Chloe returns and wants Lorna back?"

"Chloe will always be Lorna's mother and part of her life as long as she chooses. I'd like to think she won't disappear on our daughter, but Chloe has become someone I no longer know. At forty, she seems to be on a self-discovery kick."

Autumn snorts. "I know the feeling, and I'm not even forty yet."

"You are nothing like Chloe. She's turned very selfish. If she wants Peter and France, she could go, but she could not take Lorna away from me."

A heavy pause falls between us before Autumn speaks.

"I would never ask you to give her up." Her comment shifts our conversation, and my eyebrows arch.

"I know you wouldn't." There's so much more to unpack with her statement, but I need to get back to my apology. I've already told Autumn how I felt. I only want her. I don't want her with anyone else. But I've also screwed up. More than two weeks is a long time without communication in a new relationship.

Suddenly, the front door swings open, and Mila runs inside, followed by Lorna.

"Furniture is here!" Mila yells to the open entryway, allowing her little, loud voice to travel in all directions.

I glance at Lorna, who smiles at me before she winks. My sweet eleven-year-old winks at me for encouragement, and my heart skips a beat. Lorna and I have had long meaningful talks about her mother's decision and dating in general as her parent. I might have mentioned my feelings for Autumn.

"Autumn . . ." I begin, turning back to the woman beside me.

"Time to work," she says, brushing past me and stepping toward Mila. I catch her upper arm to stop her.

"We aren't finished." My tone's sharpness has more warning in it than I intend, but softening my voice next does nothing to dispel my concerns. "We aren't done talking, and we aren't finished with whatever is happening between us."

Her eyes widen as she chews her lower lip and nods once at me. "Later."

Later. It's full of promise, and I'll take it for now.

+ + +

Later, we're all exhausted. The furniture is moved in, and rooms are rearranged. I can tell Anna is overwhelmed, and Ben is bone-tired. I don't know how I didn't notice it more during our two-week vacation. It could be that all my attention was on Autumn, but I also think Ben was good at hiding his troubles in subtle ways. Maybe now that I know the truth, I'm looking for more signs.

Zack and I don't want to overwhelm Ben and Anna, and we hadn't planned to stay the night. Zack intended to head back to Detroit for the remainder of the three-day weekend, but I wasn't certain what I would do. I had hoped to talk to Autumn and come to some kind of agreement for our future, but I didn't want to force my way into Ben's home on their first official weekend living here, nor could I invite myself to Autumn's place with Lorna in tow.

Fortunately, I don't have to make a decision. Mila begs for Lorna to stay in her room again, and Mason has space in the two-bedroom apartment over the garage for Zack and me to spend the night without being underfoot of the newly moved family. Ben insists we stay the remainder of the weekend, and I don't have the heart to argue as I really want the distraction for Lorna. Hanging out with a friend is a good way to keep her mind off the fact her mother chose France over Indiana and Peter over her.

Plus, staying gives me time to speak with Autumn, which I finally get the chance to do once the sun is down.

"Take a walk with me," I mutter to her once Lorna seems settled in Mila's room, and Ben says he needs to go to bed. Mason and Zack head into town for a drink.

Autumn and I go out the back door and down the stairs to the landing between the house and beach. I snagged a bottle of wine from the bar alcove along with two glasses, and Autumn has a blanket wrapped around her as the first weekend in September has brought cooler evening temperatures.

Once we sit in the Adirondack chairs on the landing, I pour us each a glass of wine. We remain silent a second after a wordless toast to her.

"Seems I'm constantly apologizing for being a dumbass toward you on this landing," I start. "I'm sorry I didn't call."

With her gaze off toward the dark lake, she softly chuckles. A single solar-powered light illuminates her outline. "After those first few calls, I didn't want to appear needy, and I didn't want to intrude."

"How would you have been needy?" I ask, keeping my gaze on her. She turns her head to face me.

"I just wanted to talk to you."

"Autumn, sweetheart. We can talk anytime you want, about anything you want." I'd wanted to talk to her, but I didn't know what to say. Chloe's decision was sucking everything out of me, and the more time that passed, the less I knew how to reach out. It occurs to me Autumn had things on her mind as well like baby-making and motherhood, and maybe even Ben.

"Lorna is more important."

"Could I have talked to you about Lorna?" I ask, leaning on the armrest of my chair. I wanted to talk to her about Lorna. I just . . . I don't know why I didn't call.

"Of course."

"Then I want you to feel the same way with me," I reply to her immediate response. I certainly hadn't reinforced the offer, though.

"I didn't want to be a bother."

"You aren't a bother," I repeat. Where is the confident woman, the one taking charge of her life and wanting a baby despite everything? Softening my voice, I question, "What's going on?"

"I have a habit of taking over. A man in need, and I'm all over him, trying to help, trying to soothe. I insert myself somehow. I hear things that aren't really said, and the next thing I know, I've got a man living with me that I'm taking care of, and he's not taking care of me in return. I didn't want to do that with you."

"I'm not looking to move in with you." I laugh, brushing off ideas that had whittled their way into my thoughts over the days we were separated. If Chloe could run off to France to be with Peter, could I run off to Lakeside to be with Autumn? It seemed like such a ridiculous notion, especially as I have Lorna full-time. I couldn't just quit my job, move my child, and shack up with a woman, even if I've known her all my life.

"But that doesn't mean I don't want to spend time with you," I quickly add. "I want to be with you, but I dropped the ball this week. Lorna had to be my priority."

"I understand that," Autumn interjects.

"It doesn't mean I wasn't thinking of you. Every second of every day. I just . . . I should have called. My fingers hovered over your number a hundred times, but I didn't know what to say." *Come to me. Be mine. Hold me and tell me I can have it all—my child, your child, you.*

"Same," Autumn softly says, and I laugh.

"We're so stupid."

"Speak for yourself." Her lips slowly curl, and her eyes search mine.

LIVING at 40

"And you're too far away," I quietly admit of her seat over there while I'm sitting here. Setting down her wineglass, she comes to me and positions herself on my lap. I tug her back to my chest, reminding me of when she sat on my couch, between my thighs, and we watched a movie. I want more nights like that and more moments like this. "Tell me I'm forgiven. Tell me we can work this out."

"Every two weeks," she mutters. *God, what have I done to earn this woman?*

"As much as we can."

"Three hours is a long distance," she states.

"It's not so bad." I echo her words from when she drove to my place. "Please," I whisper to her neck before pressing a kiss to her cool skin. The blanket is still wrapped around her body, tucking in her arms and covering part of her legs.

"What would it mean?" Her hesitant voice warns me I'm on thin ice. I need to get this right.

"Phone calls," I quickly state. "And phone sex. Dirty texts. Dates. And sex. Coordinating calendars, and more sex."

"Is sex all you want from me?" she teases. *That's all we were supposed to have at first.*

"Yes." I laugh. "But no." I suck at her neck a second time. "I want to talk to you and hold you. I want to hear about your day and tell you about Lorna. I want to be around you, and I want you to spend time with my daughter and me."

"I'd like that," Autumn quietly says. "And we can take better precautions about baby-making."

Shifting her on my lap, I force her to look at me. "Why?"

"Because I don't want you to feel like the endgame is a trap. I don't want you to feel obligated or responsible or that I only want the sausage—"

"Shut up."

"Excuse me?" Her lids blink at my quick interjection.

209

"Shut. Up. There is no endgame. This isn't a game to me, Autumn. I'm all in with you. I want to be with you. That's the end. However we get there."

She stares at me like she doesn't understand, so I do what I think will get her on the same page as me. I lean up and kiss her hard and deep. My tongue thrusts forward, invading her mouth, wanting her to hear my words, swallow them, and feed off me. My hand cups the back of her neck, under her hair, holding her to me.

"I want." I suck at her tongue and nip her lower lip.

"To be." My mouth crushes hers, forcing her to follow mine.

"With you." There will be no more words.

Pressing at her hips, she takes my meaning and moves to straddle me. Her center hits my rock-hard dick, and we both moan at the nearness, but we aren't close enough.

"Missed you so much," she mumbles against my lips.

"Same, sweetheart. Same." My hands are in her hair, and she's rocking on my lap. My dick nearly weeps with excitement and desire for her, but I won't press. I'm following her lead. We kiss like we haven't seen one another in years instead of half a month.

"Need you," she whimpers.

"Here?" It's dark enough, and we're technically below the house, obstructed from view by the drop from the backyard.

"Here." Autumn scrambles off my legs and removes her shorts and underwear. I quickly work at lowering mine to my ankles and suck in a sharp breath at the cool wood under my ass. Autumn climbs back over my thighs, draping the blanket over her shoulders as a weak shield.

"No protection. We're going for this, and whatever happens happens." I know what I want. I want her to get pregnant, and I want the baby to be mine. Then I'm going to invest everything I have in this woman—heart and soul.

"Whatever happens happens," she repeats before positioning me at her soaked entrance and slowly taking me within her.

I groan—a heavy, lusty sound of relief. She's so warm, so wet, and so mine. My mouth captures hers again while holding her hips and helping her dance over me. After one sharp movement, I break from the kiss. "God, I've missed this. I've missed you, Autumn. End of long, lonely days. Bringing on sexy nights."

She giggles. "Why do you add those lines?" Her words stammer as she moves over me.

"Because your name is a beautiful season meaning change." And I'm so ready for one in my life. I'm ready for her.

"Some think fall is the end of things."

"Nope." Her quick slide up my thick shaft and sudden drop to engulf me in her hitches my breath. "It's a new beginning."

Her mouth seeks mine, and we move in silence other than sharp intakes of breath and subtle moans of pleasure.

"Gotta come," I warn her too quickly, but I won't go without her. Her hand lowers between her spread legs, and her knuckles brush at the coarse hair against my pubic bone. Her fingers work her trigger spot, and I drop my gaze to watch. "Fuck, that's hot."

With her head tipped forward and her breath short, she losses herself in pleasure over my body. I'm lost as well, wanting her more than anything else. We'll find a way to make us work. I won't mess up again.

"Logan," she whimpers, but I don't need the warning. I already know the signs of her body. The clenching. The shortness of breath. The increased thrusts. She breaks over me, and I hold her hips to keep her pinned in place as I go off just as quickly.

This is it. I'm going to get her pregnant, and then, I'm going to marry her.

27

[Autumn]

My legs are still trembling by the time we enter the house. The orgasm was so intense I saw stars and not just the ones peppering the sky. Logan held me over his lap until he'd gone soft, and a shiver ran up my spine. Between Ben and Anna's final move and the surprise of seeing Logan, plus what we'd just done, I am drained.

"I'd love for you to come to my place," I admit as we silently enter the back door.

"I know, but the guys are expecting me over the garage, and I want to stick close for Lorna."

"Where were you?" The sudden shriek of Mila from the dark kitchen surprises us both.

"Mila, honey, what are you doing down here?" I ask, surprised by my niece's harsh voice. Her little arms cross over her chest, and her hip juts out to the side. *Is she tapping her foot?* And why do I feel scolded by a ten-year-old? Without waiting on an answer from her, I answer her question. "Logan and I went for a walk."

"Well, Lorna's crying."

"Okay. I got this." Logan gives me a quick kiss on the side of the head and steps forward, but Mila lifts a hand.

"She wants to know if Autumn will come instead."

"What?" Logan and I say together.

"It's a girl thing," Mila announces, shrugging her bony little shoulder.

"Oh." Logan chokes around the sound, and I reach for his wrist. "Do you want to handle this?"

"Um." He swallows hard. I have faith Logan can do this. He can address his daughter's issue, but he appears a little shell-shocked.

"Is this her first time?" I quietly ask, not wanting to embarrass him.

"I think so." His wide eyes and stunned expression confirm his uncertainty. "Chloe hadn't mentioned anything and . . . Lorna hasn't said."

I smile as I softly pat his arm. "I've got this."

"Okay." His voice feels distant, and then his shoulders relax. "Okay. Thank you. Let me know if she . . . needs anything." He's got this, but he also needs a minute. Eleven years old seems early to me, but I know girls are having periods younger and younger, and Anna's already had the talk with Mila just so she's prepared.

After pressing a kiss to his jaw, I walk forward, gesturing for Mila to lead the way upstairs.

"Is Logan your boyfriend?" Mila asks once we hit the staircase.

"I—" *Is that who I am to Logan?* I'm not certain how to answer, nor do I think it's my niece's business. Her teasing voice reminds me she's young, and this isn't her concern. "Where is Lorna now?"

"She's in my bathroom."

I continue to follow Mila down the hall to her bedroom, where she has a bathroom inside. "If he's your boyfriend, do you think he and Lorna will move here? You could get married, and then Lorna and I could go to school together."

Oh my. It's a sweet thought, but Mila and Lorna wouldn't be in the same grade. I'm not even going to address the idea of marrying Logan. It's a dream I've had since I was young, but not one I want to hope for as I'm older. I'd say wiser, but I can admit I'm just a fool for love, and I wanna be in love with Logan. I am in love with him, but I want him to love me in return.

Stopping before the bathroom door, I rap softly at the wood, dismissing my niece's questions again. "Lorna, it's Autumn."

"Come in," her quiet voice offers.

Stepping inside, she's still seated on the toilet, underwear at her ankles.

"Oh baby," I quietly say, lowering to a squat. "You know what this is, right?"

213

She gives me a look like, *of course she does*, but her eyes are also full of panic. Do I let her know she's a woman now? It's scary and exciting, and it means her body can do amazing things at some point. When she's older, of course. *Much older.*

"Are you prepared for this? Do you have pads? Or did your mom mention tampons?"

"I have stuff in my bag, but I was afraid to leave the toilet."

"Okay, honey. Let me get your things."

Slipping back out of the bathroom, I find her backpack and carry everything into the smaller space. Inside the pack, I find a change of underwear for her and a small zipper case with a few items inside.

"You're going to need more than this, but we can go to the store tomorrow. Your dad can get whatever you need."

"Can you do it?" she sheepishly asks.

"Of course. But your dad knows about these things. You can talk to him about it or anything." I'm confident I'm not speaking out of turn about her father. Despite his stricken expression downstairs, he's got this with his daughter. For a moment, I'm sad Chloe missed out. This should be her domain, but she made her choice. "Or you can call your mom tomorrow."

"My mom's in France, and there's a time difference." Her voice rings bitter, and I think better of having mentioned Chloe.

"Okay. You hand me the dirty pants, and you change." Rinsing them out in Mila's sink, I hang them discreetly beside a towel on the rod.

"Where were you and Dad?" Lorna asks after concentrating on her fresh underwear and the new-to-her strangeness between her legs.

"We went for a walk."

"Is he your boyfriend now?" The question catches me off guard, and I peer down at Lorna, who isn't looking at me as she straightens her sleep shirt.

"Um . . ."

"Bethany Simone told me when a boy asks to walk you down the hallway, he wants to be your boyfriend. Did my dad ask you to be his girlfriend? That's how it's done now. I saw you kissing this morning. Bethany says when a boy kisses you, you're his girlfriend."

Well, Miss Bethany . . . I don't know what to say to Lorna, and she's already lost so much with her mother's choice to move away with her boyfriend. Will she be upset if her father has a new girlfriend?

"Mom used to kiss Peter in front of me all the time. That's how I knew he was her boyfriend."

I stare at her, wondering if that's appropriate behavior. Did she mean a little soft kiss or full make-out sessions?

"I don't really like Peter, but I'm okay with you kissing Dad."

Okay then.

"I really like your dad," I try to reassure her, finally finding my voice.

"He really likes you, too. He talks about you all the time." She rolls her eyes, and I recall finding her outside the house before I saw Logan inside this morning. The girls were waiting for the moving van, drawing with chalk on the driveway. Lorna gave me a hug just like Mila did. Surprised to see her, I blurted out my first thought.

"Are you staying in America?" It was a terrible question to ask her and could have triggered all kinds of things, but as Logan and I hadn't spoken, I didn't know what was happening for her. She told me her mother left last night. Then she ran back to Mila to continue her chalk art, and I stood there stunned.

Chloe left her daughter behind, and Logan had Lorna full-time.

I felt both elation for him and deflated for me.

Then we made love on the landing, like crazed teens. *Again.* Yeah, I liked her father. I loved him.

"I'm glad to hear your dad was talking about me, but let's talk about you. What else do you need tonight? Do you have cramps? Headache? Backache?"

Lorna twists her waist and then touches her temples as if she can't decide which part hurts, if either.

"I think backache." I want to tell her it's not multiple-choice, but I let it slide.

"Let me get you some ibuprofen. I'll be right back." When Lorna hesitates, I add. "You can leave the bathroom."

Holding the door open, I step out of the smaller space. I have ibuprofen in my bag, which is downstairs. Stepping into the hallway, I find Logan standing just outside the door to Mila's bedroom. His arms are full of supplies.

"Hey. Is she okay?" He presses off the wall.

"She's fine. She wants to know if I'm your girlfriend, just asked me if we were off kissing, and then told me you were talking about me nonstop."

He softly chuckles. "Oh boy."

"Yeah. Do you think she's going to be okay with us? Is it too much since her mother just ran off to France with her boyfriend?"

"This is different. I'm not concerned. Don't worry." He firmly nods, and I want to absorb his confidence. There's more at stake here than just Logan and me, though. "Now, how is my girl?"

"She's a young woman now, and you're going to have your hands full because she's so beautiful."

"I lov—" He catches himself, but the smile on his face at the compliment to his daughter says a lot. He'd tell me he loved me because I praised his child. It wouldn't mean more.

My eyes drift to his arms. "What's all this?" I question to dismiss the nearly spoken words.

"Ibuprofen for cramps. Peroxide for her underwear. Pads. Some chocolate. It's the best I could find raiding Anna's bathroom downstairs."

He's such a good girl dad. Patting his chest, I state, "Let me go get a glass of water for her." When I turn for the stairs, Logan calls out for me to stop.

"I did talk about you all the time, and I'm going to be kissing you more." Then he leans forward for another quick one before turning for his daughter in Mila's room.

28

[Logan]

"How's my girl?" I ask as Lorna stands in Mila's room.

"Dad. I'm not a little girl anymore." Did her first period just flip the switch on her attitude? I knew it was coming, but does it have to happen so quickly?

"Okay, young lady," I state, dropping my random wares on the bed. I step up to her and pull her against my chest, pressing a kiss to her hair. I mutter into the soft, fuzzy downs. "You okay?"

"Yes. Autumn went to get me something."

I nod against her head. "I brought you ibuprofen, peroxide, and pads. What else do you need?" I can do this. I can discuss her period with her. I'll just keep things vague.

"Mom already set me up, but Autumn said she'd take me to the store tomorrow."

"I can take you," I tell her, pulling back and holding her by her shoulders.

"Dad," she quietly groans. "Let Autumn take me."

"Okay. Okay. But you can ask me anything or tell me anything. I'm here for you." In all ways possible, I'm here for my daughter.

"I know, Daddy."

I press another kiss to her forehead and walk her over to her bed opposite Mila's. In the time it's taken for Autumn to help Lorna, Mila has crawled back into bed and fallen asleep. Does Mila know about these womanly things? Do I need to be worried that Lorna scarred her? Am I going to be okay as a girl dad? Can I do all this again with another child?

When Autumn enters the room, the second I see her, I know the answer about another child, and I want it with her. Her reassuring smile tells me she'll have parenthood handled, but so will I. I've already had eleven years of practice.

"Here you go, lady," Autumn says, handing over a small bottle of water.

"Dad, are you still staying in the apartment with Mason tonight?" The question surprises me, and I tuck the blankets around her legs.

"Yes. Why?"

"Just wanted to know where you are." The statement breaks my heart a little as I don't want her to be worried that I'll leave her.

"Autumn, are you staying here tonight, too?"

I glance up at Autumn. Will she decide to stay down the hall? Could I sneak into her room and then cross the drive to Mason's apartment in the morning?

"No, baby. I'm going to my place tonight. Why? Do you need something else?"

"But you'll be back in the morning?" Lorna asks for reassurance, and I sense her fear of being left behind. I have a long road ahead of me with my child and the assurance she needs that I'm not going anywhere.

Autumn reaches forward and cups Lorna's face. "I'll be here in the morning. What do you want for breakfast? We need to celebrate."

"What are we celebrating?" I ask like a dumbass.

"Womanhood," Autumn states, winking at a blushing Lorna.

"Okay. Time for bed." I check that her phone is on the stand and point at it. "Call me if you need anything."

I've had restless nights the last few weeks, worried I'd sleep through another desperate call from Lorna or, worse, get a call that Chloe kidnapped her. I didn't want to think so poorly of my ex-wife, but she developed a deep fear in me.

"Night, Dad," Lorna says, nestling down into the blankets. "And thank you, Autumn."

"Anything you need, honey," she sweetly responds to my little girl. *My little woman*, excuse me, and God help me.

+ + +

I walk Autumn to her car, where we kiss hot and heavy for a few minutes before she pulls back and settles into the driver's seat. I don't want her to go, and I fight a whine similar to Lorna's, begging Autumn for reassurance that she'll return. Instead, I press a hand to the window once she starts the car, and she matches mine on the other side of the glass before she sets the car in reverse and backs out of the drive.

"Loverboy," Mason announces once I enter the apartment above the garage. His voice slurs as he holds a bottle of tequila against his thigh. *Shit.*

"What's going on?" I say, collapsing on the couch next to Zack, whose eyes are half-mast.

"We're celebrating," Zack says, or at least I think that's what he said as it sounded more like *celibating*, but I'm certain he's not going celibate.

"And what are we *celibating*?" I tease.

"Zack is divorcing Jeanine." Mason holds up the tequila bottle in salute.

My head swivels on the couch back. "What?"

"My wife went to France to fuck an intern while I was on vacation here."

What the fuck is it with France?

"He's ten years younger than us. Aren't I supposed to be the one looking for someone younger?" He slurs through the question.

"You're married. You aren't supposed to be searching for anyone," I remind him.

"Is that what love and honor, and faithfulness in the vows mean? I no longer remember their definition."

Fuck. "Zack, man, I'm so sorry."

"Not as sorry as me."

I'm not convinced Zack really loved Jeanine as much as he wanted to do the right thing by marrying her. He wanted to be present for his children unlike his father, who wasn't there for him. He wanted to offer Jeanine the support his father didn't for his mother.

"Loving someone sucks," Mason states, and I narrow my eyes at him. What does he know about loving a woman? He's never been in a serious relationship.

"I didn't love her." Zack's dismissive tone isn't a surprise.

"But you married her," Mason reminds him.

"She was pregnant, remember?" Did he feel trapped? *I don't want you to think the endgame is a trap.* Autumn's concerns come back to me.

"I'm still sorry. Divorce sucks," I interject. It can be a painful process, even if he didn't love his wife. Plus, he still has two unruly boys connecting him to Jeanine for the rest of his life.

"So does marriage." Zack swipes a hand into his hair and pauses on the top of his head. "What the fuck am I going to do?"

"Zack, man, you have this." He's capable and intelligent. He already has a nanny, but he might need to cut back some hours at work and do a little better at being present as a father for his boys.

"You fuck the nanny. Hire a full-time au pair. Fuck her, too, and then you quit your lame ass job and come work for Four Points," Mason states.

"Mason." *What a dick.* "We aren't discussing au pairs."

"I'm not giving up my monsters to Jeanine. She doesn't want them anyway."

"How do you know she doesn't want the boys?" I ask, shifting on the couch cushion to better face my friend, who slouches into his like he wants to melt into the material.

"Because she said she never wanted children, and she never loved me, and now she's going to go off and fuck her little toy while my dick shrivels up."

"Oh my God, Zack. Shut the fuck up. Your dick is not going to shrivel up. Not that I want to discuss your dick. I'm sure it's a very nice dick, but we aren't talking about it."

Mason starts to laugh, and Zack smiles. "That's why I love you, man." His hand limply smacks at my knee. "Funny man."

"Well, funny man wouldn't know about dick shriveling. His dick is getting some serious use, lucky bastard." Mason lifts the bottle for a quick drink, and I don't know how he has the stomach for such action at our age.

"My dick is not overused, but we aren't discussing my dick either," I tell my two drunk friends.

"Better than abused," Mason sarcastically mutters.

"As if your dick has been abused," I snark.

"Too many women want it. Not the right woman."

"Who?" I snap, curious. We've all thought Mason might harbor some resentment toward an old crush gone wrong, but we have no clue who it is. I'm doubtful it's Samantha, Lynlee's mother.

"No can say," he mumbles through a drunken half-smile.

"Don't say," Zack rolls his head back and forth on the cushions like he knows the answer Mason should never share the truth.

"You are one lucky man, though," Mason adds, pointing a limp finger at me around the bottleneck in his fist. "Autumn has had the hots for you since she was a teen, and now look at you two. Making a baby together. Getting married."

"What?" Zack turns to peer at me with unfocused eyes.

"You had to know," I remind him. He was part of the discussions. "Remember her list, although she never really had a list."

"Right, right," Zack slurs. "A list. I should make a list. Maybe one of all the women I'd like to fuck, or the positions I want to try, or the things I want to do as I haven't had sex in so long I'm not certain I remember what it is."

Dear God, that was more than we needed to know about our Zacker. Mason snorts but turns his attention back to me.

"Seriously, though, congratulations, man."

"On what?"

"I told you I'd be the first to congratulate you when you get engaged." Mason's comment reminds me of when he said such a thing outside Crossroads Café.

"I'm not getting married," I huff. Although I thought it less than an hour ago, I'm not admitting it yet to these clowns.

"You're getting married?" Zack's voice rises an octave like a surprised and excited schoolgirl as if he wasn't part of our conversation two seconds ago. "I'm married, too. But now I'm getting divorced."

"Zack, buddy. You need to head to bed." Zack and I share a room, the one with two twin beds, while Mason has the other room with a queen-sized bed.

"I need a bed," he whispers. "I need to get laid so bad." His lids start to close, and our friend is at the end of his tequila threshold.

Glancing over at Mason, I notice him watching me, but I don't have any more words for him. I have a phone call to make to my hot as fuck girlfriend. We're making this official, effective tonight.

29

[Autumn]

Logan: Will you be my girlfriend?
My phone lights up with the text as soon as I crawl into bed, and a smile instantly graces my face.
Logan: I'm told it's not official unless I ask.
Me: Let me guess? Miss Bethany Simone?
Logan: ugh. <tongue out emoji>
Me: Not a fan?
Logan: Bad news girl.
Me: Sorry.
Logan: You didn't answer my question. I want to go steady. Will you be my girl?
Me: Do people go steady anymore? What does that even mean?
Logan: Answer the fucking question.
I laugh.
Me: Yes.
Logan: Also answer this question. Are you thinking of me?
Me: Yes.
Logan: Want me in your bed?
My breath hitches, and I momentarily wonder if he'll say he's outside my door, but the thought quickly dissipates. He needs to stay at Ben's place for Lorna.
Me: Yes, but it's late and—
The phone rings in my hand.
"Now I'm in your bed with you," he says the second I answer, and I laugh again. "God, I want to be next to you."
"This is torture," I admit, softening my voice as I want to curl up next to him as well.
"But we're doing this." A question lingers in his tone.
"We're doing this," I affirm.
"I'll see you tomorrow then."

"Technically, it is tomorrow," I tease.

"Alright, lady. Get some rest."

"Night, Logan."

"Night, beautiful." His voice lingers in my head once we hang up, and I could get very used to this every night.

+ + +

The following morning, I need to work at Crossroads Café and take a rain check on my breakfast plans with Lorna. As I hadn't planned on Logan being in town, I hadn't taken time off to spend with him and his daughter. He surprises me by showing up at the café, and I take a five-minute break to kiss him like crazy just outside the building.

"Later," he mutters as he pulls away from me, both of us breathing heavily. "Can you spend the night at Ben's?"

I'm certain I can, but I'll still check in with Anna first. "Why do I feel like a teenager sneaking around?" I tease before he kisses me once more.

"Because you're still a baby compared to me."

I laugh as that isn't true, but I do feel young and energized whenever I'm around him.

"Later," I whisper.

Later, I head to the beach to join the guys. Anna kicked everyone out of the house, overwhelmed by guests on their first weekend. I offered to help her when I arrived, but she told me to get lost as well.

"I still think we should do it if we can get pansy-ass on board." Mason's voice carries as I approach.

"Leave him alone," Ben defends.

"We can't do this without him," Mason whines, and I'm wondering what's going on.

"What's up?" I ask, announcing myself. Logan shifts in his seat as his back was to me when I hit the sand. Slowly, he smiles as he looks at me over his shoulder, and then he stands. I want to step up to him, sink into his chest, and hold him, but I scan the beach for Lorna.

"Hey," he whispers, reaching out to rub his hand up my back before tugging me by the back of the neck to him for a quick hug.

"Where's Lorna?" I ask, keeping my voice low like we're sharing a secret.

"She's down the beach with Mila. Come. Sit." Logan steps back like it was totally normal to hug me before his friends, and I glance up to find my brother staring at me.

"Is this official?" Ben points back and forth between us, not mincing words.

"It's official," Logan says, reaching over for my hand as we sit in beach chairs next to one another. Lifting my hand for his lips, he kisses my knuckles. "But new, so don't be a dick."

I chuckle at Logan's scolding of my brother.

"The only one being a dick is you," Mason mumbles.

"Mason, leave it," Zack mutters behind dark sunglasses and a ball cap on his head.

"What's going on?" I ask, glancing around the circle of men before focusing on Logan.

"It's nothing," he says, looking away from me a second, but Mason interjects. "If it's official, you shouldn't keep secrets from her."

I don't care for his tone or his meddlesome suggestion. He's stirring up trouble, and he knows it because now I know Logan isn't telling me something, and I can't simply ignore that.

"Tell me," I teasingly whine.

"Mason has this idea that we should work together," Logan explains, narrowing his eyes at his friend.

"Really?" Excitement flows in both my response and my immediate thoughts. *Does this mean Logan would move closer to Lakeside?*

"When we were in college, Mason had this idea—" Ben begins.

"We had an idea," Mason interjects, correcting Ben's explanation.

"*We* had an idea to go into business together. We'd be a full-service construction company complete with landscape design. Zack would handle legal for us."

I scan the group again. "Wow. That sounds amazing. What happened?"

"Logan won't commit."

"It's not that easy," Logan defends.

"Because you need to live here?" I wonder.

"Among other things," he replies, lowering his voice and avoiding my eyes. Sitting forward, he releases my fingers to balance his elbows on his thighs. "Mason thinks it'd be easy to just leave my job with benefits and dive into this project that involves a four-way investment from each of us."

I sympathize if Logan doesn't have the money. I didn't have the funds for Crossroads Café until my father passed and left me a little nest egg he'd been saving for me.

"I could front your portion," Zack says, and Logan sighs. I'm sensing this has already been a part of their discussion.

"Do we really need to keep rehashing this? I have Lorna to consider. Life is . . . complicated. I'm sorry, but I'm not interested." Logan stands and saunters toward Lorna, who is returning to this portion of the beach with Mila and Bryce.

Glancing at Ben, my brother shrugs, brushing off the awkwardness that remains.

"Maybe he doesn't have the money," I state, lowering my voice to defend Logan.

"Maybe he's just chickenshit to make a change in life," Mason snaps. It's an unfair argument as Logan has gone through a major change with his ex-wife leaving the country and obtaining full custody of his daughter. A change he hasn't had the time to adjust to quite yet.

"It's not as easy for everyone else to just pick up and go," Zack argues, inferring Mason's sudden move to Ben's garage, or maybe Ben's rush to move to Lakeside.

"Whatever," Mason mumbles like a petulant teen. "I need out of the sun." Mason presses himself up from his chair and stumbles off for the wooden stairs leading upward.

"Is he drunk?" I ask, watching Mason sway as he walks through the sand.

"He's hungover," Ben answers.

"We both are," Zack admits. "The devil is named tequila."

"Oh God. Aren't you a little old for the worm?"

"Yes." Zack chuckles. "But then again, I never want to feel too old for anything ever again." It's an ominous statement, and I don't know what he means. He stands next and follows Mason, picking up a cooler that must be empty and carrying it with him up the stairs.

"Was it something I said?" I ask as the circle of chairs is now clear minus myself and my brother.

"It's not you. It's them." Ben looks off toward Logan and Bryce tossing a football over Mila's and Lorna's heads.

"Is everyone acting weird because of . . ." I can't bring myself to say the words.

"Yes," Ben answers adamantly, squinting off at his children. "Maybe I shouldn't have told them yet. Maybe I should have waited."

"Ben," I whisper and clear my throat. "They're your best friends. They would have wanted to know, and they wouldn't have wanted to stay away. They're here for you. For Anna and the kids. We all are."

"I know," he replies quietly. "I don't know what I've done to deserve such good friends." To my surprise, Ben blinks several times. *Shit. Please don't cry.* My fingers twitch, eager to reach for him, wanting to comfort him, but I'm afraid if I touch him, I'll start crying.

"So. You and Logan, huh?" He chuckles as he swipes at both eyes with one hand, drawing his fingers to the bridge of his nose. When he looks up at me, I pretend I don't notice the liquid in his eyes. "I couldn't have picked a better man for you."

"Ben." I softly laugh. "I don't know if it's like that." Heat creeps up my chest, and I lower my eyes from my brother's stare.

"You've always had a crush on him, and he's crazy about you."

"How do you know?" I ask, lifting up to peer at him.

"I just do. And I know Logan. Once he's in, he's in."

"Right now, he's out with Mason and this idea, though." I'd never heard of this secret business plan amongst them.

"He's out because I'm out. I can't ask Anna to invest in this when we don't know what the future holds, and Logan wants things to be solid before he commits to anything. He's always been like that because of the losses in his life. He's slow on the uptake, but once he makes a decision, he's all in."

I consider what I know of Logan—losing his father as a child, his mother as a teen, and his wife to divorce in his thirties.

"If he's in with you, all I ask is the same of you," Ben states. "I love you, kid, but don't hurt him."

"Me?" I'm shocked at my brother's warning as I'm the one typically hurt by the men in my life.

"You're strong, Autumn, and you always recover." I stare at my brother, wondering where his idea of my confidence and strength comes from. He's the one who said men were phases. Then again, based on the number of relationships I've had and the longevity of each, Ben knows I'm loyal to a fault.

"He's strong, too," I defend, especially when I consider Logan's willingness to give me a baby and not be involved. At least at first, that was the plan.

"He'll make a good father," Ben states as if reading my thoughts.

"He already is," I remind him. "But so are you."

Ben nods, watching Bryce tease Mila as he holds the football over her head before tossing it to Logan. Ben's going to miss so much, and my heart breaks at the thought. Unable to resist, I reach out for his wrist this time, and he glances down at where I touch him.

"You know I love you, right?" he says, saying it more openly since his diagnosis.

"I know," I tease as my heart rips open a little more. "I love you, too, big brother."

After that, we both remain silent, watching his kids play on the sand with the man I'm in love with, who happens to be one of his best friends.

30

[Autumn]

"God, yes." Logan huffs into my neck as he hikes me higher against him. "Fuck yes."

I'm pinned to the back of my bedroom door at the Cottage as Logan drives into me like a man on a mission. "Oh. My. God." I stammer as he thrusts into me, feeling like he can't get deep enough. My legs wrap around his hips, and my back rubs against the door for support. Our position reminds me of our shower sex when we declared no more wall sex in order to keep what needs keeping inside me. Tonight, we just couldn't wait for the bed.

"You're so wet," he mumbles into my neck. "I'm sliding all over."

He's working so hard he's slightly clammy under my palms. Sweat beads on his forehead, and he licks my throat.

"Logan," I moan, clutching at his shoulder blades, scrambling to hold onto him as we glide together. He's so slippery. "It's going to be big."

He chuckles at the warning, but something's off about the sound.

"Logan," I cry out and lower my mouth to suck at his neck, diminishing my scream into his sticky, moist skin. Instantly, Logan follows, spewing into me in a rush, but just as quickly, he pulls out and almost drops me to the floor. My feet catch me, but my knees buckle. Logan steps back, swiping at his face, haphazardly brushing his hands through his hair back and forth.

"Oh God." I chuckle, exhilarated while weak. I'm a mess, and I lower for my underwear on the floor. I'm still wearing my beach dress, but Logan had tugged off his shirt the second we entered the room. His shorts rested just off his hips. He wasn't wearing boxers.

"Give me a second," I breathlessly say, stepping toward the powder room in my bedroom. Glancing over at Logan, I find his eyes are wild, and his coloring has drained from his tan skin to a pale, sickly color.

Sweat not only beads on his forehead but also above his lips. He hasn't made a move to right his shorts.

"Logan?" I question, reaching toward him, but he steps back. He looks at me, but it's as if he's looking through me. His eyes wander, a bit rabid, like a trapped animal, and his head twitches. His fingers fist at his side.

"Logan," I whisper, taking a step toward him, as he shakes his head faster like he's trying to settle something inside. When I reach out for him again, he swats at my hand, slapping it hard.

"Don't touch me." The aggression surprises me, and I stare at him as he stumbles backward. His shorts still dangle at his hip. He knocks into the rocking chair behind him and tumbles to the seat. His hands start to slap at his head.

"Logan. Oh my God." His diabetes immediately comes to mind. My eyes fall to his pump near his hip, but I don't know what to do for him. Because he was overweight, he was misdiagnosed as Type 2 diabetes in his thirties. He told me how he has LADA—late autoimmune diabetes in adults. He jokingly called it Type 1.5, but I looked it up and found he wasn't kidding. In short, his pump regulates the insulin his body needs to function properly.

I scream for Ben and immediately hear little feet running down the hall. Stepping up to Logan, I try to right his pants enough so he won't be compromised, but he pushes at me. I narrowly miss what would have been a powerful slap.

"Daddy!" Lorna yells, and I turn to catch her before she gets close to her father.

"Do you know what to do?" I work hard to fight the panic coursing through my body as I speak to Logan's child. "Juice, right? Or candy?"

"He should have sugar," Lorna states as Ben rounds into my room.

"What's going on?" He notes Logan over my shoulder and rushes to his friend.

"Lorna, does your dad keep sugar sticks in his pockets?" Ben tries to search Logan's shorts, but Logan's swatting at him to stop the effort.

Logan is bigger than Ben, and I'm worried he'll hurt my brother in Ben's efforts to help.

"He should," Lorna admits.

"We have Pixy Sticks in the candy jar," Mila suggests, and Lorna runs down the hallway with Mila following after her.

"We need orange juice for him, too," Ben states. "And maybe some peanut butter and crackers."

I stand still, frozen for only a second, as Ben cups Logan's face with one hand and talks to his friend, who is telling Ben he hates him.

"Autumn!" Ben hollers at me, keeping his eyes on Logan. "Move."

I pass Lorna coming up the stairs with Mila and Anna behind her as I head down. My hands shake so uncontrollably, I'm spilling juice as I pour it, and then I'm spilling more as I hustle back up the staircase.

As I re-enter the room, Ben is pouring sugar under Logan's tongue. Logan grips Ben's wrists, trying to fight him. His hair is wild like he was pulling at it. I race to Ben's side, nudging Lorna out of the way.

"Should they be in here?" I hand Ben the glass of juice, and he quickly glances over his shoulder.

"Anna. Peanut butter and crackers," Ben snaps at his wife, who directs Lorna to the hallway. Shit, I'd forgotten the crackers. As Ben holds the juice, he forces Logan to drink while talking to him in a coaxing voice.

"Drink the juice, Logan." Ben's voice is calm but demanding. Some juice spills out of Logan's mouth, but a good portion enters despite his struggle against Ben. Time feels like it moves in slow motion as Ben administers the sugary drink to Logan along with encouraging words despite Logan's attempts to stop my brother. Anna returns with an entire box of snack packs of peanut butter and crackers, and I take the package from her with shaky hands.

Slowly, Logan blinks, and his agitated state seems to settle. He's still clutching Ben's wrists, no longer fighting him but holding on to him. His entire body continues to tremble.

"That's it," Ben says, still holding the glass at Logan's lips until he drinks more than half of it. "You've got this."

"What happened?" I whisper.

"I could ask you the same thing," Ben states, finishing with the juice and pulling the glass back from Logan's mouth. "I think he had a diabetic episode of some sort."

Tears fill my eyes. *What did we do?* I consider the sex. Did I hit his pump? Did it dislodge? My eyes fall to the device. I don't know anything about his condition.

Ben firmly holds Logan's jaw as he stares at Logan, whose eyes appear to return to focus. He's still shaky and sweaty, though.

"What happened?" Logan croaks, eyes wild but not dazed like they previously were.

"You tell us," Ben says. "I think you went into a diabetic state."

Logan looks down at his pump and touches the equipment. His head pops up, and he glances from Ben to me and back at Ben.

"I'm sorry," he whispers and my mouth gaps.

"You did nothing wrong." My shrill voice is full of shock. He has nothing to apologize for.

"I think I overexerted myself."

"What were you doing?" Ben asks and Logan's eyes shift to me. His color is still too light to hint at blushing but my cheeks heat. "Never mind," my brother mutters.

"What did I do?" Logan addresses me as if he already knows something happened. "Did I hurt you?"

"No," I whisper, but distress fills my voice. He lifts a shaking hand for my face, but something makes me flinch from his touch.

"Autumn," he whispers before his eyes return to Ben. "What did I do?" The trepidation in his gaze, along with the dread in his voice, nearly breaks me. Tears I want to hold back slip freely down my cheeks.

"It's nothing, man. What can I do for you? What else do you need?"

"Crackers. Peanut butter." Logan's voice is still weak.

"I have them." I've been clutching the box so hard I dented the packaging; however, my fingers are so shaky I don't have the strength to break the plastic wrapping.

"Autumn," Logan says in a firmer tone. A clammy hand covers mine to still my frantic motions. "Talk to me, sweetheart. Are you okay?"

"Are you?" Panic laces my voice which cracks.

"Just tell me." He wants to know if he hurt me, but I shake my head. He reaches for me, wanting to tug me down to him, but I'm afraid to touch him. I'm afraid *I'll* hurt him. *What did I do?*

Silent tears continue to glide down my face. I stare down at him, clasping my hands together so I don't grab him and pull him to me. His head lowers with shame, but he has nothing to be embarrassed about.

"I need to learn what to do for you." I never want to feel so helpless again. Quickly, I turn my attention to Ben, who is holding out a cracker for Logan.

"Thank you." I've never been so grateful for my brother. His quick reaction. His steady hand. Red marks cover his wrists, and Logan reaches up to run a finger along the razed skin. His eyes widen.

"I'm so sorry, Ben," Logan whispers.

"It was nothing." Ben keeps his eyes on his friend. A thousand words are passed between the two of them without a single one spoken. "This hasn't happened in a while, right?"

Ben's comment surprises me as if he's had experience with this reaction in Logan.

Logan shakes his head. "It could have been a number of things, but I'm thinking it was the . . eh, zealous activity."

My face heats again at the hint.

"I have a kit in my room. I'll do a finger prick in a bit," he adds.

I should know all these things.

"Teach her everything," Ben demands.

Logan nods and turns back to me, directing his words to me next. "I'm sorry, sweetheart."

I shake my head again and finally give in to touching him. Cupping his face, I stroke over his stubbly jaw. "You have nothing to apologize for." I can't deny the fear inside me that things could have escalated. This could have gone terribly wrong. The tremble in my arms is uncontrollable as is the racing of my heart, but Logan did nothing wrong.

"I'm the one who is sorry." My voice remains low, apologetic, as Logan chews a cracker. He glances down at his shorts which are partially zipped, barely covering him.

"Shit." He glances up at Ben and then back at me. After placing the cracker between his teeth, he reaches for his zipper with shaky fingers.

"Zealous activity?" Ben teases, trying to break the tension between all of us.

I briefly close my eyes again, before Logan reaches for me, tenderly circling my wrist with a cool, clammy hand, forcing me to look at him.

"Tell me. Did I hurt you?" Anxiety fills his wide eyes.

"No," I state again. We were finished with sex before he started falling apart, or at least, I think his reaction started afterward. Maybe that's why he was so clammy instead of sweaty. Maybe that's why he was so rough and determined.

"Please don't lie to protect me."

"I'm not." I glance at Ben and back at Logan, giving him a weak smile.

"Daddy?" A meek voice comes from the hallway, and I glance over my shoulder as the door to my room slowly opens. Logan hardly says a word before his daughter is racing to him, wrapping her father in her arms. Tears fall from her as she must have been just as frightened by what happened.

"I'm okay, baby," he coos to his daughter, stroking over her head while his hands continue to tremble.

"I brought you sugar like you taught me," she says, sounding proud of herself.

"Good girl," Logan replies, his voice weak and full of concern. He's still stroking over her dark hair, just as afraid he hurt her.

"She was very helpful," I assure him. "Ben took over once she brought up the candy."

Logan sighs in relief. "I usually carry honey sticks in my pocket." Logan pats at one. "But I didn't have any on me. So stupid." He whispers the last two words.

"Why don't I take you back to your room?" I suggest to Lorna. "And let Ben finish with your dad." I keep my eyes on Logan. He needs some space from being the center of attention and privacy to regroup. He can talk Ben through whatever he needs next. Logan gives me a subtle nod of gratitude before glancing back at his daughter.

"I love you, baby girl. I'll be all good in a little bit."

"I love you, too, Dad." Lorna hugs him again, holding him a little tighter. Logan squeezes her in return, pressing a kiss to the side of her head before patting her back to signal she needs to let him go.

I wrap an arm over Lorna's shoulders and guide her to the door, taking a final glance back to find Logan watching me. Smiling weakly at him, he returns mine without strength. Ben says something to Logan, and he glances back down at his pump. With that, I close the door, leaving the friends to sort things out.

31

[Logan]

It had been a long day of sunshine and annoying friendship, and I'd counted the minutes until I could be alone with Autumn. I was a little light-headed when we went to her room, but I ignored the sensation as too much sun and a shitty mood. Sex with my woman would make up for all of it. But something happened as I was thrusting into her, exerting the energy to please her and ignoring the signs wasn't smart. An out-of-body experience I rapidly lost control over occurred.

I hadn't had a diabetic episode in a long, long time, and it could have been attributed to any number of things. Add in vigorous sex, and I'm not certain what happened. No matter what, I feel terrible, and I'm riddled with concern that I've hurt both my girls tonight. Lorna and I have talked about my diabetes at great length, but it isn't her responsibility to take care of me. In her reaction to me, Autumn's hesitancy tells me she feels guilty as though she did something wrong when it wasn't her fault either. It's just my body. We haven't discussed the particulars of my disease. It's not exactly sexy talk, but Ben is right. I need to inform Autumn. I typically keep glucose tablets or honey sticks in a pocket, but I didn't have any on me tonight. It was irresponsible on my part.

While I'd like nothing more than to curl up next to Autumn and hold her tight, reassuring her of everything, I need to get my glucose levels back in range and desperately need a shower. Ben guides me back to the apartment over the garage, where I do a finger prick test from a kit and drink more juice. Ben hovers. He suggests I go to an urgent care facility for a check, but I don't want to go. My body will regulate once the glucose tablets flow. I have a call-in number for my pump.

Returning to the main room once I've showered, Mason and Zack both watch me. Ben has obviously informed them about what happened. It hits me hard that it's been an interesting forty-eight hours. Chloe's departure. Lorna's and my arrival in Lakeside. The reunion with

Autumn. Lorna's period. My diabetes. I'm whipped, and the stress on my friends' faces adds to my exhaustion.

"I'm sorry to worry you, man," I admit, falling on the cushion next to Ben.

"What happened?" Zack asks from his seat on a second couch in the room.

"Zealous activity." I swipe a hand through my wet hair, waiting out the next question.

"What? How?" Zack asks. When I was diagnosed with diabetes in my thirties and told the guys, Zack suddenly became a medical expert on it. He wanted to know what to do should something happen. I have no doubt he's suddenly investigating pancreatic cancer on Ben's behalf.

"Do I want to hear this?" Ben interjects, quick to cut off unnecessary information while tipping up a brow.

All eyes are on me, waiting for an answer, wanting more details. "I was with Autumn." It's embarrassing to admit only from the standpoint I could have hurt her.

Mason chokes from his position in the kitchenette area, pouring himself a drink. "Way to go, man."

"Fuck," Zack groans, swiping a hand over his head. We're all silent for a moment.

"I don't want to be like that," Ben quietly states.

"What do you mean?" I ask.

"I don't want Anna to worry about me or see me going into some kind of state." I'm not offended by Ben's statement. He doesn't mean anything malicious. I didn't want Autumn to ever see me like I was either, and I'm still concerned I might have said or done something to her. But I also realize I need to educate her. We need to talk about my condition so I don't scare her in the future, should something happen again. I'm confident Anna already knows as much as she can about Ben's situation, and she loves him. She'll do anything for him.

"Ben," I warn, knowing what happened to me is different than what will happen to him.

"That's why I'm here." Mason attempts to tease as he circles around to the couches and takes a seat near Zack. He holds a small tumbler in his hands.

"I don't want anyone responsible for me like that," Ben admits. "Especially not Anna."

Hearing Ben's concerns are a bit of a reality check. My insulin-producing cells have attacked my pancreas, yet I'm able to manage my life accordingly. Ben has pancreatic cancer, something that could be managed with chemotherapy, but not for long. Neither of us can be cured. One of us has fate at our door sooner rather than later, and guilt punches me in the gut. It isn't fair.

"I don't want to hurt her," Ben whispers, speaking of his wife, and my eyes lower to his wrists. Ben finally broke and told me I was trying to fight him off, pushing at him to release me while he administered the juice. If it had been Autumn, I could have broken her wrists. I swallow hard at the notion.

"It won't happen," I try to assure Ben, but he looks at me by rolling his head on the back of the couch.

"You need to talk to my sister. If this is happening between you two, she needs to know all she can to help you."

"This is happening with your sister," I tell him, hoping to end this conversation while taking his warning.

"I have a serious question for you, then," Mason interjects.

"Mace," Zack warns.

"If you and Autumn are happening, how will it work? Long distance?" Mason swipes a hand through his artful hair. "Phone sex. Frequent texts. Lonely nights without her."

"Do not say phone sex and my sister in the same sentence," ·Ben warns.

"I'm just being realistic. We aren't kids. This could be the real deal for you." Mason's strong tone surprises me. I stare at my old roommate and first friend in college. Admittedly, I'd grown closer to Ben over the years, but Mason was still my roommate, which gave us our own bond. How do I answer him? I wanted to give and be given love. I wanted to

238

be accepted for who I am. A decent man. Still a little chubby. A guy with diabetes and a daughter. Without answering Mason, he continues. "Do you want to keep overworking the nine-to-five grind? Do you want to live there when your girl is here?" He points at the carpet, but he means Lakeside. "Just think about it."

"Is this about Four Points?" I question. Is this more about his investment idea than my personal preferences?

"Ignore him," Ben states.

"This is important, dammit," Mason continues. "Are you living or existing?" Once again, I don't have an answer for him, and my former roommate hastily stands.

"Think about it," he states before disappearing into his bedroom and shutting out the three of us.

"He may be on to something," Zack admits. "What do you want? It's your life, Logan. What's going to make you happy?"

"I didn't know I was unhappy."

"Neither did I," Zack cautiously states. "I thought Jeanine and I were just who we were. Not everyone can be Ben and Anna." He pauses for a moment, and I can sense the wheels spinning in his head. "You've been committed to Chloe even though you were no longer married to her. You stayed in Indy for her and Lorna. But now what? Nothing's holding you back. You can move onto something bigger, better, *other*. I understand, man. I'm re-evaluating a lot in my life, and I'm noticing how empty it's been."

I understand where Zack is coming from, but I'm well past the newly divorced phase and into the single parenthood stage. I have responsibilities, and I need to be rational. I can't just pick up and move.

"Even you, Ben," Zack continues. "What do you want? You still have a life to live. What will you do with it?"

"Love Anna. Be present for my children. Live a simpler life here at the lake."

"No offense, man, but you aren't dead yet. What about your head? How will you keep busy? What will stimulate you?" Zack smacks the side of his head.

"I'm going to consult at Dad's company."

"You could grow it. Move it into something more," Zack encourages.

"Are you seriously in favor of this idea?" I question Zack.

"I wouldn't have offered to pay your portion if I wasn't." I'm a little surprised. Zack's been quick to jump on board with Mason's dream. *Our dream.* And I'm still in shock how easily he offered to foot my initial investment in this possible venture.

I glance over at Ben, who stares at Zack.

"Mason's right. Just think about it," Zack says before he stands and exits to the bedroom we've been sharing.

I turn to Ben. "Just ignore them," I repeat his words from only moments ago.

"But I can't ignore it, can I?" Ben says. "I don't have time ahead of me to pass on things for later, and I really do want to be happy. Until my last breath, I want to do what I want with my life."

He pats my thigh and stands, leaving me to ponder everything.

32

[Autumn]

I could have killed a man having sex with him. *Okay, maybe not quite that extreme.* But still, my thoughts race, and I can't sleep. Eventually, I slip from bed, check on Lorna—who peacefully sleeps in the bed opposite Mila—and sneak out of the house.

Crossing the driveway, I know where the spare key is kept for the apartment, and I climb the stairs to let myself inside. Zack and Logan are sharing a room. As I step into their room, I find Logan sitting up in bed, reading something off his laptop. He isn't wearing a T-shirt and looks as if nothing happened to him, but the dark circles under his eyes give him away. He watches me silently cross the room and lower to kneel next to his bed. Reaching for his hair, I brush my fingers through the soft, dark locks and chew my lower lip.

"Sweetheart, what are you doing in here?" he quietly asks.

"I couldn't sleep." I try to keep my voice lowered as well, so I don't disturb Zack.

Logan reaches for my hand and brings it to his lips, pressing a kiss into the center of my palm.

"Are you okay?" he asks.

I shake my head. I'm not okay. "Are you?"

He softly chuckles. "I've been better, but I'm even better now that you're here." He gives me a more genuine grin than earlier this evening, and his dimples show. I can't help smiling back at him but my lips quiver.

"Get up here," he softly demands. I press upward, scrambling onto the twin bed next to him while he sets his laptop to the side. Wrapping my arms around him, I still worry my touch alone will harm him. Yet I need to hold him. I need to feel him against me. I need to hear his heartbeat, and I slip a palm to his left pec, pressing my hand there.

"I checked on Lorna," I whisper to him as he strokes my hair and slips a hand under the weight of it to cup the back of my neck. He tugs me tighter against him.

L.B. DUNBAR

"You're sweet," he mutters to my temple.

"You're both sweet, but I feel like I'm in fucking college again."

Logan chuckles.

"Sorry," I mutter over my shoulder. Zack lies on his back, face up to the ceiling but an arm over his eyes.

"No worries. Do I need to place a sock on the door or something once I leave?"

Logan laughs harder, and Zack flings back the covers. Glancing over my shoulder, I try not to admire his tight body. It's been a shock to see how fit he's become as a man in his forties. He's always been attractive, but he's sporting a serious six-pack. When I see something protruding from his boxer briefs, I quickly turn back to Logan's chest.

"Get an eyeful?" He teases me as Zack exits the room, softly closing the door behind him.

"I'm only looking at you." My head tips up to gaze at him. He flips back his covers, so I can crawl in next to him. The bed is only a twin, and it's a tight fit for two bodies. He slips us lower, but I hesitate where to put my hands.

"Please don't be afraid to touch me."

"You need to teach me everything." I speak to his abs and his pump before glancing up at his face. "I don't want to ever feel so helpless again."

Logan tugs me tighter into his side. "It wasn't you," he states, adding an extra squeeze to my shoulders. "This was not your fault."

"I didn't—"

"You don't have to tell me anything. I saw it on your face. You thought you did something to me, and you didn't. I was already worked up. It's my stupid body. I know better."

"Don't say that about yourself. Just teach me so I know more," I whisper, pressing a kiss to his left pec. "I don't want to be a danger to your health."

Logan softly chuckles. "You're not. You're perfect. I've told you before, while this disease has tons of information about it, it's also highly individualized. And I will tell you more, but not tonight. I don't want to

242

keep talking about this." His frustration rings through his voice, vibrating in his chest, and I stroke over the coarse hairs curling there. "I just wanted to make certain you were feeling better."

"I'm amazing now." He presses another kiss to my forehead.

"I'm serious." My voice is full of the concern and guilt I still feel.

"So am I." His lips on my forehead linger a second, and I close my eyes, inhaling the scent of him. "You know, we could have some fun with this. If I dip again when we're in the middle of sex, I could lick chocolate syrup off a spoon while you lick chocolate syrup off me. Or better yet, I could drizzle honey on your body and lap it up, especially one place in particular."

His teasing tone does nothing to ease my anxiety, but I giggle as his hand lowers under the covers and hitches my legs over his.

"Hold onto me," he whispers against my hair, and I tighten my arm around his middle. "Much better," he whispers. "I'm sorry I scared you. Tell me the truth. I can get mean or even pushy. Did I do that to you?"

I press another kiss on his pec and tell him what happened. His arms tighten around me until I'm certain we can't get any closer.

"I would never hurt you like that. Never. Don't be afraid, okay?"

"I'm not." I pepper his chest with kisses, intending to soothe his worries. I want to take care of him. I need to take care of him. "I don't want to lose you."

"I'm not going anywhere," Logan states as if answering an unspoken question. *Could he die from this?*

We remain quiet for a while, holding each other like we'll never let go before I ask something else that's been on my mind.

"What was all that earlier with Mason?"

Logan reminds me of what I've already learned about the business proposal when they were four drunk boys in college. "With Ben's announcement, Mason's really pushing things. Like he's self-reflecting on his own life goals or maybe just wanting Ben to fulfill a fantasy designed when we were young and foolish."

Thoughtful before I respond, I ask. "Was it really foolish to think you could work together? I only know the general concept, but it sounds like a plan that uses each of your talents."

Logan sighs. "It's only a concept. We don't have a plan. And it involves a financial investment that I can't give right now." The doubt in Logan's voice quietly warns me not to push the idea. However, other thoughts occur. Ones involving him moving here. We could live together. He could move in with me. He could save money that way, and I could . . . *what?* What would I do for him? We've just committed to dating, but what more does he want? I know that I don't want to lose him, and an honest fear creeps in, considering Ben's current condition.

Tugging Logan tighter once more, I wish for things I shouldn't wish for.

33

[Autumn]

As Labor Day weekend drew to an end, it brought another heartfelt goodbye between Logan and me, but this one was without tears. I would be seeing Logan in a week as I planned to visit him in Indianapolis. I suggested I get a hotel room as I didn't want things to be weird with Lorna. Logan only has a two-bedroom townhome, but he assured me he'd talk to Lorna. He wants me with him at his house. We won't be able to have sex all over the place as I'd hoped, but I am just as happy to spend time with them, learning more about Lorna.

"I hate middle school." Those words start the next weekend as we pick Lorna up from school. Logan wants to show me around the city, and then we'll be heading to dinner—the three of us. As the SUV door slams, I glance at Logan, who shifts in his seat to peer at his daughter.

"What happened?"

Lorna's crossed arms and red face tell me it's bad. She stares out the window and doesn't answer her father. He glances over at me, and I shrug but also shake my head. I remember these days, and it might be best to let her stew. Maybe it's more than middle school. Maybe it's me being here or her mom in France. She has a lot going on, and middle school can be the worst years.

We take an awkwardly quiet tour of Indianapolis before Logan parks by the barbecue place he ordered from when I first visited. Once inside, Lorna and I take a seat while Logan places our order at the counter and waits for our drinks.

"Is it me?" I ask, hating how much I feel like a middle schooler asking Lorna, but I want to be cognizant of her feelings. She has a lot happening in her young life.

"Lucas DeFranco called me fat." Lorna focuses on the tablecloth before her, and her lids blink rapidly. I slide my hand across the table and cover hers with mine.

"Boys can be jerks," I tell her, understanding exactly how she feels. "Extra stupid jerks when they don't see the lovely girl before them."

"Bryce isn't like that."

"My nephew?" *Oh boy.*

Lorna nods. "Why can't the boys in middle school be like him?"

"Well, first, Bryce is a little older, and now, he's officially in high school." Not that a few years gives him more maturity, but a few more years of experience does give Bryce a better sense of how to treat others. I'd like to think my nephew knows how to be respectful and not judgmental.

"Bethany Simone laughed when he said it."

Oh, man. Sometimes girls are meaner than boys. "You know, I was once like you."

Her head pops up. "I was a little bigger than my friends. Everyone was petite with small bones and tiny bodies that fit skinny pants. I hated them, but not really." I recall some of my girlfriends from younger years and my feelings toward them.

"I was athletic and solid, my mother liked to say, but I didn't find it a compliment. In high school, someone once told me boys like big butts, but I didn't want a boy to like my butt." I wrinkle my nose, and Lorna slowly smiles. "I had the biggest crush on an older boy too because he was always nice to me, but he thought I was just a kid."

Lorna's face falls. I'm not trying to sting her, but Bryce isn't going to look at Lorna yet because of their age difference. In a few years, it won't matter, but presently, it's everything.

"I held on to the idea of that boy, though. He didn't see me as fat. He teased me, but it was always good-natured because he was a sweet guy." I smile larger.

"What happened to him?" Lorna asks, and I lean forward.

"He's your dad." I wink at her, and her mouth falls open.

Lorna smiles wider, but then her face falls. "But you aren't . . ." Her eyes roam my body. "Fat."

"I'm healthy," I say as I pat my stomach. "I learned to eat better, and I exercised more, but you're already exercising with soccer, and you eat well because of your dad's needs. It takes time for your body to change, and it's already gone through one big change this summer." I smile, recalling her first period last weekend.

"That doesn't help me now," she wisely states.

"I know. Some days you need to grin and bear it. But you also need to ignore those negative comments because one day, those kids won't matter. That's not easy to hear now, but it's the truth."

Lorna sighs. "I wish we could move."

Blinking at her, I pull my hand back. "Move? Honey, you can't run from your problems like that."

"I know, but Dad doesn't love his job, and Mom's gone, and I don't really like my school. Mila already made her new school sound so fun."

I'm certain my niece is putting on a brave face—grinning and bearing it, as I've just said—because her life is in turmoil as well.

"You know it's different for Mila, right?"

"Because of her dad."

"What do you know about Ben?"

"He has cancer. Mila looked it up. He's going to die."

Oh God. "But not soon. Not tomorrow or even a year from now." I hope. I can only hope for a miracle to help him and prolong his life.

"When Dad had his diabetic episode, I worried he'd die too." Lorna sits up and wipes at her eyes. There are so many emotions rumbling around in her young head.

"Baby, he's not going anywhere. He's not moving away. He's not dying. He's right here for you every day." I'd like to be here for Lorna as well because I have such a kindred connection with this girl.

"Hey," Logan says, placing our drink tray on the table and lowering to a seat beside Lorna. He looks from me to her and back. "Everything okay?"

Lorna answers for us. "Girl talk."

Logan nods but glances at me once more to make certain Lorna's speaking the truth.

"We're perfect, just the way we are." Lorna sheepishly looks up at me, and her slow smile tells me she'll be okay.

+ + +

"What was all that at dinner?" Logan asks me once we're alone on his couch. I'm between his legs, leaning against his chest in the position we were in a few weeks ago. A blanket drapes over my thighs, and he toys with my hair.

"Kids at school are picking on her." Logan stills his twirling of my hair. "Some of it's typical immaturity, but it hurts. You know Lorna's sensitive about her size."

Logan leans forward to kiss my head. "I hate kids."

"No, you don't." I chuckle.

"Boys are assholes."

"Girls can be mean, too." I'm reminded of my own youth and remember how Logan spoke about me once. "More than once, a boy might break her heart or hurt her feelings."

"I know." His voice softens. "But I want to protect her from all that pain."

Shifting, I glance up at his face. Those deep eyes. That scruffy jaw. Those beautiful lips. He's had his share of pain as well.

"You're a good dad," I remind him. "And a great man."

His face slightly colors at the compliment. "Is it too soon to tell you I love you because I do."

I shift completely between his thighs to better face him. "It's not too soon." My face heats, and a smile pulls at my lips. "I love you, too."

Warning bells go off in my head, telling me to keep cool, settle down. *Don't read into the phrase.* But everything in me says this is right. We are right. I'm finally with the man I've crushed on half my life.

Our lips meet, and the remainder of the night disappears in tender kisses and soft caresses, reminding us both that we survived the rough teen years. We're adults, and we can do as we please. And right now, we only want to please each other.

34

[Logan]

By the middle of October, I'm overwhelmed. We have three new projects at the firm. Chloe rarely checks in with Lorna. My daughter is suffering at middle school, and I hardly have time to see Autumn. It isn't fair to her, and I argue it isn't fair to me. I can't do it all. When scheduling blocks cut out another weekend to see one another, I'm done.

"I don't think we should continue to see each other." The words almost gut me, but I'm convinced it's the right thing to do. I feel like a perv having phone sex with my hours-away girlfriend when my daughter is in the next room. However, I'd still be a perv if my girlfriend was in my bed because I fucking miss Autumn and the freedom to be with her.

"Logan, what's going on?" she softly says to me through the phone. I'm sick of video conferencing and text messages. I want to touch her. I want to physically see her. I don't know how people in the military do this kind of thing. I can't be distant from my girl.

Everything feels off lately. The timing of Autumn in my life. The time I spend at the office. The time I wish I had with Lorna.

"I can't do it. With Chloe here, I had a break every other weekend. I'm not begrudging having Lorna here. I'm not. It's just everything I do revolves around her. I don't get to see you between work piling up and her crazy schedule."

It's not like I can just hire a sitter or even trust Lorna home alone for a few hours and go on a date. My girlfriend lives three hours away.

"Why don't you come here this weekend? We can work something out with Ben and Anna. Give yourself some time off."

"No," I snap, harsher than I should at Autumn. She's not the person I'm most upset with; Chloe is. She's Lorna's mother, and she's nearly disappeared. How could she do this to our daughter? On top of all the activities I try to keep my daughter involved in, I have to worry about her emotional state, which is off the charts lately between conflicts at school, fluctuating grades, and this new surge of hormones every month.

"Okay," Autumn slowly states.

"I'm sorry. I can't be what you want me to be."

"Wait a minute. I don't want you to be anything other than who you are," Autumn defends, but I barrel onward.

"I can't add another kid to the mix." Instantly, I regret the words. I told her I wouldn't feel obligated. I told her I could do this with her, but I just don't see how.

"We haven't been talking about babies in the last six weeks." She's right. I know she's right, but it's all too much.

"I don't want it," I lie. I do want it. I want everything with her, but I can't envision us together. "I can't be what you need."

"You're exactly what I need," she states, frustration filling her voice.

"How?"

"You're a good man. You're kind and nice to me. You love your daughter and—"

"It's like you're telling me I have a great personality."

"What's wrong with that? You do have a great personality. You're funny and typically easygoing. I don't understand."

I'm silent a second, not able to explain myself. I don't understand me either. Having diabetes can sometimes make me moody or crabby, but this is more than a mood swing. I'm just off-balance.

"Do you want me to tell you how sexy you are? How much I think about you? How I can't sleep because I crave you next to me?"

Actually, yes. Yes, I do want those things, but I shake my head, dismissing the truth. We've said I love you, but somehow, it's not enough. "Don't humor me."

"Logan, what am I missing here? Did I do something wrong?"

She's perfect. This is all me. I need more. Three hours and two hundred miles separating us is too much. I can't race off to see her on a whim or push away my child just to have a life. I already let my ex-wife do that.

"I need to go." It isn't true, but I can't linger on the phone. I don't want to prolong the pain. The urge to call and break things off consumed me, and it felt best to rip off the bandage.

"I don't understand. We love each other," she says, and it crushes me. After our declaration, we've spent the past month telling each other every chance we get. She needs to hear it as much as I do, but it's more than words. We need to be together.

"I don't," I whisper, closing my eyes and pinching the bridge of my nose.

"You don't what?" Her voice hardens through the phone. "You don't love me?"

My heart shatters in a thousand pieces as I know I'm hurting her, but it's for the best. This isn't going anywhere.

Fat chick upstairs hungry to be in my pants. Told her my sausage was more than she could handle.

The comment comes back to me. Not that I remember the night or even Autumn trying to kiss me, but I believe I said what I said to protect myself. I hurt her so she couldn't hurt me, and that's my underlying fear. One day, she isn't going to want this distance anymore either. She's going to want that baby and a man by her side to raise a child, and I can't do that from here.

"It's better this way," I say. I hear her gasp my name through the phone, but without more to say, I hang up. Turning off my phone, I toss it across my office, where it clatters to the floor after hitting the wall. I spin away from the damaged device and glare at my draft table, staring down at a set of drawings for another building I don't care about in a town I don't love anymore.

+ + +

"When can we go back to Lakeside?" Lorna asks me two weeks after that fateful phone call.

"Probably not until summer. Why?" I swallow around the thought. Returning to Lakeside would only be torture, knowing Autumn is nearby. Thankfully, summer is months away. I've been worried about Ben as he's been short with me lately, knowing I broke up with Autumn. Mason already called to chew me out for breaking her heart. He has no idea how much mine is broken as well.

"It was only sex," I cavalierly told him.

"I don't believe that for a fucking second, and neither do you. And because it's Autumn we're talking about, go fuck yourself."

Mason had no idea how much I felt I already had. For the first time in my life, I had a woman who really wanted me, and I gave her up.

"I don't want to wait until summer. I have a three-day weekend coming up. I miss Mila. Don't you miss Autumn?" Lorna pauses. "She hasn't been back to see us."

I didn't discuss what happened between Autumn and me with Lorna. Whenever she's asked about seeing Autumn, I simply said Autumn was busy, but Lorna's sharp, and she's noticed I haven't been speaking to Autumn every night. Sometimes Lorna would pop into my room and say hi through the video chat. They even started texting one another although I don't ask if Lorna's heard from Autumn or vice versa. They developed their own bond that first and only weekend Autumn came here.

"I miss everyone," I admit. Even that pain in the ass Mason has been on my mind often lately. I've been thinking more and more about his business proposal, arguing with myself that I'm forty, and I can't turn back the clock to fulfill some drunken dream-statement said in college. This isn't some let's-get-the-band-back-together revival. We each have our own lives in separate directions.

Four Points.

Yet two points are closer together, and Zack is struggling as well as I am lately with single parenthood. We should be helping one another like those best friends who live in cul-de-sacs and raise their kids with a village mentality.

"We should go there this weekend," Lorna says, and I look up from the file I've been working on at the kitchen island.

"Lorna, we aren't going anywhere," I snap.

"You know, since you broke up with Autumn, you've been extra crabby."

I still, staring at my child over the kitchen island. "Who told you we broke up?"

"Mila. She said her aunt is sad. And you're sad. And I don't know why you'd do that. I like Autumn."

"I like Autumn, too." I love her, but this is for the best.

"Then I don't understand. Why did you break up with her?"

"It just . . . wasn't going to work out."

Lorna's quiet for a long moment. "Because of me?"

"No. Why would you say that?"

"Because Bethany Simone said her mother broke up with a man because he didn't like Bethany."

"Well, Bethany doesn't know what she's talking about. Autumn adores you, and it had nothing to do with you." My voice gives away my frustration.

"Then it was all you?" My eleven-year-old calls me out.

"Fine. Yes, it was all me."

"Dad, are you being an extra stupid jerk?"

"Hey," I snap again at her.

"Autumn says extra stupid jerks don't see beautiful girls before them, and it sounds like you're not seeing Autumn."

I'm quiet for a second, staring at my child, who schooled me and leaves me wondering when she got so wise. I was being stupid and a jerk.

"You need to get Autumn back. I suggest groveling, flowers, and taking us to Lakeside." Slipping off the stool, my daughter gives me her back and stomps to her room, which is good because I was about to send her there myself.

+ + +

As if the moment with my daughter wasn't enough, Mason calls a half hour later.

"You need to get your fucking head out of your ass," he greets me.

253

"Is it Ben?" My heart races. *Did something happen?*

"No, it's Autumn."

That racing heart chokes me. "What's wrong?" I lean on the kitchen island to support myself.

"And I didn't think you had it in you, but you're a total asshole."

"What are you talking about?" I demand, not liking his tone or the continued insults.

"You need to man up. Call her. Or better yet, get up here."

"Fuck off, Mason. Just tell me what happened?" My fingers fist, and I pound on the countertop.

"You happened." He's quiet for a second, and I have no better understanding of what he isn't saying. "It's your life, too, man. Like I said before, are you living it or just existing in it?"

"What are you even talking about?" He's really pissing me off, and it's all the more reason to decline the Four Points idea we had when we thought we were invincible.

"If you don't show, I'm putting myself on the list."

My racing heart comes to a halt, knocking the wind out of me. "What list?" I choke around the question, knowing the answer. Autumn moved on.

"The man-up list." With that, Mason hangs up on me, and I stare at the phone in my hands. Between Lorna's suggestions and Mason's cryptic call, I suddenly fear I've made the biggest mistake of them all.

35

[Autumn]

To say I didn't see the breakup coming would be a lie. Men just do not commit to me, and I took poor consolation in the fact Logan hadn't cheated on me. I almost wished he had so I could hate him instead of yearning for him like I do. I understood we hadn't been able to coordinate. Things were crazy here for me, too. I was trying to support Anna and Ben as best I could despite Mason being here, plus I had the café. My sweet spot was headed toward a slower season although the fall colors tour—the final burst of tourism—provides an extra boost before winter sets in and the beach crowd dwindles to nothingness.

I wanted to forgive Logan, but two weeks after the breakup, I didn't. I'd grown angry, and I had no one to blame but myself. I'd gotten what I expected. Men did not stick with me.

Pouring myself a glass of wine, I lift the glass for a sip but think better of it.

No more wine for you, missy.

A sharp knock comes on my condo door, startling me from my thoughts. As I'm not expecting anyone, it must be a lost delivery person at the wrong address. I'll be all alone tonight as I am every night. In fact, I'm looking forward to a night alone. I've had weeks to get used to the idea, and tonight, I relish it. I'm tired.

A second knock—that's more like a subtle pounding—forces me forward. Yanking open the door, I freeze at the man on my stoop.

"Logan?" In his hands is a large bouquet of fall flowers.

"Hey." He hesitantly smiles at me, and I hate how my heart flutters and my belly flips. His damn dimples are on display, and I'm blinded by how good he looks. Instantly, I remind myself this man broke up with me after a whirlwind affair and declarations of I love you. I know better. Nothing lasts forever, especially for me. "May I come in?"

Still holding the door, I actually contemplate whether I should let him enter. I don't trust myself not to easily give in to whatever he wants.

Reminding myself he's Ben's best friend, I step aside, wave him forward and then glance outside the open door.

"Where's Lorna?"

"She's with Anna and Ben." He enters my place and stops in the middle of my small living room.

"Is everything okay?" I ask once I've closed the door, concerned for his daughter. I've been in touch with Lorna but prudently avoid any mention of her father.

"I want to talk."

Are there any worse words? "We don't need to do this." I pause by the overstuffed chair facing my balcony.

"I wanted to see you."

I don't believe him although his presence negates my thought. "What do you want?" The question is sharp. My tone harsh.

"Mason called me."

Crossing my arms, I glance away from him, staring toward the large, glass double doors leading out to my balcony. In the distance is the quiet, calm lake under a hazy fall sky. *Mason.* I shake my head. He's almost as meddlesome as Anna.

"He told me there's a new list."

"Oh. My God," I nearly scream, lifting my head to face the ceiling and clench my fists at my side. I cannot believe these clowns.

"There wasn't a list," I groan in frustration. "Anna suggested a list. Not me. Not ever. I only wanted one thing, Logan."

"What?" He steps toward me, but I step back.

"It doesn't matter." Lowering my head, I gaze at the floor and draw a circle with my toe on the carpet. *I wanted you to love me.* More than just saying the words but truly love me.

Nevertheless, I've come to realize that something is seriously wrong with me, and perhaps I came on a bit strong because of my desire for a baby. *For my phase*, as Ben called it. My phase for motherhood and marriage and more.

"Of course, it does." Logan sighs.

256

"Go home, Logan. As you said, we're over." Summer's over. The two-week visit is over. The baby-making business is done.

Logan exhales, lowering the flowers he's been holding at his chest to his side. "I made a mistake."

"No, I made a mistake," I state loud and clear, pointing at my chest. "Don't say that about us." His eyes widen. It's true, though. I did this. I believed we could be something other than having sex to make a baby for me. *Only me.*

Logan takes another step closer, but I take another backward, bumping into the chair.

"Marry me."

"Don't do this." Tears instantly well in my eyes. *Not this.* "Don't make a mockery of marriage. Don't turn this into your sausage joke. This I cannot handle."

"I'm not joking." His eyes widen even more, and those dark orbs plead with me, but I can't do this.

"You broke up with me two weeks ago."

"I was a fool. As I said, I made a mistake. Big mistake. Huge mistake." He expands his arms, flowers waving in the air, but it's not enough. There's no excuse for his behavior that doesn't point right back at mine. I had a crush on him. I wanted to have sex with him. I wasn't good enough for him.

"I won't play into some competition with Mason. There's no list. You're free of . . ." *Obligation?* He was never obligated to me. We made no promises. You can still love someone and not have it move forward into something more. I know. I've been in this position numerous times in my life.

"Actually, the list Mason mentioned was called the man-up list, and I'm here to do it."

A lump forms in my throat, and I swallow around the thick blockage. My arms cross, holding myself together.

"You have nothing to man up over. I'm fine on my own." I straighten my back.

"But I'm not," Logan says, lowering his voice. He takes a deep breath and continues. "Remember when you told me that statistic about men and marriage? How men don't want to be alone. I don't want to be alone." He points at himself. "There's been a void in my life. One I didn't even see was there until you began to fill it."

"Logan," I whisper, shaking my head and facing the floor. My toe digs at the carpet.

"And remember when I asked you why you weren't married, thinking every person who didn't ask you must have been a fucking idiot? You said the right man hadn't found you. But I did. I just . . . I got a little lost on the way here. I'm also a fucking idiot, but I'm—"

"Stop it," I whisper, tears blinding me.

"I want to be with you. I want you to be with me."

He takes another step closer to me, and as I'm plastered into the chair at my back, I have nowhere to go. He's filling my space and clogging my senses. I close my eyes as if that will block him out.

"There was something there," he whispers, reminding us both of when I got my period, when I went to him convinced I had to be pregnant because I felt so different. That difference had been him. He was the something there, and now he was here, but I'm so confused.

"I'm sorry," Logan says. "I'm always apologizing to you, and I'll continue apologizing until I get you back. We aren't over."

My lids open, but I can't look at him. I can't fall into the trap of falling for him again.

"I'm tired, Autumn. I'm tired of only existing in my life instead of living it."

My head pops up at his words as I've heard Mason saying something similar. Even Ben professes he plans to live out the rest of his days truly living them.

"I'm going into business with Mason."

"What?" I blink.

"I haven't been happy for a while now. When we started, I knew I'd been missing out on something more in my life, but I just didn't know what it was. That more is here, with you, with the guys. Then everything came crashing in at once. Ben's condition. Chloe leaving. And Lorna. My poor baby girl is so unhappy, too."

My chest aches when I think of Lorna. She misses her mother and doesn't understand how her mom could leave her behind. She's mentioned that Logan's been crabby and working hard. She's lonely. And I never want to hear the name of Bethany Simone again.

Logan pauses, softening the desperation in his eyes. "We need you."

Words I've always wanted to hear fall far too freely from him, and I want to believe him, but I can't. This man broke my heart only weeks ago.

Logan bitterly chuckles when I don't respond to him. "Lorna told me I was an extra stupid jerk. Extra stupid jerks don't see the beautiful girl before them, and she's right. I blinked for a moment and lost sight of what I had, what I want most. Grovel, she said. Flowers." He lifts the bouquet, still held in his hand. "And go to Lakeside."

I glance off toward the balcony glass doors, chewing at my lips.

"I'm going one better. Lorna and I are moving to Lakeside."

"What?" Glancing back at him, I can't believe what he said.

"And I'm going to marry you because, like Mason said, everything I want is right here." He reaches for me, brushing my hair over my ear before cupping the back of my neck. He leans his forehead to mine and drops his hand to touch mine.

"And in here." He places my hand over his heart which races under this shirt.

"And here." He lifts my hand once more to kiss my palm. "You hold me in the palm of your hand. You hold my heart. And I'm going to carry yours. You'll see." Logan leans forward and kisses me so softly, so sweet. It's quick and over before I know what's happened, and I'm left still standing by the chair when I hear my front door click shut, and the flowers lay on the seat of the chair at my back.

+ + +

The following morning, Crossroads is as busy as I expected. It's a beautiful fall day with lingering warm temperatures. The town will be buzzing with people soaking up one more weekend before out-of-towners permanently leave their summer residence and year-rounders settle into the quieter pulse of our small community. When the day finally comes to an end for me, I find Ben outside the back door of the café with two bikes.

"What are you doing here?" I ask, chuckling as Ben and I haven't ridden bikes together since we were little kids.

"Take a ride with me."

"How did you get here with two bikes?"

Ben shrugs. "It doesn't matter. Just ride with me a bit."

Hopping on the bike Ben offers, we travel down Beech Street to the inner drive and head in the direction of Lakeside Cottage. Ben remains quiet as we pedal beside one another. This isn't a race. We aren't teasing one another or showing off with feats of balance. We simply take our time to push the pedals and glide along the fall-colored drive. The trees are in full display, and a crisp smell filters through the air. Change is coming. I have so many questions, all of which I want to ask Ben, but I don't. I savor this moment, adding it to a new list. The one where I hold every memory of my older brother before he goes.

We pass the cottage, which surprises me, but I follow Ben's lead traveling further down the road. We pass Zack's old home, which is right next door, and the historical inn. We pass a Spanish-inspired home that has always intrigued me, and then we near my house, as I affectionately call the place.

The one where I dreamed of living one day with a husband and child of my own. The place wasn't as flashy as the cottage house of Anna's family, but more your traditional lakeside home. It was perfectly situated on a raised lot, and Ben slows as we near it. The FOR SALE sign that once sat in the yard is now gone.

"It sold?" My heart breaks at another dream shattered.

"I think so," Ben says, hopping off his bike but turning it onto the drive.

"What are you doing?" I ask, still straddling mine. Ben walks up the drive. Distance grows between us until Ben stops and tilts his head. "Come on."

Removing myself from my bike, I hold the handlebars and walk it up the gravel drive. "Ben, this is trespassing."

He chuckles. "Might be the last time you get to peek inside then," he teases. He stops short of the front walk and lays his bike on the lawn. I follow his lead and walk the broken path to the front door where Ben has stopped before the entrance. He turns to me.

"You know there's nothing I want more than for you to be happy, right?"

I tip my head to the side, curious where his comment is leading. "Of course." He's always been the best of brothers.

"This is the happiness you deserve." Ben reaches for the doorknob and presses it to open the door.

"Ben," I whisper, narrowing my eyes as my heart races. "What did you do?"

"I didn't do anything." Ben slowly smiles. "It was all him." Ben holds out a hand, and I hesitate as I cross the threshold of the house I'd always dreamed of owning to find Logan standing inside.

36

[Logan]

As Autumn enters the house, she looks as nervous as I feel. I swipe my warm hands down my jean-covered thighs and wait as she cautiously steps farther inside. I'm going to owe Ben big for this, as I called him before I made a decision. I wanted his approval and his help.

"Welcome," I say, biting off the second word I want to share with her. I hold off as I have more groveling to do and more explaining, but I wanted this moment first.

"What are you doing here?" she asks, sidetracked by the old fireplace and built-in bookshelves. A large bay window looks out toward the water, unencumbered by the house across the street as it sits lower on the incline, pitching toward the lake. The sun is setting earlier on this mid-October day, but it's no less striking than a summer sunset.

"What do you think of the place?" I question, having a hint as Lorna knew about this house.

"I love this house." Autumn pauses, glancing around the open space between the front room and the dining area where I've set up a card table with flowers and a linen tablecloth. Her head tilts.

"Want to tell me about this house?" I ask, hoping to reel her in and open her up to me about it.

"I've always admired this place for some reason. It seems more cottage-y than Anna and Ben's place, and I've always wanted to own a house, not a condo." Autumn's place is a newer build pressed up to the waterfront in town. It's nice and modern with a great view but lacking character.

"Lorna told me you called this *your house*." My daughter mentioned how they drove by it one night, and Autumn called this place her home. Mila and Lorna also rode bikes past the house, and Mila called the swing in the front yard her spot.

"I did." She softly chuckles. "But Ben told me it—" She stops, holding still in the empty front room while I remain by the makeshift dining table.

"It what?" I slowly smile, nearly ready to burst.

"It sold." Her voice drops as she stares at me. "Did you buy this place?"

"I did." My voice rises with excitement, fighting the anxiety underlying the phrase.

"Why?"

"I want to give us a home."

"Logan." Her shoulders visibly fall, and her lips purse. I've stressed over being too late to win her back, but I'm more determined than I've ever been to do this with her.

"Welcome *home*," I state. Autumn stays where she is, and I slip my hands into my back pockets. I muddled things up a bit last night when I went to her place. It would have been too easy if she had accepted my botched proposal, and I'm a little glad she didn't. I regrouped today once the realtor gave me the keys to this place and then recruited Ben to get her here. I didn't want to mess things up again.

"I almost missed you," I state, and her head pops up. "You said the right man hadn't found you, and I almost missed you. I was searching out there." I wave a hand to mean the larger world. "When you were right before me all the time. You were here the entire time."

Autumn lowers her head, and I take a few steps to be closer to her. I don't want to feel like I'm shouting my words. She needs them up close. She needs to feel them from me.

"You thought destiny missed you. I felt the same way, but it hadn't. It's been before us all this time. I'm the one."

I reach for her and rub my hands up and down her arms. "You're the one."

Liquid fills her eyes as she gazes up at me but quickly turns her head away. I reach under her hair and around her neck and tip up her chin with my other hand so she faces me.

"I'm no Prince Charming, but I promise you won't need to search anymore. I'm here."

A tear leaks from the corner of her eye, and she quickly swipes it away. I stroke my thumb over her cheek and lick my lips before continuing.

"I cannot live without you. A lifetime will not be long enough. And I know you're capable of doing everything alone, but I don't want you to do it alone. *I* don't want to be alone. I want to be here with you. For you. And for a baby. For all the babies."

Her mouth pops open, but I use my thumb at her lips to stop her from speaking.

"I need you and not in some creepy needy way, but just an aching need to have you with me. Take care of me but let me take care of you. I'll hold your hand. I'll hold you up. And while I might not always get it right, I'm damn well willing to try until I figure things out. You feed my ego because you're so fucking gorgeous, and I'm a chump. Let me remind you every day how fucking gorgeous you are."

More tears fall from her beautiful eyes, and I swipe at them.

"Marry me, Autumn. Let us be the couple who was made for each other."

Autumn breaks into a sob, covering her face as she cries, and I'm thinking I've really fucked this up. Not a little mess up, but full-blown fuckery. Her head tips toward me, and I catch her in my arms, wrapping them around her back and stroking up and down her spine. I press my lips to her hair as she shudders against me.

"Would it really be that bad?" I question, thinking back to when she refused to sleep with me at first, and I took it personally. Maybe she hadn't wanted me. Then I learned she'd always wanted me, and I'd been a fool not to see her. An extra stupid jerk as Lorna reminds me.

Autumn shakes her head against my sternum. "No," she says, and my heart crashes to my feet. Her head continues to wag side to side. "No, it wouldn't be that bad."

I pause and press at her shoulders so she'll look up at me. "What are you saying?"

"I have something to tell you first."

I stare at her red-rimmed eyes and her swollen lids. She looks so broken and sad, and my chest hurts because I did this to her.

"You can tell me anything, sweetheart."

"I'm pregnant."

My heart stills, and then it hammers. Blood rushes to fill all my veins at once. "What?" The question is soft and strangled, surprised.

"I was going to tell you. I just wanted to let it sink in a little bit and—"

My mouth covers hers. I keep it tender and slow, sucking at her bottom lip before covering them both as I absorb what she said. When I pull away from her, I lean my forehead against hers.

"We're doing this. Together."

"Logan, I don't want you to feel—"

My thumb covers her lips once more. "The only thing I feel is love for you and our future." I drop a hand to her belly. It's almost unbelievable, yet I'm thrilled.

"When do you think it happened?" My palm still covers her lower belly. There's nothing to feel yet but one day, she'll swell, and I'll be here to watch it all happen. We'll experience it all together.

"I'm thinking the Adirondack chair on the landing."

"You're not very far along," I state, counting the weeks backward. That was Labor Day weekend. It's now the middle of October. "Maybe six weeks."

Autumn fights a grin. "Six weeks."

"How do you feel?" *She's pregnant.*

She shrugs, but she smiles larger as her hand covers mine over her stomach.

She's going to be a mother, and I'm going to be a father again.

"We're going to have a baby," I whisper to her.

"We're going to have a baby," she repeats.

"I'm going to fill you with them." Taking a deep breath, I glance up at the ceiling in need of repair before blowing out a breath and noting the hardwood floors that need refinishing. This house is a project, but I'm excited to take every step of it. I'm excited to live here with her. My Autumn. A new beginning. A permanent change. "I'm going to fill this house with them."

"Maybe we should take this one baby at a time," she teases.

"One baby at a time," I say, leaning forward to kiss her again. I want nothing more than to devour her and lay her out on this cracked wood floor. I want to bury myself inside her, and celebrate this moment, but we have other repairs to be made first.

"I'm going to love you the right way every day. You'll see."

37

[Autumn]

For the next weeks, I do see.

The house was the first gesture. Logan bought it under Lorna's guidance. He told me how they had a long talk about each of their futures. What they wanted. What would make them happy, and Logan admitted that he'd been holding back because he didn't want more change to disrupt Lorna's life. Lorna was happy to let her life change one more time. The kids at school knew too much of her story. Her mother left her behind, and it hurt.

Logan and Lorna wouldn't officially be moving to Lakeside until they closed on the house, which would be another month, but Logan's place was up for sale. He gave notice that he'd be leaving by the holidays to his architectural firm and sought the means to invest in Four Points.

For us, the next thing to happen was phone calls and virtual dinner dates through video conferencing. In a sense, we returned to who we had been, but this time it was more. It wasn't just sex. In fact, there was no sex between us. Logan teased and flirted, but he didn't press for naked video time and sexy texts. We learned more about one another.

When I had my next doctor's visit, Logan took the day off, drove three hours, and attended with me. He swore he didn't want to miss a minute. We agreed not to tell Lorna until I was past the first trimester, which wouldn't be until after the holidays. For now, it was a moment just for us.

Every weekend, they traveled to Lakeside. Lorna's soccer season was over, and Logan allowed her to quit piano lessons.

"What did you tell Chloe?" He didn't let Chloe take their daughter overseas, but he was removing her from their original home state.

"Chloe?" He snorted when I asked. "My ex-wife has hardly called her daughter. Hell, you've had more contact with Lorna in the past months than her mom."

I'd been vigilant to maintain a relationship with Lorna, mainly because we shared that kindred spirit I felt. I wanted to be a pseudo-aunt or fairy godmother to her, if I wasn't going to be anything else. I still had not accepted Logan's marriage proposal, and he hadn't asked again after that first weekend. Still, we moved forward in preparation for his closing on the house.

When Logan came to Lakeside, he stayed in the garage apartment with Mason, allowing Lorna to sleep in Mila's room. The two girls really were the best of friends, and the separation allowed Logan some of the free time he needed. He spent those extra moments with me.

We talked. We held hands. We kissed, but we did not take it further than heavy groping and some torturous grinding.

"I'm not making love to you again until we're living in the same zip code," he teased one night as we sat on blankets in the empty house he would soon move into. It was unorthodox to enter the house before Logan officially signed on the line, but Mason knew the realtor. She was someone he hooked up with once, and she owed him a favor, so Logan had keys to enter as needed to discuss things with the contractors. We sat in our familiar position of me between his legs, my back to his chest. "In the same house."

"Are you asking me to move in with you?" I tease. Logan's place had sold rather quickly, and the timing coordinated that he'd move here and virtually close on his place.

"Yes." His adamant response startles me.

"I'm kidding," I tell him, lessening the pressure.

"I'm not. I want us in the same house, same bed."

"Don't you think it's too soon?" I question. "Lorna will need time to adjust to the move, and you'll be busy, and—"

"I think it shows Lorna how truly committed I am to us. While her mother ran off to live with a man in France, I'm bringing Lorna with me to live with my future wife. Plus, you're having my baby, which will be her little brother or sister. We've been apart long enough. I'm ready to start living with you day in and day out."

Logan speaks openly about us marrying. He isn't feeling me out, questioning if it's something I want. He's simply making a statement. We will marry.

"Your wife? Gosh, I hope she doesn't mind you spending time with me," I tease again.

Logan shifts, and I adjust to face him between his spread thighs.

"Oh, my wife will approve."

He leans forward to kiss me, hard and fast. Our touches have grown desperate under his rule not to have sex until we are together all the time. Pressing at his shoulder, he falls to his back and takes me with him, so I blanket his body with mine. Soon enough, I may not be able to lay like this with him, but for now, I love it. And I'm ready to beg him to sleep with him, desperate to know how much longer we'll keep up the ruse of abstinence. Pregnancy has made me horny, and this man just does it for me.

"Are we finally ready to have sex again?" I tease at his lips.

"Are you finally ready to be my wife?" he asks, stroking his hands up and down my back.

"You haven't asked me anything," I joke back, keeping my lips against his.

"Then I guess it's time to ask again." Reaching into his pocket, he pulls out a ring and holds it between us. "Autumn Kulis, will you do me the honor of making, and raising, babies with me, as my wife?"

"I—" I stare at the ring for a moment. *Is this really happening to me?* Am I really going to have it all: husband, child, house? It doesn't seem real.

"You just had this in your pocket?" I tease while choking on the words.

"It's been there since I returned in mid-October."

"I—"

"I know I come with a teenage daughter, but she approves. She adores you. She loves you like I do."

Softly, I laugh. "It could get tricky trying to make babies with a teenager in the house."

"We can be creative," he says, leaning forward to take my mouth for a quick kiss. "We'll need to be creative anyway as we'll be having more than one baby."

I chuckle at his joke, but his face turns serious.

"I'm going to fill you up, sweetheart. I'm going to give you all the babies you want and all the love you deserve. Marry me." He wiggles the ring in his fingers.

"Yes. Yes, I'll marry you." Cupping his cheeks, I take his mouth with mine and kiss him with all I have. His palm comes to mine, and without even looking, he slips the ring on my finger, not missing a beat as he continues to kiss me. Eventually, the weight registers, and I pull back to stare down at the ring, placing my hand on his chest as I balance over the length of his body.

"This looks familiar." I stare at the simple cut and silver band.

"I didn't have my mother's engagement ring to give to you." It's a reminder that Logan has no family but his friends and my family. "This is your mother's. She gave it to me, saying it brought her years of happy marriage and two wonderful babies."

Tears well in my eyes. My father bought my mother an anniversary diamond, and she eventually wore that ring every day. This ring is her original engagement ring and means everything to me. It means my mother approves of my marrying Logan.

"Wait? You asked my mother for permission to marry me?"

"I asked Ben. Your mother just happened to be in the room. I wanted to do it all right for you."

He said he wasn't always going to get it right, but he was willing to try until he did. I'd say he'd put forth plenty of effort to do right by me after our early hiccups.

"I love it," I whisper, still in awe that my family approves, and this sentimental gift rests on my finger. "I love you."

"I love you, too, sweetheart."

+ + +

That night, we show off my ring at an impromptu engagement party. Logan must have called the family together somehow because when we return to Anna and Ben's, all are gathered, including my mother. Lorna immediately hugs me once her dad announces I said yes, and Mason makes a crack about diamonds being the way to win a woman. He might have said they were the way to get in a woman's pants, but I'm giving him the benefit of the doubt because young ears were listening.

I pull my mother aside to thank her for the ring.

"This really means everything to me, Mom," I say, glancing down at the diamond and silver combination on my finger.

"Your father would be so proud of you. You finally have everything he would have wanted for you."

Tears fill my eyes again. "Mom, I have something else to tell you."

She waits me out until I blurt, "I'm pregnant, but we aren't telling everyone until we tell Lorna." Somehow, she doesn't appear surprised.

"Well, I was wondering when you were going to tell me." She chuckles.

"Logan told you, didn't he?"

"Wild guess," she says. "I know I recommended Mason at first, but I think you made the smartest choice from the list. You need a man who knows your worth, and he is pretty hunky in his own right."

"Mom," I drawl.

"I might be old, but I'm not blind."

"How did Logan get the ring?"

"He came to see Ben before he sought you out at your place. He didn't have a ring yet, so I immediately gave him mine."

"He didn't know I was pregnant then," I state. He couldn't have told my mother when he told Ben he planned to marry me. Actually, Logan demanded I marry him twice before I told him I was pregnant.

"No, but he said he planned for it to happen."

I softly chuckle. Such confidence.

"It appears he's a virile man as well." She wiggles her brows. "He's also attractive, but the best thing about him might be his sweetness and his humor. If a man can make you laugh, there's more chemistry in that

271

trait than anything else." She softly smiles, and I remember the laughter of my parents. My dad was a funny guy.

"The best thing about Logan is he loves me," I whisper.

"I would have settled for nothing less for you, honey. That's why I gave him the ring." Unable to stop myself, I wrap my arms around my mother.

"I love you, Mom."

"Ah, honey. I love you, too."

We both know it's important to say these things.

Epilogue

The Following Summer
[Logan]

As we both wanted Ben present in a healthy condition, we held a micro-wedding on our new property in the spring. Standing on the front lawn of our new house, we stated our vows before family and friends with the sunset as a backdrop. The setting was as gorgeous as my blushing bride, who was rather pregnant at the time. Her long flowing dress disguised her baby bump, but she would pop soon enough.

Lorna stood up as a maid of honor along with Anna as matron, and Amelia, Anna's younger sister, as another bridesmaid. On my side, I have my brothers from another in Mason, Ben, and Zack. It was a small affair, but it was everything I could have asked for—friends who are now family.

Ben had weathered a storm of ups and downs with experimental drugs. Shortly after our wedding, he took a turn for the worse and then recovered. The unknown wore on Anna, but the perfect couple remained the perfect couple. I was no longer jealous of them because I had my own perfect love with my new wife and the family we were creating with Lorna as a big sister and the future baby.

Near the beginning of July, on what felt like the hottest day of the year, baby Anders arrived. Unfortunately, Ben was in the hospital at the same time. I rolled Autumn to the oncology unit in a wheelchair with the baby on her lap. We had to have special clearance for such a thing, but as a small-town community, the local hospital staff knew the story of the Kulis siblings.

One was dying while another was giving birth.

"Hey." I knocked on the door of Ben's room, hoping today was a good day for him. Anna slowly rose from her seat beside her husband. She'd been up to visit us shortly after Autumn and the baby were cleaned up. She cried as she held our little one, and Autumn cried just as hard. I wanted them to be happy tears, but I assumed it was a mixture. I shed a few myself because I couldn't believe I was where I was. A father again. A married man. Truly in love this time.

"Hey," Ben's hoarse voice reached us as he was propped up in the bed. He still looked like Ben in his eyes and his smile, but my friend was slowly leaving the body of the man before us.

"We have someone who wants to meet you," Autumn stated, elevating her cheerful voice as she struggled to pretend she wasn't shocked by her brother's appearance.

"Who's this?" Ben asked although he was already aware we had a baby.

"Benjamin Michael Anders meet Benjamin Traverse Kulis."

Ben blinks as Autumn hands baby Ben to me, and I pass my son to him. Anna stepped up to cradle her hands under Ben's arms as he held his namesake. A tear fell down Ben's cheek, and Anna was quick to swipe it from his face.

"He's so beautiful, Autumn."

My own eyes burned as I watched my best friend gaze at my newest child.

"He definitely takes after his mother."

I softly chuckled. "Hey."

"But I know you'll have the heart of your father," Ben stated as if he already knew my son. I can only hope he'll live up to every letter of his namesake.

Autumn swiped at her face and reached for my hand, and I squeezed her fingers with my own. Slowly, Ben lifted his head and looked at his wife.

"It's time to go home, my love," he stated to her, and Anna's eyes widened.

"But—"

"No buts. I want to go home." There was no bark to his words but still strength in his demand. Ben didn't want to end his days in a hospital, and we all knew what he was requesting.

Ben wanted to return to Lakeside Cottage.

+ + +

It's a blustery day in mid-July, roughly two weeks after the birth of my baby boy. Zack and his boys are present, staying in the garage apartment with Mason. Anna and Autumn plan to entertain the girls as Autumn is desperate to get out of the house. A trip to the beach didn't seem wise to me at first, but with baby Ben strapped to my chest, we begin the laborious trek down to the water from Lakeside Cottage.

Mason and Zack take turns carrying Ben down the one-hundred-fifty wooden steps, resting at the landing to change carriers. Bryce and Calvin have gone ahead with Zack's little terrors, who seem to be even more hellacious in their mother's absence.

When we finally arrive on the sand, a pop-up canopy covers two sand chairs, and Ben is settled into one of them. I take the other, keeping the baby in the shade while Mason and Zack hover on the edges. Silently at first, we watch Bryce and Calvin toss a football as Trevor and Oliver run between the older boys as if they can catch the ball floating over their heads.

"Those kids are crazy," Mason states, watching the younger set run back and forth, back and forth.

"I know," Zack moans, rubbing a hand down his face. "But they're also kids."

"Nothing you can really do but love them," Ben states in his permanently graveled voice. A large beach towel wraps around him despite the warmth of the day. The brisk breeze cools things off, but the sand bites at my ankles.

"That's the future of Four Points," Mason says, still watching the boys, and I realize he's correct.

Our business venture began around the new year, and we've worked hard to get every project started. Ben hasn't been as involved as we hoped, but he's been present when he could. Mostly what he's done is update files and plans, leaving things in place for someone to take his place in the landscape division. We offered the position to Anna, but she wants to continue subbing at the local high school in hopes of a permanent position this fall.

"It's the cycle of life," Ben suddenly states, staring off at his sons. "You live and love, lose and learn, and then you start all over again."

Ben isn't wrong. In many ways, we lived different lives when we were younger. We fell in love, and some of us fell out of it. We lost parents and wives. We learned hard lessons, and in my case, started over again. Autumn has been the life change I needed, along with the new business, the move, and the baby. And, of course, having Lorna full-time has made a big difference.

"To the cycle," Mason states, holding up a beer he grabbed from the cooler one of the boys lugged to the beach.

"To the future," Ben states, his eyes still focused on his children.

"But also to the past," Zack adds, staring at our sick friend. He's the one who brought us all together. He'll always be the True North that points us home.

"To friends forever," I say as I did on our first reunion last summer.

"Must you sound like a thirteen-year-old girl?" Mason teases, still holding up his beer.

"I like that," Ben says, and I turn my head to find him looking at me. In our wedding vows, I promised to love Autumn with everything I had. It's something Ben asked of me. *Love her with everything, and she'll do the same for you.* In some ways, I think it's how he viewed his relationship with his sister. He'd loved her with all he had like he loved each of us, and in return, we loved him for what he'd given us.

The best of friends in the best of men.

"To thirteen-year-old girls," I state, and Mason groans.

"Do you know how wrong that sounded?"

"Just drink," I tease, and Mason does, but I glance back at Ben, whose gaze has fallen on my son, tucked into my chest.

"This is the best," Ben whispers, eyes still on my child, and I'm not certain if he means a sleeping baby or a child nuzzled to a chest. Or just sitting on the beach with friends. I'll take all those moments and roll them into one.

"I've had the best of lives," Ben says. "Because I lived every moment of it."

"Ben," I choke, sensing he's trying to impart some wisdom on us.

He slowly smiles and turns back to watch his own boys torturing the younger ones.

In a maudlin moment a while back, Ben asked me: *"If you live another forty years, my friend, what will make you happiest?"* The answers were simple and came quickly. His sister. My daughter. Our new child. The home we were building together. The life we planned to share as a family.

"That's all I'd ask of any of you," he had said because Ben knew what was important. In his cycle of life theory, he recognized that we followed a pattern.

And while we might be forty-year-old men, we're still those four college boys inside, striving for what we wanted most in life.

And when we were forty, we still had so much life left to live.

As Ben intended we should.

Second Epilogue
[Zack]

July

Ben was dead.

There was no easy way to sugarcoat the truth. Our best friend had died after a short life and a brief struggle with pancreatic cancer. I'm still dressed in my funeral attire minus my sportscoat. My tie is loosened, and I gawk out the second-floor, bedroom window into the yard next door. Anna's family calls this place Lakeside Cottage, but for the past year it was the permanent residence of one of my oldest friends and their family. My family used to live next door—once upon a time.

Swiping a hand through my hair, I sigh. The past eleven months have been hell. Just shy of a year ago, Ben told us about his diagnosis. He'd already been through treatment without success. Ben Kulis. *Clueless Kulis*, we teased him in college. The nickname came about because he only had eyes for one woman. That woman would become his wife, Anna. They were sickly sweet, madly in love, and now she was a widow too young. Ben was the best of men. Loyal to a fault, he saw the good in most people even when they didn't recognize it in themselves. Having been Anna's friend first, my friendship with Ben happened second but was no less important than hers.

Staring out the dark window, I'm distracted when a light from the house next door illuminates a portion of the yard. A yard that was mine once upon a time. My childhood dreams were built there until everything shattered when I was a teenager.

I hate this room. I hate that it faces what I once had. I hate that facing what I once had reminds of all that I've lost.

A house. A home. A wife. A friend.

Ben would have told me to let it go regarding that house next door. I'm certain he said something similar to that before the phrase—*let it go*—became so popular. It was only a house, he probably said, but it had been my house. My home. Home is where you plant your garden and sow your seeds, he might have added being a landscape designer who loved planting metaphors. Instead of that house being a special place, I was uprooted as a teen and forced to bloom elsewhere.

Regarding my ex-wife, he told me to let her go as well, and I did.

Suddenly, a woman enters the yard, distracting me from my thoughts of shattered dreams and broken homes. Her hair appears golden in the dim light, flowing behind her like she's a mystical creature from a child's bedtime story. She wears a dress that's light in color and fabric, covering her from shoulder to ankle and yet leaving nothing to the imagination. In profile, I see the outline of her form. Pert breasts. Long legs. And that hair like a veil drifting behind her in the light wind.

She looks like an angel.

And I must be losing my mind.

This must be the neighbor who arrived around the time we visited last summer. Anna and Ben claim they never formally met her, only passed friendly hellos through the tall shrubbery between the homes. Anna's best guess is she's roughly our age. We all turned forty the year of the great reunion where Ben dropped the bomb about his situation. Now, we are forty-one.

Roughly loosening the remainder of my tie, I continue to stare into the mostly dark yard. The patio is illuminated by the soft glow of light coming from the house. *The kitchen.* I recall my mother cooking there, my brother doing homework at the oval table, and my father's laughter. Tonight seems to be a night of memories. My childhood home. My best friend's passing. And this woman is invading them both.

With my room two stories up and steeped in darkness, I remain submerged in my dismal mood but mesmerized by her presence.

Why tonight? Of all the times I've visited this home in the last year, why am I seeing her tonight of all nights? And why does she look so beautiful, so peaceful, just standing in my yard—*her* yard—facing the lake off in the distance? Her head tips back and I imagine her closing her eyes, allowing the soft breeze to coast over her face, caress her skin, kiss her lips.

I'm not a romantic at heart but I'm definitely turned on. The idea of being the one to touch her cheeks, stroke down her nose and stare into eyes I cannot see from this distance overwhelms me. *And that hair.* I want to comb my fingers through that spun gold and curl a fist in the silky-looking threads. My mouth waters at the possibility of kissing the column of her throat, visibly on display with her head tilted backward, face aimed upward. Heaven is calling her.

Ben.

My eyes prickle. My throat tightens. If I were a man who believed in something mystical, I'd think Ben placed this angel in my old yard just for me.

'Mine' whispers through my thoughts. *Why?*

I can't seem to turn away from the window when I know I should. Staring down upon her makes me feel like a voyeur, like a man witnessing something private, almost intimate. I want to stand in that yard with her. I want to rub my hands over her shoulder where the edge of her dress slips downward, exposing the curl of muscle at the top of her arm. I want to kiss her there.

None of it feels appropriate—*watching her, wanting her*—on this day, when I buried a friend. Still, I stare out the window at a stranger next door. My fingers curl into a fist on the window's trim, balancing me upright, holding me in place. I can't seem to look away.

Then, she looks at me.

Her head swivels so quickly, I remain caught in eyes I can't see as her face angles toward the second floor, toward this window, toward me.

What does she see? The miserable man that I am. The shitty husband I once was. The poor father I've been.

I don't want to be any of those things, but I don't know how to change. I don't know what to do, what I want. I only know I want to be better. I want to *feel* better inside.

Staring down at her, I'm certain she sees me until I remember I'm covered in darkness. The lights remain off in my room and I'm at the edge of the window. She can't possibly see me. I've been so good at pretending I'm something other than who I am, I don't think anyone knows the real me.

Not even me.

Thank you for taking the time to read this book.
Please consider writing a review on major sales channels where ebooks and paperbacks are sold and discussed.

SCAN ME

For a bonus scene of Autumn and Logan.

Next at Lakeside Cottage: *LEARNING at 40*.
Zack Weller can't keep his eyes off the woman next door, and she's hard to miss as she's naked over there.

If you like small lake towns, you might also enjoy:
THE HEART COLLECTION

More by L.B. Dunbar

Scrooge-ish
A flirty, over four, silver fox, second chance holiday romance.

Road Trips & Romance
3 sisters. 3 destinations. A second chance at love over 40.
Hauling Ashe
Merging Wright
Rhode Trip

Lakeside Cottage
Four friends. Four summers. Shenanigans and love happen at the lake.
Living at 40
Loving at 40
Learning at 40
Letting Go at 40

The Silver Foxes of Blue Ridge
More sexy silver foxes in the mountain community of Blue Ridge.
Silver Brewer
Silver Player
Silver Mayor
Silver Biker

Sexy Silver Foxes
When sexy silver foxes meet the feisty vixens of their dreams.
After Care
Midlife Crisis
Restored Dreams
Second Chance
Wine&Dine

Collision novellas
A spin-off from After Care – the younger set/rock stars
Collide
Caught

Rom-com standalone for the over 40

L.B. DUNBAR

The Sex Education of M.E.

The Heart Collection
Small town, big hearts - stories of family and love.
Speak from the Heart
Read with your Heart
Look with your Heart
Fight from the Heart
View with your Heart

A Heart Collection Spin-off
The Heart Remembers

BOOKS IN OTHER AUTHOR WORLDS
Smartypants Romance (an imprint of Penny Reid)
Tales of the Winters sisters set in Green Valley.
Love in Due Time
Love in Deed
Love in a Pickle

The World of True North (an imprint of Sarina Bowen)
Welcome to Vermont! And the Busy Bean Café.
Cowboy
Studfinder

THE EARLY YEARS
The Legendary Rock Star Series
A classic tale with a modern twist of rock star romance and suspense
The Legend of Arturo King
The Story of Lansing Lotte
The Quest of Perkins Vale
The Truth of Tristan Lyons
The Trials of Guinevere DeGrance

Paradise Stories
MMA romance. Two brothers. One fight.
Abel

Cain

The Island Duet
Intrigue and suspense. The island knows what you've done.
Redemption Island
Return to the Island

Modern Descendants – writing as elda lore
Magical realism. Modern myths of Greek gods.
Hades
Solis
Heph

(L)ittle (B)its of Gratitude

It all started with a pandemic. Not the best way to start a story, but it's true. We needed to get out of the house, and my youngest wanted to go blueberry picking. It was June and the blueberries in Michigan weren't ready yet. Strawberry picking it was then. My husband convinced us to stay the weekend. *Take a break.* With safety measures in place, we traveled to southwest Michigan, spent days on the shores of Lake Michigan, and people watched. It's how I get much of my inspiration.

Four men sat on the sand surrounded by children, but only two women. I made up their storylines in my head. Then, I plotted their life with paper and pen. The stories had to wait a full year before hitting my computer, and this is the start of that spur-of-the-moment getaway during the pandemic of 2020. I'm hoping to make history here, in a better way.

It takes a village, or in my case, a small town of people to produce a book, so I'd like to thank a few.

Shannon: Another amazing cover. Thought you might clobber me over this one but when we finally got it right, it was right.

Regina: I don't know you personally, but your images are breathtaking.

Mel: Cheesus, I can't even start with you, but know this, as a first reader, turned follower, turned friend, turned editor, this book publishes pretty close to the anniversary of that first book, so seven years, my friend. Seven years. And I thank everything in the universe for putting you on my path and joining me on this journey.

Jen: For making my words better.

Karen: For finding the words I forgot.

A new Jenn: For taking on the role to help me organize bloggers, bookstagrammers and the release tour.

Sylvia and Tami: My unsung heroines who keep up Loving L.B., the best reader group ever, filled with the most loyal, inspiring, hot-mess-heroines who keep me going. Every. Single. Day.

And to my family: Mr. Dunbar, MD (and D), MK, JR and A. You're all part of how I live my best life, over fifty!

For more information about diabetes, I highly recommend: Beyondtype1

About the Author
www.lbdunbar.com

L.B. Dunbar loves sexy silver foxes, second chances, and small towns. If you enjoy older characters in your romance reads, including a hero with a little silver in his scruff and a heroine rediscovering her worth, then welcome to romance for those over 40. L.B. Dunbar's signature works include women and men in their prime taking another turn at love and happily ever. Along with her #sexysilverfox collection, she's made Amazon Top 10 in Later in Life Romance with her Lakeside Cottage and Road Trips & Romance series. She is also a *USA Today Bestseller*. L.B. lives in Chicago with her own sexy silver fox.

To get all the scoop about the self-proclaimed queen of silver fox romance, join her on Facebook at Loving L.B. or receive her monthly newsletter, Love Notes.

+ + +

Connect with L.B. Dunbar

Printed in Great Britain
by Amazon